P9-DJB-752

**ACCLAIM FOR GEORGE D. SHUMAN'S
GRIPPING DEBUT**

18 SECONDS

'What appears at first glance to be a garden variety cop novel is actually a thrilling read when a dash of the supernatural is thrown in.'

—*The Cairns Post*

'Shuman handles the intersecting storylines well and the book builds to a taut and surprising conclusion. A good example of how to skilfully interweave the extraordinary into a tough, gritty police novel.'

—*The Canberra Times*

'. . . a corker. Fast-paced, it keeps you on the edge of your seat . . . Great book, even better ending.'

—*Herald Sun*

'Combines gritty storytelling, richly drawn characters and police procedure to brilliant effect.'

—*Townsville Bulletin*

'. . . bustling but carefully woven plot.'

—*The Sun-Herald*

'What distinguishes this novel is Shuman's skill at characterization . . . [He] has the talent to put . . . evil on the page and make it specific and real.'

—*The Washington Post*

'A convincing, perfectly paced novel. You won't be able to look away.'

—Paul Lindsay, author of
The Big Scam and *The Führer's Reserve*

'In this dramatic, highly imaginative first novel, George D. Shuman delivers an explosive thriller—brutally authentic in detail and absorbing from beginning to end.'

—Robert K. Tanenbaum,
author of *Counterplay*

'With a brilliant concept, truly human characters, and a *Sixth Sense* sensibility, *18 Seconds* is terrifyingly authentic. Sherry Moore is a memorable heroine who promises to have many more adventure ahead of her.'

—Brad Meltzer, author of
The Zero Game and *The Tenth Justice*

'Intricate, compelling, and real, *18 Seconds* is suspense at its up-all-night best . . . Welcome a new and substantial talent to your bookshelf.'

—John J. Nance, author of *Pandora's Box* and *Orbit*

'A thrill ride, no doubt about it. Shuman grabs you and pulls you into his chilling, twisty plot, never letting you go until you finally close the book.'

—Jillian P. Hoffman,
author of *Last Witness* and *Retribution*

A Sherry Moore Novel

18 SECONDS

GEORGE D. SHUMAN

SIMON & SCHUSTER
AUSTRALIA A CBS COMPANY

First published in 2006 by Simon & Schuster, Inc.
1230 Avenue of the Americas, New York, NY 10020

This edition published in 2008 by Simon & Schuster Australia
Suite 2, Lower Ground Floor,
14-16 Suakin Street, Pymble NSW 2073

This book is a work of fiction. Names, characters, places and incidents are products of the author's imagination or are used fictitiously. Any resemblance to actual events or locales or persons, living or dead, is entirely coincidental.

National Library of Australia Cataloguing-in-Publication entry

Author   Shuman, George D. 1952-
Title   18 Seconds / George D. Shuman
ISBN   978-0-7318-1378-0 (pbk)
Notes   A Sherry Moore novel.
Dewey Number: 813.6

Cover design by Xou Creative
Printed and bound in Australia by Griffin Press

The paper used to produce this book is a natural, recyclable product made from wood grown in sustainable plantation forests. The manufacturing processes conform to the environmental regulations in the country of origin.

10 9 8 7 6 5 4 3 2 1

To Susan, whose special gift to this world is her innocent love for all things.
To law enforcement friends, brothers and sisters who made the ultimate sacrifice.

18
SECONDS

1

Easter morning, March 27
Pittsburgh, Pennsylvania

Sherry stepped off the courtesy cart near the hotel kiosk in the ground transportation level of the Pittsburgh International Airport. The customer service agent driving the cart laid Sherry's single bag on the floor and made a noisy three-point turn before he sped away.

She braced herself as small feet thundered in her direction. Screaming children circled her in a game of Monkey in the Middle, soon dashing off into the murmuring crowd. She could hear the tinny voice of Elton John on someone's headphones, a couple arguing over who last had the camera, a policeman's radio announcing an accident in short-term parking.

A baggage conveyor lurched forward under a dissonant horn and a stampede ensued, someone colliding with her shoulder; she began to reel until sizable hands reached out to steady her. "So sorry, my dear," a nun chortled. "God bless you!"

She felt a chill as the doors leading outside opened and closed. She was dressed in black slacks, a smartly cut red wool jacket, and practical shoes.

A ruffled man in a long dark trench coat watched her from the opposite side of the kiosk. He was standing with his hands in his pockets, trying to concentrate on the faces around the luggage carousel, but his eyes kept straying back to her. She was exquisite, he thought, simply exquisite, and it took all of his effort to pull his eyes back to the crowd.

There were several candidates for his rendezvous at the carousel; one in particular fit the image he'd conjured. She was wearing a khaki safari suit and hiking boots, her long red hair braided into a pigtail. Of the two runner-ups, one was a platinum blond who wore a black jumpsuit and stilettos, and the other had a gray ponytail and wore a purple sweat suit and running shoes.

It occurred to him that he could have had young Mr. Torlino research the woman on the Internet, perhaps pull up a picture of her to bring along, but neither he nor Torlino had managed to sleep more than four of the last forty hours, much less surf the Internet.

The crowd was tangled around the conveyor, some struggling to extract their bags. He took a moment to steal another glance at the dark-haired beauty by the kiosk. People stopped to talk to her, mostly men who appeared to offer assistance, but she smiled them all away with her magnificent smile. He was ashamed that he wanted to walk over to her and say something trivial, just to see her smile for him.

The crowd began to disperse in twos and threes. The safari lady joined a bearded man with a camouflage hat, and they walked off with two netted bags. The woman in stilettos called over a porter for a tapestry steamer that would have held his entire wardrobe. The purple sweat suit collected a husband

and three clutching children. He swept the concourse for a single female, checked his watch and then the door. There were two lonely bags circling the carousel, but no more candidates.

Something rolled against the side of his foot; he looked down at the back of a child's curly head. A chubby hand reached for a rubber ball, the face nearing the cuffs of his trousers, and he wondered if the child could smell death on his shoes.

The man shifted his weight, self-consciously scraping his shoes across the carpet, thumbed another Life Saver from the roll in his pocket, and popped it into his mouth.

A heavy woman stepped onto the descending escalator and waved frantically in his direction. She had a blond bouffant and heavy makeup. A shopping bag hung over one arm and a small white dog squirmed in the other.

"Yoooo-hooo," she trilled, and he closed his eyes, wondering if his idea hadn't been too desperate. A moment later a dowdy man with a straw hat ran past him to join her. He sighed in relief, turning back to look at the kiosk.

Could she have been delayed getting down from her gate? She might have become ill and gone to the ladies' room. Maybe she was waiting for him in another part of the airport. He supposed there were other hotel kiosks, but he had specifically said the one at ground transportation.

And here there was only the beautiful lady in red, still waiting patiently for whomever to come collect her.

An electronic voice announced that unattended vehicles would be towed and bags removed. He hesitated, then stepped toward her, his expression somewhere between uncertainty and embarrassment. She was standing tall, arms at her side, back straight. There was a calmness about her that belied the commotion around them.

He saw her head turn, her face registering his approach.

"Forgive me, ma'am," he apologized, his face already drawing heat, "you wouldn't be Miss Moore?"

"Sherry," she said, sticking out her free hand. The other clutched a long red and white walking stick. "Captain Karpovich?"

He stepped back and put his hand to his mouth.

Thick chestnut curls bobbed on her shoulders. Her lips were arcs of autumn red that matched her jacket. She was tall, full-breasted, and ever so sensual.

She pulled a strand of hair behind her ear with the hand holding the red and white walking stick, then put it down so that the stick touched the floor again. He took her hand quickly and it was warm. "Please call me Edward," he said. Her beauty and affliction were inconsistent, the appeal practically heart-wrenching. He unconsciously covered her hand with his own, patting it gently. She was thirty-something, he guessed. "I'm so sorry, Miss Moore. I wasn't expecting you to . . . ah . . . come by courtesy cart."

"It's quite all right, Edward," she said cheerily. "Which way do we go?"

He grabbed her light bag and hooked an arm

under her elbow, forgetting all about his mission for the moment, then led her proudly toward the sliding glass doors. "Our car is just outside."

"It feels very cold," she said.

"Rain," he told her, patting her arm, "and flurries are possible in the mountains."

"Ugh." She smiled and he patted even harder.

The cold temperatures hit them full-face when the doors whooshed open.

A black sedan idled at the curb; it had government tags and an impressive array of antennae. A plume of white exhaust hovered over the trunk. Edward laid her day bag on the backseat and helped her slide in next to it.

The interior was warm, and she could smell the driver's good cologne. "Mike Torlino," a voice said. She sensed a hand being thrust in her direction.

"Sherry Moore," she said as she smiled, reaching for it.

The older man got in the passenger seat and Torlino retrieved his hand, shaking it like it had been burnt. "H-O-T," he mouthed to Edward, which earned him a frosty look.

"I'm afraid I didn't dress for the weather," she said. "It was almost sixty when I left Philadelphia."

"It's coming off Erie." Torlino lowered his head to look in the outside mirror and pulled into traffic. "We lost ten degrees in the last hour. Are you staying in Pittsburgh tonight?"

He adjusted his rearview mirror to look at her face.

"I was hoping to make it a day trip if we got finished in time," she said.

"We'll have you back in plenty of time." Karpovich glowered at his partner. He put his arm over the seat and turned to look at her directly. "Plenty of time, Miss Moore."

They motored south on 90 and east across the turnpike into Donegal and working farmland. Sherry put her forehead to the cold window and listened to the rain and the beat of the wipers as she thought about her nightmares. They would start innocently enough and always decline dreadfully. The face in the windshield lingered on in her memory, clear yet not clear, familiar yet unknown.

In the nightmares, she would be sitting in a car as someone pulled an oversize red fisherman's sweater that smelled of body odor and fuel over her head. There would be a scream and a woman's face slammed hard against the windshield in front of her. She would look up into those terrified green eyes and see crimson blood trickling from a cut lip, smearing pink around a pale flattened cheek.

Then the face would be jerked away, vanishing in a mere instant, the blood washed away by a cold, steady rain.

The nightmares were worse this winter: more frequent, more violent. She was told she suffered everything from parasomnia to post-traumatic stress disorder, always with the caveat that no one could honestly predict what the side effects of her work might be.

Torlino swerved gently to miss something in the road and her head rolled on the cold glass, startling her from her reverie. It was good to be out of the house today, she had to admit, good to be thinking about something else besides her nightmares.

"What's it like outside?" she asked, absently tugging an earlobe.

"The rain's turning to snow," Karpovich said.

She could hear the patter of beaded ice where she pressed her forehead against the glass.

Karpovich didn't stop there. He began to describe the farmland, his voice soothing and patient like a good storyteller's. She could sense he was tired, yet he spared her no detail, reminding her of her neighbor, Mr. Brigham, who would read her mail to her on so many lonely nights. She wondered if Edward's skill was practiced at home or in a nursing facility on some sad, bedridden soul.

The hills were craggy and the farms poor. Cattle and sheep were anchored knee-deep in the mud. Strings of last year's Christmas lights framed the porches and windows of old farmhouses. She tried to imagine the farms in her mind. The scent of wood fires, beds unmade, breakfast dishes caked with eggs and apple butter; coats on the door smelling of sweat and machinery, boots caked with manure.

In time the land began to level, rolling pleasantly along the base of Laurel Mountain. Working farms gave way to green pasture bordered with ribbons of elegant estate fence. Magnificent horses nuzzled the grass in quilted blankets of green and blue.

It was to such a property they came, turning sharply between stone pillars chiseled with the name Oak View. They climbed a meandering lane toward a large ranch house overlooking the rolling plateau.

There was a marked state police car in the driveway and a white van on the lawn.

Torlino parked next to the police car, and Karpovich turned to look over the back of his seat. "Would you like something for the smell, Miss Moore?"

She shook her head. "I'll be fine."

A trooper waited inside the door, staring curiously as they passed.

"We'll be walking across the living area, then a few steps down to the kitchen," Karpovich said softly. "I'll tell you when we're there. Are you ready?"

"Okay," she said. "Let's go."

The house smelled musty and it had the unmistakable stench of death.

"They weren't found for more than a month," Karpovich said. "The wife was in a bedroom off the hall behind us."

"You have the note with you?"

"I do," he said. "Would you like me to read it?"

"Please, Edward."

He liked that she used his name.

He slipped a hand inside his jacket and removed a postcard-size piece of paper, a handwritten version transcribed from the original. He shook open his glasses and began to read.

It will be March soon. Maggie liked March,
liked to invite the neighbors over for a party
after her first spring cleaning, but that was all
years ago. We stopped seeing people. Or
maybe they just stopped seeing us?

You know, of course, that she suffered depression. For years she begged me to take her life. I was too selfish to let her go before me. I made her wait until it was my time.

I want to confess to you about another matter, however. Her name was Karen Koontz. You'll find her in your files as a missing person from the early 1970s. She died here on the farm. Her sister came looking for her with the police. I had to lie. I knew it would make things difficult for my residency.

She loved the farm and the animals. Please give her a proper burial and a stone. She deserves a nice stone after all those years in the field. I used to look out there from my chair and think about putting one up myself, but Maggie didn't know about her. I couldn't let Maggie know. It would have upset her so.

You forensic types will be interested that she died of asphyxiation. The ligature will still be around her neck. We were experimenting with drugs and sex, and things just got out of hand. An accident of excess, I guess you would call it. Life is incredibly fragile, isn't it?

My will provides for any expenses you will incur. As for Maggie and myself, there are plots in Easthampton, Massachusetts. The details are with my attorney. Please see that we arrive together if possible.

For what it's worth, I'm sorry for the way things turned out.

Donald S. Donovan, M.D.

Karpovich removed his glasses and returned them to his pocket. "The letter goes abruptly from giving the girl a proper burial to the arrangements he wants made for him and his wife without providing the location of the body. He seems to have lost the thread before he died."

"I imagine he was under a great deal of stress."

"Indeed," Karpovich said. "Indeed he was. There are a hundred and fifty acres of field back there, Miss Moore."

"Have you tried infrared?"

"Too long in the ground," he answered.

"Did you identify her?"

"Karen Koontz was reported missing in 1973, two years after Donovan bought the farm. They had been seeing each other for several months, according to her sister. She was a waitress at the Westmoreland airport and he was learning to fly, so it's likely they met there. The restaurant called the sister one day and told her Karen had stopped coming to work. They had a paycheck she hadn't picked up. She tried to call the doctor, but he never answered the phone. When she got suspicious, she told the police about him. They handled Karen like a missing person, which meant little or nothing in those days. They didn't have cause to search the doctor's farm, so weeks went by before they came out and asked him for permission to look around."

"And she was never seen again?"

"Never. The commonwealth would just as soon put this case to rest, Miss Moore. You can imagine the argument of digging up a field on so little information. The girl's sister died many years ago and she was the last of her family. Since the doctor is now dead, there is no one to prosecute, even if we found her. In other words, it wouldn't mean a hill of beans to Pennsylvania if she was left here or not."

"Except that it bothers you, Edward," Sherry said softly.

He coughed and shifted his feet nervously.

"I've earned a few favors in the last thirty years, Miss Moore. I used most of them to get you here today. Family or not, she doesn't deserve to be left in a field."

"Well then," she said, warming to the old man, "are his hands exposed, Edward?"

"The right one is draped over the arm of his chair. The gun he used was on the floor beneath it."

"Can you put a chair alongside him?"

"He's quite decomposed, Miss Moore."

"Yes," she said, "I would imagine so."

"Very well then."

"Good," she said. "Then we might as well get on with it."

He opened the door and the stench hit her full in the face.

Sherry could hear the window blinds rattle; the cold air from outside did little to minimize the smell.

"Ten more steps," he told her, then reached for a chair, dragged it next to the body, and helped her into it. "I'll be by the door. You call me when you need me."

He watched her from the ledge of the open window, not knowing what to expect. After a few minutes her head tilted to one side and he thought he heard the slightest moan escape her lips.

The walls were painted oxblood. The furniture was heavy, dark wood and leather splintered with cracks, everything covered with a somber layer of dust. Karpovich knew he would never forget the sight, not until the day he died—the beautiful blind woman holding the hand of a putrefied corpse. It was surreal.

She washed her hands in the kitchen sink and dried them with paper towels. "I'd like to walk to the field, if I may."

"Of course," he said hoarsely. He led her out the door past Torlino and the trooper.

Karpovich held up five fingers before he closed the door and Torlino nodded.

"You're cold," he said, reaching for her hands and pushing his gloves into them.

"Thank you, Captain, but what of your own?" she asked.

He patted her on the arm. "The field begins here behind the house and runs to the mountainside. The nearest neighbors aren't visible."

He sneezed and removed his handkerchief, blowing his nose and wiping it.

"Just a hundred feet ahead there is a cluster of trees. Midway is a cement drinking trough for the cattle. There haven't been any livestock here for years, but the field is still cut up from their trails."

Sherry looked ahead. "Take me to the trees, Edward."

"The grass is high, Miss Moore. Your feet will be soaked."

"It's all right." She took a step forward and he jumped to catch up with her, grabbing her arm for fear she would fall on the uneven ground. The going was awkward at times, the tip of her walking stick collecting chunks of sod, her boots becoming covered with grass and hayseed.

"What does the house look like now?" she asked. "You said it hadn't been cared for?"

"It looks like they stopped living five years ago. That's about the time he quit the hospital and sold off the animals. They had become recluses, according to the neighbors. Not even the postman had seen them for months. There is dust and trash in every room. The roof could use new shingles; they get lots of wind up here. There is grass growing through cracks in the patio and pool."

A stiff breeze pelted them with icy flakes of snow. She stopped for a moment to turn from the wind. Then she started out again, her hands thankful for the gloves as she continued toward the grove.

"Take me under them," she said. "I'd like to stand there for a minute alone, if you don't mind."

"Pretty woman," Torlino said. He'd come around the gate to join his partner.

"Beautiful, actually," Karpovich responded. He was standing by the gate, breathing hard from the walk uphill. His hands were cold, and he buried them in his pockets.

"Shame, good piece like that. Know what happened to her?"

Karpovich looked at him. "I didn't ask."

They could see her tapping her walking stick and stamping her feet to get the layout of the ground. At last, she put her back to a tree and seemed to be staring in their direction. Then suddenly her body started to sink down and Karpovich leaped, too late realizing that she was only crouching with her back against the tree.

He looked to his partner in embarrassment, but the younger man pretended not to notice.

"So what happened in there?" Torlino asked.

"She held his hand," Karpovich said distantly.

Torlino looked at him. "You're kidding."

Karpovich shook his head.

"That's it? She didn't say anything?"

"Not yet."

Torlino looked at her and pointed. "What's she doing now?"

"She wanted to be alone under the trees," Karpovich said. The snow continued to blow off the slopes of Laurel Mountain to their east; it lay for a moment on their heads and shoulders before it melted. "Please get us the umbrellas, Mike."

Torlino rolled his eyes and turned for the car.

Sherry crouched and felt her heart beating. She felt the moisture of her breath around her nose. She smelled the man's rotting body all the way into her sinuses, tasted it in her mouth. She removed her hand from the glove and traced the roots of the oak behind her. This was the frustrating part of what she did. Trying to interpret the images she had just seen.

Karpovich had said the tank was for watering cattle, not sheep. But she distinctly saw and smelled sheep at her feet as she was holding the doctor's hand. Why were sheep so important to his last seconds of life?

She grabbed the trunk for support and managed to get herself back on her feet.

One leg had cramped and her fingers were cold. She bent them back and forth, pulling the glove on as she heard Karpovich's labored breathing. "Here," he said as he took her arm. She could sense the umbrella above her head and huddled closer to him for warmth.

"Could we walk by the water trough?" she asked.

He led her to it and she leaned forward, the front of her thighs against the cold, rough concrete.

"It's rather high," she said. "Too high for sheep to drink from, is it not?"

"Yes." He looked at her oddly. "I would think it would be."

She stood there, eyes straight ahead, staring toward the Blue Mountains as if she could actually see them.

"I know where she is," she said at last.

The airport was crowded for March; the booths were filled in the small TGI Friday's next to the C-gate walking tram. Torlino had ordered a beer and Karpovich a ginger ale. Sherry ran her finger around the salty rim of a margarita.

"You really don't have to wait with me," she said. "I'm boarding just across the corridor."

"There is no place I'd rather be, Miss Moore," Karpovich said. "I can only thank you again for taking the trouble to do what you did for us."

"Very well, but please don't give me any credit," she warned. "Not yet. It doesn't always work out the way I imagine. You could dig for a week and not find anything."

Karpovich smiled. "It will still have been my pleasure," he said warmly.

"I read something about your role in the Norwich case," Torlino said.

Karpovich, who had observed a thousand interrogations over the years, caught the faintest tic at the corner of her mouth. She was uncomfortable with the subject.

"Can you tell us how you do what you do?" Torlino asked.

The older man was about to cut him off, but Sherry leaned forward, seeming to welcome the change in subject.

"I'll tell you what the doctors tell me." She folded her hands in front of her. "I suffered brain damage as a child, a head injury followed by cerebral blindness, which means that my optical nerves are intact but something in my cortex prevents them from working. I also suffer retrograde amnesia, meaning I have no memory of the injury or anything prior to it. Damage to the cortex imitates the electrical anomaly of an epileptic. My brain has electrical storms, though I don't have the seizures."

Her smile was disarming, Karpovich thought. She had none of the inanimate characteristics associated with the blind. Her eyes were light sensitive and looked quite normal behind her tinted glasses. She followed conversation with her face and used her hands as she spoke.

"One day when I was quite young I took the hand of a dead girl in a funeral home and saw images that were not my own. When it happened again years later, I saw a crime taking place. The police got involved and more or less verified what I had told them. One thing led to another and people started asking me for help.

"Scientifically speaking, I'm told I'm tapping into the short-term memory of the deceased."

"Uh-huh," Torlino said, stuffing a pretzel into his mouth.

"The frontal cortex of the brain houses short-term memory. Every time you compare cereal box labels in the grocery store you draw information from your memory reserves and bring them into short-term memory to assist you in making a decision. STM holds only what you are thinking about at the moment, about eighteen seconds' worth, so if you had a heart attack while comparing cereal box labels, there might be glimpses of what you were reading along with people running or kneeling over you trying to help. You might even retrieve the image of someone dear to you or someone like your family doctor. If you were shot instead of having a heart attack, you might focus on the face of the shooter. If you pull anything into the eighteen seconds of memory, like the face of someone you loved, you push something else out."

She took a drink and dabbed her lips with her napkin.

"Okay," Torlino said. "So it's like the RAM memory in a computer."

Sherry nodded. "Essentially."

"But what exactly is it that your body is doing to reach it?"

"In a sense, I am completing an electrical connection." She wiggled her fingers. "I am electrically charged, just as you are electrically charged. We are all wired with millions of receptors from our fingertips to our toes. Brush against something and the receptors stimulate neurons. Neurons send signals to the brain, retrieving interpretations. Your brain tells you if the object is hot, cold, dull, sharp, whatever. Everything we touch, just like the Braille I read, is interpreted by various parts of our brain in short-term, or working, memory for real-time evaluation."

She took a breath.

"When my skin receptors touch a dead person's skin receptors, my live electrical system—which is to say my central nervous system—makes contact with the circuitry of the deceased person's central nervous system. I am hot-wiring myself through their central nervous system to their brain."

A woman sitting at another table turned to look at them.

Torlino lowered his voice an octave and leaned toward her. "What does another person's memory look like, Miss Moore?"

She shrugged and tilted her head to one side. "It's like a homemade movie, but every one is so very different. I once saw nothing but words on the pages of a book—the whole last eighteen seconds of that person's life were immersed in a novel. Most often, when people are under stress, they move from one thing to the next without warning, although you can tell pretty much what is real time and what is not. Sometimes, though, the memory of something or someone in the past may be so vivid that the thing seems to be standing right there in front of you. The tricky part is trying to interpret the difference, to understand real time versus the recollections of a dying human being."

She put her hands palm-down on the table. "In any event, the images come and go, a second here, two seconds there, until the whole eighteen seconds is exhausted. Eighteen seconds is a lot of time." She turned a thumb toward the corridor behind them. "Consider what you have been thinking for the last eighteen seconds and what it might look like on film. You would undoubtedly be thinking about what I am saying right now, my face might be there, but what else would be on your mind?" She smiled. "You might also be thinking of a flight attendant who just walked by, and so her face or some part of her body comes to mind."

Torlino smiled and tried to roll his eyes.

"If your thoughts strayed to tomorrow's dental appointment, you might envision your dentist's chair or his face, or maybe your mind is on the date you had last night. I must tell you that not all of what I see is

PG-13. Can you imagine trying to interpret those images out of context? Let's say you were shot in the back. I could see the women I just mentioned, but without the benefit of your specific knowledge of who they were, I couldn't know if one was your wife or your sister or your murderer unless I actually saw her kill you. And those are the easy ones. When death comes slowly, there are a great many images of unknown relevance in a person's last few seconds. The dying often forget about the present and start to recall old friends, family, lost loves—it all comes to mind, sometimes things that no one else ever knew about the person."

"You mention images. You can't read thoughts, you just see images?"

She nodded and smiled. "Ironic, wouldn't you say? A blind woman who can see images."

Torlino smiled and looked up at the ceiling. Then he shook his head back and forth, as if to unclog it. "No," he said, "more like unbelievable."

Sherry picked up her glass, pressed one finger against it, and lifted it up for them to see. "Who would have believed two hundred years ago that a man could be identified by leaving his fingerprint on the side of a glass? Who would have believed fifty years ago that the blueprint of our existence would be found in the oil that makes up that fingerprint?"

She put the glass down and folded her hands. "If the brain is more sophisticated than any computer we ever hope to devise—and I daresay we don't use a tenth of its capacity—then given the right conditions, couldn't it tap into other human systems and read the data? That's a pretty simple task to ask of a computer."

"So you're saying your mind is acting like an EEG or whatever, but you're reading images, not electrical waves?"

"I don't even know if it's that sophisticated, but yes." She nodded. "Something along those lines."

She tapped the table. "I believe that the aggregate of all we've ever experienced is etched into the cerebrum when we die. Picture our brains as saturated with data just like the hard drives we throw into the trash when we outgrow them. That I am able to see a few seconds of it surprises me not at all."

"Then why wouldn't you be seeing images every time you shook hands with someone?" Torlino asked.

"Think about it," she said as she shook her head. "If a living neurological system were exposed to outside stimuli, it would be compelled to reject it. Its primary function is toward self-preservation, and it does that by maintaining a closed system. In other words, nature itself wouldn't permit it." She wagged a finger. "But turn off the power and the wiring's open to invasion."

"Any side effects? I mean, how do they end?" Torlino asked.

Sherry's fingers curled into a ball. She smiled, and crossed and uncrossed her calves.

Another question she didn't like, Karpovich thought.

"Side effects?" Sherry repeated. She put her elbows on the table and folded her hands, seeming to contemplate the question.

How did they end? A very good question indeed.

How did you ever forget the sound of earth being tossed on your grave as you're being buried alive? How could you ever forget the taste of a plastic tube taped in your mouth, the plane going down, or the muzzle flash when a gun is pointed straight at you? Could you ever forget making a mistake that cost a life?

"No effects, really," she said.

Even now she was defying her doctor's orders. *"Your little horror shows are catching up with you, Sherry, aren't they?"* The doctor never liked what she did and thought it caused her harm in ways that no one could comprehend. She'd been told that her work was at variance with nature and that just because she was already blind didn't mean that worse couldn't befall her.

She knew what the doctor was thinking—the nervous tic that sometimes appeared at the corner of her mouth, the nightmares and obsessions.

"Post-traumatic stress disorder can lead to dozens of forms of psychosis, Sherry. You must consider the side effects."

But people managed to cope with complex emotions all the time. Cops, emergency workers, soldiers—they all took on horrible memories. The fact that she was seeing it through the victim's eyes hardly seemed relevant. It was still only a memory, and no one ever died of a memory.

Besides, the thought of not doing it terrified her even more.

As a child in the orphanage, she had dreamed of becoming someone important, some extraordinary woman that other people looked up to, a woman like the doctors and politicians and astronauts in her textbooks. She wanted to go to a university to discover new theories and ideas; she wanted to contribute to society in some distinctive, meaningful way.

But the dream had only been a dream. She was, in reality, a penniless orphan. Not only was she an orphan, but a blind orphan with no past. It quickly became apparent to her, as other children came and went, that no one was going to adopt a blind girl with no history. She knew that without the kind of financial help that only parents could give, she would never realize her dream.

It was ironic that only now, after Sherry had become a minor celebrity with more than enough money for college, that universities were throwing themselves at her feet, that doctors and scientists rallied to study or educate or even save her from herself.

No. She had made it this far on her own. She had fulfilled the dream on her own and she had no intention of going back, no desire to live in darkness or go through life afraid. She would take life head-on, even at the risk of her sanity.

Torlino continued to nod, seemingly impressed by the expression on her face.

"No dreams?" Karpovich asked. His voice was so soft, so gentle that the question barely registered.

She turned her smile away from them. "We all have dreams, Edward; you dream about what you see at work, I dream about what I see. Even our victims have dreams. Dr. Donovan was thinking about that concrete trough in the last moments of his life because he must have thought about it most every day for the last thirty years. And sheep. I know you mentioned it was a cattle farm, Edward, but I saw sheep beneath my feet."

"Sheep?" Torlino repeated.

She finished her drink. "What if the whole purpose of the cattle was to justify the trough and the whole purpose of the trough was to cover a grave? According to the inventory, there was more than adequate machinery to set the tank there by himself."

"But why go to the trouble?" Torlino asked. "Why not just bury her at the edge of the forest?"

Karpovich put a hand on the younger man's arm, feeling foolish for not thinking of it himself. "Because he didn't know when the police were going to show up, and the last thing he wanted them to discover was broken ground."

"Exactly," Sherry said. "The tank looked natural because water slops out and the earth around it got trampled as a matter of course. Can't you just imagine those officers walking around those buildings and fields, and right there in front of them, just fifty feet from the house, was a herd of cattle, ankle-deep in the muck around a trough, as if they had all been there for years? Who would have thought otherwise?"

"So what's with the sheep?" Torlino asked.

"My guess," Sherry said, "is that there were sheep in the field prior to the murder. I think he was remembering a time right after the killing. He was standing among the sheep and trying to decide what to do with her. Finally he decided to drop a concrete trough on top of the grave, a trough so large and so heavy that nobody could move it without machinery. The sheep were too small to drink from such a tank, so he sold them and surrounded it with cattle."

2

SUNDAY, APRIL 10
TEXHOMA PANHANDLE, OKLAHOMA

Dirt devils danced on a sea of brome, jagged shards of lightning intermittently blazing on the charcoal sky. The storm front stretched across the Oklahoma horizon, clouds twisting, merging, rising from an untold fountain of energy, feeding the violent thunderheads that grew larger and darker with each passing minute.

A church bell tolled, for it was Sunday, and those who elected to worship were ushered from their blocks into various congregations. Earl Oberlein Sykes, who chose not to, watched the storm's approach from his cell.

A buzzer sounded in the bowels of the building, electronic doors opened and closed, followed by shouts and cadent footsteps.

The April winds howled through the bastions, slapping snap hooks on flagpoles with a monotonous clanking of steel on steel that reminded Sykes of sailboat riggings in the stormy harbors of his youth.

The inner walls of the prison measured four stories

high and six feet thick, a fortress of red brick topped with rolls of razor wire and miles of filament so hot it would liquefy your belt buckle. Two outer perimeters of twenty-foot cyclone fencing were similarly electrified, with three additional coils of razor wire and pressure-sensitive alarms built into the ground. Guards walked the towers with SIG Sauer sniper rifles; heat-sensitive infrareds panned the complex's concentric tiers of security, all of them autonomous and all of them lethal.

Beyond the walls lay hundreds of thousands of square miles of barren plain—a no-man's-land with no signs, no roads, no lights, no landmarks, and no hope of outrunning a helicopter in pitch darkness.

Sykes no longer dwelled on the walls or on what was on the other side. Oklahoma wasn't his concern anymore.

He backed up to his bunk and sat in boxers that were soaked, like his body, with sweat. His sallow flesh sagged for lack of sun and bore faded green tattoos on both arms—one an evil leprechaun, the other a naked woman. He wore LOVE etched across the knuckles of his left hand and HATE across the knuckles of his right. His eyes were a liverish brown and draped with reptilian lids. A thick, wormlike scar ran jaggedly down the front of his neck, where an inmate had cut his throat with soup can lids soldered together. A brown, cauliflower-like tumor had formed behind one ear and another grew on his groin. A quarter-size patch of dead skin, which he would scratch until it bled, rankled the back of his neck.

Sykes wiped his underarms with a hand towel and

dabbed his face. Sweat continued to pour from his temples and his brow and belly and, Jesus, it was hot.

Rain splattered the window and abruptly stopped. He pushed the towel against his abdomen and bared his teeth, rolling off the cot and moving fast for the toilet. Something repugnant slithered in his belly and his bowels let loose all at once.

He'd been thinking about Susan Markey again this morning, all the usual things—wondering what she was doing right now, where she was living and with whom. Wondering when she last thought of him, if she'd thought of him, and what she would think of him now. If she knew.

He saw her in his mind's eye in his old Chevy van, cross-legged in her hippie skirt, lips smeared red, eating from a basket of strawberries that she would buy—or more likely steal—from the truck stands outside the Pine Barrens. Her green eyes were always wild, waiting in rapt attention for him to tell her where they were going next, what they were going to do; the anticipation drove her crazy.

A chill ran down his spine. He finished on the toilet and pushed the button to flush, then got unsteadily to his feet and made his way to the bunk, wiping his mouth with the hand towel once more.

The sweating stopped abruptly, his arms and legs prickled with goose bumps, and he shivered. Hot and cold, cold and hot. It had been like this all week.

A hollow ringing sounded on the steps. More gates slid open and closed. He stared at the steel bars, then at the steel walls, the ceiling, floor, mirror, sink, toilet, bed—everything steel. He hated the sound of metal more than anything else on this earth. He was a monkey in a cage, marking time by the opening and closing of his master's doors. The waking time, the feeding time, the exercise time . . . all preceded by their own unique metallic noise.

The shivering worsened. It was nerves, he knew. He'd been warned about getting the nerves. They said it would happen like this. Even the toughest of inmates went through it, though he had never imagined it would happen to him.

Syko Sue, her friends had begun to call her. The play on words stuck and he'd gone around Wildwood painting it on railroad trestles, overpasses, concrete walls, and boardwalks.

She was anti-everything and liked the name, liked to think of herself as an anarchist and despised authority of any kind. She would have joined the Weathermen or the SLA if she'd moved to a big city. In small-town Wildwood, she did the next best thing. She joined Sykes.

She was into sex, oh Jesus, she was into sex, but it wasn't about sex or a lack of inhibition with Susan. Susan wanted to obliterate her past. She wanted to escape the shattered dreams of a once-perfect childhood; of an abusive, pious father, a former police captain who got himself indicted for racketeering; of her pretty mother, who walked into the ocean rather than face the humiliation.

She wanted to hurt someone, anyone, even herself. She wanted to inflict pain on other human beings. And in the bucolic seaside resort filled with the hippies of the Love Generation, it was only natural that

Sykes, who simply radiated wrong-side-of-the-tracks appeal, caught her eye.

He wasn't like the others, all beads and blather. He was pure, unadulterated disorder, and it pulled her to him like a moth to the flame.

He knew she liked the reactions they got when she brought him around her friends from school. She especially liked to shock her father and his cop friends who used to visit the house for holidays and backyard barbecues. Back before the rumors of an indictment came around.

But Sue Markey wasn't all show. She had an insatiable appetite for danger. There wasn't anything she wouldn't do, save murder, and she knew that Sykes's tastes ran even stronger. Susan had been to the bus. Susan knew what happened to those women in the bus.

He threw the dirty towel in a corner and looked at the Timex Indiglo he wore on the underside of his wrist. Rain hammered on the window once more, this time continuing. He scratched the dead skin at the base of his skull and something wet gave way. *If the cancer doesn't kill you, the cure most surely will.* He hacked and spat at the sink.

Sykes had never had money growing up, not even the middle-class kind of money that Susan Markey was accustomed to, but he knew all too well what money looked like, smelled like. He'd been bused from his ramshackle trailer park out of the Pine Barrens to Central High in Wildwood. He'd seen the Northside mothers picking up their daughters in their shiny new convertibles, gold glittering around their necks, their skin scented with nice perfume; how badly he had wanted them. How badly he had wanted to be one of them.

"Want a ride?"

Bianca Ashley was one of them: long hair down to the hem of her miniskirt, brand-spanking-new Mustang convertible for her sixteenth birthday. She'd caught him staring at it after school. The black paint was so liquid it looked like you could put your hand through it.

She brushed by him and threw her books in the backseat.

"Say pretty please."

They had never spoken before that moment. Bianca had ignored him all of the seven years they had been going to the same schools.

"Come on, boy. Beg a little and I'll give you a ride."

Sykes had just stared at her, not knowing if she was serious. She jumped behind the wheel and her checkered skirt leaped up to reveal a pair of pink panties that she was slow to hide. His eyes fixed on her long bare legs. *"Yeah, cool,"* he heard himself say. *"Yeah, please. I'd like a ride."*

She turned the key and when he stepped toward the door she punched the accelerator, flinging mud all over his jeans as she fishtailed her way out of the parking lot. *"Yeah, right, Syko,"* she'd laughed over her shoulder.

In that moment, Sykes knew that whatever he wanted in life he was going to have to take. That no one was ever going to give him anything. And he knew that one day he would meet Bianca Ashley again, and when he did, it would be her turn to learn about pain.

But that was all a very long time ago. Now was what mattered. Sykes had to concentrate on now. On what was left.

The small-town cops never connected Sykes and Markey to their crimes. They were far too busy with the thousands of hippies swarming the coastal communities, overwhelmed with human emergencies when most of them had only ever written parking tickets before. The state police were called in to assist on the more serious cases, but the locals were jealous of them and there was so much enmity between the two divisions that little was ever accomplished.

Meanwhile, Sykes and Markey kidnapped, robbed, and burglarized with impunity.

Their union was more than mere occasion; one could say it was a cataclysmic event. Individually they posed a societal threat, and each was certainly destined for a life of judicial intervention. Together they formed a uniquely chilling menace. A predator with two minds and one will. Markey wanted the dissolution of society. Sykes wanted to take what he had been denied by birthright. They complemented each other in some twisted way, brains and brawn, different backgrounds, different triggers, but equally extreme and depraved. If Sykes hadn't panicked and run that bus off the road, the cops might never have caught on to them, at least not for years. Not back then. Not in the chaos of the seventies.

His recollection of the accident was still hazy. It was winter; Susan and he had been breaking into vacant luxury homes on North Beach for several days while bingeing on speedballs. They used a set of masters he'd bought from a cleaning contractor. They were soaring high when they picked up a shivering hitchhiker and her kid on the road out of town. Markey took care of the toddler while Sykes raped and then disposed of the woman in Blackswamp. When he went back to the van, it was gone, along with the kid. Susan Markey had taken them both.

He'd walked home, borrowed his neighbor's car, and driven the strip on Atlantic Avenue. She wasn't in any of the usual places. No one had seen the van.

Looking back, there had definitely been something going on with her around the holidays. She was having mood swings and he remembered their fighting over something that last day, though what it might have been, God only knew with all the drugs they had been doing.

Sykes was driving between his trailer and the boardwalk for the second time that afternoon when a police car rolled up behind him. He stepped on the gas and started to flee because he was still wearing the pants he'd worn when he'd killed the woman. He was just pulling away from the police car, a mile or so from the Atlantic Avenue strip, when he rounded a corner into the lane of a school bus.

He never did see Susan Markey again. She never showed at any of the hearings or trials. He never read a word about the kid or any of the half-dozen women who had gone missing in the Wildwood area during those years.

Years later Sykes received a letter from Susan while in prison. She told him she was glad about what had happened. She said she'd found God and prayed that he would do the same. Markey, who once thought the world was God's pigpen and he its perverted master, had found God. She—who said that no one ought to feel good; who moralized that the world's populations died of starvation while the rich cheated on taxes, gorged themselves with alcohol and food, whored and sent their children to schools to learn how to become just like them—had told him they deserved to get fucked. Fuck all of them. If Sykes and she happened to come along and fuck up someone else's life, it was no worse than they deserved.

Sykes knew she hadn't ratted him out. If she had, they would have taken him back to New Jersey and tried him for murder. If someone had found all those bodies in the junkyard, it would have made national news. But no one ever did, which meant that Markey hadn't wanted to confess to her crimes beyond some priest behind a confessional, and that she and God were content to leave well enough alone as long as he was in prison.

Now it was twenty-nine—nearly thirty—years later, and Sykes had spent most of the days of his life in prison—all for a fucking traffic accident. How ironic was that?

It had taken him a long time to come to the realization—the realization that he'd gotten life. The public defender assigned to represent Sykes told him to plead guilty to involuntary manslaughter, which would get him two years with probation. It was what all the drunk-driving fatalities were getting in the seventies.

But Wildwood police chief Jim Lynch wanted more and when he presented papers to prosecute Sykes for second-degree murder rather than manslaughter, the voters rallied around him and an election-year judge was all ears. Murder two was defined as "taking a life while engaged in the commission of a crime." It did not require the specific intent to murder. Chief Lynch proffered the argument that because Sykes was operating a motor vehicle under the influence of illegal narcotics when he obliterated the seventeen lives on the school bus, he was guilty of murder, not manslaughter.

Sykes was indicted, tried, and sentenced to life times two. The other fifteen trials were set aside in the interest of justice. Sykes had his life sentences. More trials would serve only to delay the healing that the town so badly needed. Only the mercy of an otherwise liberal judge allowed the sentences to run concurrently.

Like most serial rapists and killers, Sykes had thought a lot about his crimes over the years. The difference between Sykes and most other cons was that his crimes had gone unnoticed. The killing frenzy and the ease with which he kidnapped and disposed of his victims provided a veritable kaleidoscope of images: arms, legs, stomachs, hair, wild eyes, and pleading lips. He thought of Susan's own beautiful body and the deliriously erotic games they'd played. Looking back on the early years of his incarceration, he could remember thinking about little else. All he had then were his memories.

But now they were coming back to life. Susan had become a liability again. Susan, who knew what no other person on earth knew—where the bodies lay.

Sykes pulled on khaki trousers and heavy shoes and took a Marlboro from a pack on the stainless steel table, tapping it down on the face of his watch. He struck a match and raised it to the cigarette, admiring the way the woman's breasts swelled on his bicep, just the way they had when he was seventeen years old. He stood and threw the match at the stainless steel sink, hawking up something yellow that he spat into the toilet.

He blew smoke at the ceiling, the cigarette dangling from his lower lip as he rested his shoe on the sink and laced it, and wondered how it would feel.

A door opened at the end of the corridor. He could hear footsteps approaching. He dragged fingers through what was left of his dull gray hair, scratched the sore on the back of his neck, and approached the bars.

It was time.

Ice pelted the ground as they escorted him across the recreation yard. Though it was still morning, the sky had gone dark and the floodlights glared brightly. He was wearing orange coveralls with his wrists shackled to chains around his waist, which were shackled to chains around his ankles.

Low, chalky clouds raced over the walls, luminescent in the spots along the tower. Lightning stabbed through the darkness, revealing a lone silhouette at a fourth-floor window. The prison's psychiatrist. Sykes could make out the soft tapering of her shoulders in the shifting strengths of light. He looked up at her and smiled.

On the perimeter, a beacon switched from red to green and revolved slowly as heavy steel gates silently rolled back on Teflon bearings. He looked next at the men pacing the catwalks, rifles at the ready, razor wire flashing in the arc of the searchlights. He stepped into a wire chute and walked between his escorts to a small outbuilding at the base of the sally port. The gates rolled closed and the beacons switched back to red.

The heart of the storm struck all at once, dropping small spirals in the recreation yard, rattling fences, whistling through the brick turrets, bombarding hail, and hammering the steel rooftops of the outbuildings with machinelike precision until the noise was deafening.

The guards ran with Sykes, slamming the door behind them. Then advanced him toward a scarred metal desk, where he submitted his thumbprint and a signature. The guards led him to a small room with a bench chained to a wall. They removed his shackles and coveralls, which they flung in a canvas bucket, and gave him a belt and a denim shirt, a check for eighteen thousand dollars, and a fifty-dollar bill. Then they led Sykes to a door on the far side of the wall, where one of them pushed a button that released a heavy mechanical latch. The guard opened the door and let Sykes out into the storm. A plain white van idled outside the fence with its taillights glowing red and its double rear doors wide open.

The hail came in waves as thick as the rain and he raised his face to meet it, welcoming the stinging cold on his forehead, his neck, his mouth open and filling with ice as one of the frozen slivers drew blood from his lips.

He put a foot to the bumper just as another bolt of lightning illuminated his face. His eyes were wild with excitement as he stepped into the darkness, licking the blood from his lips and thinking how sweet it tasted to be free.

3

SUNDAY, MAY 1
WILDWOOD, NEW JERSEY

Lieutenant Kelly Lynch-O'Shaughnessy parked her cruiser in the Cresse Avenue public lot, climbing the ramp to the boardwalk and looking north toward Strayer's Amusement Pier. The pier extended over the dark ocean to where the first line of waves was breaking. It was a dismal sight this time of year. Wooden scaffolds and frames of amusement rides stood dormant until Memorial Day weekend, when the tourists began to trickle back into town.

She crossed to the opposite side of the boardwalk and descended the stairs to the beach. A crowd of policemen milled about; pink-faced rookies wearing yellow rain slickers walked a grid search back and forth along the beach.

It was a gray, unseasonably chilly day. She could feel the sand overtaking the sides of her shoes and reached down to remove them. Her panty hose would not survive, but heels were impossible in the sand.

She wore a navy plastic poncho—with LIEUTENANT stamped across the back—over her church clothes, a silk blouse and green wool skirt. She'd had to leave the girls with friends seated in a nearby pew.

She kept a long metal flashlight tucked under one of her arms and a portable radio clipped to her waist behind her gun. She could hear the garbled conversations between crime lab technicians under the boardwalk and cops in the public parking lot where they'd found the victim's car. She waited, alone, shifting her feet in the cold sand until they emerged from the darkness. She watched them cross the drainpipe that jutted out from under the boardwalk, their cameras slung over their shoulders. The pipe was at least three feet off the ground, difficult enough to cross in slacks; she wondered how she was going to manage it in a skirt.

"All through, Lieutenant," the first of them said.

She nodded. "What am I looking for?"

"Looks like she made it about halfway under and tried to hide behind the pipe," he replied, pointing toward the boardwalk. "That's where the blood trail ends. You'll see it easy enough. Up on top of the pipe there are drag marks; lots of handprints, most likely hers. Lots of hair, too, long hair." He held out his hands to indicate a foot or more. "Plenty of that around."

"Thanks," she said, rummaging through her pockets for a Nicorette. After a minute she popped one into her mouth and followed the pipe into the shadows.

"Lieutenant bars, my ass." Russell Dillon shook his bald head in disgust. "I've been taking that test since '91 and no one's going to tell me some broad can ace two back-to-back exams without some kind of help from above."

Doug "Mac" McGuire sighed and jotted notes in his book.

"Good ol' girl network. City manager is looking after her 'cause of her old man. You think I was born yesterday?" He lit a cigarette and belched.

McGuire looked up from his notes. "She wrote better papers than us. You can't fault her for being smart."

"Smart? Yeah, well, maybe you think she's smart. Some of us ain't that gullible."

"It's not being gullible, Dillon. I know her. I work with her."

"No, Mac, you work *for* her; there's a difference. She took your job out from under your nose and you don't even have the balls to stand up to it."

"Stand up to what? She outscored me. End of story."

Dillon looked at him and shook his head. "What? Are you in love, too?" He shook his head and stepped back. "Jesus Christ." He laughed. "A pair of tits walks into the building and suddenly everyone's too stupid to wipe their own ass. Well, not me. Chief makes the promotions come out the way he wants. That's just a fact of life. Blacks and women will always do better than us workingmen." He put on his hat. "Tell her I said one good fucking deserves another. Maybe she'd be interested."

"Tell her yourself," McGuire spat.

"Yeah, well, maybe I will. See yah later, *Sar-geant,*" he sneered. It was a look that was supposed to convey that Dillon knew something to which the rest of the world wasn't yet privy.

O'Shaughnessy shivered in the dark. She could smell the ancient timbers covered with barnacles and sea-weed. She played her light overhead, then ran it down the length of the pipe and around her feet in a circle. Water dripped from the cracks between the boards above, plinking hollowly in the cavernous chamber.

How different, she thought, from the church she'd been sitting in an hour ago. More and more frequently, she'd be with the girls one minute and out on the street the next, often in the middle of the night. But that was part of earning her new rank, she knew. It brought the respect of the men and women who had to be out there day and night, seven days a week. That respect didn't come easy. Besides, it wouldn't last forever. The girls probably wouldn't even remember it when they got older.

Graffiti covered the big drainpipe, mostly initials and dates and profanities. A leak at the bottom of the pipe allowed a stream of water to cut a gully through the sand. A heavy black stain marked the side of the pipe next to a smudged handprint. Mac said a dog found the scene. This is where it would have been. She could see the blood smeared across the pipe. This was where the victim had tried to hide from her captor.

O'Shaughnessy crouched where the handprints had dried on the near side of the pipe and tried to imagine what had happened. She placed her feet where the girl's feet would have been and leaned forward with her head touching the pipe. One large smear above her looked as if the girl had rested her hand there, bleeding all the while from her wound.

On the other side of the pipe lay crushed beer cans, bottle caps, and broken glass.

She rolled the beam of her light across a splintering timber, then back to the pipe and to the top of it again, finding more bloody splatters and smudges that could have been caused by someone's clothes. This was where he'd pulled the girl back across.

O'Shaughnessy played the light at her feet again, reaching for a red plastic hair clip. There was rust on its hinges, so she tossed it aside. To her left, she saw broken cinder blocks and a stack of broken planks, discarded angle brackets, and hundreds of galvanized nails.

She looked back toward the beach and the line of pale daylight coming from where she'd entered. McGuire was still there, kneeling in the light, his yellow slicker in stark contrast to the gray morning. She watched him raise a radio to his mouth and a plume of warm breath form around his head.

Sounds were immensely exaggerated beneath the walk—dripping water, footsteps clopping overhead; she could hear her bare feet grind the wet sand.

The mist had already made her skin and clothes slick, and the old timbers had shredded her stockings when she brushed against them. Something flashed in her light, farther under the pipe. She bent down, stretching for it, and plucked a woman's gold wristwatch from the sand. It bore no rust. In fact, it looked new and expensive. Someone had put it there intentionally. For someone else to find?

She turned off the flashlight and lifted her skirt to her waist. Then she put one leg over the pipe and followed with the other, tugging the skirt down over her hips when she was on the other side. Then she turned the light back on.

The ceiling was getting lower as the sand began to rise; soon she had to stoop as she continued toward the street side of the walk.

Radio static sounded on her belt, but she was no longer listening. She was fascinated by the graffiti overhead. *LCMR High—'94 Champs, Allison loves Christy, Beejun's suck,* and *Surfers Rule*—but someone had put a *D* in front of the *R* to make it read *DRule. Beatles, Talbert, Wishbone, EP loves FS, Fuck Gerald,* and *Bay Side Blows. I love Paul, Pat loves Rocky, SSM 96, BH is a cunt, Green Day Dookie, Merchant Marines, Syko Sue, Kurt Cocaine, Curly and Moe.*

Who spent so much time under here? she wondered. Druggies? Had the victim come here willingly?

She had never really thought about what went on under the boardwalk before. It didn't exist for her. She'd grown up in Wildwood and had gone to the beach parties. She'd even hung out with some of the girls on Strayer's Pier, but if there had been life beneath the timbers she'd missed it somehow. It had never occurred to her all these years that there could be people gathered down here right under her feet.

She tried to imagine them sitting in the dark, hot coals of their cigarettes floating about their heads, drinking beer and pointing their hissing cans of paint at the beams to write their epigraphs.

O'Shaughnessy continued to the parking lot and stepped out alongside the pipe. The dull light shone on the wet asphalt. Uniformed officers were gathered around a wrecker that was lifting a dark green Explorer onto its hook.

The jack lay next to the right front tire, which was flat. A woman's jacket sat on the passenger seat. O'Shaughnessy knew what was in the pockets—an unwrapped condom and a tube of lipstick.

She stood another minute, glancing between the Explorer and the dark boardwalk from where she had just exited. Then she looked toward Atlantic Avenue. If the woman had been near her car when her attacker pulled into the lot, then why hadn't she run toward the lit street instead of going under the dark boardwalk? She took the radio from her belt and keyed the mike.

"Cruiser three."

"Go ahead, three."

"Have we got a return from Randall yet?"

"Yes, Lieutenant. He states negative on the hospitals; we're still checking the twenty-four-hour reports with the state. Copy?"

"Copy," O'Shaughnessy said.

* * *

An hour later she returned to police headquarters on Pacific Avenue carrying a Styrofoam cup full of coffee. She was hungry, but ever since she'd stopped smoking, she had been fighting off the weight.

O'Shaughnessy peeked into the sergeant's office, where McGuire had a phone cradled to his ear. She could tell by his expression that he was on hold. "Anything new?" she whispered.

He mouthed the word "Chief" back at her and pointed toward her office. She waved her thanks and threaded her way through the detectives' desks toward the glassed-in enclosure with a sign that read "Lieutenant."

Loudon was on the sofa thumbing through an old edition of *The New Yorker.*

"Chief." She put down her coffee and stashed her purse under the desk, then shook off the rain parka and hooked it on a tree.

Loudon looked up at her and recrossed his legs. "I heard on the radio you were heading back. Thought I'd make myself comfortable."

Her hands were filthy. Her stockings were torn. There was a streak of something black across her forehead.

"You all right?" he asked, looking over the top of the magazine.

She nodded, sliding into her chair and prying the lid off the Styrofoam cup. "Just chose the wrong outfit again."

She sneezed.

"God bless you," Loudon said, tossing the magazine aside.

"Want to share?" She held up the cup.

He shook his head. "But thanks."

There was a pack of photos on her desk: early copies of the crime scene from this morning. The lab chief had rushed them.

O'Shaughnessy kicked off her shoes and began to rub her feet together under the desk. She took a sip of coffee and removed a notebook from her purse, flipping open the cover.

"We've got a fresh scene," she said. "Six to ten hours old at the most. No body." She looked up at the chief. "I'm writing it as a kidnapping. Woman was jogging with her dog along the beach when the dog ran under the boardwalk. When he came out, his muzzle was bloody. She thought he'd cut himself, but when she checked him out, he was fine."

The phone rang in the outer office. The chief got up and pushed the door closed.

"The woman called nine-one-one and we sent a patrol car."

She nodded at the envelope.

He opened the seal and shook the pictures out on the desk. There were flashbulb bursts of bloody handprints on pilings, blood pools in the sand, blood smears on a drainage pipe.

"First officers on the scene found the Explorer in public parking. Doors were unlocked, keys in the ignition." She pointed to a picture in his hand. "Tire's flat on the driver's side, there's a hole in the sidewall at least two inches from contact tread. A woman's jacket was found on the passenger seat, no IDs, but there was a registration under the visor. Matches the tags. Car is listed to Jason Carlino, 10 Faring Way in North Beach. We sent uniforms, but no one was home. His neighbor says he goes out of town a lot on business. Drives a Lincoln for a company car, and it's not at the house."

She took a sip of coffee. "Wife's in her late thirties, name is Elizabeth. She owns Guppies, the day care on New York Avenue. There's a daughter, Anne"— O'Shaughnessy flipped through her notes—"she's seventeen. We left a note on the door of the house and have been calling there hourly. No sign of anyone yet. Possibly they are away for the holiday, but that doesn't explain the Explorer."

The chief grunted.

She looked down at her notes again.

"Jason is the CEO of Echo Enterprises, a communications consulting firm. We have an office number for him, got it from the company that monitors his security system. Mac left a message on his voice mail. Hopefully he checks it often."

O'Shaughnessy turned a page and sipped more coffee. "Uniforms conducted a grid search of the lot and beach. Negative. Only two businesses are open late night on Atlantic this time of year. The Texaco and the 7-Eleven. We woke up both clerks and neither of them remembered anything unusual. You know what it's like down there in May. Ghost town."

Sergeant McGuire was on his feet and coming toward the window. He pushed a sheet of bond paper up to the glass that read: "Your daughters are home with Tim. Cat is missing."

She sighed and nodded, raised a hand to thank him, then looked back at her notes.

"Morning Public Works crew comes on at four. Mac has a guy at the dump looking through last night's trash."

Loudon grunted. "What else?"

"Under the boardwalk, over here." She leaned forward and took the photos back, fanning through them until she found the one she was looking for. "This drainpipe runs across the parking lot and under the boardwalk. That's where she went in. The blood trail follows it. When she gets halfway under, she crosses to the other side. Then she tries to hide under it."

She pointed to a dark smudge on the film. "This is where he pulled her back across." Her finger slid to the bottom of the picture. "I found a woman's wristwatch right here. I think she left it there on purpose."

Loudon's eyes met hers over the desk.

"It rained pretty hard last night, so the lot's clean. Sand is too deep to get usable footprints. Maybe they'll have better luck with whatever they find inside the car."

"Get that blood typed," Loudon said. "Maybe it isn't human." As he spoke, he flipped through the photos—some with bright white spots where flashbulbs reflected off the white-paint graffiti. "I've seen some pretty weird hoaxes around here."

O'Shaughnessy nodded. "I thought of that, too. Meyers got samples to Mercy Hospital first thing. It's A-positive and definitely human."

"Yeah, yeah," Loudon whispered, as though it was foolish to hope for good news.

"I checked the emergency rooms at both hospitals;

there are no Jane Doe admissions in the last twenty-four hours."

"Can we get into the Carlino house?"

"McGuire has a call in to Hamilton. He's working on an affidavit with Judge Merrell."

"Good job, Kelly. Let me know if anything changes."

"The press," she said quickly. "What do you want me to give them?"

"Nothing. Not until you've talked to the family. We need to know who's not accounted for before we start crying wolf."

She nodded. "But if we do reach the family and either of the Carlino women is missing, I want a photo of them on the eleven o'clock news."

"Do what you think is right. You need anything from me?"

She shook her head.

He made a steeple of his fingers and touched his lips. "You heard about Elmwood?"

She nodded. "I sent McGuire when we finished. I'll stop by myself as soon as I get out of here."

"Don't bother." Loudon shook his head. "I went over myself. Body's in the morgue, building's in lockdown, nothing you can do until tomorrow."

O'Shaughnessy raised her eyebrows, wondering why the chief would respond to a slip-and-fall death in a nursing home.

"Any scene to speak of?"

He shook his head. "Nothing inconsistent with an accident, although I don't like people falling down stairwells in the dark. Always looks too neat. Even old people in nursing homes."

"Maybe he cheated at hearts."

"Or he was hitting on some great-grandma and her main squeeze found out." Loudon smiled.

"McGuire could have managed until I got there." The question loomed.

"I knew him," Loudon said at last. "Name was Andrew Markey. He was a captain on the PD when I came on."

"No shit."

"Didn't end up well for him." He shook his head. "Got involved with organized crime in Atlantic City and earned himself a few years in Poughkeepsie."

"So the fall down the stairs really does bother you?"

He shook his head. "Nah. All that's ancient history now. Slip-and-fall is all it was. I guess I was just curious."

"You want me to do anything special?"

He shook his head. "Autopsy should tell you enough. You're going to have plenty on your plate with this boardwalk thing, so get yourself into some dry clothes and find that cat. Let Mac take it for now. Mac can handle it just fine."

O'Shaughnessy finished the dishes by eight, put scraps of cold lamb in Chester's bowl, and changed into workout clothes after she tucked the girls in for the night. Tim had stayed with them until she got home. In retrospect, he had tried to start a conversation, but she'd been unreceptive. Maybe it was all that had happened today or maybe she just didn't want to make things easy for him.

She didn't play the 911 tape until she was on the exercise bike in her bedroom, eating a celery stick and trying to manipulate the cassette player with her free hand.

"The time is 5 . . . 54 and 20 seconds," a voice announced. There was silence followed by static, then a loud clicking noise before the voice of a female dispatcher: "Wildwood Central. Go ahead with your emergency."

"My name is Cathy Rush," a woman said. Her accent was very heavy Southern. "I'm, uh, visiting a relative in town, and I, uh, I was jogging and my dog went under the boardwalk and came out with blood all over his face. I checked him out real good, and the, uh, blood cleaned up, but something is under there. I, um, yelled out, but nobody answered. It's pretty dark under there and I didn't want to go under alone—"

The dispatcher broke in calmly. "You say this is under the boardwalk?"

"Uh-huh, near the big pier with all the rides on it."

"Is that at Rio Grande?"

"I'm not sure of . . . the street name, there's a . . . there's a shop here on the corner, I'm just visiting for the weekend, T-Tops, the store's called T-Tops, the carnival rides are just across from me."

"Look at the top of the ramp; there should be a metal sign across the top of the ramp with the street name on it. Can you see it from there?"

"Just a minute," the woman said. A moment later she was back. "Yeah, Rio Grande—just like you said."

"All right, ma'am, that's Strayer's Pier. Can you stay right there where you are? We'll need you to show the officer where your dog went under. Can you wait long enough to show the police the way?"

"Uh, yeah, I can wait."

"All right, Cathy, they're halfway there now, you just hang on, all right?"

"All right," she said.

The tape stopped, but O'Shaughnessy pedaled on, thinking that at any minute her own phone would ring. McGuire should certainly have found one of the Carlino relatives by now.

She thought about the foreboding she'd felt under the boardwalk this morning, how eerie it all had seemed. It was like another world down there. She thought about the graffiti and the beer cans and the cigarette butts and the idea of people walking up and down the boardwalk with someone crouched beneath. The pier no longer summoned the good feelings it once had.

Strayer's Pier was where all the teens hung out in summer; it was no secret to the Wildwood police that there were drugs around. Even in winter, when the weather was decent, there were crowds. Had Anne gone to buy drugs and returned to her car to find her tire flat?

O'Shaughnessy stopped pedaling and jotted a note on a pad she kept next to the bike. *Check service stations about other tire repairs from parking lot.* Maybe it was a robbery that turned bad. You wouldn't report it to the police when someone stole your drugs, but you still had to get your tire fixed.

She jumped off the bike, disappointed that she hadn't heard from McGuire. It had been nearly twenty hours and they still didn't have a name for their victim.

She took a hot shower, then crawled into bed and tried to read.

McGuire called at eleven. He explained that the judge had issued a warrant so that the police could enter the Carlino family residence to check on their well-being. McGuire used the alarm company's keys, searched the house, and picked up messages from the answering machine. A young woman wanted Anne to call her immediately. A young man simply said, "Call when you get a chance."

A calendar on the refrigerator displayed school events, dentist appointments, and an oil change for the Explorer. Today's date had a line through it with "Dallas" written in pencil on it. McGuire picked up an address book from a desk in the dining room and left a note for the family to call him upon their return.

O'Shaughnessy could hear a phone ringing in the background as they talked. "Wait just a minute, Lieu," McGuire told her. "That might be them."

Five minutes later he was back.

"That was Mr. Carlino. He's at the Airport Hyatt in Dallas with his wife. The daughter, Anne, is still here in town. I explained that we found his car and he said his daughter would have been driving it. She's supposed to be staying at a girlfriend's house in Wildwood. He called there as soon as he got our message, but the line has been busy and he can't get through. I told him I'd head straight there and call him back.

"The girlfriend is Jennie Woo. Needless to say, the

father's upset. They're booking a flight home now. You'll be in Trenton tomorrow?"

"Yes, but call me when you get to the Woos'. I can sleep on the way to the conference."

The call came at 1:00 A.M.

"Jennie Woo said that Anne lied to her parents about staying at her house. When her parents leave town, Anne's boyfriend always sleeps over at the Carlino house. It was a thing they had going on."

O'Shaughnessy looked at the Nicorette box on the dresser and forced herself to remain in bed.

"Anne was supposed to hook up with the boyfriend at Strayer's Pier after ten."

"Didn't she worry her parents might call the Woos' house?"

"Jennie said they had a routine. Anne's mother always called to check on her in the morning. Anne would spend the night at her parents' house with her boyfriend and beat feet over to Jennie's in time to intercept the call. She said they'd done it two or three times before. She said her parents never talked to the Carlinos so there was little chance the families would compare notes."

"Didn't her friend worry when she didn't show up for the call?"

"She did. When Anne's mother called this morning, Jennie lied and said that Anne had just run to the store for orange juice. She thought maybe Anne had had too much to drink and was sleeping it off with her boyfriend. That's when she left the message we heard on the machine."

"Who's the boyfriend?"

"Name is Larry Wilder. Jennie already called him."

O'Shaughnessy grunted and swung her legs out of the bed, walking to the dresser for a piece of the gum. "One of Bud's sons?"

"Oldest. He said he was on Strayer's talking to another girl when Anne showed up and it turned into an argument. He said he left her standing there and went out drinking with the guys. Larry is twenty-two and Anne is seventeen. He told Jennie he thought Anne had gone straight to her house. His was the second call to the Carlinos after he talked to Jennie."

"Get over to his house and see if he'll give you a consent to search his car. If not, secure it until we can get a warrant. Someone had to drive her out of there, and whoever did has blood in their car."

"On my way."

"One more thing. Check out the parents' flight to Dallas. Make sure it jibes with what he's telling us."

"I'll ask Randall to confirm it."

"Good. I want a picture of Anne on the news the moment the parents return. Pick a good one. I'll write the press release and fax it to you when I reach Trenton."

"That it?"

"That's it."

She lay back on the pillow and chomped on her Nicorette for a while. Then she took it out of her mouth and laid it on the edge of a magazine for morning.

Thirty minutes later she was awakened by a sleepy eight-year-old Reagan in flannel pajamas. The two snuggled tightly, but for O'Shaughnessy, the night was sleepless.

4

WEDNESDAY, MAY 4
PHILADELPHIA, PENNSYLVANIA

Sherry was bundled in a sweater on a lawn chair overlooking the Delaware. She could hear the growl of a tugboat heading upriver and the chop of the waves slapping against the bulkhead. The evening sun was warm on her face and along the shoreline someone was playing music. Laughter traveled easily across the water. Happy people, touching people, the kind of people she wanted to be.

Sherry was nearly five years old when her life began. A maintenance man found her unconscious on the stairs outside a Philadelphia hospital. It was in the early-morning hours and the city was glazed by many hours of freezing rain. Investigators later speculated that she had neared the top and lost her footing on the ice, stumbled backward, fallen, and fractured her skull on the concrete landing. Her face was so thoroughly frozen to the ground that the skin over one cheek tore in their haste to get her inside. Only an adult-size red fisherman's sweater that someone had put on her saved her from hypothermia. But she suffered brain damage resulting in the bilateral destruction of the occipital cortex, leaving her blind and without a memory of her past.

Philadelphia made a fuss over her for quite a while: money poured in from well-wishers all over the country, much of it used to pay her medical bills. Police used the media in their search for her parents, and doctors tried for months to break down the psychosomatic walls that her brain had erected to protect her. Neither came to fruition.

Sherry was eventually named for the deceased daughter of the janitor who'd discovered her and packed off to a city-managed orphanage. It was there—at age eleven—that Sherry first experienced the loss of another human being, of someone she knew.

It was in the springtime, when windows are left open and green buds dot tree branches. One of the girls at the orphanage fell ill and was rushed away.

Four days later the children were bused to a funeral parlor where they lined up with single carnations to carry to the casket. Sherry, who had been instructed to keep her hand on the shoulder of the child in front of her, instead reached for the dead girl's hand to press the flower in and was instantly overpowered by visions not her own: a drab steel cabinet, a glass bottle, the black-and-white tile floor. The girl was vomiting; her eyes were at floor level watching a green-colored translucent bottle rolling in a circle by her face. There were letters on it: C O C A – C O L A.

When Sherry was next aware of her surroundings, she was kneeling on the wet step in front of the casket. There were hands on her shoulders; she had vomited all over her dress.

Later she told one of the children what she'd seen. When the staff learned of it they sent her to the headmaster, who made her apologize for lying. Sherry could no more know the color green, the headmaster told her, than she could read Chinese—or English—for that matter.

Many years later a detective in the Philadelphia Police Department would pull the files on the death of the young girl at the orphanage and discover that the maintenance people were storing strychnine concentrate for rat control in soft drink bottles in an unlocked cabinet on the children's floor. The child's death had been ruled accidental by the coroner, he told Sherry. The headmaster had received a slap on the wrist.

It was her second experience with death at age twenty-three that would bring Sherry's remarkable ability to the attention of authorities and soon after, the world.

The incident was in late November, during a snowstorm when tire chains jingled merrily throughout the city. She had just departed the bus at Passyunk and Washington to a street corner transfer, tasting spits of snow on her tongue and thinking about a boy she had met at work. Suddenly she heard a woman's scream and something heavy fell against her. A strong hand grabbed her wrist and pulled her down to the sidewalk. There were more screams, then movement all around her; she was dazed, but heard the word *ambulance*.

She turned in the direction of the person who had grabbed her, his hand fiercely clutching hers now; snow covered the side of her face, stuck to her eyebrows and hair. "He's not breathing!" someone screamed. "He's not breathing!"

Someone else grabbed her shoulders. "Are you all right? The ambulance will be right here."

There were more footsteps, then sirens and people crowding against her; suddenly the hand went limp. The moment the big cold fingers relaxed, she saw a woman, then a man behind a desk, a truck, a barrel filled with holes, a finger coming out of one of the holes, the finger moving, the barrel falling, striking water under a bridge, bobbing for a moment, then sinking beneath the surface.

Sherry's injuries were minor. Separate ambulances took her and the heart attack victim to Nazareth Hospital, where a police officer later told her that the man had died on the street.

Sherry wanted to tell him about the man in the barrel. But it wasn't easy telling someone what you thought you saw when it was clear to the person that you were blind. She recalled the sharp rebuke from the staff at the Halley House Orphanage and kept her mouth shut.

But later that night in her apartment, she remembered thinking that she was withholding something vitally important. What if the police were looking for a man? What if they would know what she was talking about?

Sherry called 911 and convinced someone to let her talk to a detective. A young rookie named John Payne answered the phone, and agreed to come to her apartment and meet her.

She was still second-guessing her decision when he arrived. He sat on her threadbare sofa and listened as Sherry described what she'd seen. He was sensitive, or at least polite. He asked her questions about what had happened during her fall; he was curious about how hard she'd struck her head, but who could blame him? When she talked about the barrel on the truck drilled full of holes, he prompted her to recall what the barrel was made of and whether or not it had any markings or imprints on it or if she could see anything else in or around the barrel or the river that could tell them where it was. Sherry remembered that there had been a blinking red light on the concrete support below the bridge. A navigation light?

The detective promised to check reports of missing persons in the city and let her know if anything unusual came up. She was sure he also called the hospital to check on her head injury. Whether it was her story or the next morning's news article in the *Inquirer* that motivated him, she would never learn. All she knew was that the following afternoon Detective Payne was back in her apartment carrying the newspaper.

The headline, he told her, read "Teamster Boss Missing." The article went on to describe how Joseph Pazlowski, recently indicted by a federal grand jury for pension fund fraud, was rumored to have been making a deal with the U.S. attorney's office before he mysteriously disappeared. Pazlowski was last seen near Christ Church on Market.

The man who had had the heart attack and pulled her to the sidewalk was Frank Lisky, better known on the waterfront as "Little Franky." Lisky had a record for freight hijacking and homicide.

Payne was particularly interested in the solid gold

tractor-trailer-shaped clip they found on Lisky's necktie in the hospital. Sherry couldn't have known he was wearing one. Sherry was blind. But Pazlowski, the missing Teamster, had owned one just like it. In fact it had been custom-made for him by Peterbilt, and he'd worn it every day of his life including the last on which he was seen.

The detectives put boats and search teams on the rivers under bridges. Divers did the rest, and when they finally found Pazlowski's body in an olive-oil barrel drilled full of half-inch holes, a very frightened Sherry Moore was brought into the U.S. attorney's office in Philadelphia District Court for interrogation.

The United States attorneys and organized crime investigators grilled her for hours until they were satisfied she had no prior knowledge of Pazlowski or Lisky and that her unexpected meeting with Lisky on the sidewalk had been just that. How she knew what she knew, they didn't dare to contemplate. In fact, all mention of Sherry Moore's testimony was stricken from the case files, and the department credited an anonymous caller's tip with leading them to the body.

No way did they want some defense attorney screwing up a murder indictment if they were lucky enough to make arrests on whoever ordered the hit.

Unfortunately—or fortunately, depending upon how you looked at things—a clerk in the U.S. attorney's office leaked Sherry's story to the press and she was immediately set upon by the media.

The front page of *The Philadelphia Inquirer* read "Blind Woman Sees Dead in Philadelphia." Detective Payne, fearing that halfwit mobsters might be planning to dispose of Sherry lest she see them committing crimes, began to stop by her apartment to check on her.

She got crank mail now and then and some odd and obscene calls until she dropped her listed number. Eventually the ruckus quieted down, but a letter that came a few months later from a lady in Minnesota would change Sherry's life forever. The woman had written to ask for Sherry's assistance in locating her husband's body. The missing man, Sherry would later discover, was the CEO of a national car rental company who had gone hunting in Canada with his best friend. Neither had been seen or heard from for weeks until her husband's friend had washed up in an Ontario Indian village on Rainy Lake.

Sherry's first friend outside the orphanage was Jolet Sampson, a neighbor who used to help Sherry go through her mail and pay the bills. She was sitting in Sherry's apartment laughing over the letter until it came to the part about the fee. Then Jolet went silent.

"What's it say? What's it say?" Sherry coaxed.

Jolet started again, but the mellifluent qualities of her voice were gone. "She wants to pay you fifty thousand dollars," she said, her voice quiet, speaking more to herself than to Sherry.

"Okay, yeah, yeah, tell me what it says."

"Sherry, I'm not kidding. The woman wants to pay you fifty thousand dollars."

Sherry laughed and told her friend to throw the letter away.

But Jolet's attitude had changed. "I don't know

what you think you're going to do in this world, you and your walking stick and your public school education. Do you have any idea what this place looks like, girl?" Jolet threw her arms out. "This ain't the fucking Ritz. This is a roach-infested slum, you idiot. You call that woman and you call her now. You be a damned fool if you don't. People like us don't get no second chance. If you don't call that lady, then I have nothing else to do with you, girl. I ain't hanging 'round with no fool. Not Jolet Sampson. You hear me?"

Sherry couldn't bring herself to make the call. Not even when Jolet failed to look in on her the next day and the day after that. For one thing, she wasn't even sure she could repeat what had happened on the corner of Passyunk and Washington. She couldn't take money for something she didn't know how to do in the first place.

Of equal concern was the fact that Sherry had never been beyond the ten square blocks in which she had been found and raised. Going out into the world by herself was an overwhelming prospect for a blind twenty-five-year-old. Maybe this wasn't the Ritz, but she was living on her own and that was a leap from the orphanage in her mind.

She did the only thing that made sense to her. She threw the letter away and hoped that Jolet would come to her senses.

The following Saturday, a man knocked on the door to her apartment. Sherry could hear the chains rattling down the hall as neighbors peeked out to see who was visiting. Jolet later told her the man had gotten out of a "big ass" limousine parked in the circle in front of their building.

His name was Abernathy, he said, an attorney, and he worked exclusively for a woman in Minnesota who had written her concerning her missing husband. Mr. Abernathy said that he was authorized to hand her a check for ten thousand dollars if she would only allow him ten minutes of her time. Sherry, who wouldn't have refused him under any circumstances, let him in.

He explained, over what turned out to be an hour, that his client had "friends" in Philadelphia who gave credence to Sherry's part in the Teamster matter. Because of them, he said, his client had come to believe that Sherry could help the police learn what had happened to her husband. He said the woman was prepared to give her an additional fifty thousand dollars for forty-eight more hours of her time. After that, no strings attached, she could keep the sixty thousand and Mr. Abernathy would see that she was returned to her doorstep.

Sherry protested that she honestly didn't believe she could help, but the attorney would not take no for an answer. He assured her his client's money was going to end up in someone's hands and that the next person might not be as scrupulous.

Charles Goldstone had gone on a hunting trip with his best friend, Bernie Lennox. Dropped in a camp on the Canadian border, they hiked into the woods as they had done a dozen times before.

The men had been missing for three weeks before Bernie's partial body washed up on the shore of the river that ran through an Indian reservation. Mrs.

Goldstone simply wanted to know where Charles had met his end. She held little hope he was still alive, but could not bear the thought of leaving him in the wilderness for eternity.

Sherry didn't even know what to wear. She had three outfits to her name, all dark polyester pantsuits that she wore to work. For the first time in her life she left the city limits of Philadelphia, flew on an airplane, rode in a limousine, and slept in a hotel.

The next day she flew in a four-seater from Rochester, Minnesota, to the Ontario border, then was driven to a small hospital in Fort Francis. Abernathy had warned her the previous night not to eat anything exotic. She wasn't sure what exotic meant, but now that she was having the first stirrings of what she was about to undertake, she got the message. "Exotic" meant anything she couldn't keep down.

This was no fallen man on a street corner that she was about to encounter. This was the partial remains of a man pulled out of a river, and God only knew what had been nibbling at him for so many weeks.

What would he smell like? How would his skin feel? She had a very limited knowledge of what happened to a body after it died. She knew of course that it must rot, but how long did that take? Weeks, months, years? Maybe she wouldn't be able to concentrate long enough to feel anything. Maybe it wasn't even possible to feel anything with someone who had been dead that long.

A very young and proper police officer had picked her up at the plane; the bitter winds had buffeted the small plane during the landing and Sherry was doubly glad she hadn't eaten breakfast that morning.

She felt the slippery tile underfoot as they left the snowy sidewalk, and was startled by a blast of hot air from above as they crossed the threshold into the reception area. A female physician met them at the counter and led them to an elevator in which they descended to the basement. Sherry couldn't say anyone was unpleasant to her in Fort Francis, but she couldn't say they were warm, either. Undoubtedly they were as skeptical of the whole affair as she was, and likely feeling foolish at the expense of some rich woman. In the morgue, the physician took her into a chemical-filled room and offered her a hard, molded chair to sit on.

"I will wheel the cadaver alongside you," the woman said. Her voice had a peculiar accent, something not even hinted at in the languages Sherry had yet been exposed to.

"It has been cleansed—not cleaned," she said, "and wrapped in plastic, except for the arm." Meaning there was only one arm?

"Please do not handle the skin roughly. It will come off. I have a mask for you if you'd like."

It took all of Sherry's will not to get sick. The hand felt like a rubber glove filled with ice water, and there was never a smell in her experience more putrid or powerful than the stench of that body. But the moment she took the hand she saw snow beneath her feet and the images started to pop like flashbulbs.

Something glimmering . . . a river . . . bloody hands . . . rushing water . . . last rock in a line of rocks . . . an arm in an orange coat sticking out of the snow . . . a massive boulder with pits for eyes, it had a shadowy crevice for a mouth and limbs and branches caught up around its base in the river like a dark fur collar . . . he jumped . . . underwater . . .

It took only seconds. Sherry dropped the hand and pushed her chair away from the corpse. Hearing the door open, she said, "I'm ready to go now."

If the woman was expecting an explanation, she didn't ask, nor did Sherry provide one. It was a private matter, she felt, something between her and the woman who had paid her. She thanked the doctor and left with the young policeman, stopping first at a lavatory to wash her hands and then taking his arm out to the car.

"Do I smell bad?" she asked the officer on their way back to the airport.

He laughed. "What do you mean?"

"I mean, do I smell bad?"

"You mean like that body?"

She nodded.

"It's in your head," he told her. "Literally in your head. It gets in your sinuses and taste buds and won't go away for days."

"So I don't smell bad."

"No." He laughed. "You don't smell bad."

Sherry sat with her head against the headrest, feeling two conflicting emotions. One, the horrible ordeal the man had gone through, the cold, the hopelessness—the heartache of his surrender to the river.

Then there was the elation of achieving what she had come to do. She had done it! She had purposely reached into another person's mind and read his thoughts. How unbelievable, she thought. How incredible. How uniquely her!

Mr. Abernathy was waiting for her in Rochester when she landed.

"Mrs. Goldstone wondered if she could meet you in person. She lives an hour from here. I took the liberty of making another night's accommodation for you if you decide to stay."

"I would love to spend another night," she said sincerely. "More than you can know, Mr. Abernathy. But I have to be at work in the morning or they'll fire me."

"The Department of Motor Vehicles," he said dryly.

"Yes."

Sherry thought about her overnight bag. She hadn't even brought extra underwear, let alone clothes for a second day. She knew, too, that she couldn't risk her job, no matter how much she wanted to prolong the adventure. And she couldn't take Mrs. Goldstone's money. Not for something as simple as telling her someone else's thoughts. Besides, everything about the trip had been a learning experience, terrifying and exhilarating, but oh how wonderful, and she thought it was payment enough.

No, she didn't want to return to her puny apartment in South Philadelphia and the halls that smelled like burnt grease and roach spray. She wanted to lie in the luxurious bed at the Hilton and eat twice-baked potatoes and taste the milk chocolates left on the fresh-scented sheets.

Abernathy sensed her dilemma. "I would be happy to pass on your message to Mrs. Goldstone since you are unable to, but what if I were to arrange another day off for you at work? Do you think you might reconsider?"

Her face lit up. "That's not really possible, Mr. Abernathy, is it?"

"Everything is possible, my dear," he said kindly.

"Then yes, but may I ask just one more question?" she said.

"Of course," he answered.

"Do I smell bad?"

Sherry spent two hours with the woman. She might not have eyes to see, but Sherry could tell the size of a room when she entered one, and if rooms were supposed to be like this, then she had been living in closets all her life.

"A truffle, dear?"

"I'm afraid I don't know what they are."

"Then take one," the woman said, placing a napkin in her hand. "I've never known anyone not to like them."

The old woman put Sherry at ease, assuring her that she had long been prepared for news of her husband's death. As Mr. Abernathy had said, she only wanted to know where he was, so she could put him to rest.

Sherry told her about what she'd seen: her husband's friend Bernie at the river's edge, trying to cross the rocks, but then falling in. Mrs. Goldstone was gracious and tranquil in spite of the news, sitting by a fragrant fire afterward and reminiscing about her husband.

Sherry listened with rapt attention for nearly an hour. She had the impression that the woman rarely had an opportunity to share her feelings about Charles with anyone, that her wealth had somehow isolated her. Mrs. Goldstone had lost not only her husband but her best friend as well.

This, Sherry thought, was the relationship she had been trying to articulate all these years. This was the kind of love she sought for herself, the marriage of friends and lovers.

"Oh, what good friends we all were. I miss them so." Mrs. Goldstone sighed. "And I'm afraid I've bent your ear all evening long. Finalizing Charles's affairs has drawn all of my attention, and then the children came and the board of directors; I seem to have been engaged since this happened. I haven't had the time to think of my memories just yet. I'll have Dan wire your money in the morning and see that you get home safe and sound. Is there anything else I can do for you, dear girl?"

Sherry nodded. "Mrs. Goldstone, I can't accept the money you offered. It was far too much to begin with, and you have given me an experience I'll never have again."

"Nonsense," the old woman said. "I always do what I say, and you should endeavor to do the same. The money will be wired as discussed. Remember, Sherry, that you have a gift, a rare gift, and I have a feeling you'll be doing lots more traveling before it's all over."

Sherry smiled and said thanks, thinking nothing could be further from the truth.

"Miss Moore."

Abernathy had appeared out of nowhere; his car was idling under the covered drive.

Sherry turned quickly. "Ma'am, there is one more thing you could do for me, if you don't mind me asking." She looked pathetically embarrassed.

"Please tell me, girl."

"Might I have another truffle?"

Indian guides knew of the face in the rocks that Sherry described. Starting on the opposite shore, they retraced Bernie's route and found the remains of Charles Goldstone only a few hundred yards away. He'd been killed by an ice fall while walking under a ledge. Bernie, badly wounded, had gone for help, but was too weak to manage a river crossing.

Word crept out of Fort Francis about Sherry's vision, and soon Sherry was famous. *Entertainment Tonight*, *People* magazine, *Popular Science*, *Newsweek* . . . Everyone was interested in the girl who could talk to the dead. The big four networks tried to get interviews, late-night talk shows called, and schools for the blind solicited her for speaking engagements.

Mrs. Goldstone was better than her word, depositing an additional twenty thousand dollars in Sherry's bank account the day they found Charles's body. She also sent her a box of truffles and continued to do so every year on the anniversary of their meeting.

The letters came rolling in by the hundreds.

Mail began to take on a whole new meaning to Sherry. She no longer worked at the DMV, but lived off the interest of her earnings. She accepted several "consulting" projects and was eventually recognized by some of the more liberal circles in law enforcement.

In time, she moved out of her little apartment and purchased a home on the Delaware.

Her gift brought her money and her money brought her security, but it was the sudden need that everyone was showing for her that rewarded Sherry the most. Their need gave her purpose, and purpose was a real reason to live. It was a dream fulfilled.

She had lived in the stone house for almost nine years now. Detective Payne helped her move her few things in and bought her her first housewarming gift—a golden kitten she named Truffles.

She soon met her neighbor, Mr. Brigham, widowed and well into his seventies, full of boyish energy. He was the tinkering sort, always hauling things around behind his lawn tractor. He took an interest in her immediately, sharing his evenings to read her mail or just chat over a glass of his beloved port.

So life had turned out better than she ever could have imagined; she had always been grateful for that, but she had never forgotten the sound of Mrs. Goldstone's voice as she recounted the stories about her husband. To have that kind of love was to have everything. That was what everyone lived for and so few experienced. That was the one thing that remained beyond her reach.

Sherry's world was small, even though she was making friends across the continent. She had no social circle and no events to attend, other than those

Detective Payne or her neighbor Mr. Brigham might drag her to, and they were mostly Christmas and retirement parties where couples dominated.

There were, however, three suitors over the last nine years. One, the result of Brigham's attempt at matchmaking, was a political science professor who held a civilian position in the defense department. He was also an avid football fan and, much to her delight, invited her to an Eagles game for their first date. Sherry was impressed that someone could understand how a blind person might find excitement in a stadium filled with people. Most people never saw her as another human being; were concerned with what she did, not who she was; wondered what she was thinking when she took their hand, if she could somehow read their minds. Either that or they treated her like an invalid.

She saw him a second time, for the symphony, and a third and last time over dinner. He had been made an unexpected offer in the Middle East, the details of which were sufficiently murky to suggest CIA to Brigham, but who would ever know? Brigham told her later that his colleague had sold his home and was never heard from again.

Then she met a police captain in Dallas on a case in Fort Worth. They saw each other monthly throughout 1995 and 1996, though monthly seemed to be enough for both of them. It was a purely sexual relationship, if she was honest with herself.

Most recently it had been the doctor from Denver whom she considered the biggest heartbreak of all. They'd met while she was working on a privately funded project in Pueblo, an archaeological dig by an internationally known salvage hunter named McKeewan. She'd worked for Gavin McKeewan before and was said to have put millions in his pockets. The focus of the dig was a mummified Indian embedded in the cavernous walls of an old copper mine; McKeewan was looking for gold, not copper, and the Indian carrying primitive tools had a bag of pure nuggets in his pocket. Sherry's attempt to read him produced nothing, but that's how it went. Nothing was ever for certain, not when it came to the dead.

Since it was winter, she considered the trip a welcome respite from the gloom of her house. Sherry was a summer girl in spite of her sightlessness, and the cold seemed only to work against her state of mind.

On the evening before her departure, the treasure hunters crowded into a saloon at the foot of Cheyenne Mountain. The salvage boys liked the place for its hearty stews, but the real appeal was the local beer.

A physician who was friends with one of the salvage crew came to the table and ended up buying a round and staying. The night grew old before the salvagers decided to leave; they still had an hour's drive back to Pueblo, but the doctor stayed on, and Sherry, who was booked at the Broadmoor a block away, could think of no reason to leave.

The Bee, as the saloon was known, was packed and noisy by midnight. They drank half-yards of beer and the waitress threw the trademark bumblebees that stuck to their clothes. One o'clock came and went, they had begun touching each other's arms as they talked, getting louder and laughing harder, and trips to the restroom aside, Sherry believed she had not had so much fun in all her life.

He called her cell phone the next morning and again that night when she was back in Philadelphia. He sent her a snowball packed in dry ice with a note that read "You're It." When Brigham opened it and put it in her hands, she knew she had left her heart in Colorado.

They talked on the phone all that week. On Saturday, he flew in to take her to dinner; he stayed at the Radisson rather than in her guest room. On Sunday they bundled up for an open-bus tour of downtown Philadelphia. He was funny and interesting. He seemed to know when to do something and when not to. He didn't dance around the fact she was blind and he didn't overcompensate. She could tell that his words came from his heart rather than his mind, and they reached her every time.

The following weekend she was back at the Broadmoor. He waited in the spitting snow with horse, carriage, and driver. She would never forget the jingling reins, the soft clomp of the animal's hooves, the driver's gentle nudges, and the old seat creaking as the doctor put his arm around her and pulled her into his shoulder.

She stayed at the foot of Cheyenne Mountain all that week and half of the next. And the year 2000 became the happiest year of her life.

She looked back on that wistfully. Things changed over time. The trips weren't always possible; his shifts

were long and he had other obligations as well. Sometimes she was on the road, too. Then his calls came
less frequently, and reluctantly Sherry had to accept
that he was moving on.

The answering machine kicked on and she heard
Detective Payne's voice. "Sherry, are you there?"

She pushed the cat away and got to her feet,
making her way to the wrought-iron table and felt
around for the phone.

"John, I didn't hear it ring."

Payne was the only person in Sherry's life with
whom she could be open. He was someone on whom
she could dump her troubles during those very rare
occasions she chose to open up her heart.

Sherry counted him as the first person ever to take
her seriously and their friendship had grown steadily
on that cornerstone. From the media attention she'd
gained over the Teamsters, to the shores of Lake
Francis to Arkansas and Colorado, Payne had always
been there when she needed him most.

She had to admit that in the early days she had
been more than just curious about him—curious in
a female sort of way. He was a detective, after all,
which was exciting enough when you're twenty-five.
She remembered her disappointment upon discover-
ing he was married. A silly thing, she'd thought
later; what detective would have wanted a blind girlfriend to take around?

To be honest, the doctor she'd met in Denver reminded her of John Payne. Neither man was given to
alarm; everything about them spoke of calm and
order. There seemed nothing they couldn't fix, no

problem that couldn't be solved. Both men were most capable yet exhibited a quiet modesty. They were men given to action rather than words, she thought.

Payne had introduced Sherry to his wife, Angie, soon after the Teamsters incident. The three of them socialized on a number of occasions, but then Angie stopped going out and Payne explained that she preferred to stay at home. Sherry accepted the excuse, but instinct told her something more was wrong.

Nine years later, Payne was still her best friend. She knew that he cared more for her than he would like to admit; there was always something else with Payne, something he held back and something she didn't encourage. She decided it was chemistry, the not uncommon sexual tension between two people who enjoy each other's company. God knew, if she'd had the chance to become Mrs. Payne years ago, she would have jumped on it, but it wasn't like that and it never would be. Payne had never expressed that his marriage was anything but good, and Sherry didn't pry when it came to Payne's home life. As for sexual tensions, people certainly didn't respond to every feeling they encountered.

Besides, Sherry knew what it was like to feel loss; she had lost her entire past and everyone in it. The last thing she was ever going to do was interfere with a relationship. She would never wish the kind of loneliness she felt on anyone. So Sherry had become an expert at hiding her emotions from Payne.

"You want Chinese?"

"Do you want Scotch?"

"Only if you want Chinese."

"Then I'll have the shrimp with lobster sauce."

"Be there in thirty minutes." He hung up the phone.

Payne mixed their cocktails in the kitchen and carried them to the yard with the bottle, food, and chopsticks. He even managed to get it all to the picnic table without spilling the drinks.

"Are you starved?" he asked. He let the bag drop to the table and brought her Scotch to the side of her chair.

"Nah." She sighed. "Maybe in a couple minutes." She took a sip, hearing the wake of a boat slapping the shoreline. "Just sit and relax."

He watched her face in the waning light. "You should take a vacation this year," he told her. "Book a cruise. Visit Europe. Hit the beach."

She smiled. "Not that again." She heard the ice tinkle as he took a drink and sensed that he was looking at her. "It's almost spring, John. It's getting warm again. I like it by the river. Can't you hear the water?"

"Oh, come on, Sherry. You've been hiding in this house ever since Norwich."

"I went to Pittsburgh," she retorted. "You said you were proud of me for going to Pittsburgh."

"I would have been proud of you for getting a root canal if it got you out of the house."

Sherry nodded. Payne knew how hard the Norwich case had been on her. How long it had taken for her to get the images out of her mind. And he knew, no doubt, though he'd never let on, that Sherry called the Connecticut State Police every few weeks to see if a suspect had been identified. One hadn't.

If he'd known about the recent nightmares and migraines, he'd have insisted she see the doctor, but then some things weren't even for Payne. Some things were best kept to herself.

"What about you guys? When was the last time you and Angie went anywhere? I haven't heard a single vacation story from you since I've known you, John. Oh—wait—yes, two years ago you painted the bedrooms." She snorted.

Payne threw up his hands. "We're talking about two entirely different things, Sherry. Angie and I don't have to sit around the house by ourselves every night, either. Besides, we never agree on where to go. I like to relax and she likes sightseeing and shopping. Usually she ends up going with her girlfriends and I stay home and putter around the house."

Sherry started to say something but nixed it. She raised her glass to salute instead. "To the river," she said.

"The river," he agreed.

They sat in silence until the sun gave in and the temperature began to fall.

"We'll have to microwave the food," she said, knees to chest and hugging herself against the chill.

"I'd forgotten about the food, actually. What say we have another Scotch, then go in?"

"You're the detective." She smiled, squirming to get her feet under her behind.

5

WEDNESDAY, MAY 4
WILDWOOD, NEW JERSEY

Sykes reentered Wildwood with none of the fanfare he'd received going out. Not even a byline in the *Patriot*, though he'd been front-page news for five weeks running in the fall of 1976.

Few would remember his name and even fewer would recognize his face; he didn't at all resemble the wild-looking youth he'd been at twenty-five. Now he was scarred, older than his years, with patchy gray hair and a tumor growing on the side of his neck. Most people avoided eye contact with him. They tended to stare down or look away when he came around, like the woman in her bed in Elmwood Nursing Home, who saw him mopping the green linoleum floor of Andrew Markey's corridor.

But Andrew Markey would have remembered him. That was what had mattered. Maybe not his face after all these years, but Susan had seen to it that he would remember his name. She had wanted her father to know who she'd ended up with after he went to prison. She wanted him to imagine his daughter fucking that same kind of trailer park trash he'd spent a lifetime trying to protect her from. *Hypocrite.*

So when Andrew's daughter was found murdered, people would come around to see him. And he couldn't allow Andrew to answer their questions.

* * *

The only condition of Sykes's release was employment. There were no drug or alcohol screens to contend with, so he reported to a harried parole officer in Trenton who accepted phone calls rather than personal visits to lighten his workload.

His prison earnings in Oklahoma, which mandated that prisoners be paid something for their work, amounted to three decades of labor at forty-six cents an hour, monies from which Sykes bought a used house trailer in Paradise and a Jeep.

He looked out at the rutted dirt road and the tops of dead trees over his neighbor's battered trailer. Junk cars and old tires were scattered around along with discarded appliances and mattresses and box springs; garbage bags were picked apart by crows and litter was dragged through the trees by homeless dogs.

His own trailer was royal blue and perched on stacks of gray cinder blocks. Three television antennae jutted from the roof above heaps of rusting tin cans. The small creek behind the trailer smelled of raw sewage, which was bearable in the winter but stunk to high heaven in August.

Wind coming through a broken window that had been mended with cardboard and duct tape disturbed a tattered curtain. Sykes fished a pack of Marlboros from his pocket and thumped one out on the heel of his hand. He dug at the bleeding sore on the back of his neck with his fingernails and tossed the pack on the counter, scattering roaches.

Sykes had been raised only a few hundred feet

from here. His father, Oberlin, had brought his mother to the Pine Barrens just after World War II when young men debarking ships from France were fleeing the cities for suburban life. Oberlin hadn't been a soldier returning from war, however. Oberlin was getting out of Newark's medium-security prison and thinking there were fewer policemen to deal with in the suburbs than in the city.

But rural life hadn't been any kinder to his father than city life had been. Tempting fate once too often, he had been shot and killed trying to rob a gas station on the outskirts of Avalon.

There was an open phone book on the kitchen table with "J. Lynch" circled in black. The former chief's name was Jim. When Sykes drove by the condo at 26 Atlantic Avenue and checked it out, however, he found that the name Lynch had been replaced by O'Shaughnessy.

Likewise there were no Markeys in the book, which meant that Sue had either died, married, requested her number be unlisted, or moved away. Finding out where the former police chief and the ex-girlfriend were living was going to require help.

Sykes lit his cigarette and pulled the faded drapes wide open. His neighbor's trailer sat only thirty yards away. He could see the magazine pinups stapled to her living room wall. Eighties rock stars, NASCAR drivers, and centerfolds from *Playgirl*.

He let the curtain go and emptied the bag on the counter, then put the beer, mustard, bread, and bologna into the refrigerator. Lottery tickets and Twinkies, he tucked in his pockets.

The furniture, like the Jeep, was easy to obtain. No cosigners, no collateral. He didn't even have to make payments on it for a year. A year, he'd laughed at the saleslady. A whole fucking year! If only they knew.

He'd been thinking about Jenson Reed lately and remembered meeting with the woman shrink that first day. Sykes had been doing time in Lewisburg, Pennsylvania, when the government started leasing private prisons as part of a federally funded reform program. As a nonviolent offender under a lifetime sentence, Sykes qualified for rehabilitation. They transferred him to Texhoma with the first seven hundred and fifty cons to live in Jenson Reed.

Private prisons were like nothing Sykes had ever seen before—they had art in the administration corridors and carpeting in the common rooms. Music was pumped through recessed speakers in the mess halls, and the recreation rooms looked like spa-quality health clubs.

"It's nice to have you with us, Mr. Sykes," the doctor said, offering her small, dry hand to shake. "I trust you'll find us more accommodating than the folks in Lewisburg."

Under stylishly short blond hair, she wore red teardrop earrings that looked to Sykes like long drops of blood. She leaned close and crossed her legs with a whispering graze of nylon. He could smell the expensive powder on her body. It was a pleasant fragrance, expensive, not the stuff his mother used to slap on the folds in her flabby neck until she looked like she'd been hit with a sack of flour.

"Would you like some water, Mr. Sykes?" She'd

poured it from a stainless-steel pitcher. Ice tumbled in the glass with a melodious tinkle.

Frost formed on the edges of the bulletproof panes and fragile spits of snow danced in the air. He stared at where her blouse had puffed between buttons, exposing a flat, white belly.

"Do you like it?" she asked after a few seconds.

Sykes looked up at her face but didn't answer. He had never seen anything like her before.

"I will afford you every opportunity to express yourself, Mr. Sykes. There are rules in Jenson Reed, but never against speaking your mind."

Her words came out slowly, in measured portions like the individual cubes that tumbled into his glass. She extended her arm toward the window, palm up, directing her bloodred talons at the world. "Do you want to go back?"

He only looked at her.

"Reflect on the educational experiences of your youth. You had no opportunity to succeed. There was no mechanism in place to save you. Your family and teachers and policemen sculpted you into what they thought you would be and you did not disappoint them."

She recrossed her legs.

"You must learn to contain your emotions, Mr. Sykes. You must learn to safely vent your rage. You must maintain a constant vigil on your anger. You must find a safe place to dump it all, Mr. Sykes, for those are the rules of society and the key to your return."

Return. Could he really return?

Sykes worked in the metal shops and dairy barns at Jenson Reed. He studied small engine repair and received a GED, last in a class that no one ever failed.

They would need to learn skills, the men were told. Those who might be paroled would be provided jobs—nothing fancy; they would become mechanics and repairmen, starting out cold at minimum wage; forty and fifty and sixty years old.

Each day the sun rose and set, months blew by, then years; the seventies became the eighties, which became the nineties, and soon another century arrived. Once a week the shrink scheduled fifteen minutes in which to change his life, and in all the years he had been at Jenson Reed, only one thing had ever changed.

She had.

Sykes grabbed his cigarettes and clamored down the steps to his Jeep, startling a scavenging tomcat. He drove under the garish wrought-iron arches of wheat and cherubs—a monument to the founder of the park who envisioned post–World War II families gathered around the community swimming pool, barbecuing, playing badminton under spotlights in Jersey pines—and onto State Road. Though Paradise had never become a summer campground or a vacation spot for tourists. Paradise was best known as a haven for bikers, addicts, and prostitutes.

The state road took him to Grassy Sound, where he turned to follow the irrational course of Nescmhague Creek. This section used to be a freight road, a marvel of forties' civil engineering. Now it was only a place for gulls to crack their oysters and for odd-looking snakes and turtles to sun.

The older people remembered its origin—a blistering summer in 1942 when a battalion of loggers bludgeoned their way into a woodland marsh full of elegant cranes and water moccasins. The scholarly effort was a rung up on the ladder of technology at the time, a solution to the northeast's escalating waste problems. It called for using the New Jersey swamps to dispose of hazardous waste from the laboratories, chemical research facilities, hospitals, and clinics in New York City and northern New Jersey, where it would bring the state new revenues and do the oceans no more harm.

They hired locals at eight dollars a day to drain the swamp back into Nescmhague Creek. The old-timers remembered the summers of sun poisoning and spider bites, endless bouts with poison ivy—sickness from the heat, infections from scratching the insect welts, diarrhea from the water, and the agonizing venom of wolf spiders and water moccasins. They also recalled the constant sound of derricks pounding day and night under the stench of mosquito torches, digging into the wet sand—not for water or oil or gas, but just to make more holes.

In 1944, when they finally finished draining and perforating the marsh, they let the trucks roll in, dumping drums and barrels and bags into hundred-foot silos.

No one thought much about it for decades, not until revelations about carcinogens and biohazards came to light. Not until the marsh was filled with drugs and body parts, human organs, diseased tissues, serums, X-rays, carcinogenic waste . . .

Not until the swamp had turned black and oozed into the creek, polluting Nescmhague halfway back to the coast—and by then it was most commonly known as Blackswamp.

The government halted the work in the early sixties; the trucks ceased to run. They sent steelworkers to cap the holes and highway crews to erect security fencing to contain the perimeter. One final initiative served to cover the area with the glut of junk the state had been storing outside Newark: old service fleets of police cars, buses, safes, filing cabinets, stanchions, highway signs. All the steel a bureaucracy outlives.

In time the forerunners of modern environmentalists came to understand the seriousness of what had been done and issued health warnings to the residents around the swamp. They even bought up land and helped relocate families to other parts of the county.

Legends developed of eyeless rats and two-headed snakes, shell-less turtles and hairless raccoons. It was said that birds in flight over the swamp might suddenly be overcome by poisonous updrafts and die in midair. There were reports of spiders the size of saucers and worms with fangs. For years, not even fearless teenagers would venture near the fence with the signs showing a green skull and crossbones.

To Sykes, it was a personal playground. A boy's dream come true—plenty of things to shoot at and break and no one around to tell him what to do. When he became a teenager, it was a place to hide his contraband. When he became an adult, it was a place to bring and hide his victims.

He passed the fence, still placarded with signs, but instead of the old skull and crossbones, he saw futuristic-looking rings of the modern BIOHAZ symbol. He hid his Jeep in the tangles of ivy alongside the fence and approached a section of wire that had been snipped out like a door; he pushed through it, and closed it behind him.

The ground was glazed with a crystal frost. He could see the footprints he was leaving as he walked between the towering stacks of cars and trucks, could smell the stench of the infected earth, even in the cool spring air.

In the maze of a thousand vehicles he came to a row of early-twentieth-century buses, some on their rooftops and some on their sides. One with a FLAT-BUSH AVE placard was rusting away on its bottom without axles or wheels. He tapped a Marlboro on the face of his watch and brought it to his lips, lighting it with a match. Then he walked to the open door.

Sunlight glinted from a broken mirror. A pale rat scampered over the hood of an overturned vehicle. He took a long pull on the cigarette and tossed it, then climbed the steps. The seats had been removed from the rear of the bus and replaced with a mattress and a kerosene lantern. A sheet of plywood covered a section of the floor midway back; he made his way between the front seats and knelt before it. And lifted it away.

Fumes seared his throat and burned his eyes as he stared into the black abyss. It had once been capped with an iron plate that had split in two when the crane dropped the bus on it in the sixties. One of the halves of the cap had fallen inside and in time the acidic vapors had rusted a hole through the bottom of the bus. That was how he'd found it as a boy.

There was no way to know what was really down there; cesium 137, radium, mercury—certainly those and more; radionuclides and isotopes that doctors had found in the marrow of his bones and some with a half-life of four million years.

They had gone so far as to talk about investigating the area of New Jersey he had grown up in. That scared him and plenty; God knew what they would find if they traced his cancer back to Blackswamp. But in the end they wrote it off to one of life's mysteries, which meant that no one cared one way or another how a dying convict developed a mutating, cancerous radiological disease.

He lay on his stomach and reached into the pit, patting his hand around the edge until he located a revolver hanging by a railroad spike driven into the wall of earth.

The gun was small and dark and pitted with rust, and he stuffed it in his waistband before replacing the sheet of plywood.

Now to make up for lost time.

He put a coin in the pay phone and dialed a number.

"Radio Shack," a man answered.

"Yeah," he said. "Is Ricky there?"

Sykes used his thumbnail to scratch a lottery ticket, looking at a TV screen in the store window. Whoever thought of this shit was brilliant—millions of fucking dollars for scratching one lousy ticket.

"Hold on a minute," the man said. "He's just in the back." A grinning Bob Barker was standing next to a woman holding a sign shaped like the state of Texas— now there was another guy who hadn't gone any- where in the last thirty years.

"Ricky," a voice said.

"Yeah, it's me. You got the stuff?"

"I got it," the boy said.

"I'm right outside."

Seagulls congregated in a V on the glistening pavement, the door of the Radio Shack chimed, and a gust of wind lifted tinsel off a posterboard girl inside. The acne-faced teenager whom he'd met in the video arcade off Atlantic Avenue walked out the door, looked in both directions, and headed toward him.

"Fifty bucks," Sykes said, pushing fives and tens into the kid's hand.

The boy looked around once more, then reached into his shirt pocket and handed Sykes a three-by- five. "It's all there, everything you asked for. Got it right off the Internet."

Sykes stared at the three-by-five all the way back to his trailer. She was alive! Her name was no longer Markey. He wondered what her house looked like. Did she have any money?

William and Susan Paxton, 1515 Quail Avenue, Gloucester Heights, New Jersey. The kid said it was outside Philadelphia, which meant she'd probably gone to visit her aunt and uncle after all. Probably the same day he went to jail.

He snapped a beer and used his thumb to press numbers on the phone.

"'Lo," a boy answered.

A child?

At her age?

"Is Susan there?" he asked.

"Gram's at work. She don't get home till seven."

Sykes looked up at the television: Magnum PI was dueling with his boss on a lawn overlooking a pale green ocean. "This is Mr. Higgins from the church. I had a question about food donations. You have her number there?"

The boy rattled it off.

"Thanks," he said. Sykes dialed and tried to imagine what she would look like after all these years.

"Carmela's," she said.

The voice was a little deeper, a little huskier than he remembered, but only a little. "Yes," he said, his own voice hoarse, his hand drifting to the back of his neck, feeling something old and painful at work in the pit of his stomach. He imagined her wet hair on his chest, the smell of strawberry shampoo. Everything was always strawberry with her: strawberry ice cream, strawberry lipstick, strawberry chewing gum—it was the one childish indulgence she maintained.

Would she have let her hair go gray, or would she have dyed it? he wondered.

"I was just wanting directions to your store."

6

Susan Markey Paxton was going through the day's take when her husband called for the third time.

"The kids want KFC instead of hot dogs. Do you mind stopping?"

"How much longer are they staying with us?" She pretended to whine.

"Hey, it was your idea to take them in. And wasn't it just last year you said you wanted another one of your own?"

"I'm approaching menopause," she said dryly. "Women say anything when they're approaching menopause. I'll stop on the way home, but don't let them snack. They chomped through a week's worth of cookies last night and didn't eat their supper. I don't want Lindsay thinking we fed them junk all week long."

"When do they get back?"

"Two days, William," she said, exasperated. "Two days. Don't you ever commit anything to memory? Call up Greg and have him put some steaks aside."

"It's supposed to rain all weekend."

"Then you'll need to wear a hat," she said merrily. "I want steaks and I want them on the grill the way you do them."

"Oh, right, butter me up."

"And keep them away from the cookies. I'll be home soon. 'Bye, dear."

"'Bye."

Susan looked out over the sales floor at her newest addition to staff. The girl was seventeen going on fifty. Shakra. Who in the hell would name their daughter Shakra? She had five earrings in each ear, a pierced eyebrow, and a pierced tongue.

Shakra's first question when Susan interviewed her was about her employee discount.

Susan would have turned her around right then and there, but Shakra was the daughter of a judge who was dating the owner, so it really wasn't an interview as much as it was an introduction to her new employee.

"I think she's stealing."

"How could she be stealing?" her Irish friend asked. "The inventory is tagged, we have a camera on the registers, she can't under-ring and she can't void without an authorization. Look, Susan, she's certainly not my cup of tea, but if Carmela wants her, Carmela gets her."

Susan shook her head. "I know she's stealing. I'd bet my life on it."

"Then how?" The older woman sighed, pulling a scarf from the coatrack and tying it over her silver hair.

"I don't know how, I just know it is so," Susan said. "I know her type. I can read her like a book." She squinted until her eyes were mere slits and pursed her lips together for effect.

The older woman laughed. "Oh, you can, can you

now? And how is it you know about such things, girl?"

"Because I was just like her, Ellen." Susan put her hands on her hips. "Actually I was worse. She's stealing, Ellen, mark my words."

"You were worse than our little Shakra here?"

"I even had a nickname, Ellen, and don't ask. It wasn't flattering."

"Fine, catch her stealing, but do it tomorrow. Let's get out of here and find us some warmth for the night. One more day and it's the weekend." She beamed. The woman grabbed her raincoat. "See you tomorrow."

All the clerks but Melissa were gone by five. Susan locked the door, leaving the key hanging in the lock on its long wooden tag. She pulled the plug on a window display and looked outside.

The rain was coming down so hard she could barely see across the street. Commuters with umbrellas and hats pulled low on their heads dashed between the cars and the puddles. Melissa could have gone home with the others, but she liked to stay and close. She was a timid youngster who lived with her grandmother near the marketplace on Washington. Quite forgetful at times but seldom when it came to money. She loved to fold and reorganize the misplaced stock each night—a job all the other girls hated.

"Go on and get yourself out of here early for a change," Susan said. "I'll tidy up and pull stock for tomorrow."

"I don't mind," the girl said sincerely, but Susan shook her head firmly.

"Out!"

Melissa gathered her things and went to the employees' break room to get her raincoat. When she returned she waved and turned the key to let herself out. Susan heard the door chime tinkle as it closed.

The register tapes showed that it had been a good day. Next month they would be getting their fall stock and she'd have to flip the entire store. Another summer gone and it hadn't even officially begun. Time waited for no one.

Susan finished tallying the tapes and wrapped them in an envelope with the cash and checks and deposited them in a drop safe. Then she walked the sales floor and started putting loose clothing back on the racks.

She was going through the sweaters on a carousel when the door tinkled open. She could hear rain slapping the sidewalk from the flooded gutters. It was a cool rain and a chill touched the back of her neck.

She was crouched over a pile of sweaters and squinting to read the size tag in her fingers. "What did you forget this time? You know you do this every night, Melissa. Maybe you should try ginkgo?"

There was no answer.

She stood and turned, sensing something was wrong.

It was the same strange man who had been in during the lunch hour, wearing a raincoat and a floppy hat pulled low over his forehead. He wasn't the kind of man who bought presents for his wife, let alone expensive labels like Carmela's. Susan hadn't liked him then and she didn't like him now.

"I'm sorry, but the store is closed," she said firmly.

She looked up at the security camera for emphasis, wishing she had taken the time to lock the door behind Melissa.

She remembered thinking this afternoon how interested he had seemed in the cameras and their locations, how he would pick things up and lay them down without really looking at them. Susan had begun following him around the store until he seemed to get annoyed and left.

"We closed at five." She shooed him with her hands. "You'll have to come back tomorrow."

The man smiled with bad teeth; a horrible scar crossed the front of his neck diagonally. An ugly brown growth protruded from behind one ear. She didn't know him, of that there was no doubt. You didn't forget a face like that, and yet there was something—

The man picked up a stack of sweaters lying next to him and extended them toward her, then smiled.

Suddenly she felt ill; the image of a Manson-like youth appeared before her. Two loud reports reverberated around the walls of the store.

Susan's legs buckled and she dropped to her knees, arms still clutching the sweaters. She looked up at the man in disbelief. One bullet lodged in her back, the other passed through the soft tissue in a shoulder and continued on.

Sykes? she thought. Earl Sykes? It couldn't be.

Sykes put the gun against her forehead and fired once more, watching her body jerk backward, then forward. The bullet mushroomed out the back of her skull.

She fell face-first into the carpet.

He pulled his hat low and turned, looking down and away from the cameras. Then he exited with the key, locking the door from the outside and joining the hundreds of other hats and umbrellas on their way home.

Carmela's BMW was idling in front when the police arrived. It wasn't yet daylight, but the street cleaners and trash trucks were out.

Susan's husband had spent all of last night and the early morning hours looking for her. He'd called the Pennsylvania and the New Jersey state police to see if she had been in an accident. The Gloucester Heights police took a missing persons report and contacted state and Philadelphia city police, who checked out the store where she worked. It was dark and all looked secure.

At 3:00 A.M. a New Jersey state trooper found Susan's car in a commuter lot near the Walt Whitman Bridge. A near-hysterical William Paxton called Carmela at home, asking her to meet the Philadelphia police and open the store so they could have a look around.

Carmela turned the key and found the light switch behind the display window. One officer went with her to check the office, and two others milled around the door uncertain what to do next. The store was quiet and everything looked in order. Cash drawers, per closing procedure, were emptied and turned on top of the machines.

Finally the senior of the two officers pointed to the

back of the room. "Hey, Fresco, why don't you go over and check out the dressing rooms."

"Yeah, okay." The doughy rookie waddled off with keys and cuffs jangling on his belt.

"Everything seems to be here," Carmela told the officer. She was worried for Susan, but whatever had happened obviously hadn't happened here. She closed the books and put them in the drawer. "Do you want me to open the safe?"

The senior officer looked across the sales floor to where Fresco was weaving his way through the clothing racks. "No, ma'am, I think we've seen enough."

Just then Fresco made a grunting noise and disappeared from sight, all of his heavy equipment crashing to the floor. Then came a bloodcurdling scream.

The story would be told around precincts for all of time, becoming a legend that was embellished over the years until it was horrid beyond description. Fresco would be too traumatized to repeat it, however. He had tripped over the dead woman's shoe and fallen face-forward in the mess that was once the back of her skull.

Detective Payne arrived at five-thirty to take charge of the scene. His hair and face were soaked; there was a cup of Seattle's Best in one hand.

He already knew that his corpse had been contaminated, not a great career move for the rookie—dipping his face into someone else's brains—but Fresco was gutsy enough to clean himself off and stick with the scene, so Payne patted the young officer on the shoulder as he passed. He knew plenty of other rookies who would be looking for post-trauma therapy so they could sit on their fat asses in a desk job for the next thirty years.

He listened to the briefing by the senior officer while Fresco stood by the door and logged all entries.

The mobile crime lab arrived at dawn and began their fingerprinting routine.

"Try to get that safe in the back office. I want the owner to get in there next."

The technician nodded.

Payne walked along the back of the room and then around the body, looking at it from all angles. He knelt and took her hands, lifting each of her fingers with the tip of his pen. Then he studied what he could see of her face, lifting her hair away with the pen and feeling a pang of sorrow when he saw how pretty she had been. The head shot was pencil thick between the eyebrows and apple-size where Fresco's face had been, but there was no slug in the wall or on the floor.

He took out his penlight and swept the carpet under the clothing racks, then crawled between them until he was at the other end of the store. Nothing.

The bullet would have been badly deformed and traveling slowly after passing through her skull. Not enough punch left for the hardwood shelving or concrete wall in the back of the room. He concentrated on the clothing racks just behind her.

There was a mist of red over a carousel of white blouses, spreading in an ever-widening cone away from the body. He followed its path to several neat stacks of oatmeal-colored turtlenecks and stood over them. He crouched and surveyed each one until at last he shone his light on the telltale gray mark on a folded edge.

He looked at it more closely from both sides and then lay on his back and looked up at it. Finally he knelt and lifted the sweater with his pen. The slug was lying between two sweaters in perfect condition. It could not have been the head shot. One of the rounds in her torso must have passed through without meeting bone or sinew.

"I've got a bullet," he yelled, pointing down to the stack of sweaters. The technician who kept on dusting nodded in acknowledgment.

Payne propped the sweater up with his pen so the bullet was visible and walked to the front of the store to talk with the owner.

Once they were finally able to open the safe, Carmela found the day's cash and credit card deposits as well as checks and voids balanced out in Susan's handwriting. There was even a petty-cash box with three hundred dollars and a book of business checks.

In fact, the only thing that seemed to be missing was the tape from the security camera, but that turned up later in the pocket of a new employee's coat. Her name was Shakra.

Of one thing he was now certain. Robbery wasn't the motive. Whatever had happened here was personal. He needed to talk to the husband.

The phone rang, and Carmela snatched it up without thinking.

She was a handsome specimen of a woman, Payne

thought, and successful, too. An article Payne had perused in some magazine mentioned that she had stores in Boca, Boston, and Washington, D.C., and was moving into the gentlemen's market.

Carmela's hair and makeup appeared to be perfect, even though she'd been called out in the middle of the night. She had a presence about her; it was easy to see how she connected so well to the elite.

But the beautiful face began to disintegrate when she pressed the phone to her ear. Her lips trembled, her eyes lost their luster, and her face took on that vacant look he'd seen so many times before. Payne could hear a voice calling out to her, a man's voice on the other end of the line. "Hello . . . Hello . . ." Payne reached out and took the set from her hand and found William Paxton on the other end.

He spoke softly to the husband, telling him to put the uniformed policeman who was sitting with him on the line. He knew it was going to be a long hard day in that house and that tomorrow, when the realization set in, things would be even worse.

He spoke to the officer, then pushed the button to disconnect and dialed 911 for an ambulance. Carmela might be one cool lady in her element, but this wasn't it. He watched her lips turn blue as he put his coat around her. Carmela was going into shock.

A collage of glossy photos thumbtacked to the wall showed people around a birthday cake; a group at a summer picnic in shorts and polo shirts; three women—one of them Carmela, another Susan—drinking champagne on a boat. It was easy to tell who Susan was in the pictures. Susan, with her bronzy complexion and big wide eyes, wore no makeup and let her hair fall straight. Even at forty-something, Susan looked happy and healthy.

But happiness was relative, and husbands and wives did run astray. Everyone had something to hide if you looked hard enough.

Everyone.

7

SATURDAY, MAY 7
WILDWOOD, NEW JERSEY

A cold front had dipped out of the Great Lakes that first week of May, laying a rare glaze of ice on the beaches. The Carlino abduction remained a front-page story in the papers along the Jersey seaboard. Today's read: "Echo Enterprises Puts Up $50K for Information Leading to Arrest." Beneath it was the line "Police Baffled."

A hotline received a deluge of calls from across the state, though none panned out. A trucker on a run from New York to Delaware saw a girl who looked a lot like Anne on the Lewes Ferry. She was in the company of an older man and she was wearing a scarf that covered not only her hair but also her mouth and most of her forehead, which he thought had a scratch above one eye. "Well, then, what color were her eyes?" the detective had asked, wondering how the man connected a pair of eyes with the missing teenager.

"Didn't notice," he replied.

They thanked him for his help.

There were dozens of "Anne sightings" in the rest stops, hotels, and gas stations along the Garden State Parkway, and not a few from the casinos of Atlantic City. None led anywhere, and nothing brought them closer to finding Anne or even a witness.

As for evidence, the blood type on the drainpipe matched that of the missing teenager. Several hairs taken from the scene matched samples from a hairbrush in Anne Carlino's bathroom. The expensive gold wristwatch found in the silt under the pipe turned out to be a February birthday present from her parents. Gus Meyers, the forensic chief, found an unidentifiable residue in the links of the wristband and sent it to the FBI for identification.

Forensics picked up green fibers that had snagged on wood splinters under the boardwalk. Mrs. Carlino remembered a dark green sweater that was no longer in Anne's closet. Her boyfriend couldn't remember what she was wearing, but said whatever it was, it definitely wasn't white. Aside from her wristwatch, she wore a gold ring with a smooth oval face engraved AMC and four studded earrings in each ear, a pair of which were gold stars. The ring they added to the broadcast. The star earrings they left out in case they got a confession and wanted to validate it.

Among the dozen or so teenagers who had been identified as being on the boardwalk that night, none had seen a man or a car that seemed out of the ordinary. No strangers, no strange cars.

They could do little else now but wait.

O'Shaughnessy saw the Explorer every day she came to work; it was parked in the police impound lot adjacent to her parking space. Looking at it always made her gloomy. The motor pool mechanics determined that the sidewall of the tire had been punched with the blade of a half-inch knife.

O'Shaughnessy had begun to suffer the effects of a full-blown cold and had an impressive array of remedies on her desktop. Between tissues and sneezes she hung blowups of the drainpipe photos around the walls of her office. It was a somewhat dramatic gesture, but a week had gone by and she didn't know what else to do.

Some of the pictures had starry white back flash around the graffiti. She knew the words by heart now: *JM loves PJ, Ron & TS 1983 forever, Surfers DRule,* and *East Hills Conference Champs 81. Syko Sue, Patrick B. and Jacko, Beatles, Horsley Eats Shit,* and *Grateful Ded.* Photos also showed the bloody handprint on the pipe and the brushlike swipes that had been made by the girl's blood-soaked hair.

She could imagine two very different scenes below the boardwalk. One of teenagers drinking beer and fumbling with each other's clothes; the other of a frightened girl crawling on her hands and knees, badly injured, maybe even stabbed or shot. She would have been scared out of her wits, trying to be quiet and run at the same time. Every sound she made must have seemed amplified a hundred times, every hollow breath, every beat of her heart.

She must have thought that hiding was better than

running, which bothered O'Shaughnessy. Did she turn to the dark recesses under the boardwalk because she was too badly injured to make it to Atlantic Avenue? She must have known at some point that she couldn't make it out onto the beach on the other side and so tried to cram herself under the drainpipe. She must have heard him getting closer and closer until she realized he was going to find her.

O'Shaughnessy also wondered if Anne had been a random victim, or if her abductor had known she was Jason Carlino's daughter. The Carlinos had money. Could it have been planned as a kidnapping for ransom and something had gone wrong? Six days was a long time to wait to make a demand.

Jason Carlino had done more than put up a reward for his daughter's return. He had begun to campaign the city manager to request state police assistance. He wanted horsepower, not some local cops with limited resources.

But Wildwood had jurisdiction and unless it could be determined that the girl had been taken across state lines, the city didn't have the power to relinquish the responsibility. That was the statement O'Shaughnessy gave to the press, though it failed to mollify Carlino.

O'Shaughnessy wiped her runny nose, picked up the case jacket, and went through it once more. It was gaining weight, was becoming a thing—the forensic reports, interviews by detectives canvassing the strip, interviews of Anne's friends and informants and a handful of prior offenders.

Anne's boyfriend had given the detectives written

permission to search his truck. It was clean and his alibi was bulletproof. When he'd gone barhopping in town the night of her disappearance, dozens of people had seen him throughout the night, calm, cool, and without a drop of blood on him. The city manager's own son had dropped him at home, and his mother, who had been up late reading, fixed him a sandwich and watched him take it to his room.

Cruel as it sounded, O'Shaughnessy would have at least preferred a body. Maybe then they could get evidence and stop whoever had done this, could prevent it from happening to someone else's daughter. Unless, of course, Anne Carlino showed up on her parents' doorstep one day—but that scenario seemed less likely as the days went by.

O'Shaughnessy had been sleeping poorly since May Day, dreaming about the cavernous place beneath the boardwalk. In her dream, someone was chasing her and she could hear his heavy breathing behind her. Water plunking from overhead conduits, she threw herself under a drainpipe, knees wet in mushy sand. She put a bloody hand on the pipe to steady herself and was trying to hold her breath when a hand reached across and grabbed her wrist.

"Line one, Lieu."

Startled, she sat up, snatched the phone from its cradle.

"Lieutenant O'Shaughnessy, this is Detective John Payne with the Philadelphia city PD. We're working a homicide from last evening and trying to locate relatives. You have a nursing home there, Elmwood. My victim's father is supposed to reside there, but the staff won't tell me anything and suggested I contact you. Can you tell me what's going on down there?"

"What's his name?"

"Andrew Markey."

O'Shaughnessy squinted. "He's dead," she said. "Fell down a concrete stairwell and hit his head. May first."

Silence.

"Detective?"

"Jesus, Lieu. Clear-cut accident?"

"I haven't seen the autopsy report, but my sergeant was on the scene and said it looked okay." She made a face. "We were told there was no next of kin."

"Yeah, I think there was a problem between father and daughter. My victim's husband says she barely acknowledged he existed. What happened, anyhow?"

"He opened a door to a storage area and fell down a dark set of stairs. Staff said the door should have been locked but wasn't."

"No witnesses."

"Uh-huh," she said, feeling less certain about the "accident" every second.

"You know he did some time in prison."

"I heard something about that. Way back," she said. "Mid-seventies?"

"Did you hear he testified against his codefendants."

"No," she said.

"And that one of them was Anthony Scaglia."

"Scaglia?"

"He's an underboss in the Gambino family now,

Peter Gotti's successor."

"He wouldn't hold a grudge that long."

"I don't know," Payne said. "The last two generations of organized crime in New York City were nothing less than bizarre."

"Tell me about your victim."

"Susan Paxton, her maiden name was Markey. Caucasian, forty-five years. She was the manager of an upscale women's clothing store. One adult arrest, hashish possession in her teens. After that, not so much as a parking ticket. She was a saint, according to everyone who knew her around here. Plenty of friends, lots of activities, bigger than life in the church. The priest said it would take weeks to rechair all the committees she led. If she had a secret life, she had one hell of a time squeezing it in. Anyhow, my shooter comes in after closing and pumps three bullets into her, one in the head and two in the chest. Then he walks out the door without taking anything. No sex, no robbery, no motive. This didn't look like sport shooting, Lieu. I think that whoever shot her knew her."

"She keep ties here in Wildwood, other than the father?"

"Zip. She treated the coast and her childhood like it didn't exist, and that's for the last twenty-some-odd years."

"I'll get the autopsy on Andrew Markey. Give me twenty-four hours and a fax number."

"Hey, Lieu. Can I ask you to keep that body on ice?"

She thought about it a minute. Thought she might

want to talk to the medical examiner about it herself. "Shouldn't be a problem. How long are you thinking?"

"Just a week or two. I shouldn't need more."

"The morgue's rarely busy. I'll do what I can. As long as family members don't come out of the woodwork objecting."

"Don't think you'll find any, but let me know if you do. I'd like to meet them. And I appreciate it."

He gave her his fax number.

The blinds to the outer office were open and O'Shaughnessy could see Sergeant McGuire at his desk, phone cradled under his left ear, staring at the ceiling and rolling a quarter back and forth across the knuckles of his hand.

Sergeant McGuire was tall and curly-haired, a detective most of his twelve-year career. Everyone had considered Mac a shoo-in for the commander's job when O'Shaughnessy's predecessor retired, but she'd written the better paper on the promotional exam and the city had no choice but to offer her the job.

She never forgot Chief Loudon's advice that day: "Win McGuire and the rest will follow. He's the key to your success."

Winning McGuire was much easier than she'd expected. He had no ego. They worked well together. Mac didn't seem to mind working for a woman or anyone else as long as the job got done. Ever since she'd been promoted, she made it a point to include him in everything. When she wanted his advice, she had no qualms about asking for it in front of the men. She knew the all-male office had a lot of respect for him and that they were constantly looking for his reaction when

O'Shaughnessy asked them to do something.

It was her third week without a cigarette and he'd joked with her this morning that the guys were getting ready to chip in for a carton. She knew she'd been getting edgy since the Carlino incident Sunday. She also knew McGuire had been kidding, but she sure as hell didn't want the guys thinking she was cracking under pressure.

She pinched the bridge of her nose, thinking about Andrew Markey. She'd looked at Detective Randall's report on the accident again. Nothing seemed wrong about the scene when you considered the man's age and mental capacity. Still . . .

She punched a button when McGuire put the phone down on his desk.

"Mac," she said, "you're not going to believe this one."

8

SATURDAY, MAY 7
PHILADELPHIA, PENNSYLVANIA

Sherry Moore sat in the ponderous silence of her home. It had been over a month since she'd returned from Pittsburgh and she had yet to cross the threshold of her door. She was still having the nightmares, but not nearly so many and not nearly as debilitating as they once were. Soon spring would bring the sun's healing warmth.

Winters were awful under the best of circumstances, she thought. It was a conclusion she'd come to as a very young woman. She had once joked to a friend that she suffered from light deprivation, but it wasn't, in all truth, a joke to Sherry. There was a difference, a palpable, indescribable difference between light and dark, never mind that she was blind. *Never mind that she had been collecting images from the dying for half of her life.*

She could have lived anywhere she'd chosen, of course, a climate more to her liking. But leaving Philadelphia would mean leaving the only place she had ever known as home.

An old Belgian clock ticked loudly from its place on the mantel. Crystal butterflies sat on either side of it. There were more butterflies on the nightstand in her bedroom and in her study and some silk ones in the sunroom. For a time she couldn't stop touching them, holding them, surrounding herself with them. At every opportunity, she had Brigham or Payne take her shopping for one. She still thought about them, but not so obsessively.

She yawned, her stomach rumbled. She tugged on her earlobe, thinking she should eat, have a cup of tea, try to sleep on the couch. Blind or not, it felt safer to sleep during the day. Days were when she finally rested. Thank God they were getting longer.

The branches of a sugar maple scratched dully on her windowpanes. She listened to them, slipping in and out of sleep, recalling similar branches on similar trees, scratching the windowpanes of her childhood. The cat jumped to her lap, pressing its face to her breast, startled when a screen rattled.

Her house was on the Brooklawn shores of the Delaware. The real estate agent called it baroque, its facade greatly emphasized, but Detective Payne called it Gothic and proclaimed it Castle Moore. He said it was large and dark and scary.

Sherry knew it was an imprudent dwelling for a blind person—it had more staircases than most houses had rooms—but she hadn't bought it for its design. She'd bought it for its massive brick sunroom and a lawn on the shore of the river. It was the closest thing to being in the city and the country at the same time.

The wind rose to a howl, lifting pages of a Braille book on a desk; dust swirled in the open hearth, sucked up the three-story chimney. The old house groaned. She put the cat down and stood, making her way toward the kitchen, annoyed when her elbow collided with a door frame.

White lace curtains rustled over a stainless steel sink, cool air pushed through the crack of an open window. She turned on the gas beneath a scorched teapot and let herself fall heavily on one of the kitchen chairs.

Hadn't there been enough lonely days, Lord?

Brigham would be here any minute now. Dear Mr. Brigham. But company did not always dispel the loneliness.

She had dreamed of Karpovich last night, the state police captain she'd met in Pittsburgh. The Pittsburgh trip had been the only exception to her self-imposed exile, a favor to a friend and partly to appease John Payne, who had been pressing her to get out of the house. She took it mostly because the job was eminently safe. No one's life was at stake. Either she would be able to solve the thirty-year-old mystery of the missing woman or she wouldn't.

A lot of her work was safe. She'd worked with historians and treasure seekers at archaeological sites around the world, far from the heart-pulsing business of life and death, far from places like Oaxaca City, Mexico, and Walnut Ridge, Arkansas, far from Norwich, Connecticut. She'd more than had her share of those kinds of places.

In her dream Karpovich is standing in a field, his sad eyes watching a backhoe lift a cistern from the ground, chains creaking against the weight of a vault, and later, the onlookers stare witlessly as the tooth of the bucket catches a threadbare suitcase, dumping its rotten contents in the trench.

She looks down into the hole and sees a body bag. It is labeled "Pittsburgh General Hospital" and through a tear in the bag she can see a woman's face, a beautiful woman with long chestnut hair. It was a sad dream, a profoundly sad dream, and as always, the face was that of the woman on the windshield.

The letter had prompted the dream, of course. Brigham, her neighbor, had been reading the mail the evening before, describing the grainy aerial photograph that Captain Karpovich had sent. It was a Polaroid of the Oak View Estate, a long, heavy Cadillac in the drive, a herd of sheep in the field behind the house. Scribbled handwriting on the back of the photo read "Oak View 1969."

Karpovich would have found it in the house. She smiled at his thoughtfulness.

Brigham was a retired admiral, a widower who lived in the ivy-covered monolith next door. He taught political science at the university, but his classes were in the afternoon and he liked to keep late hours, so he came around every evening and looked in on her, read her the mail, and drank a cup of tea or some of his port, which he inestimably preferred.

Her personal mail was easy; Sherry had an accountant to handle her financial affairs, so it was mostly junk that they decided to throw away. After tea came the serious stuff from the PO box that Sherry used to receive her public mail.

There had been a time, in the early years of her notoriety, when she could get through it all in a week, and had even attempted to respond to the more compelling entreaties.

Now they were far too many, the majority unopened in boxes stored in the basement. Tens of thousands, the last anyone dared guess.

Sherry knew the mail ritual was macabre, godlike even, since she was choosing whom she would help and whom she would not. It left her with no small amount of guilt. She had given her gift to many over the years, yet it seemed too little in a world so filled with pain.

Brigham arrived promptly at nine. There were the usual letters from universities asking her to speak. There was a letter from Mexican authorities confounded by a serial killer at the Basilica de Guadalupe. There was a letter from a schoolteacher in the Virginia Blue Ridge Mountains about the death of one of her fourth-grade students. There were silk panties from a woman in Jasper, Alabama, who wanted to know the name of her husband's mistress. There was hair from a man looking for his lost twin, and dried blood from a leukemia victim in search of a donor. Most people had no idea what she really did; they just clung to the hope that someone out there could help them.

There were love letters, always lots of love letters, some poignant, some lewd; she had even received a request years ago to pose topless for a men's magazine.

When they were finished, she asked Brigham to go back and read the letter from the fourth-grade teacher.

It was about a nine-year-old boy named Joshua Bates who had fallen to his death in the Blue Ridge Mountains near Luray. A clipped newspaper article stated that he had wandered off on the mountain while his father was cutting wood. A search the following day found the boy at the bottom of the Hughes River Gap. He had apparently walked off the edge of the cliff in the darkness.

The envelope contained a photo of a young boy with big brown eyes taken in a school auditorium— most people didn't know that Sherry was blind, and sent her pictures.

"May I hold it?" she asked.

Brigham handed her the envelope and went through the other documents. Sherry liked to touch things.

"Here's another clipping," he said.

"Go on," she encouraged, rubbing the picture between her thumb and forefinger.

Brigham murmured under his breath for a minute, then began: "'Busloads of volunteers from Staunton arrived in Luray Tuesday morning, focusing on the area east of the Gap. Volunteers were called off just after one o'clock when it was announced a body had been found on the riverbed. Officials declined to comment, but one volunteer called it a tragic accident. An autopsy will be held in Harrisonburg following the weekend.'"

There was a handwritten letter from the boy's schoolteacher, a Mrs. Gretta Mitchell, who wrote that she had been documenting complaints to the Virginia Child Protective Services about signs of child abuse by the boy's father. She said she had both seen the injuries and talked to the boy about them, and had warned the state repeatedly that the child was in danger. Now that he'd died, they were calling it an accident, and she was incensed that no one was going to speak up for the child. She said that she'd read about Sherry's work and hoped she would help police put this boy's murderer in jail. She ended by asking her to please contact the Page County sheriff.

"So what do you think?" Sherry asked.

"Well, I guess if I was just itching to go off and do something, it might be this," he said. "It's certainly a compelling story, but I'm not sure the locals are going to see it the same way."

Sherry knew that was all too true. Cops, especially

small-town cops, weren't generally receptive to out-siders meddling in their business. On occasion she'd been turned around at the airport.

"Call the airlines," she said. "Maybe there won't be any seats."

She went to the kitchen to fix them a decaf, and when she returned, he told her she'd better get her things together.

"It leaves godawful early."

SUNDAY, MAY 8

Sherry flew a turboprop from Philadelphia into Har-risonburg, landing just before nine. She tried to reach the schoolteacher at home, but there was no answer.

Next she called the Page County sheriff's office and reached a Sheriff Ringold, who told her the case was considered active until their coroner ruled next Mon-day. That meant the body was still considered evi-dence and that no one was getting near it until that time. Not even a relative, he said.

She was sure that after a long fall on the rocks there would be a closed casket after the body was re-leased to the funeral home, if in fact the boy's father didn't have him cremated. Petitioning the father would be unproductive if there was any truth to the teacher's story.

"Could you at least try to reach Mrs. Mitchell and tell her I'm here? That I'm coming up to Luray and would like to meet with her." Maybe that would loosen things up, she thought. It was a small town.

Maybe the teacher had some influence with the sheriff. She left him her cell phone number and told him she would try to arrange transportation to Luray.

Ringold advised her not to waste her money.

Twenty minutes later she was sitting on the cold backseat of a large rattling car that she could only further describe as smelling like an ashtray. The driver had a hacking cough and the worst case of body odor she could ever recall in her life. But for fifty dollars plus gas, he agreed to take her where she needed to go and see that she got in and out of buildings with assistance.

Twenty-five miles and forty minutes later she was sitting in the office of the Page County sheriff, listening to a gum-smacking receptionist blather about a weekend romp in the Poconos.

Sheriff Ringold let her sit for fifteen minutes, then came out to meet her. If he was at all taken aback by her lack of sight, his voice didn't betray it, which meant that he had probably used the last hour researching who she was.

"Bill Ringold," he said, taking her elbow and leading her into his office. It was a decidedly warmer room smelling of copy paper and gun oil. He closed the door.

"Miss Moore," he began, "I am an elected official of the county, which means my legal responsibilities are to the constituents of the county. That includes the boy's father, Custer Bates. You do understand that, don't you?"

She nodded. "I didn't come here to interfere with

your investigation, Sheriff. I came here at the request of one of your *constituents* who indicated doubt as to the father's innocence. The news article sent to me stated the autopsy was scheduled for next week. I thought if I came right away I might have a chance to see the boy before he was sent to Harrisonburg. That's all."

"I made a call to Gretta Mitchell, Miss Moore," the sheriff said. "Gretta is a good woman, a very good woman. She takes her job seriously."

The sheriff's words came out one at a time, ponderous and heavy with emphasis.

"But she doesn't sit in this seat and she doesn't have to take responsibility for my actions. A body is evidence until the coroner releases it, which means there is a chain of custody, just like there is a chain of custody with any other kind of evidence. When a policeman starts putting evidence on public display, he violates that chain, and when he involves other people, he's putting a lot of careers in jeopardy."

"What I am asking to do is no more intrusive than holding the boy's hand, Sheriff. Everyone who helped bring that boy off the mountain handled him." Then she raised her hand and sighed. "You know you're right, Sheriff. It was a hasty decision on my part. I usually don't come into things this way. It was Mrs. Mitchell's letter and there was little time."

She heard his chair slide back and his boots on the tile floor. He had come around to her side of the desk and sat on the corner directly in front of her.

"I also made a call to a friend in the Pennsylvania

State Police this morning," he said. "We went to the FBI Academy in Quantico together. He made some calls in turn and told me there's a couple of major crime detectives and a U.S. Attorney up there in Philadelphia who think you're the cat's meow."

Sherry looked straight ahead.

"I never liked Custer Bates. He's a drunk, and he's a mean one at that. And he never was no kind of father to that boy. Everyone here knows that. Why the state didn't take that boy was beyond our understanding, but that's just the way things are sometimes." He stood. "Now we are going to take a ride in my car to Page Memorial Hospital and I'm going to give you a tour of a three-body morgue in the basement because your distant cousin Jeanette Granville is down there. Jeanette died of kidney failure yesterday morning and is going to be cremated at the behest of blood relatives living in California. When I leave you for a moment to visit with her, you will find a body on the table in front of you, though it will not be Mrs. Granville's. Ten minutes later I will return and drive you back to the office so you can meet your cab. I would not want any of this to be repeated ever again, so we will discuss it only once on our trip back here. Then we will discuss it no more. Is that acceptable, Miss Moore?"

"That is acceptable, Sheriff," she said softly. "Thank you."

The sheriff took her arm and led her to his car. "Miss Moore, the coroner knows about the abuse allegations. There aren't many secrets around Luray. I know he expects to find bruises on the boy that preceded his death, but they won't prove murder. Absent a witness, I don't know how anyone could prove the boy's death was caused by anything but the rocks at the bottom of that gap. In other words, no matter what you see, the ruling is still most likely going to be accidental."

"I understand, Sheriff," she said.

The morgue was cold and smelled strongly of antiseptic.

Sheriff Ringold left Sherry and closed the door. She reached across the table to find a small shoulder and traced it down to the boy's small squishy hand. Hands were always different, large or small, soft or callused; sometimes she could feel the character of them, sometimes it was already gone. This one felt defenseless.

Exhaust vents rattled, and she could hear the faint chatter of a police radio in another room. She felt a bone protruding from under the skin, the smell of antiseptic growing sour like spilled whiskey.

"Whiskey?" she whispered.

Twigs snapping, running, tears in her eyes, one of her boots unlaced, a voice—"I'll kick your ass, you worthless little shit"—he was drunk, a creek ahead, shocking cold water, her mitten caught on the thorns, came off, she had to hide, she needed more time, he was always better after time, OH MY GOD! He was in front of her somehow, there was a chainsaw in his hand, he was coming toward her, she tried to run. "I didn't mean to spill it, Pa. We can get more whiskey."

She made the last flight out of Harrisonburg, thankful that she didn't have to spend the night in some small hotel.

The house was damp when she entered it. She let the cabbie put her bags in the hall and tipped him, closed the door, and turned up the heat. Then she drew a hot bath and called Brigham to tell him she wasn't up for company. Not tonight. She slept through noon and woke up feeling like she had picked up a touch of the flu. Brigham came, but only stayed for tea. She still wasn't up to talking.

There was a message on the answering machine that afternoon.

"Miss Moore, this is Sheriff Ringold. I wanted to tell you how sorry I was that I couldn't honor your request on Sunday. I hope you didn't take my decision personally.

"Oddly, there has already been a change in the status of the case. The coroner found a wound on the back of the boy's head that wasn't consistent with the rocks he fell on. On a hunch, one of the deputies checked Custer Bates's tools in his pickup and found that an oil cap on the underside of his chainsaw matched the diameter of that wound. We will be seeking a grand jury indictment for the boy's murder in Harrisonburg this afternoon." She could hear the strain in his voice. "I just wanted to tell you that. You be well now. Hear?"

Sherry put the phone back down and sat on her sofa.

And then she cried.

9

Saturday, May 7
Wildwood, New Jersey

Tim was waiting in front of the house when O'Shaughnessy got home. The babysitter was sitting on the front steps with the girls, who both had their backpacks on, ready to run. It was Saturday and the beginning of another week with their father.

O'Shaughnessy gave them hugs and watched them dash for their father's SUV. "You guys be good for Daddy," she called. "Make sure you wear your seat belts."

"We will, Mom," the older one groaned, her eyes rolling in mock exaggeration.

O'Shaughnessy caught Tim's look and nodded curtly, then quickly turned away to pay the babysitter. She knew he'd wanted her to come over to the car with them, but she stood her ground.

Dinner was a can of tuna with a hard-boiled egg and saltine crackers. She vacuumed the house and dusted the furniture, put laundry in the machine, and baked cookies for a school fund-raiser.

She hated television but flicked through the channels until she hated it even more, and then she put her feet up on the recliner, wondering what she was supposed to do about Tim.

They had agreed to equal time with the kids, at least for now, which meant that the children switched houses every week. One week it was hers, the next it was his or his mother's if he called and said he had to work late. She loved her mother-in-law; the girls did, too, so it wasn't really a problem of who they were with. They'd already lost one grandma; her own mother had died last fall. She knew that Tim was home with them every night he could be, so there was no arguing that one parent was any more available than the other. But the constant uprooting was taking its toll, and their grades were slipping because of it. Just last week she'd gotten a note that Reagan hadn't done two nights of homework.

On top of that, she was sick and tired of packing and unpacking bags for them. The girls needed a home—one home, one bed, one place to do their schoolwork. Someone was going to have to give in soon. Someone was going to have to be sensible.

God, she thought. Her younger girl was only eight years old. If things were this bad now, how would they be a decade from now? And what happened in between all that time? New stepmom? New stepdad? How do parents and kids get through this stuff?

She lit a scented candle and was considering running a bath when the phone rang.

"Hey, I'm surprised you're home."

"Where else would I be?" she asked. She sat down on the recliner and tucked her feet under her butt. "I thought you were surfing in Bogotá."

"I was sailing and it was in Baltimore. I just got back and am ready to boogie. How about you?"

"I told you, Clarke. I'm not the boogying type."

"But there's still hope. I can teach you."

"Now there's a scary thought."

"Look, you know Kissock's. We'll grab a snack there. They have great spiced shrimp. Say nine o'clock? I'll be the one with bells on."

"You better have more on than bells," she said, laughing.

"So you'll be there?" Clarke sounded a little more than surprised.

She looked around the room and then at the television. Someone in safari shorts was holding a snake up to the camera. "Nine," she said, "but I can't stay late."

Clarke Hamilton was the district attorney for Cape May County. He'd always been a little playful around her, nothing improper, but enough to signal that he was interested. She didn't know how he'd heard about her and Tim, but a month after their breakup he was sitting in her office asking questions about some bogus case. What he'd really come for was to ask her out, which she'd declined then and three times since.

Clarke was a good-looking man, to be sure, maybe even a little too good-looking for Wildwood. His family had money; DAs didn't drive Porsches and live in mansions overlooking the ocean, at least not in this part of the state. He was a gym rat; he wore thousand-dollar suits and a platinum Rolex on his wrist and was into exotic vacations. She'd heard he'd rafted the Amazon and climbed two Nepalese mountains, though she wouldn't have remembered their names if she heard them.

Naturally Clarke was part of the local gossip in Wildwood. She'd heard his name kicked around the hairdresser's; they talked about Clarke in the super-markets; they even talked about Clarke in church. He was gay, his family was *connected*, his face had been reconstructed after a car bombing, he had a gambling problem, he had a drinking problem, he had a drug problem, his wife had died mysteriously—all the single women had something scandalous to say about Clarke and all of them would have dropped to their knees if he'd come walking through their door.

Personally she thought he was funny and clever, and if there was anything quirky about him, she could not have cared less. She wasn't looking for a man. Not at this point in her life. Right now she had the children and a new job to concentrate on, which only left her with the guilt of being separated and seen in public with single men.

Come to think of it, if Tim hadn't been the cheating asshole he was, she wouldn't be sitting here right now wondering what people might think if she and the district attorney were seen together.

Tim had been good for her. He was thoughtful. He was kind. He was generous. He was good with the girls and a wonderful lover. In fact he was everything a woman could want—except that he was a man and men were thoughtless, conscienceless creatures who stalked the earth to get laid. A tear started pushing its way forward and she chomped harder on her gum, taking in a few deep breaths.

She knew it would take a lot more than three months to get him out of her system, but she was sick and tired of tearing up every time she thought about him. Damn him, she thought. Just damn him!

The tear fell anyway and she wiped it away with a finger. Life had to go on, and whatever else Clarke Hamilton might be, he would be company for a night, and that was something she'd had too little of lately.

She showered and dressed in a skirt and turtleneck, brushed out her hair, and applied lipstick. It was still cold and she grabbed her leather jacket, then headed for the door, thinking that as long as Clarke understood that they went different ways at the end of the night, everyone would get along just fine.

She drove along Atlantic Avenue, noticing lights in a few of the shops that had been closed for the winter. The snowbirds were returning from Key West or wherever it was they wintered.

A steady breeze off the ocean required wipers to move away the mist. She pulled her car in front of the neon lights at Kissock's and noticed Hamilton's metallic 911 Cabriolet on the opposite corner. She'd seen his car plenty of times at the courthouse, used to call it "that silver convertible" until McGuire punctiliously corrected her. Men!

Kissock's was always dim with lots of dark wood and candlelight. She could smell the spiced shrimp boiling and hear the low chatter on the dining room side of the beams.

The bar was crowded for a May weekend. Most were early tourists getting a head start on the season, but Ben King was there, the strip mall magnate who'd recently divorced, and he was sitting next to Jan Winkleman, a loan officer at her bank who was definitely not single. O'Shaughnessy was overcome with curiosity until Clarke Hamilton's white smile flashed across the room and suddenly she realized that she was about to go under the microscope herself.

Clarke stood as O'Shaughnessy slid onto the stool beside him, rubbing his hands together to make heat. "What's your poison?" he asked. "I always figured you for a rum kind of girl."

"Then I'll have a margarita," she said.

The prosecutor smiled and turned to admire her. Her hair was a mixture of caramels and blonds lying just on top of her shoulders. She had a softly defined jaw and her lips were brushed with wet gloss.

She turned to him and smiled while Kissock ground a goblet in salt.

"You guys ready for the blitz?" Kissock asked.

"Ready as we'll ever be," O'Shaughnessy said.

"Hard to beat Roman candles on top of the Ferris wheel and naked chorus girls singing 'I Love New York' across two lanes of Ocean Avenue? Quite a year, I'd say."

She smiled. "It teaches one to be humble and never say never."

"Amen to that." The old man grew serious. "How's Gus holding up, anyway?"

She looked at Clarke, then back at Kissock.

"You know, those two are about the nicest two people I ever met. I just can't believe it's true."

O'Shaughnessy looked concerned. "I'm sorry?" she said. "What about Gus?" The only Gus she knew was Gus Myers, the department's forensic chief, and she'd left him only hours ago.

"Ah, shit. Am I talking out of school again?" Kissock leaned on the bar with both elbows. "Agnes," he whispered. "Stomach cancer." He patted his stomach, straightened up, and poured tequila in the glass. "Terminal, I heard."

"No," O'Shaughnessy said, taken aback.

He nodded. "She's just about the sweetest woman who ever walked the face of the earth. I sure hope things work out for them."

O'Shaughnessy knew that Gus had taken his wife to the emergency room several months before; she was having stomach pains around the holidays and Gus thought she might have an ulcer. He'd said their youngest daughter was moving back into the house after a nasty divorce and that Agnes had already been under a great deal of stress at having to put her father in a nursing home. It was one of the rare times she'd ever heard Gus mention his troubles, and she never heard him talk of it again.

"Ah, jeez, I hope that's not true," she said to Clarke.

Kissock returned with a blender full of margarita, poured hers first, then set a Sierra Nevada on the bar for Clarke. Two more customers entered by the back door and Kissock left to greet them at the far side of the bar.

O'Shaughnessy scanned the dining room for people she knew and was grateful not to find any.

"Shrimp or a menu?" Clarke asked.

He had narrow fingers and perfectly formed nails. Besides the Rolex, which was comfortably plain, he wore no other jewelry. She liked his hands.

"Shrimp," she said.

"You know, I was a little surprised that you agreed to come out tonight."

She smiled. "Actually I was a little surprised you called me at home." She lifted her glass and took a drink.

He looked down at her hand; O'Shaughnessy still had her wedding ring on.

"But you *are* separated?" he asked cautiously.

She nodded and sipped the margarita; Clarke's expression seemed to relax.

"I hope it wasn't the wrong thing to do?"

"I'm here." She patted his arm. "It's fine."

Ben and Jan were scratching lottery tickets and drinking shots of something clear; Jan caught her staring once and O'Shaughnessy thought her expression looked conspiratorial.

Kissock lit a cigarette, which made O'Shaughnessy squirm. "It's all new to me," she blurted out, "the separation thing."

Clarke looked at her curiously.

"You know what Wildwood is like. It's easy to become street talk around here."

He took a sip of his beer, nodded. "Did you know I'm in the witness protection program?"

She laughed, circling the rim of her glass with one finger. "No, I hadn't heard that one yet. But don't you have a rather high-profile job for someone trying to remain inconspicuous?"

"They don't actually think when they make up these stories," he said. "It's just like the news; they go for the shock and awe."

She laughed again.

"Fact is, I'm not even sure if Tim and I are over yet. We have things to work out," she said. "I guess that's the best way to describe it."

Reagan and Marcy were the largest part of what they had to work out. Every time they came back from a week at Tim's, they wanted to know when Daddy was going to move back in. She thought at first that Tim was putting them up to it, but the more they talked, the more convinced she became that he wasn't. It was what they really wanted to happen. It was what they expected the two of them to do. Work it out.

She reached in her purse and pressed out a Nicorette. "Shitty habit, huh?" she said, popping it into her mouth.

"I didn't know you smoked."

"Started when I was studying for the sergeant's exam. Stupid thing to do, but it helped me relax. After that I only smoked in the office and when I went out for a drink with Tim, which was pretty much next to never."

She smiled and looked embarrassed. "We had plenty to do, with the kids."

She scraped nervously at a piece of caulking that had come loose along the edge of the bar. Kissock's was a blue-hair crowd; Andy Williams was singing "Moon River," a song that had made her want to cry ever since her mom died, but then more and more things made her want to cry lately, one of the seven signs of depression she'd read somewhere.

"You never married? Never had any kids?"

He shook his head. "Close, but I escaped in the

eleventh hour. No—let me amend that." He smiled. "*She* escaped in the eleventh hour."

O'Shaughnessy smiled. She liked Clarke; he wasn't full of himself like so many of the other lawyers and cops she knew. Men who had a whole lot less reason to be.

"This is the first time I've been out since we split," she said.

"Well, I can't say you surprised me there." He smiled. "You're a little more than nervous." He nodded toward her finger digging at the caulking and she quickly stuffed her hand in a pocket.

"I don't think the occasion rises to a date," she said, "but whatever it is, it feels weird, I must say. Don't take that personally, it's me, not you."

The shrimp came. They ate and talked. Clarke told her about his sailing trip in Maryland, an annual law school reunion. The boys and girls crewed a boat from Baltimore to St. Michaels on the opposite side of the Chesapeake. You had to be there to get the shirt.

They talked about their childhoods and they talked about the weather. They talked about the savings and loan case he was working on, the Carlino abduction, and the ex–police captain who fell and cracked his head open five days before his daughter was gunned down in a Philadelphia clothing store.

O'Shaughnessy ordered a second margarita, thinking Clarke was fun to be with. He was educated, socially adept, polite, handsome . . . She wondered what was wrong with him.

"What say we go to Trippers for a nightcap," he said. "It's just a little more invigorating there, don't you agree?"

"Trippers?" She laughed. "We're too old to go in there. They have rules against people our age."

"Oh, come on," he said. "Don't tell me you don't dance."

She looked at him as though he couldn't possibly be serious, but when he reached for her hand and squeezed, she squeezed back.

"It'll be fun. Something different." He discreetly dropped her hand and waved to an older couple leaving the bar.

His hand had been warm and felt good in hers. She thought of Tim. She missed touching.

The wind picked up, bending the tops of the trees in her front yard. She could see them from the street lamps as she pulled into the wet driveway. She got out and entered the house through the unlocked kitchen door. It was well after midnight and she was tired, though far too wound up to sleep. She took a bottle of water from the refrigerator and sat in her recliner, feet curled under her, watching the lightning flickering behind a blur of rain on her windowpanes.

She put her head back and closed her eyes, remembering the kiss. They'd walked out of Trippers hand in hand. Dancing *had* been fun. Tim might have been the best husband and father in the whole wide world, but he never took her out dancing. Never.

It was very late when they got back to her car.

Kissock's was closed, all the lights were off, and everyone had gone home for the night. She wondered if anyone noticed her car sitting outside. Just then she'd had the exhilarating feeling of being wild like when she was young.

They sat in his car, everything dark and warm, quiet but for the wipers sweeping the rain away.

"Thanks for a great night," he said.

She looked at his face in the dim light, rain pattering softly on the roof. He was so good-looking, she thought.

"Me, too. It was fun."

She reached for the door, but he gently took her arm and pulled her to him, leaning across the console to kiss her on the lips.

She couldn't say she completely opened up to him, but she couldn't say she pulled away either. The kiss was long and good, his smell was good, the touching was good, oh yes, the damned touching was good.

Then he let go and put his forehead against hers. "Can I see you again?"

She looked back at him, scouring the door with her right hand to locate the latch, and when she found it, she pulled it open and said "Yes" as she stepped out into the rain.

Sykes sat in his truck a few blocks away in a public parking lot off the boardwalk near Cresse. It was cold and the lot was nearly empty for a Saturday night. In just another month the population would explode, the beach and boardwalk would be overflowing with people, and the music of the Ferris wheel and the

Gyro and the great pirate ship would carry up and down the coast.

The winds sprayed chilled sea mist on his windshield. The sea smelled strongly of fish. The dark silhouette of Strayer's Amusement Pier jutted out over the sea in the distance.

This was how he'd spent his teenage years. This was where he'd met Susan Markey.

Sykes's hair—what was left of it—was patchy and short. He wore a green jacket with the Wildwood City seal sewn over a breast pocket, green trousers, and new construction boots splattered with blood.

His job had been arranged through the State of New Jersey, driving a truck for the public works department in his hometown of Wildwood. The doctors said he could live normally for a year or more on chemo pills in combination with intravenous treatments. Still, the pain would steadily increase and the day would come when he would no longer be able to function on his own. The government would provide a hospice after that, but Sykes had no intention of being around for it.

The job they provided wasn't a very good job; in fact it was the bottom of the ladder in the sanitation business. The "meat wagon," they called it. Scraping dead animals off the streets, hauling their maggot-infested carcasses to the county incinerator. Even the kids who rode on the back of the container trucks made more money than he, but Sykes wasn't working for the money. Sykes was working to keep the government from checking on him.

The job had its benefits. It was a one-person assignment, so he could do pretty much as he pleased. All he had to do was answer radio runs when his boss or some police officer wanted something dead removed from a public space or a highway. Other than that, he just drove around, supposedly looking for roadkill.

He worked the evening shift, and there was only one night manager to deal with, a man who stared at God knows what on his computer screen the whole eight-hour tour. No one ever came out to check on him. No one ever asked him what he was doing. He was more or less invisible, blending into the background along Atlantic Avenue.

He heard voices and glanced up at the rearview mirror. Someone was coming from the steps of the boardwalk. There were two cars under a flickering halogen in the lot besides his own, a red Miata and a Lincoln Navigator parked side by side.

He slid below the headrest and waited until the voices passed before he peeked over the wheel. The woman went to the red sports car and the man followed her, unbuttoning her coat and putting his hands inside and all over her body.

She was laughing and pulling away from him; finally she opened her door and climbed behind the wheel, then closed the door and lowered her window to kiss him once more.

The man stood tall and rapped his knuckles on the roof of her car, then walked around the back of his Lincoln.

He left first, tapping the horn on the way out to Atlantic Avenue. The Miata remained a moment longer.

He saw the interior light go on and the woman's head moving around; she was doing something with her face in the rearview mirror. Then he saw the light go off and the brake lights flash as she put the car in gear.

"Yeah, baby," he said to himself. "Take me home."

He waited until she was on Atlantic before he turned on his headlights, followed her to New Jersey Avenue, then to Spruce.

At Spruce she bore left to Taugh Creek, then west on Wildwood Boulevard. Only a handful of cars were out, since it was the off season, but he was merely a set of headlights on a city truck in her rearview mirror.

She took the northbound ramp to the Garden State Parkway and Sykes accelerated, trying to close the distance between the small dump truck and her sports car. Chains rattled in the bed and the steering wheel trembled in his hands. He advanced to within fifty feet when he reached for his jacket and removed a small revolver from the inside pocket. He would get closer, then come alongside her in the passing lane and turn on his yellow beacon and interior light. When she looked over, he would point to her tires.

He was just about to edge into the passing lane when headlights appeared in his rearview mirror and they were coming up fast. Sykes let off the gas and pushed the gun under his thigh. Then he gripped the wheel hard to keep the truck from weaving. When the car got nearer, he could make out the outline of the beacon on its roof.

"Jesus," he hissed through clenched teeth.

He knew he would never pass a sobriety test, and if

they happened to search his truck and found a gun, he'd be headed straight back to prison.

But none of that was going to happen. Sykes had already made his life-and-death decisions in prison. There would be no more prisons in this life.

He let off the gas until he was holding at fifty-five, wanting the sports car to get as far away as possible if the policeman pulled him over. It would have to be quick. Wait until he was at the window, shoot point-blank, and clear the scene fast. If he could get off the parkway before anyone saw his truck, he'd get away with it. No one would suspect a city worker in a city truck.

The headlights got closer; the patrol car was almost on him when suddenly the blue lights started flashing. "Shit, shit, shit." He thumped the wheel, but the words no sooner left his mouth than the cruiser accelerated past him and hooked in behind the sports car.

Sykes slowed to fifty, unable to believe his luck, scratching the sore on his neck and cursing out of nervousness, then taking deep breaths. The Miata was beginning to edge off onto the berm with the trooper trailing behind it. He passed them both without looking over, taking the next exit and using Route 9 to parallel his way back toward the county incinerator.

He was carrying two dead deer, a collie, a seagull, a rat, and a stiff tricolored cat that he'd had to scrape off the asphalt with a flat-bladed shovel. The dog had a collar and tags, but Sykes burned it all to avoid more paperwork.

Back at home, Sykes sat on his new sofa drinking beers from his six-pack, trying to calm his nerves over the near miss on the parkway.

The woman in the red Miata would be home by now, complaining to her husband—on whom she had been cheating—about a policeman who wrote her a ticket on the parkway. The policeman who had saved her life.

10

THURSDAY, MAY 12
PHILADELPHIA, PENNSYLVANIA

The city was having an unseasonable heat wave with temperatures soaring into the low nineties. It looked like it would hold for a few days—intolerable weather for a Philadelphian in the second week of May.

Summer predictions of scorching weather had people scurrying to scoop up rentals on the shore or book vacations in Maine or Ontario.

Sherry took advantage of the sun on her back lawn. She was wearing a black two-piece bathing suit. Her legs were propped on the lawn chair, water bottle and telephone next to her. Her Oakley sunglasses were fashionably frameless, a gift from Payne, who'd said he'd gotten them for a steal. She didn't believe him.

Payne walked through the house, grabbed two

Heinekens from the refrigerator, and elbowed his way through the swinging screen door to the backyard.

"A regular bathing beauty," he said cheerily.

"Is that you, Detective Payne, or one of the Chippendales gone for beer?"

"John Payne. City detective at your service."

She made a pouting face with her bottom lip.

He didn't ask her how she knew he had the beers in his hand. Sherry heard everything. Absolutely everything.

Payne twisted the top off one and reached out to touch the back of her wrist. She took it from him and put it to her forehead.

He set the other beer on the ground, unbuttoned his shirt, and fanned himself with it for a moment.

"God," he said. "How can you stand this? You know there's air-conditioning in your house."

Sherry put the beer to her lips and sighed with delight. "This, John Payne, is what I live for."

"Yes, well, take this and double it in the city. If this is May, I can't wait to see what August will bring. I think I lost five pounds today."

He grabbed the back of one of the Adirondack chairs and turned it to face her; then he fell into the seat and picked up the beer. His eyes traveled to her stomach and followed it to the swell of her breasts.

He was silent a moment.

"I had a murder on Friday. High-end clothier's called Carmela's. You ever hear of it?"

She shook her head.

"Nice-looking lady, middle-aged. Husband home

with two grandkids. The daughter and son-in-law were in Alaska on an anniversary cruise."

"Ugh," Sherry said.

"Someone walked in and put three bullets in her." He took another drink. "Nothing is missing, no sex, no motive. Husband's as clean as they come. Saints, the priest called the two of them. Like Thomas Aquinas and Mother Teresa. Then I call Wildwood, New Jersey, to talk to her father and find out he died from a fall on the first of May. It turns out the father had mob connections back in the seventies. One of them is Anthony Scaglia."

Sherry would know the name. She listened to New York news radio every day. She turned to face him and raised her eyebrows.

"I know," he said. "The police down there are calling it an accident. It was in a nursing home: man's elderly, they say he wandered to an unlocked door and went down a set of stairs in the dark."

"Except that you don't believe that?"

Payne sighed. "I guess I'll have to until someone proves different. Autopsy shows a head injury consistent with a fall. I hate coincidences in homicide investigations, but anything's possible. Anyhow, he's their problem for now. Sherry, there's something about this case. Something tells me I can close this if I just do a couple of right things."

"Am I one of the right things you need to do?" she asked lightly.

He looked at her with an incomprehensible expression, something on his tongue, but he bit it back. "I think you could help," he said instead.

Sherry was in a good mood, in spite of, or maybe because of, the heat. She'd been sleeping lately. Her complexion looked good. He'd seen her working out in her gym wearing her karate gi. Sunning herself in dead heat paled in comparison to what she could put herself through kicking air with Sensei Whatever-his-name-was. She probably liked it a lot hotter than this.

"This is a first," she said. "I thought you told me we should never mix business and friendship?"

"I've got four open cases this year, Sherry. Four dead ends with four families I can't face. Now this one is slipping away, and it's going to end up as number five if I don't find out what my victim knew."

"When is the funeral?"

"I released the body this morning. Some of the extended family needed time to get back into town, so it will probably be Sunday. We could go Saturday night."

He looked at her legs, crossed, calf bouncing lightly. A bead of sweat ran down her side, a breeze stirred the hair around her ears. He knew she was thinking about Norwich. That she was afraid of making another mistake.

It was hard to read Sherry. She didn't give out a whole lot, not even to those closest to her. He wondered what she thought of him. He knew she liked him, of course, but how much? When she put her arm around him or when they walked together or even when their hands touched by accident, it was with that same firm, assertive contact that is universal among friends. Nothing more.

He'd sensed in the very beginning that there could have been more, but neither of them had ever acted on it. Now, who knew?

Sweat ran down his temples and into the collar of his shirt. He stripped the shirt off and draped it over the back of the chair. Then he walked to the bulkhead.

He saw the river go white beneath a thirty-foot Scarab, the Scarab's bow rising like a missile launched for the bridge. She had to know how he felt about her; she was too intuitive not to. Sherry caught vibes like spiders caught insects.

The Scarab skimmed across the river on its stern and he followed it until it disappeared under the bridge. Payne knew the danger of asking for Sherry's help. Hell, he knew the danger of having her for a friend. One hint around the courthouse that he was friends with the famous Sherry Moore and he'd never again be able to testify in court, not without some smart-ass defense attorney haranguing him about his more intuitive leads.

"Isn't it true, Detective Payne, that you confer regularly with a psychic—a woman who communes with the dead?"

"Objection."

"Sustained."

"I'll rephrase the question, Your Honor . . ."

Which, of course, would make him useless as a homicide detective, which of course would put him back in uniform or in some miserable desk job for the rest of his career.

But there was another and far more important reason for trying not to involve Sherry in his work. He had never wanted Sherry to think he cared about her gift. It was the person he had always been interested in, had always loved. Not what she could do with the dead.

"I'll do it, you know."

He turned and saw her wiggle her toes. "Thanks, Sherry," he said after a moment. "That's very cool of you."

"Cool," she repeated, raising the beer to her lips. A drop of condensation from the bottle fell, striking her collarbone, and it slid down her chest between her breasts. She trapped it with a fingertip. "It's not cool, John. I just like to see you happy." She turned to face the water again, toes wiggling, and brought the finger to her lips. She licked the drop off.

"So what do we do next?"

Sherry was occasionally asked to do something publicly for law enforcement, usually for the higher-profile cases where the media's sympathy was a factor: a missing child, a ransom deadline. But most of her work was done in secret. Private organizations and private donors looking for clues from the dead. Generally, these citizens were hunting for valuables or historically significant artifacts. They didn't want competition or scrutiny.

The few police departments that considered Sherry credible could hardly admit they were contracting out investigative leads to civilians. Especially civilians with claims of paranormal abilities.

Sherry didn't take it all personally. She honestly believed there was a scientific—not a paranormal—explanation for what she did, but she also understood the difficulty police officers and jurists would have in accepting it.

"You really don't mind the funeral home?"

"I've been asked to be quite creative lately, haven't I, John?"

She was thinking about children in holes.

11

FRIDAY, MAY 13
WILDWOOD, NEW JERSEY

Lieutenant O'Shaughnessy had been staring at her desk, at the note from Clarke inviting her to his home for dinner. He wanted to cook for her, he'd written. Cook?

She left a message on his voice mail, begging for a rain check. She hadn't given herself enough time to think about where they were headed or what that meant to Tim and the girls. Maybe she was just putting it off because she didn't want to explore the feelings, but she had to admit she liked him. A lot.

She recalled that night in his car, his breath on her neck, an arm around her shoulders, one hand caught between his thigh and her knee. The feeling she had way down low, wishing for more, wanting his hands to move and hating herself for it.

No, dinner wasn't a good idea, she told him.

There were things that needed to be done at home, laundry for the girls, groceries bought and bills to be paid. *And by the way, Clarke, I really can't come over tonight because if I did I'd end up fucking you, because that's what people do once the preliminaries are over, isn't it?*

If there were ever going to be other times and they did have sex, her life would have to take a whole new direction and it was a direction some of the other people she loved were not going to appreciate.

"Lieu," Detective Randall called. She looked out her office glass window and saw Randall holding up three fingers. She punched a button on the telephone. "Lieutenant O'Shaughnessy."

"Detective Payne again. Philadelphia."

"Detective Payne," she said. "You got my autopsy report?"

"Everything, I just wanted to say thank you."

"So I can take Andrew Markey off the ice."

"Actually I was going to ask you not to."

Payne didn't think it would come to it, but he didn't want Andrew Markey's body to disappear if there was a chance his death wasn't an accident. If there was a chance that he might need to take Sherry to Wildwood after she visited Markey's daughter in the funeral home tonight.

O'Shaughnessy tapped a pencil on her desk and pushed back in her chair. "I suppose so." She put the toe of a shoe on the side of her desk. "How much longer?"

"Just a few more days. Just until I know where this case is going."

12

FRIDAY, MAY 13
WILDWOOD, NEW JERSEY

A breeze stirred the ground, raising hills of brittle leaves in tiny whirlpools that crossed the yard and settled in similar mounds nearer the shed.

It came with smells like ocean salt and something old and timeless and decayed.

Jeremy ran to the window, curtains fluttering in his face. Flat dark nimbuses approached from the east, great barges of doom drifting slowly across the cape. Thunder rumbled in them and leaves rattled on the trees in a gust of wind, something screeched, and he let the curtains fall and backed away.

The house was deathly still; he could smell coffee and bacon downstairs. Was anyone home? They should be calling him for breakfast by now. They always called him for breakfast by now.

The screeching grew louder by the second. He looked around his room; baseball cards blew off the nightstand, medals that he'd draped across trophies clinked together in the breeze. He glanced up at a citation from the mayor that was hanging on the wall and saw that it was shaking.

He looked at the window, east across the rooftops in the direction of the sea, and then he ran to the hall and down the stairs by twos until he hit the first landing; the picture window exploded as a wall of green seawater slammed into him.

The room flooded. He was trapped under the ceiling, using his hands to push himself down and work his way toward the stairs; a lunch pail floated by, a pair of eyeglasses; his chest felt like there was an elephant on it and blood wiggled from a tear in his pants leg.

Drip, drip, drip . . .

Somewhere in the recesses of his brain, he understood.

But what was dripping?

Drip, drip, drip . . .

Slowly he opened his eyes; across the room beneath a rusty sink he saw the source, a blue coffee can beneath a leak from a rusty drain trap.

He rolled to his side on a bare damp mattress, his brow soaked to the hairline as he sat up on the edge of the bed.

His right arm was twitching so badly he had to grab it with the other as he looked around the room nervously. The nice curtains were gone, replaced by a stained white towel nailed over the window. The dresser with trophies didn't exist; there were no baseball cards on the floor.

Jeremy rose and pulled on his only pair of trousers, trying to control the spasms in his arm as he dragged a broken comb through his hair. Then he went to the bathroom and scooped cold water onto his face. Cold was the only temperature water came in, according to his landlady. Mrs. Lester also controlled the heat, which she kept low most of the winter "because heat rises and what heated her rooms was more than sufficient to keep him warm." So he would cover himself with blankets he found in the trash.

Before he left, he pulled on the filthy tan trench coat that he wore every day of the year, high rubber boots, and fingerless gloves.

It was foggy out, the air so thick you could wipe it from your face. He walked his quickest pace, toes pointed inward and favoring his right leg. His white canvas sack hung from his shoulder, his paper spear was firm in his trembling fist as he set out toward the harbor to get his morning coffee.

The tide was high this morning; the dark swells washed over the jetty, leaving frothy suds and crabs for the gulls to pick apart. He thought about the dream again and felt sad for reasons he couldn't explain.

The Crow's Nest was a fisherman's bar, a small square building tucked between the icehouse and bait storage.

There was a modern jukebox and a phone bolted to the bar so no one would throw it out the window. Tables and stools were similarly screwed down. Cueballs and sticks would have been out of the question at midnight, so there was never a need to buy a pool table. Instead the fishermen gambled away their earnings with a jar of bar dice.

He left his canvas sack and paper spike outside; Janet told him it smelled too bad to bring inside the bar. The room had plank floors and a cast-iron woodstove for winter. The bar was L-shaped and sat only ten stools. He walked to his usual place by the window, stepping over someone's brown dog curled outside the men's room. A fisherman's oils hung on a hook just above it. He heard a toilet flush behind the wall.

"Hi, Jeremy."

Janet poured a Styrofoam cup full of coffee that she set on the bar along with the sugar and cream.

Jeremy smiled back at her with a look of love.

"Moorrniiiinnggg, Janet."

She smiled her best smile for him.

Janet pitied Jeremy; he was still a handsome guy beneath the rags. Even someone who didn't know him had to admit that. If you trimmed his hair a little and dressed him up, you might even think he was something special from a distance.

His arm twitched as he picked up the cream, but he managed to pour it without spilling. Then he proudly set it back down and picked up the cup.

A dragger was motoring out of the harbor, nets riding high on steel plates that looked like wings. Jeremy heard its horn blow and looked up just before its lights disappeared in the fog.

Janet turned to finish the glasses, wondering how things might have turned out for Jeremy. She often wondered if he would have wanted to live or not if he knew the truth about himself.

"Did you get another haircut, Jeremy?" She asked it loud, for he was deaf in one ear.

"Yeeeeesssss, Janet," he lied, wiping his hand over his hair. She reached across the bar and patted the side of his head. "Looks real smart, I'd say, very short here at the sides; that's the way the guys wear it these days."

Jeremy was in heaven.

The toilet flushed again and a fisherman in rubber overalls came out. Janet set his Budweiser on the bar and Jeremy looked into his coffee and tried to find his reflection.

Janet had been about ten years behind Jeremy in school, but everyone knew his story. He hadn't been just an honor student. He was the only MVP ever to hold the title for three years and not just for football; he was the baseball MVP as well. And then there was all the gold he had brought home from the state Olympics.

But that was then, and then might as well have been never, for Jeremy could barely drink his own coffee now without spilling it all over himself.

There were times, though, that people said they thought they caught a glimpse of someone in there. He might hear a familiar name and his eyes would flash, or he'd see the sports highlights on the TV over the bar and there was something in his expression searching for God knows what, and then it was gone in an instant.

He didn't even know his own parents after the accident. They tried to take care of him for years, but finally left town brokenhearted, realizing they would never make him any happier than he was on his own. Life had ended and then started over again on that day in 1976 for a lot of people.

Janet reached for a glass to dry and Jeremy shoved a quarter her way so she could see it. She put the smile on once more.

Jeremy of course had not become anything. She

often wondered if he had an inkling of what was going on around him. Did he ever see his high school sweetheart and her three grown children on the streets? Did he ever notice the picture of himself in his football uniform with the rest of the '76 Warriors hanging in a black-draped frame in the window of the shoe shop on Main Street? Would he even know himself if he had?

Did he know the cheerleader Debbie McCormick had posed for *Playboy* or that Derrick Hunter had died in the Twin Towers? Did he know that Bill Grant and Gavin Thomas died of AIDS and that the Michelson brothers crewed in an America's Cup race?

She put down the glass and leaned close to Jeremy, picking up the quarter. "Thank you, babe." She patted him on the hand. Then she turned so he wouldn't be embarrassed getting off the stool, which he had difficulty doing.

It was 8:20 A.M. when Jeremy slipped out the door. He gathered his paper spear and placed the empty coffee cup in his sack before he set off through the alleys that would eventually lead to Ocean Avenue.

Trucks were unloading in delivery zones and shop owners were dragging bundles of newspapers in their doors, cleaning windows, and organizing displays. Cars began to sound their horns and Jeremy slipped between them, alley to alley, street to street, following a schizophrenic path that ended precisely at Twenty-sixth Avenue and the boardwalk at 9:00 A.M., rain, snow, sleet, or hail.

He never wondered why he went by the high

school or looked at himself in the reflection of the gymnasium doors. Or why he cut through faculty parking until he reached the football field. He never suspected that cheerleaders once yelled his name or that crowds of people stood and roared as he drove toward the end zone. A utility road took him past the stadium gates and a boarded-up hot dog stand to a strip of trees that he entered and exited on Barclay.

The beach and boardwalk were Jeremy's only assignments. Not on top where people walked, but below, where people threw their trash and where all kinds of things blew away from the crowds on the beach. In the morning bicycles thrummed overhead; later came the clopping footsteps and then the whine of the long motor trams.

Mostly his work was kneeling and reaching under the boards, but sometimes there were places to stand and he could see up through a knothole in the wood or a crack between the boards, and flashes of color caught his eye as people went by.

He loved the smells around the boardwalk, the roasting peanuts, the taffy and sausages and pizza. He loved watching the sunbathers as he walked along the beach.

He stabbed a sock, a candy wrapper, and someone's discarded brassiere that he held high to inspect before he dropped it in the sack. "Bbbbbraaaaaaaaa." He smiled.

The fog was lifting and the sun was getting whiter. Soon the haze would burn away and there would be a startling blue sky to take its place.

Jeremy's rubber boots tread along the sand, his

eyes alert for objectionable litter. An airplane growled its way up the coast, dragging an ad banner. He stabbed a prophylactic and a gutted fish, then two paper cups and a hamburger wrapper. The bag filled quickly and he climbed the steps to the boardwalk and dumped it out in a bin. Then he returned to fill it again and again until noon, when he left his sack and spear on the sand beneath Pedro's and went up to get his Styrofoam cup full of black beans and rice. He sat under the walk and ate half of it, saving the spoon and the rest of the container in his pocket for dinner.

It turned out to be another bright, clear day and the beaches were packed with people. He watched them playing Frisbee and badminton and football, something that always looked like so much fun to Jeremy.

The girls were dressed scantily and he grinned at them wearing only their bbbbrrrraaaaaassss and ppp-paaaantiiiiieeeesss. There were only a few out now, but in a month the beach would be covered, bodies slicked in oil as far as the eye could see.

He rarely ran into people under the walk and when he did he made certain to walk around them. If they said anything mean to him, he was not supposed to listen. He was there to pick up the trash and they were there to leave it and that was all he needed to know or think about, his boss Ben Johnson told him.

The late afternoon sun cast shadows on the strip of tall hotels to the south. Lifeguard candidates were doing their rescue drills with an orange boat in the surf, and a small crowd of tourists had gathered to watch.

Just before five he came to Strayer's Pier and then to the drainpipe, which he followed midway where it began to rise on trestles and slipped under it. He stabbed a napkin trapped under the boardwalk and saw another beneath the pipe. Jeremy was six feet tall and hitting his head was a problem under the walk, so he was careful to look up when he got too far under, which was exactly what he was doing when he noticed the shiny object stuck between the cracks of the boards.

He used the handle of his plastic spoon to dislodge it and found a small ring caked in crusty brown gunk.

Jeremy left his bag under the walk and stepped out into the sun, shielding his eyes from the blazing light until he could see once more. Then he made his way around an island of towels and proceeded toward the ocean. At the water's edge he stopped and watched tiny holes appear when the tide receded, and then crouched there waiting for its return.

Gulls sailed overhead, watching for the telltale glimmer that betrayed food, soaring north across Strayer's Pier, turning west over the boardwalk and Ocean Avenue, looping once more toward the surf. One landed next to him as he put the ring in the water, rubbing it between his thumb and fingers, and when all the brown stuff was gone, he stood again.

The ring was gold and it had the letters AMC on it.

Jeremy found rings and other jewelry from time to time, most of them were just plastic, but some were metal like this one. He used to call his supervisor every time he found something, but Mr. Johnson said he was tired of driving out for every piece of junk he found, so he told him that unless it had a big sparkling white stone in it, keep it.

He put the ring in his pocket and went back to re-trieve his sack. He started south again, picking up more trash until he was at Cresse Avenue and the end of his day.

It was after five and Jeremy was late again. Some-times Mr. Johnson would come by in his pickup at five and let him climb into the bed under the tarp—because Jeremy wasn't supposed to ride in the back and never in the cab because he smelled too bad—and drive him back to Mrs. Lester's rooming house. He might have shown Mr. Johnson the new gold ring if he had come today, but he was late and Mr. John-son had already made his rounds.

A football game was under way on the beach by the Cresse Avenue ramp. He sat under the walk in the shadows, watching the men set up plays, passing tight spirals, diving to catch the ball.

Football was one of those mysterious things to him. He couldn't explain it, but when he saw people playing, it was like a happy and a sad feeling all rolled up in one. He had those feelings when he woke from some of his dreams as well, always imagining himself as someone else in some other room and then finding out that he was only lying in his own bed at Mrs. Lester's. He felt that way when the leaves turned in the fall and when a school bus passed and the kids were screaming from the windows. He felt that way when he saw the black-draped picture in

Mr. Coco's shoe repair shop. He'd heard about those boys who died on that bus; he had heard about it more than a few times because people used to whisper about it every time he came near. But that was a long time ago, and no one talked about that so much anymore.

Maybe on the way home this evening, when he was by the fields behind the high school, he would try to run a few steps himself. He smiled at the thought.

13

SATURDAY EVENING, MAY 14
PHILADELPHIA, PENNSYLVANIA

It was nine-thirty on the last night of the Paxton viewing. Payne chose the time because most visitors had come and gone and the family was weary of walking up to the casket by now. They all sat there, washed out and whispering to one another. Children were gathered on one side, adults on the other.

Susan Paxton would have had many regular customers in her years at Carmela's—people the family couldn't have known—so an attractive, well-dressed blind woman visiting the casket wouldn't be all that remarkable. And a blind woman who had taken the time and effort to come here would be expected to stand a few extra minutes with the departed before she left the room.

Payne needed to divert the family's attention. He didn't want them walking up and putting an arm around Sherry when she was on the brink of connecting.

"Detective Payne," Mr. Paxton said, surprised.

"Mr. Paxton," Payne acknowledged him.

"I—didn't expect—"

Payne nodded and took the man's hand, putting his arm around his shoulders. "I didn't want to come when you were so busy with family. Might we walk up and see Susan?"

"Of course, of course."

Paxton led the detective to his wife's casket. "They did a nice job."

Payne's eyes strayed to the entry wound on her temple. Paxton was right; they *had* done a nice job. "I'm sorry it took so long to release the body."

"It's fine," Paxton said. "It kept the family together a little longer."

They stood a moment looking at her, then Payne turned and led Paxton to the back of the room. He was looking down toward his shoes, seemingly on the verge of saying something, seemingly unsure of himself at the same time.

"Is there something new, Detective? Something you wanted to tell me?"

Payne shook his head. "Not new exactly." He walked toward a corner. "But I wouldn't mind talking with you a few minutes if you don't think it's bad timing."

"Certainly," Paxton said.

There was a small commotion at the door and

everyone turned to see a beautiful woman wearing tinted glasses and carrying a white walking stick. She was on the arm of the funeral director and heading for the casket when the director noticed William Paxton in the rear of the room and diverted her to him.

"This is *Mr.* Paxton, Susan's husband," the director said. "Miss Moore?" The director skillfully patted her hand as he talked.

"Yes." She smiled. "I'm so sorry, Mr. Paxton. I was a customer and friend."

The director looked questioningly at Payne.

"John Payne," the detective said, reaching for her hand. "Very nice to meet you, Miss Moore."

Paxton smiled for the thousandth time that week. "Thank you so much for coming. It is so incredible to us to discover how many lives Susan touched."

"She was a saint," Sherry said, and Payne winced. "I didn't want to interrupt you, though. Please, may I walk up and spend a moment with her?"

"Of course, of course, let me walk with—"

"No, no, please let me spend a few minutes alone, if that's all right? You two go back to what you were doing."

"Of course," Paxton said. "Of course, and thank you again for coming."

They watched the funeral director lead the blind woman away.

"It's this business with her father that's been bothering me," Payne said, pivoting Paxton away to break the spell.

"I told you she didn't have any relationship with

him. Really, Detective, none at all."

Payne motioned toward two folding chairs. "Yes, I know, but the mob might not care about that."

Paxton wheeled around. "The mob?"

Sherry asked the funeral director to position her mid-casket and assured him she could manage from there on her own. She whispered conspiratorially that it would also give her some time to catch her breath. "I don't get out that much and the effort tires me easily."

"Yes, yes, Miss Moore." He patted her hand. "Take all the time you need. Just raise a finger when you want me to come forward. I'm only in the back of the room."

She waited until he was gone and reached for the rim of the casket, fingers tracing the satiny material to the woman's arm, then down to an exposed hand. The room was warm; the hand was cold and dry.

Someone sneezed well behind her; she could hear conversations, separately at first, then all together like the distant hiss of a waterfall. She squeezed Susan's hand and—

. . . a pair of small white patent leather shoes, toes swinging back and forth over a mound of dirt, chubby legs kicking outward to gain speed, chiffon dress filling with air, climbing to dazzling sunlight, plunging past a ring of yellow lilies.

A woman was crying at a dining room table, a man wearing a floppy hat and raincoat with horrible scars on his neck was looking at clothes, he was in the store where Susan worked, she thought. A customer . . .

Her arms reached out, pulling a heavy red

fisherman's sweater over a dark-haired child, pushing the child toward a set of glistening stairs that climbed to a snow-covered angel.

She saw a vintage bus with a metal placard that read FLATBUSH AVE.

Her nose wrinkled.

Something sweet, the smell of . . . strawberries filled her head; a policeman smiled down at her, a man in jeans handed her a rose, a priest laughed.

S Y K O   S U E. *The letters were spray-painted white on a board, a bearded long-haired boy with crazed black eyes came toward her—she saw a gun, then a muzzle flash. Suddenly she was in a car looking out, could smell gasoline and dirty clothes; a woman's face was slammed against the windshield, lip split, smearing blood around a pale flat cheek. One green eye stared in at her, the eye open wide in terror, pleading, the face suddenly ripped away as the woman was flung aside.*

Sherry felt hands on her shoulders, people whispering excitedly behind her; she was being pulled off the floor and helped to a chair. Someone made a hushed command for water. A moment later a paper cup was put to her lips, then more hands on her shoulders.

"There, there, Miss Moore, are you okay now?"

She could smell Payne's fruity cologne, a Christmas gift from his wife two years ago.

"Yes." She held up a finger for everyone to give her a moment. She needed to catch her breath. She wanted to go back to the casket, to take the woman's hand again; she needed to know how the nightmare ended. Her nightmare!

"More water," the man commanded, and small footsteps pattered across the carpet.

She shook her head, overwhelmed by the scent of strawberries. "I just need some air," she said. "Just some air and I'll be fine."

How strange the feeling, yet what could it mean? How could Susan Paxton have known what she dreamed of? Was it even possible for two people to have the same dream?

Or maybe, as she had long suspected, they weren't dreams or nightmares at all. Maybe they were memories.

"Shall I call someone? An ambulance?"

"No," she said firmly, a tic quivering at the corner of her mouth. "No, I'm all right now." She trembled. She could still feel the woman's hand in hers, still see the woman's face against the windshield, and the sight of her was heart-wrenching.

"Just a touch of the flu," Sherry managed to say. "It's been coming on for a while." She blotted her forehead with her sleeve. "My cab is waiting outside. If you can help me to the door, the air will do me good."

Fingers snapped and she was helped to her feet. "Here, Miss Moore, take my arm. I've got you now, steady there, I've got your cane."

"What happened in there?"

Payne thought she looked worse than she had at the funeral home. He walked into the kitchen and put a kettle on the stove for tea. A few minutes later he put a cup in her hands and she wrapped her fingers tightly around it.

Sherry sat silently, a shawl around her shoulders, holding, not drinking, the tea.

There was a rap at the door.

"Mr. Brigham," she said softly. Her neighbor had come by to read her the mail. "Please tell him I'm not feeling well. Tell him I'll call him tomorrow."

The experience with Susan Paxton was more than personal. The face on the windshield had never been so clear, so vivid. How could she explain to anyone else what it was like to look inside your own head?

Payne and Brigham spoke at the door for several minutes. Sherry was sipping her tea when he returned. Her amber-shaded eyeglasses were on the table; her face was ashen. She was frightened, he thought. Frightened of the shooter or something else?

"Did you see a man, Sherry?"

She shrugged and nodded. "Several."

"The man who shot her?"

She shrugged again. "I don't know, John. I think so, I guess so, I don't know for sure."

"Somebody stood out?"

She nodded. "There was a man, a young man. I think he was there just before the gun went off."

"Can you describe him?"

She nodded. "Long dark hair, bearded . . ."

"To an artist, I mean? A police artist."

She nodded again.

"You're frightened of something, Sherry?"

She hesitated. She didn't want to go into it right now. She wouldn't even know where to start.

"John, I don't know for sure if he was the killer. You know what it's like. What I see is not always in the right order."

"If there was something else, Sherry, tell me. Anything could be important."

She shook her head. "I don't know; there was a woman and her face was pushed against the windshield of a car."

"Susan?"

"No, not Susan. I don't know who she was."

"Okay, then where? Can you tell where this was?"

"No!" she said too loudly. "She saw it from inside the car." Sherry was both tired and exasperated. "She, Susan, was looking out of a car and this woman's face was being pushed down on the other side of the windshield. That's all I saw, that's how it ended, John."

"Okay, okay, back to the guy. The younger one, he was the closest person in time to when you saw the gun?"

"That's what I remember," she said shakily. "I saw his face, then I saw the muzzle flash. John, I'm all right. Maybe I really do have a touch of the flu. I'll be fine, I promise."

"Can I bring you more tea?"

She shook her head. "John, go home to your wife. She's probably frantic by now."

He looked up at her; it was a tone she had never used with him before.

She wasn't wrong, of course. He had a wife and a home of his own. He did have to go.

"We'll talk tomorrow then, okay?"

She nodded without answering and turned away from him.

"Sleep well."

"Yes," she said. "I'll sleep fine, John."

She waited until she heard his car start, then ran to the closet where she kept her medicines and rummaged through her containers until she came to a box filled with suntan lotions and tubes of lip balms. She pulled off caps and smelled them, tossing them aside until at last she found what she was looking for. Then she returned to the couch and sat, tears streaking down her face as she began to apply it to her lips. Then she covered her chin and cheeks with the strawberry-scented balm.

14

Sunday, May 15
Glassboro, New Jersey

Marcia spat into the cracked porcelain sink and rinsed flecks of clotted blood down the drain. She pushed her loose tooth to the left with her tongue; a green lump swelled above her breast.

It had been one round after another since Nicky took the week off from work, culminating in last night's knockout punch that seemed to satisfy even the generally importunate Nicky Schmidt. At least he must have been satisfied. He hadn't raped her while she was unconscious this time.

Today would be better. Sundays were quiet days. The Schmidts spared their women on weekends in favor of NASCAR on the patriarch's big-screen TV.

Marcia didn't know which she hated more— weekday beatings or Nicky's sister climbing the walls for a fix of crack cocaine while his mother, who hid her own bruises under makeup, made sandwiches and carried beers to and from the living room.

On Sunday evenings Marcia usually went home by herself, which meant a decent night's sleep. Nicky and his brothers would pass out on their parents' sofa.

Last Monday and Tuesday he'd come home too exhausted to torment her. She'd wondered how his boots and clothes had gotten so dirty. Nicky wouldn't break a sweat if his life depended on it—not at work, not at home, and definitely not unless there was something in it for him. Nicky, she was certain, was up to no good.

Marcia cringed when she heard his footsteps on the stairs. She ran to the sink and busied herself with dishes. Nicky walked into the kitchen, opened the refrigerator without looking at her, and drank from a carton of milk while opening and slamming cabinet doors. Finally he went to the torn screen door.

"I'll see you over there."

Then he walked out of the house, letting the door slam behind him.

"Go, go, go," she whispered under her breath, leaning against the sink and praying he wouldn't turn around. She waited a full minute before she dared to pull the curtains back and saw a plume of dark smoke from the back of the shed. A moment later he was backing his old car out toward the road.

She ran up to the bathroom and checked herself in the mirror. There was redness over one eye and a scratch of dried blood on her neck where he'd raked her with his ring.

The phone rang and it startled her. She ran to the bedroom and snatched it from the cradle, bringing it to her lips with both hands.

"Hello," she said softly.

"You all right, Marsh? Are you okay?"

"Yeah, I'm fine." She sniffed. "I'm fine."

"I saw him drive away just now. We could hear you guys all the way down here last night. When in the hell are you going to leave that man?"

"I've got noplace to go," she said firmly.

"Hell, anyplace is better than there, Marcia."

"Listen, Connie, you have your mom to run to. I've got nothing but Nicky and his paycheck."

"I'm sorry," her friend said. "I was just trying to help."

"I know, Connie. I know. And I'm sorry, too. I know your mom's glad to have you home."

"You tell him yet?"

"No."

"You going to?"

"Yeah."

"When?"

"I don't know. Soon. I've got to wait until the timing is right, is all."

"Just tell him we're going to my mom's for a couple of days and that you're working extra hours so you can leave him some money to go drinking with. He'll be pushing you out the door."

"All right, all right," she said. "I'll say it, but there isn't going to be anything left for me to bring to Wild-wood."

"How much you got now?"

Marcia started to cry. "Nothing. He found it on Wednesday, took it all. I'm not going to let the preacher's wife pay me anymore. Not until the day before we go."

"Shit, girl, we only need about fifty bucks between us and I've got that much myself. Finish the month and leave Nicky whatever you earn. That'll be enough."

"I don't want to impose on you and your mother." Marcia tried to collect herself.

"Marcia. The food is cheap and the men in Wild-wood will be buying us more drinks than we could finish in a lifetime."

Marcia sniffed and managed a smile. "Your mom really doesn't mind me coming?"

"She's not even going to be there, Marsh. She goes up to Atlantic City every weekend with her girlfriend. They like to flirt with the old geezers and play the nickel machines." Connie got quiet. "She feels real bad about you and Nicky. She'd do anything to help you, Marsh. She said you could stay down there at the beach till you got your feet on the ground. There's lots of jobs down there in the summer."

Marcia looked in the dresser mirror. "And what would I do when winter came? I don't know how to do anything but iron and sew."

"Maybe one of the hotels needs a housekeeper. It's just something to think about."

Marcia looked at the swelling around her eye and felt a flutter of excitement in her stomach. "Really?"

"Yeah, why not," her friend said. "Why not?"

Marcia hung up the phone and went downstairs to the kitchen, where she opened the front door and sat on the front step with her old dog Ding. The ground was cool on her bare feet. She looked at her broken toenails and thought how much fun it would be to paint them.

There was a rusty skeleton of a pickup truck in the yard and a long-dead tractor behind the barn; the straight pipe exhaust had a hornets' nest plastered around it.

The only thing that looked new around the farm was the gleaming gold padlock on the double barn doors, which at first made as much sense as the eight-hundred-dollar magnesium wheels on Nicky's rusty old Dodge, but then she climbed on top of the tractor and peeked through the cracked walls and saw a brand-new front-end loader in the barn. Nicky was renting the barn to someone and pocketing the money without telling her. Bastard!

June was only two weeks away.

I tell him tonight, she thought. Tonight is the night.

15

The sun was setting on Billy Weeks's twenty-fourth birthday—a workday for Billy in which he'd spent the afternoon pacing the sidewalk in front of Lecky's Pawnshop, leaning into cars and shaking hands. After the dinner hour, he would move to the boardwalk at Strayer's Pier. By 9:00 P.M., things should be wrapping up nicely.

He'd met a girl outside the pancake house this morning, young and ever so hot in her little tube top and miniskirt. Her parents were inside with her brother while she used a pay phone to call her girl-friend back home. Billy figured her for fifteen or sixteen, but she didn't hesitate when he asked her if she did blow. He told her to meet him at Strayer's Pier under the demon at nine—his standard line— then he beat feet down the street before her parents came out. Parents had a way of fucking things up when they saw Billy around their daughters.

He looked around for cop cars, saw none, and ducked down the alley. The air was ten degrees cooler in the shade, which was still in the high seven-ties. He was shirtless and wearing a pair of baggy shorts, a red kerchief around his neck and sandals on his feet.

He pulled a roll of bills from his pocket and

counted three hundred and sixty dollars. Not bad for two hours of work.

Cocaine sold hand over fist in Wildwood, enough to pay for his brand-new Mustang and a very cool apartment on the edge of town. The best thing about it was the risks. There were none. Not in a town like this.

Billy knew he could never do a nine-to-fiver like his old man, bringing home a thousand bucks a week and trying to keep up with a house and four little brats in school. Nor, he found out, was he cut out for the kind of work it would have taken to get through law school. Billy made a thousand dollars on a summer evening, and selling cocaine in a beach town was more like being a rock star than a dope dealer. All the chicks came to buy from him and all of them wanted to sleep with him. Billy banged a different girl almost every night of the summer.

He heard the drone of an airplane dragging an ad banner up the coast. He knelt to eject a piece of gravel caught between his toes and picked up a whiff of something foul. When he stood, he found himself face-to-face with Jeremy Smyles.

"Jesus Christ, you stupid fucking idiot!" Billy yelled. "Why don't you just fucking watch where you're going, you stupid fucking shithead."

Jeremy was used to being called bad names, so he walked around Billy, stooping to pick up a discarded cup, and turned up the alley on his way toward the bay.

Billy stood there a minute, trying to stop his own hands from shaking, then started pacing. "Fucking retard," he said, kicking at a patch of grass in front of Lecky's Pawnshop. He walked back to the alley to see the idiot once more, but Jeremy was already gone.

He was creepy, Billy thought. Very fucking creepy.

The cops had once picked Jeremy up for being a Peeping Tom, fucking pervert. That had always made Billy laugh. What in the fuck was he going to do if he saw a little tit anyhow? Yell shucks and golly?

He shook a Marlboro into his fingers and lit it with a quivering match. The nicotine calmed him some and he blew smoke up into the awning. Tonight was going to be killer.

It was dark when he climbed the ramp at Rio, winking at the girls and giving high fives to the guys along the way. Billy was dark and handsome, his hair thick and combed straight back over his head. Black Oakleys were perched on top of his head and a heavy gold chain hung around his neck.

They envied him, he knew. No midterms, no minimum wage, no end to the pussy.

Billy conducted his business near several park benches opposite Strayer's Pier. The Strayer's demon loomed above him, its long green talons draped over the gates, red lightbulb eyes flashing, tongue lolling about as it growled and opened its mouth to show the kiddies its fangs. Behind the gate he could hear the screams of teenagers and the deafening volume of the Beastie Boys.

One more weekend and it would be full swing into summer.

Summers were a sea of bodies. In no time he turned a pocket full of dust into cash.

Billy prided himself that he was no fool. He knew a girl at the selectman's office who always told him when the drug task force was in town. The beach town couldn't afford a narcotics unit of its own, and state assistance was only available for a minimum number of days each summer.

Billy knew the law, too. As long as he didn't have more than five or six bags on him, he was below the five-hundred-milligram minimum the cops needed to charge felony distribution. He kept the rest stashed in a crumpled-up Happy Meal bag near his feet.

If he was ever caught, a judge would have to consider his lack of criminal history, so he was always good for a first-time slap on the wrist and community service or, at the very worst, a couple months of probation. If he needed to rethink the risks of dealing then, so be it, but for now he was riding high and dry.

Several fat ladies sat down next to him, all wearing matching sweatshirts that said "Wildwood" and eating huge ice cream cones and giggling about how they were getting it all over themselves. Billy kept kicking the McDonald's bag away and followed it into a corner, where he pushed himself up on the handrail.

He dealt for nearly two hours and called it a night, just before she arrived.

She wore a white miniskirt and a skintight white top that clung to her nipples and showed off one bare shoulder. Even the unflappable Billy was moved.

Her strawberry-blond hair complemented her

freckled skin, which was tanned from the day's sun. She carried a small cloth purse over her shoulder that matched the beige sandals she wore on her feet.

He stepped down from the railing and casually worked his way to her, slipping his hand in hers and pulling her away from the din of the music.

Billy saw all the heads turn, the kid working for minimum wage in the Dog House, the man scooping fries, the old scarred dude on the railing. Yeah, dream on, motherfuckers. He put his hand on her ass and led her away.

They walked south on the boardwalk away from the lights and crowds. They kicked off their sandals and walked the beach to the water, where they sat and smoked a joint. The moon was low on the ocean and the waves broke gently before them. Billy spooned her some coke and then kissed her as the water rushed to their feet. Now and then a couple would walk past, but Billy paid them no mind as he groped her body.

Her name was Tracy, she told him. Tracy Yoland from Nebraska. Her parents were in the insurance business. She was a junior in high school looking forward to cosmetology college. Tracy wanted to live in a big city like St. Paul or Des Moines, where she could get a car and rent an apartment of her own.

Tracy told him her family was leaving early the next morning for Washington, D.C., and they wanted her in by eleven.

Billy guided her by the hand until they were back at the boardwalk and then pulled her under into the dark.

He took off his shirt for her to sit on, knelt in front of her, and kissed her until she relaxed. Then he pulled her top over her head and threw it aside with her purse.

They heard occasional footsteps and laughter coming from overhead. Cars pulled in and out of the public lots and doors slammed. She was nervous at first, but he lit a cigarette and put it between her lips, then he pushed her down and let her smoke while he ran his tongue over her stomach, moving lower to the line of her skirt.

"Billy—" she moaned as he lifted her hips from the sand and tugged aside her thong. "Billy, do me."

He took off his shorts, barely mounting her before he ejaculated and fell breathless on top of her.

Footsteps ground across the sand-covered parking lot just behind them. A siren wailed as it raced up Atlantic Avenue, and shoes clopped overhead. Tracy heard a sound that reminded her of Velcro being pulled apart.

"What was that?" she whispered.

"What?" he said, still breathless.

"That noise. Did you hear it?"

He shook his head and rolled off. "Are you all right?"

"Yeah," she said. "I'm fine."

He sat up and started brushing the sand off his body.

"Is my top over there?" she asked.

Billy felt around, found it, and handed it to her.

She used the top to brush herself clean, then stretched it over her head and pulled it down; the sand was gritty and uncomfortable on her chest.

She knelt and brushed the sand from her thighs, looking for her purse and thong.

"You said you're leaving in the morning."

She nodded.

"Well, look, I hate to run, but I got to meet some dudes. Are you going to be okay getting home by yourself?"

"Just leave me another cigarette," she said.

Billy shook two from his pack and gave her his matches. "Hey, it's been fun," he said, smiling.

"Yeah, me, too," she said.

Billy stepped into the moonlight and walked to the steps, where he slid into his sandals, taking the steps two at a time, then rushing north toward Strayer's Pier. Billy had to meet someone, it was true, but not a couple of "dudes" on the boardwalk. Billy had to meet the vixen Carpenter twins who had promised him a birthday ménage à trois in exchange for some coke.

Tracy heard his footsteps receding and then all was quiet.

The air was sticky like the sex. She kept brushing the sand from her body, thinking she might as well put her thong in her purse instead of feeling un-comfortable all the way home. Of course the sand in her clothes would still be there when she got back, but if her mother said anything, she would just tell her she couldn't find anyone to hang out with so she sat on the beach by herself. Her mother would believe her. Her mother believed anything Tracy told her.

She heard the Velcro noise again, but this time

it sounded close. There was probably nothing to worry about, she thought. This was the beach, after all, not the big city. Probably it was just a rat or some seagulls in the Dumpsters, but she looked harder for her purse, thinking she could just as easily step out onto the beach and smoke under the stars as sit here in the dark with God knows what running around.

"Where are you?" she whispered, looking for her purse and making circles in the dark sand with the outstretched palm of her hand.

Waves crashed in the distance; a horn sounded on distant Atlantic Avenue. She got on her knees and climbed a foot farther into the darkness. She patted the sand around her and thought for a split second about leaving, but her purse contained her brand-new learner's permit. One more minute—

The air changed all at once. Something was different, something was wrong . . . Tracy moved faster, wanting to get out from under there. Fuck it, she thought at last, small hairs rising on the back of her neck, but as she started to back away, a bolt of electricity pierced her side and she fell to her hands and knees, heat spreading throughout her body so sharply, she thought she was being electrocuted.

A second wave surged through her and she pitched face forward into the sand. Then she heard the ripping sound again and someone pulled her arms together and she felt them being strapped at the wrists.

A hand grabbed her hair and jerked her head up from the sand, shoving something into her mouth, then propped her back against a piling. The hand began winding a spool of tape around her neck and strapping it to the post.

The whole thing took two minutes.

"There now," the man whispered as he straddled her legs. Her neck was so tightly bound that she couldn't turn her head. Her legs were thrust out in front of her and she could see the ghostly white foam of the waves breaking on shore.

It was hard to make out his face; her eyes were tearing from the pain, but she could tell it was an old face and the neck below it was raked with thick white scars.

"The first thing you will learn," he told her, "is what will happen when you no longer please me." He leaned in and kissed her mouth and forced a hand between her legs. "Then we'll have some fun, what do you say?" She tried to scream, but the stuff in her mouth prevented it. He removed his hand and wiped it on her face, then pulled a strip of tape across her mouth and backed into the darkness.

Tracy felt nausea stirring in her belly. There were people walking above her, footsteps clomping just above her head. She could hear a group of older women talking merrily about a man one of them had met.

The tape that bound her neck to the piling restricted movement below the neck. She blew sand out of her nostrils so she could breathe easier.

Hours passed, filled with footsteps and voices. People walked just above her, but none of them would ever know that she was down here. Bile climbed to her throat, something shifted in her bowels; she fought back the nausea.

He hadn't intended on killing her. Not yet. He said he was going to teach her what would happen when she no longer pleased him, which meant he intended to keep her for some time. Maybe days. There was still hope that she might be saved. Or maybe, she thought suddenly, he was jerking off somewhere and was never coming back. Maybe he got his rocks off like that. He could have had her right here if he'd really wanted her.

Tomorrow the beach would be filled with people. Someone would come by and look under and see her. Tomorrow she would be rescued, if not before.

A chunk of something rose from her stomach and lodged in the back of her throat. Oh, please, she thought. Please don't get sick. Not now.

Sykes sat in the Lucky Seven drinking slow beers until the bar closed. He didn't want to drink too many on an empty stomach and not with all the pills he'd been popping because of the chemo.

It was 2:00 A.M. when he returned to the public works complex and parked his Jeep on the hillside where it couldn't be seen from the road. It was Sandy Lyons's night off, like he planned it. Sandy drove the meat wagon on midnights, and when Sandy wasn't around, no one would be looking for the truck.

He slipped in the side door to the garage and opened the bay doors to pull it out. By two-thirty he was parked alongside the boardwalk.

Sykes lifted the tarp out of the back of the truck

and dragged it into the shadows under the walk. He knew that if someone saw him, there was a 90 percent chance they'd be three states away by the time the cops started asking questions. That was how it was in a tourist town. Witnesses changed every three days and even if someone did see him, he appeared to be a man out doing his job. Most people subconsciously dismiss what seems normal. He would be doing something normal, and the cops would be asking them to remember something suspicious. He knew how the mind worked.

He also knew that something was wrong the minute he saw her. Even from behind. Her head was slumped forward and something smelled bad. Real bad. Like she'd shit herself.

The moon was low on the ocean, which gave him plenty of light when he got around front to see her. "Oh, fucking Jesus," he whispered, turning away and gagging. Her cheeks were blown full of puke around the tape, her eyes were bulging out of their sockets, and vomit had begun to squeeze through her nose. Her bowels had let loose and created a mess between her legs. She was quite dead.

He got his pocketknife and cut the tape away at her neck, careful to avoid her mouth. Goddamn it to hell. He needed to think. He'd worn gloves when he taped her up. That part was okay. He could leave all the tape behind; even if someone found it, there wouldn't be any prints on it. But Sykes was a fanatic about evidence. He needed to get rid of her. He needed to get rid of the body.

16

WEDNESDAY, MAY 25
WILDWOOD, NEW JERSEY

The last week of May brought six hundred calls for police service, one hundred and twenty-three arrests that were mostly minor, and half as many motor vehicle accidents. Crimes ranged from auto theft to shoplifting to public intoxication. O'Shaughnessy also counted a handful of narcotic arrests, two robberies, and a half-dozen larcenies of women's pocketbooks from supermarket carts. Summer was a weekend away and Anne Carlino's photos were sun-bleaching away in storefront windows.

O'Shaughnessy kept the case file on her desk rather than in the filing cabinet. Putting it even that far away was a reminder that she and her people were no closer to solving it.

She still had a few of the old Carlino crime scene photos—mostly of the graffiti on the pipes—tacked on her walls among her daughter's colorful crayoned art.

O'Shaughnessy wondered if Anne had died quickly that night or if her ordeal had continued at length. She couldn't help but imagine what she herself would be thinking under the circumstances. Would she want to die quickly or hang on for the sake of a miracle? For the sake of her children or even for the sake of Tim?

Tim? Why did it always come back to him? She

knew the answer, but of course she had always known the answer: she loved him, no matter what a jerk he had been.

The green Explorer was gone now. Anne's father had removed it finally. He remained an outspoken critic of the department's handling of his daughter's disappearance, calling relentlessly on the state's attorney general to look into the investigation. He gave the *Patriot* regular interviews, was quoted as saying that citizens were afraid for their children and that the business community should be concerned for its commerce. If there was one way to get the politicians off their asses, he knew, it was to make the business community nervous. Everyone understood that bad press didn't do a tourist town any good in season, and he was intent on keeping that fear alive.

O'Shaughnessy knew she needed a break, and she needed one fast. And when it came, it came in the form of Gus Meyers, standing unexpectedly in her doorway.

Gus Meyers was a young-looking fifty-six, nearly six foot four; his knees never seemed to find enough room no matter where he sat. He had brilliant white hair and a perpetual tan, favored dark sports jackets with elbow patches and pastel cardigans. Today's sweater was pink. His trousers were always charcoal. If you were asked to associate a hobby with Gus, it would be ship modeling or fly tying. In fact Gus liked to wreck dive; he had a china plate from the *Andrea Doria* on the credenza in his office.

She had known Gus since she was old enough to sit on her father's lap in his office. Gus was looking much older now, older than she could ever remember seeing him.

"You have something?" She looked up hopefully.

He nodded and smiled, reaching into his jacket for a plastic envelope. O'Shaughnessy recognized the contents immediately. It was Anne Carlino's wristwatch, the one she'd found under the boardwalk on May 1. Her initials were scrawled across the face of the bag in Magic Marker.

"You remember this?" He dangled it in front of her.

She nodded. Anne's mother had identified it one tearful afternoon in the Carlinos' living room.

"You remember the residue I found in the band? The stuff I sent off to the FBI?"

She nodded again; her heart accelerated.

He dropped it on the desk in front of her. "It's auto paint. General Motors."

"It is?" She raised an eyebrow.

"Uh-huh, 1993 through '97. That's when they changed the composition. The color is a dark orange, not very common—but it gets better. It's fleet paint, Kelly. They didn't use it for the general market."

"Fleet paint," she repeated.

"Uh-huh. Probably a truck or some construction vehicle. Maybe a cab, though not many of them are orange anymore. I'm trying to get the distribution lists now; that's harder than you would think with all the hubs they apportion to. It might take a week or more, but I think it's enough to start looking."

O'Shaughnessy was thinking, but not about Gus Meyers and not about the FBI lab report. She was imagining Anne Carlino, upset about the fight she'd had with her boyfriend on the boardwalk, upset about finding a flat tire on her parents' car. She would have been relieved to see an orange truck pull into the parking lot. Was that why Anne hadn't run for the streets?

Or maybe the truck was already sitting there? Waiting for her to notice the flat tire before he got out to offer help. Or maybe he waited for her to come over to him. Had he been parked near the drainpipe and attacked her there? A struggle by his truck would have accounted for the paint.

One thing seemed sure. At that distance from Atlantic Avenue, no one would have heard. Anne had seen the drainpipe and thought if she could just get under there long enough to hide, he'd be forced to leave. But he didn't leave. He went in after her and found her.

"—of course the vehicle could have been parked there by anyone," Gus continued, "and she just happened to scrape up against it. But with all the press about the kidnapping, someone should have come forward by now and said they were parked there that night, even if they didn't see anything helpful."

He recrossed his legs. "The residue I took off that watch wouldn't have stayed on it for long by itself. I think it happened when she was attacked, Kelly, and if you find a vehicle that matches that paint composition, you're going to have some very convincing evidence that it was near the scene."

She nodded and heard herself thanking him, watching the boardwalk photos on the walls come alive. An orange vehicle had never come up in any of the interviews. Would the suggestion of it jog someone's memory? She needed her detectives to question Anne's boyfriend and anyone else who was on the boardwalk that night. She needed to find out how many orange fleet vehicles were in Cape May County or the whole state of New Jersey, for that matter.

When Gus left the office, O'Shaughnessy saw that Sergeant McGuire was waiting outside the door.

"Mac, I think we've got a break."

McGuire's response wasn't cheery. "I think we might have a problem, too, Lieu. Officer Ross from midnights is with me. I thought you'd want to see him." He opened the door wide.

A rumpled-looking patrolman came in and took a seat. His neck looked stiff, his face creased as if he'd been sleeping against a wall. McGuire stepped back and closed the door.

"Shouldn't you be under the blankets, Ross? It's almost ten."

Ross had been in her squad when she was a midnight sergeant in uniform. The night shift got off at seven. He should have been home hours ago.

"I wish." He smiled tiredly. "I needed to fill your guys in on something. Mac said to talk to you directly. We got a missing person's call last night, tourist, sixteen years old. The family is all but out of their minds. They were supposed to leave town this morning. The mother says the daughter's never done anything like this before. The father agrees with his wife. Says this isn't like her."

"When did they last see her?"

"Just after eight last evening. She was going to the

boardwalk to look for other kids her age. I've been with the family since three A.M. That's when the father called us."

"What's been done?"

"All the checklist stuff. Hospitals, clinics, and shelters. I put it on the clipboard for day work, so patrol has the description. Also tried some of the hangouts, but the night owls are home in bed. We'll go back up there tonight."

"Good," she said. "Good."

"Girl's father went out at midnight looking for her. He said he drove up and down the strip and walked the lower end of the boardwalk twice. I asked them for photographs of her, but all they had was an undeveloped roll of thirty-five millimeter. I took it up to the One Hour Photo this morning. Thought if she didn't turn up, we'd at least have something to work with."

"Great idea," she said, nodding.

"Other than that, they've been sitting in their room and waiting for her to walk through the door. You know how this stuff usually turns out, but something feels wrong about this already."

O'Shaughnessy knew exactly what he meant. Anne Carlino loomed in her mind. "Shoot me copies of the pictures when you get them. I'll see that the detectives put them in their cars. You want me to notify Youth Division?"

"Already did. Celia Davis is on the way to meet them. She's really good with parents."

"Sounds like you're covered," she said. "Where are they staying?"

"Dunes, room 1212."

She jotted a note. "Thanks for the heads-up, Ross. I'll ask Celia to keep me posted."

"Thanks."

Missing sixteen-year-olds, even those staying in hotels with their parents, had been known to meet up with other teens and wake up hungover in strange houses. She hoped that's all it was.

She looked at the bloody May Day pictures on her wall.

She hoped.

THURSDAY MORNING, MAY 26

Barf, who earned his moniker at countless fraternity parties, caught the Frisbee on a dead run, managing a full pirouette before releasing the disk backhand and pitching face-first into the wet sand. It was an impressive stunt for the two-hundred-and-fifty-pound boy, except that the Frisbee soared over his intended receiver's head and disappeared under the boardwalk.

He got up in time to see his playmates ambling back to their blankets and beers and leaving him to retrieve his own out-of-control pass. Barf brushed sand and broken shells from his face and jogged determinedly toward the boardwalk, thinking it was time to put more lotion on his back.

The smell hit him from ten feet away; flies swarmed the place he had last seen the Frisbee. Something dead was under there: a gull or a small shark left to cook in the afternoon sun. If the Frisbee hadn't cost ten bucks he'd have walked away, but ten bucks was six and a half beers, so he dove headlong under the walk.

His friends said later that they saw his broad white back disappear and then reappear a minute later; he didn't turn around or come to his feet, he just knelt there in the sand for the longest time. Then he went back under.

"Hey, Barf! Barf! You gonna spend the day there?"

O'Shaughnessy looked up at the towering hotels facing the ocean. There were hundreds of people around. It wasn't like May Day when no one was in town to hear the screams. This was high season and right under their noses. So why hadn't anyone seen or heard anything?

The girl was sixteen by a month. Her curfew was at 11:00, according to the parents, so it was assumed she was attacked some time between 8:00—when her parents last saw her—and 10:45 when she would have most likely started back to the hotel. That presupposed she had been abiding by her curfew, but no one had reason to think otherwise. Not now.

The forensics people collected the dried contents of someone's stomach and the crust of human excreta Barf had plunged his hand through. Barf said he might have tossed his cookies and been on his way if he hadn't seen the white thong under his Frisbee. Then he saw the small beige purse covered in puke and above it a foot of duct tape with long blond hairs stuck all over it; someone's head had been strapped to a piling! Barf knew that whatever had happened here, it wasn't good.

Police had closed down a fifty-foot section of the boardwalk and detoured pedestrians back to Atlantic Avenue. Barf—his real name was Charles Dubois—confessed that he had added his own breakfast to the mess before running to the ocean to clean himself off. He then used his cell phone to call 911. The EMTs checked him out, handed him over to the detectives for a statement; they then released him to his friends. Reporters chasing the story on police scanners started arriving with cameras. The veteran puker was heard to say that anyone regurgitating so much blood would be in dire need of medical attention. Barf was getting his fifteen minutes of fame.

The Yolands were taken to a private conference room in the hotel while their son toured the police station. O'Shaughnessy headed to the hotel to join them. She didn't want them hearing about Barf's discovery of the crime scene on the television.

Hours later she walked around the entrance to Strayer's Pier. She wished that things were the way they used to be with Tim. She would tell him the harder things she went through, not for his advice or opinion, but just to talk about it, to get it out. She was only human and she was just as worried and helpless as the families of her victims.

The Ferris wheel was spinning on Strayer's Pier. Hundreds of people strolled along the boardwalk. The day was on its decline, and the diehard sun worshipers were pivoting their towels to claim the last bit of light.

Soon it would be the dinner hour and everyone would leave to shower and change their clothes in anticipation of churning up the town's nightlife.

She walked past T-Tops with their racks of rowdy T-shirts, past James Taffy House and Planters Peanuts and the wax museum.

At last she stopped at a newspaper stand and worked her way around the wooden rack of cigarettes to a squat man sitting on a footstool.

"How are you doing, Newsy?" she asked.

He looked up and squinted toothlessly, "Heyyy, Sarge. Ain't seen you since last summer." He took in her street attire. "You get fired?"

Newsy had gray stubble on his face and was over-dressed in a heavy flannel shirt and dirty chinos. He had never before seen her out of uniform.

"Promoted," she told him, taking a pack of gum from the rack and unwrapping it. She popped a stick in her mouth and turned to look at the green demon hunched over the steel gates of Strayer's Pier.

"Lieutenant." He grinned. "Not surprised."

"Anything new around here?" She nodded toward the pier.

"Carny trash, if that's what you're asking. They're all new. Make quite a scene down at the Anchorage after closing. Moe never had guys like that before. You looking for someone in particular?"

"A man that would drag a teenager under the boardwalk."

Newsy nodded. "Yeah, I seen them flyers this morning. Parents shouldn't let their children go around dressed like that."

O'Shaughnessy was painfully aware of the photo Sergeant Dillon had selected. Dillon had been the highest-ranking officer in the station when the film came back from One Hour Photo. He had chosen a full-body shot of the sixteen-year-old in her bikini. He later said it was the best likeness of her face.

O'Shaughnessy nodded. "It still shouldn't make her a target, Newsy."

"Now that's the truth, I swear it shouldn't, but you know how it is."

Her eyes traveled to the colorful rack of cigarettes. "Ever smoke, Newsy?"

"Sure. Everyone smoked when I was a kid. We thought it was good for us."

"You quit?"

"Thirty years ago."

"I'm trying to kick it."

"Not easy," he said. "Little bastards crawl into your mind and talk to you."

She nodded, looking back at the demon. "They do, don't they, Newsy. Keep your ears open for me." She tucked a five-dollar bill behind the register and fished a card from her pocket.

Newsy dropped it in his shirt pocket.

O'Shaughnessy walked to the other side of the board-walk and took a seat on a bench. Some of the joggers and power walkers were out taking advantage of the dinner lull while there was still daylight.

She looked around the shops: the Dog House, the ice cream stand, funnel cakes under the demon's tail. This was where the teenagers came. This was where Tracy Yoland would have ended up if she was looking for kids her age. Or if she was looking for drugs? To-morrow O'Shaughnessy would have McGuire take his detectives to meet Moe's crew on the pier. Shake them up a little; let them know they were interested.

Two handsome, middle-aged men jogged by, shirtless and buff. One turned to whistle at her and O'Shaughnessy smiled thinly, shaking her head as if he was a naughty boy. She stood and walked to the rail that overlooked the beach. The lifeguards were tearing down their stations. She watched a dog playing with a Frisbee and thought about the dog that found Anne Carlino's blood under the boardwalk. She pictured Barf's Frisbee skidding into the place where Tracy Yoland had disappeared. Nothing ever seemed to be discovered by hard work, just by dogs and Frisbees. Such circumstances reminded her of how powerless she was, that the police were only observers unless they got a break.

She looked back across the boardwalk. Someone was standing here last night. Someone had seen Tracy Yoland.

And liked what he saw.

17

THURSDAY EVENING, MAY 26
WILDWOOD, NEW JERSEY

Jeremy's run hadn't gone as well as he would have liked. He'd tripped while pretending to catch a ball and sprained his ankle.

He did find a box of tea bags in the alley behind the supermarket. No one was around to give it to, so he put the box in his coat pocket and thought he would make a cup with his dinner.

By ten that evening he was sitting cross-legged in his underwear on the filthy mattress in his room, eating the last of his rice and beans. Greasy flecks of red peppers stuck to the stubble on his chin. A pan of water was boiling next to him on a hot plate on the floor. His landlady told him he couldn't have a microwave because it took too much electricity—where she thought he could have gotten money for a microwave, he didn't know—but she never said anything about a hot plate and hot plates were easy enough to find. There were always hot plates in the trash.

He had his giant red cookie tin on the bed next to him. It contained a collection of stuff that he liked to take out and spread on the sheets. There were earrings and metal buttons, wristwatches and dozens of rings. There were two pocketknives, a tiny compass the size of his thumbnail, lots of unusual coins, a stained pair of white panties, keys and cigarette lighters, two bras, and a pack of condoms.

"Rrrrrubbberrrrrr," he said. He knew where it was supposed to be worn, but he hadn't gotten up the nerve to try it on yet.

Jeremy sat up straight and sniffed the air. He didn't have the best of memories, but he had an excellent sense of smell. Mrs. Lester did not. Twice last year he had to remind her that she'd left her oven on and both times she'd been asleep when he knocked. Why she was so grumpy with him he didn't know, but it made him think twice about waking her again. Even if he did smell something burning.

He took out the new ring and put it on his little finger. It wouldn't fit over the knuckle, but he liked it there on the tip of his finger and extended his hand to admire the way the letters were drawn.

He had tried on the panties several times. Sometime he was going to do that while wearing the rubber, but that was a secret thought and he didn't want to think about it further right now. The smell was getting stronger, like burned piecrust or blackened cookies on the sheet. He got up and put his pants on and walked out into the hall. It wasn't as strong out there, but he walked down the stairs to Mrs. Lester's door just the same and stood, wondering whether or not he should knock on her door.

It was awful late, and right or wrong he knew she would be mad. Mad like the time he pointed out the dripping faucet to the health inspector. The very next week she took his toilet seat and gave it to one of her tenants in the basement.

Then there was the time she accused him of taking her panty hose from the basement dryer. Jeremy promised he hadn't done it; he wouldn't take anything from anyone unless Mr. Johnson said it was okay, but Mrs. Lester didn't believe him.

Suddenly the smell got stronger, surrounding the first-floor hallway. He raised his fist, looked down to make sure his pants were zipped up, and knocked. A minute passed. He knocked three more times, louder.

Finally she opened the door and looked up at him

through sleepy eyes. "What is it?" she snapped.

"Yeeessssss, Miissesss Leesstter. I jusssst smmeellled sommeethiinnggg burninggggg."

"Oh my God," she yelled, her eyes rolling toward the top of her head, and Jeremy thought she was going to faint until he saw that she was looking over his head. When he turned, there were billows of black smoke rolling down the staircase from his room.

Jeremy's heart began to pound. "Mmmissssessss Lllleeeeeesssssssttttttterrrr!"

The firemen threw the last of Mrs. Lester's furniture through the second-floor windows; someone had wrapped Jeremy in a blanket and given him oxygen, sat him in the back of the ambulance while they treated the burns on his feet. Jeremy had gone back up the stairs long enough to ensure that his neighbor wasn't home. He would have liked to retrieve the cookie tin from his bed, but his room was engulfed in flames.

Fire trucks were scattered every which way, and police officers diverted traffic from as far away as Rio Grande Avenue. Wet hoses and metal couplings had ruined Mrs. Lester's wood floors and carpets. Jeremy could see the firemen walking around in his second-floor room, spotlights from the trucks playing over their bright yellow coats and hats.

Earlier, as a precautionary measure, they'd evacuated the two houses on either side, but now they were allowing the owners to go back inside.

Mrs. Lester and her tenants were not going to be allowed to go back home, however, because Mrs. Lester's boardinghouse had been destroyed by smoke and water.

Jeremy saw one of the firemen holding a twisted piece of metal that looked a lot like his hot plate in front of Mrs. Lester and talking to her. Jeremy winced when he saw the look on her face as she charged across the street with balled fists.

He had never seen her so angry. Not ever.

"You have no home! You will never have a home! You are out, Jeremy Smyles. Out!"

She could barely get the words out; her face was so badly contorted that the dentures slipped from her mouth and she had to shove them back in before she finished and stomped off again.

Then a police car rushed into the block and a uniformed man with stripes vaulted the front steps past the firemen pulling their hoses back out.

Ten minutes later the policeman returned and joined Mrs. Lester on the sidewalk. As they spoke she began pointing at Jeremy and stamping her feet. He got a very bad feeling inside.

An old metal table hit the ground, then a pane of shattering glass and a blackened lid from a cookie tin, which rolled into the street and spun like a top on its end before it fell down. The policeman with the stripes started toward him. He was short with a large belly; his hat was in his hands and his hairline receded behind his ears. He smiled, but only with one corner of his mouth.

"Jeremy Smyles?" he demanded.

Jeremy nodded.

"That your room?" The policeman pointed at the second floor.

Jeremy shook his head. "No."

"I beg your pardon?" the man yelled.

"Mrs. Lester says I don't live there anymore."

The policeman drew a breath. "But you lived there before. You lived there alone in that room up until the fire tonight. Isn't that right?"

Jeremy nodded.

"And everything in that room is yours and yours alone?"

Jeremy thought about that. He owned only his clothes and the hot plate and the cookie tin of trinkets. Everything else belonged to Mrs. Lester.

"I asked you a question." The policeman's voice went up an octave.

"I don't own nothing but my clothes and stuff." Jeremy smiled.

"What stuff?" the policeman nearly screamed. "Did you own the goddamned jewelry in there?"

Jeremy nodded. "The watches and rings and key chains and things? They're all mine. Can I have them back?"

The sergeant's smile expanded another inch.

"You are under arrest. You have the right to remain silent. Anything you say can be used against you in a court of law. You have the right to an attorney; if you cannot afford one, Uncle Sam will rob the taxpayers to ensure that you get one. Do you understand, you retarded little piece of shit?"

O'Shaughnessy cut the siren as she drove onto West Spicer.

A man sat handcuffed in the back of Sergeant Dillon's cruiser. A black Lincoln Town Car was angled sharply against the curb. The driver's door was open and chiming.

Sergeant Dillon met her at her door, leading her lazily toward a crowd that had gathered at the foot of the stairs of Mrs. Lester's house.

"What possessed you to call Mr. Carlino?" she hissed.

Dillon turned and sneered. "Whoa, lady. I thought he would appreciate knowing I broke his daughter's case. We're public servants, aren't we, Lieu? We don't have nothing to hide. Do we?"

"You ever release information on one of my cases again and I will have you in front of a trial board so fast it will make your head spin. Do you hear me, Sergeant Dillon?"

The sergeant held up a hand like he was stopping an errant motorist. "Look, lady, I don't take shit from you or anyone else. As far as I'm concerned, it's my case. I'm the one that closed it." He pointed a finger at her. "All you detectives do is prance around town with your stupid little flyers."

He pointed at the crowd. "Everyone's over there, Lieutenant," he said. "I'm sure as a lieutenant you can find your way from here."

Dillon turned his back on her and started for his cruiser.

O'Shaughnessy's first reaction was to suspend him. Insubordination was a trial board offense, but Dillon had just made an arrest in the town's most celebrated case. Tonight's events would become the morning news.

Choose your battles, she told herself. Dillon could wait. There would always be another day with Dillon.

A towering figure, Jason Carlino was wearing a silk shirt, Italian loafers, and no socks. He was jabbing a finger in McGuire's chest as she approached.

"Mr. Carlino," she interrupted.

He spun around and glared at her. "I want that bastard locked up, Lieutenant, and I don't want to hear any shit about him being crazy. You fuck up this arrest and I'll have your job." He turned and stormed to his Lincoln.

"That was pleasant," she said to McGuire.

The sergeant nodded grimly.

"What happened here?" she asked.

McGuire pointed. "Dillon has his suspect standing outside the police car in handcuffs when Carlino comes barreling onto the block. He jumps out of his Lincoln and sucker punches the man in the face. Man's name is Jeremy Smyles. He works for the Public Works department. I called for one of their supervisors." He pointed to a man leaning on an orange truck. "Name's Johnson. He's the one who helped me wrestle Carlino away from Smyles. Just what in the fuck—sorry, Lieu—would possess Dillon to call Carlino in the first place? I mean, how would he even get his number?"

"Forget about Dillon," she said. "This isn't the time or the place. Tell me what you've got."

McGuire looked at her pointedly, and O'Shaughnessy knew he was sizing her up. "Mac," she said, "this is police work. Okay? Police work. We'll deal with Dillon later, I promise."

McGuire nodded and took a couple of deep

breaths. "The firemen said they found a tin can full of jewelry and some ladies' underwear spread over his bed. They thought the jewelry might have been stolen, so they asked for a police official. When Dillon came on the scene, he saw Anne Carlino's signet ring and read him his rights."

"Did you get to talk to him at all?"

"I asked him where he got all that stuff and he said he finds it under the boardwalk where he picks up trash. When I asked him about the ring with the initials on it, he said it was shoved up between the cracks in the boardwalk."

O'Shaughnessy remembered the wristwatch that Anne had shoved under the sand. "He say where?"

McGuire shook his head. "I had a crowd around me; I didn't want to go through it here."

"What was Carlino talking about back there? About him being crazy?"

"That's the problem, Lieu. He really is crazy. And wait till you get a whiff of him."

She looked around at the crowd. Two massive gay men with goatees, sleeveless shirts, and shorts had their arm around each other's waist; a stern woman with curlers in her hair stared at her with the expression of someone who'd just bitten into a lemon. A dozen teenagers talked to each other, chewed gum, and adjusted each other's clothing all at the same time.

"Let's follow him over to the hospital and get a statement. He can give us a statement, can't he?"

McGuire shrugged. "I guess we'll find out, Lieu. I'll wrap this up with the fire marshal."

O'Shaughnessy walked over to the sanitation truck.

"Mr. Johnson?" she asked.

"Ben," he answered, offering her his hand.

"Kelly," she said. "I hear he's one of your guys?"

He nodded. "Are you charging him?"

"Right now he's a material witness in an abduction case. We need to ask him some questions. What can you tell me about him?"

"I sure as hell wouldn't figure him for a criminal, if that's what you guys are thinking."

"Why not, Ben?"

The lanky man folded his arms and leaned against his truck. He was wearing a drab khaki uniform and well-worn boots, his hands were knobby and callused, and one of his thumbnails was black from an injury. Johnson looked like your typical public servant, a laborer or a foreman, except that his eyes and voice told you he wasn't.

"You're Jim's daughter, aren't you?"

She nodded.

"When you were a little girl, Smyles was in a traffic accident. In a school bus run off the road by one of them hopheads from Paradise. He spent a lot of time underwater and it left him that way. He's slow but honest as the day is long. Best damn worker I ever had."

As the cruiser was leaving the block, Jeremy looked out at them and smiled.

"Why couldn't he be responsible for a kidnapping?"

"He's not that kind of person, Lieutenant. It isn't in his nature. And he's not that clever. Where do you think he could take a person that you guys wouldn't be able to find?"

O'Shaughnessy stood silent. He certainly had her there. She stuck her hands in her pockets and looked around at the crowd. Then she looked at the house on the corner. It reminded her that it was late and the children were at home with Tim. She'd had to drop them there on the way to the scene, and she was hoping to get back in time to take them home so they could get some rest for school. Except that to do that she would have to wake them, which would rob them of even more sleep, but what else could she do? Was the separation really all her fault? she wondered. If Tim were home like he wanted to be—and like the girls obviously wanted him to be—then the kids would be home in bed. They'd wake in the morning; they'd have breakfast, get their lunches, grab their homework, and be off with the reassurance that the next evening or the next wouldn't be interrupted by a frantic trip to their father's or grandmother's or some neighbor's down the street.

"I've got men in my outfit I wouldn't blink an eye over if you'd told me they done something like this. Smyles ain't one of them. He's too damned sensitive about people."

"That could go two ways," she said, dragging her thoughts away from her children. "Some psychotics have a distorted view of the world. They see things from both ends of the spectrum. Love and hate, it's all the same."

"He's a pussycat, Lieutenant. He wouldn't hurt anything or anyone."

O'Shaughnessy looked at Johnson.

In truth she wanted Jeremy Smyles to be guilty. She wanted him to confess and to take her to the bodies so she could get this part of her life behind her.

But Smyles's story about finding the ring made sense. She had been under that walk; she'd found the wristwatch. She came as close to feeling what Anne Carlino felt as anyone could possibly feel. The young girl could easily have removed her ring and stuck it up between the boards. She was preparing herself. She knew he was going to find her and she didn't want him to have it all.

18

FRIDAY, MAY 27
WILDWOOD, NEW JERSEY

The phones at the police station rang constantly now. Someone was doing the smash and grab on high-end cars around town, someone was breaking into condos on the bay, and a gang of well-dressed Latinos was shoplifting clothing up and down the coast.

The report was brief. Andrew Markey, male Caucasian, 78 years, pronounced at 2:13 P.M., Sunday, 12 Macy Lane, Elmwood Nursing Home.

Time of death was estimated to have been between four and ten on the morning of May 1, although no one could physically account for Andrew since the previous evening. That was the last time he was seen alive.

She looked at the photographs of Andrew lying faceup at the foot of a concrete stairwell, then the ones from the morgue.

The cause of death was listed as blunt-force trauma to the head. Other injuries included multiple rib, radius, and fibula fractures. All injuries were consistent with the scene. All injuries were consistent with a fall. She knew by now that the toxicological tests were negative.

The only remaining questions were: Who left the door unlocked? Was it intentional or unintentional? Did Andrew open the door, or did someone open it for him? Did Andrew fall or was he pushed? None of these questions would have been asked had Andrew's daughter not been murdered a week later.

O'Shaughnessy leafed through the witness statements. The majority were from staff members having noticed nothing unusual, though one was from an elderly resident, a Mrs. Campbell, who claimed to have seen a man mopping floors outside her room early Sunday morning. Early, as O'Shaughnessy read, was described as being before the day shift arrived to administer medications.

She'd heard about this witness already, and she knew that the staff at Elmwood did not consider her credible. Still, it was a story that could not be reconciled. No one was around to mop floors on Sunday mornings. If she really had seen somebody, they could not have been part of the regular staff.

The nursing home employed surveillance video, but not at all entrances and not between the nurses' stations and the emergency exits, which included the area between Andrew Markey's room and the stairwell where he happened to fall down.

"Mac." She caught a glimpse of her sergeant passing by her door. He stepped back slowly, cautiously.

"You try an Identi-Kit on Mrs. Campbell?"

"No," he said dryly.

O'Shaughnessy just looked at him.

"She didn't know what race he was, Lieu."

O'Shaughnessy cocked her head. "She said he was white or that if he was black he was light-complexioned."

"Yeah." He grinned. "That's what I said. Look, Lieu. I didn't blow her off. I spent an hour talking to her the day of the accident."

O'Shaughnessy waved a hand across the air. "Oh, Mac, I know. I know. This daughter thing is really bothering me, though."

"It bothers me, too, Lieu, and if it's any consolation Mrs. Campbell has made eleven rape complaints since she's been in the home. The suspect is always the same dark-complexioned male. One time she pointed him out on the television, screaming 'That's him, that's him, that's the man who raped me.'"

McGuire, in a rare attempt at levity, cried out in falsetto, shaking his arms above his head.

O'Shaughnessy cocked her head expectantly. "Go on," she said flatly.

"George Hamilton." He grinned.

She laughed.

"Lieu, you want me to take an Identi-Kit over

there, I'm on my way."

O'Shaughnessy shook her head. "No, Mac. No, you've got plenty on your plate already."

McGuire shrugged and started to back out of the door.

"Send Randall," she muttered, picking up her coffee cup, scowling to find it cold.

She thought she heard McGuire sigh as he walked away.

She closed her door and headed for the break room.

"How about Smyles?" the chief asked as O'Shaughnessy scooped coffee into a filter.

"I don't think he's the guy," she said. "We spent an hour with him last night. He can barely tie his own shoes, let alone chase a seventeen-year-old down in the dark." She poured water into the machine. "Everyone I've talked to says he's the real thing. What you see is what you get." She pushed the on button and turned to face him. "You know him?"

He nodded. "I know about him."

"He has an old arrest, 1996, Peeping Tom."

Loudon nodded. "I wouldn't give that arrest all that much credence. I don't think he knows to this day why he was brought in."

"What do you mean?"

"One of our rookies turned into the alley and saw Smyles standing by an apartment building in the dark. He stopped to check him out and there's a naked woman in a tub in the basement apartment below them. Can't imagine what conversation passed, but the officer calls for Sergeant Dillon, who arrives on the scene and orders the officer to lock him up."

"You don't think he was guilty?"

Loudon looked at her, trying to decide what to say. "Let me tell you what I think, Kelly. If I'd been walking down that alley and saw a naked woman below me through an open window and she looked halfway decent, I might have stopped myself for a peep. What I don't think is that he was out looking for it."

She smiled, staring into her empty cup. "What did you do?"

"Nothing. I had your job at the time. I made it a point to keep my nose out of uniforms' business. Just like you are trying to do now."

"What about the women's underwear they found in his room and his landlady, who swears he stole panty hose from her dryer?"

Loudon shrugged. "I'm not saying he's put together right, Kelly. I'm saying he's a severely challenged man. The question should be, could he kidnap a girl and dispose of a body that a city full of supposedly talented people can't find?"

She nodded in agreement. "That's about what his supervisor said."

"How'd he take it when you brought him in?"

"He didn't have a care in the world—smiled away like we'd invited him to a tea party. I sat through sixty minutes of statements about there being more green gum wrappers than red ones on the beach and how he can cut his own hair with a knife. I let the poly-graph guy look him over and he all but laughed in my face."

"So what did you end up doing?"

"I cut him loose." The coffeemaker started gurgling and puffing out steam. "We can always get Clarke to open a grand jury if we need to rearrest him. He'll have Dillon's testimony, Carlino's ring, and the women's underwear."

"You have all that now."

"And I think it's weak."

She poured herself a cup of coffee.

"I'm not arguing with you, Kelly. I'm playing devil's advocate. What are you going to tell the press when they ask you why he's out on the streets again?"

"That there's no clear evidence to suggest he was responsible. He's a material witness because he found a piece of evidence."

"Stick to it. What's this business about Dillon calling Jason Carlino?"

O'Shaughnessy leaned against a stack of unopened copy paper and folded her arms. "He was on the scene when McGuire arrived. Apparently Dillon called him and told him about his daughter's ring."

"He strike Jeremy Smyles?"

She nodded.

"Any damage?"

"He's got a black eye, but I don't think he remembers how."

"Thought about charging anyone?"

She formed the slightest smile. "Not the right timing, Chief?"

"Now you're catching on. You leave Dillon and Carlino to me. Your job is to find out who kidnapped that girl."

She poured more coffee. "Can we walk?"

"Sure." They started back toward her office.

"What happened to Smyles?" she asked.

"Bus accident. He and seventeen other boys were coming home from a football game in Cape May in the fall of 1976. A policeman was chasing a kid in a high-speed pursuit; car ends up head-on with the school bus and runs it off the road. Worst tragedy ever to hit this town."

"My father was chief."

"Your father was the case. The defense tried to argue that the police caused the accident by pursuing the kid. Your dad coerced the DA into charging murder two instead of manslaughter and they walked him through two trials and convicted him— got life times two. First of its kind for a traffic death in the state."

She led him into her office and pulled the blinds. Taking a pack of cigarettes from the drawer, she said, "Here, you smoke and I'll watch."

Loudon took a cigarette from the pack and picked up the matches. The chief was known to smoke only on crime scenes and when someone offered him one. If it took a year for either of the circumstances to come around, he waited. She hated that smoking made no difference to him.

"God, I miss those things," she said dreamily. "Gus said there were no other survivors."

Loudon shook his head.

"You said the question was whether Smyles could kidnap and dispose of a body," she went on. "What were you thinking?"

The chief blew a circle at the ceiling. "Get him tested."

O'Shaughnessy squinted. "Beg your pardon?"

"Get Clarke to write an order to have him tested by a psychiatrist. Dunmore Psychological Institute in Vineland does a lot of work for the courts. Physical ability, capacity to understand right and wrong—all that stuff."

She smiled in appreciation.

Detective Randall knocked at the door. "Phone, Lieu, it's Gus."

She nodded and the chief stood. "Stay away from those cigarettes, Kel." He closed the door behind him.

She punched the speakerphone. "It's O'Shaughnessy, Gus. I wanted you to check something for me."

"I'll do what I can."

"Can you put your hands on the city's fleet vehicle registrations?"

He thought a moment. "Yeah, I don't see why not. You got something in mind?"

"Last night at the fire we brought a suspect in with Anne Carlino's ring. I was talking to one of the Public Works department supervisors. His truck was orange."

"I'll call you," Gus said.

O'Shaughnessy drove the downtown streets for an hour, chewing gum and thinking about Jeremy Smyles. The jewelry they'd found in his treasure tin was mostly junk. There were a few nice pieces—a

ring, an earring, and a watch that had some value—
but no engravings and no hits on the stolen property
inventories in their database. Jeremy had other
problems, however. He couldn't account for his
whereabouts during either of the kidnappings. He
had no friends to vouch for him, no one who saw him
coming or going from his rooming house, no one who
could explain what he did with any of his time.

Jason Carlino had called him the primary suspect
in his daily interview with the *Patriot,* and it was getting harder each day for the city manager to ignore
him.

Yes, Smyles had been in possession of something
belonging to one of the victims, but his explanation
was plausible, O'Shaughnessy told reporters. He'd
taken detectives to the place where he said he'd found
it and it was the same place O'Shaughnessy herself had
found the girl's wristwatch. They'd just missed it the
first time around. That was all.

But to Jason Carlino that meant only that Jeremy
Smyles knew where the crime scene was. *Well, of
course he knew where the crime scene was.*

Policemen investigating the death of Tracy Yoland
had been walking the boardwalk continuously since
her disappearance. They showed pictures of both her
and Anne Carlino, trying to find anyone who might
have seen them before they fell off the face of the
earth, anyone who might have seen a suspicious orange vehicle near the boardwalk.

O'Shaughnessy was saddened to hear that Tracy
Yoland's parents had separated back in Nebraska.
Things like this could break up a marriage. She'd

seen that happen more than once.

She stopped at the corner drugstore next to Tim's office. She used to meet him there for lunch and thought for some absurd reason that he might be sitting there when she walked in. She would make some big to-do about bumping into him and they would end up sitting together for coffee and she would finally break the ice.

She ended up eating an egg salad sandwich alone and glancing at the door every time it opened, hating herself for missing him and hating herself more for letting him go. She didn't want to go on like this any longer. She was tired of being without him. The girls were tired of being without him. This was 2005. Presidents made mistakes, astronauts, preachers, sports stars . . . If she wanted blind devotion, she could have gotten a Labrador, not a human being.

She knew it hadn't been easy for him to confess what he'd done; she knew that he'd also been honest with his mother, which must have been hard as well. She hadn't given him any repose for it; he hadn't deserved that yet, she thought. But he had a conscience, and that, she had to admit, was another of the many things she loved about him.

He was only a few buildings away; she bought a package of peanut butter cups to share with him. They used to make tents under the sheets and split them with the girls when they were very young. It was a silly game, but over the years one or the other would suddenly come home with a package and the two of them would dive under the covers and eat chocolate and kiss and end up making love with peanut butter on their breath.

She pocketed the candy and stopped by the car to drop off her purchase of Nicorettes, and saw the message light flashing on her phone. The first call was from Gus; he had her vehicle records and wanted her to call him. The second was from Tim; he wanted to know if she could drop the girls at his mother's instead of the apartment tonight. He had a commitment. A *commitment!* Was that supposed to be code for a goddamned date?

The third was from Clarke Hamilton, who wanted to know if she could take a ride up the coast. Goddamn right she could. She didn't have any *commitments*.

Gus Meyers was waiting in her office when she got back. He looked like he hadn't slept in a week.

The rumors were no longer rumors. Agnes had less than three months to live.

He reached into his jacket pocket and withdrew an envelope. He handed it to her. "There are five trucks in Wildwood that fit the profile, unless they junked them in the last three months. That's when the last inventory was turned in. Now, this doesn't mean they match the paint I found on the watch. Only that they're the right years and models. Okay?"

She nodded. "So I need to get a scratch off one of them to compare?"

"Yes. If you have a particular vehicle in mind, go for it, but I think that any one of them should do. Find the fleet first and then you can look for a scratch on a particular vehicle. You want me to send one of my people over, or is this a secret?"

"I think I'd like to keep it quiet just a little while longer. How long will it take to turn around a paint sample?"

"Weeks." He shrugged. "Maybe months. The bureau has the only archives of this type and they work on prosecutable cases first. Put a suspect's name with your request and it'll get done a whole lot faster. That's my two cents."

"Thanks, Gus." She felt deflated. *Months?*

"Don't thank me. You thought of it."

TUESDAY, MAY 31

"I heard there was a pentagram on the beach this morning."

O'Shaughnessy looked over her shoulder. The chief was walking just behind her and not looking cheerful.

"It's Memorial Day weekend," she said.

She stopped at the mailroom and grabbed a handful of envelopes, then started back to her office. "It came from the tip line," she said. "I hate to admit it, but it had me scared for a hot minute."

"So what did it turn out to be?"

"Well, to begin with, it was drawn on the sand by the bandshell where everyone has to walk. Someone wrote the word 'whore' in the center and the letters AC and TY on all five sides. If you ask me it's a bunch of sickos want to read about themselves in the paper."

"Anything else around?"

"A couple of kiddie sandcastles and a one-legged seagull."

"Did it look possessed?"

"They all look possessed."

"What about phone calls?"

"Galore. Everyone who jogged by must have called. It started at five and ended about an hour ago. They said the Pagans were in town."

"The Pagans don't play in the sand," the chief said. "Not in all the years I've known them."

"We also got a call about a coven on Marshland Road, one of the old summer cottages. I sent a car over. There were shades pulled on all the windows and three couples inside. Spiked hair, black nails, black lipstick, you know the type, lots of black." She turned into her office. "Caught them eating chocolate cereal. Everybody needed a bath. Other than that, they were normal."

Loudon smiled.

She took a seat behind her desk and he sat on the edge.

"My assistant said you called?" Loudon asked.

"I need help."

He raised his eyebrows.

"You know anyone in Public Works I can talk to?"

"Concerning?"

"The kidnappings."

He nodded thoughtfully. "This about Jeremy Smyles?"

She shook her head. "Uh-uh. I'm looking for a truck." She told him about the paint scratches and the city inventory.

"Ben Johnson," he said quickly.

"I met him." She nodded. "He was on the scene

when Carlino poked Jeremy in the eye."

"He's the glue that holds that place together," Loudon said. "Not very tactful when it comes to the politicians, but he's outlasted four administrators. I've known him since I was a rookie."

Loudon reached down and put a finger on a pencil on her desk, spinning it around in circles. "Carlino's attorney filed a formal complaint against us. The city manager is taking it seriously. He wants a written response."

She turned to look at him. "About what?"

"Smyles," he said. "He's accusing us of putting a murderer back on the street. He's threatening the city with a lawsuit."

"For doing our job?"

"For negligence. Sergeant Dillon claims he has two teenagers who will swear they saw Smyles on the beach the night Yoland was abducted. Were you ever able to pin him down for an alibi?"

O'Shaughnessy looked down and shook her head. "He said he went for a walk."

"A walk?"

"A walk," she repeated softly.

The chief groaned. "You give this to Clarke?"

She nodded. "He agrees that it doesn't help, but Smyles still isn't capable."

"You talk to Clarke about a shrink yet?"

"Saturday the fourth, one o'clock. They were booked through the week. Look, Chief, you were right. Whoever took those girls from the boardwalk needed the strength to overpower them and the means to get them out of there, not to mention the brains to dispose of them. That person is not the Jeremy we interviewed."

He shrugged. "So get it into Clarke's hands. Find out who these kids of Dillon's are and get their stories on paper. You're not going to accomplish anything with Carlino on your back."

She nodded.

"Kelly. No matter what anyone tells you, myself included, don't eliminate Jeremy Smyles. Not unless you can do it conclusively. If it turns out one day that he was the guy, we're going to take a fall. A hard fall."

O'Shaughnessy nodded, knowing full well that "we" meant her.

"And leave Dillon to me," Loudon concluded.

O'Shaughnessy entered the Public Works complex just after four and was directed to Ben Johnson's office. The room was tiny and he'd had to move a chair into the hall to get the door closed so they could talk privately. Miss February was hanging on the back of the door wearing nothing but a ski cap.

"Nice tan" was all O'Shaughnessy could think of to say.

Johnson smiled and climbed behind his desk.

"Mr. Johnson, first of all, I want you to know that I am arranging a psychiatric evaluation for Mr. Smyles. It's voluntary and I hope it will resolve whether he is even capable of committing a crime."

"You're not going to charge him then?"

She shook her head. "Right now he's a material witness. Because of the ring he had in his possession. But that's it. Nothing more. Personally I don't think he's capable, but don't go quoting me. That's an opinion that is subject to change."

"Did he tell you where he got the ring?"

She nodded. "He says he found it under the board-walk when he was picking up trash. He said you specifically gave him permission to keep whatever he finds, which leads me to my first question." She leaned forward. "That doesn't sound like any bureau-cratic policy I've ever heard of. Is it?"

"It isn't." He put a foot on the edge of his desk and pushed his chair back. "But you'd have to know Smyles to understand why I treat him differently."

"Tell me," she said.

"Give Smyles an assignment, any assignment, and you can expect it's going to be followed to the letter. He doesn't have the faculty of discretion. He can't dif-ferentiate between what I say and what I mean. If I told him to pick up trash until the beach was clean, he'd never go home again. He'd always be chasing one more piece of paper. When I first hired him and told him to turn in any personal property he found, I got bags full of plastic rings and watches. There's more junk jewelry up there than anywhere else on the planet. I can't teach him what's valuable and what's not; to him everything is valuable, so frankly, I got to the point where I didn't care anymore. If he keeps a decent watch now and then, so what. He's the hardest-working employee I have and he makes noth-ing for it."

O'Shaughnessy looked at him and nodded. "So you would testify that the jewelry in his box, that he claims to have found under the boardwalk, was his to keep by your permission?"

Johnson's jaw set, but he turned it into a tight smile. "Lieutenant, this little department of mine rides on a highly unstable seven-million-dollar budget. I have half the fleet I need to get the job done and it's been that way for a quarter of a century. Do you think I care about what some broad-assed selectmen might say over a found-property policy? If they think they can come down here and do better, they will find my retirement papers on their desks so fast it will make their heads spin. Then they can have all the buckets of plastic rings their little hearts desire."

She smiled. Loudon was right. No one was going to be making much of a fuss over Smyles's little treasure box.

"Mr. Johnson, Jeremy isn't the real reason I came here today."

He looked at her, puzzled.

"I have reason to believe that there was an orange-colored vehicle in the parking lot the night Anne Carlino was abducted."

Johnson studied her face, trying to comprehend. One minute they were talking about Jeremy Smyles and now an orange vehicle. "Jeremy doesn't drive," he said, confused.

"I know that," she said.

"So now you think it was somebody else that works here? Maybe me?" The jaw tightened again. "Is this Pick on Sanitation Month or what?"

She looked at him, eyes steady. "The description we have is of an older model General Motors vehicle, early '90s series. We understand there are several trucks like that in your fleet. I just need to know who has access to them."

She took the inventory list from her jacket and unfolded it, pushing it across the desk. "Chief Loudon told me you might be able to help me out."

There. She let it out. The chief had sent her.

Johnson's eyes narrowed as he pulled the paper toward him. He picked up his glasses and a pencil and started tapping the paper.

"This is a pretty specific list," he said. "You mind telling me how you got it?"

"I can't right now," she said. "But I promise you'll be the first to know when I can. Right now I'm just trying to determine the credibility of the lead."

He looked her over carefully.

"Look," she said. "I'm sorry for what happened to Mr. Smyles the other night. Jason Carlino is a grieving father. I'm sure it's easy to put yourself in his shoes."

Johnson didn't need to be coddled. "You're looking for criminal histories on my drivers?"

She nodded. "You said yourself you had a couple of potential kidnappers."

"I said that?" He smiled, then snorted out a laugh, shaking his head at the memory.

"Something like that," she replied, smiling back lightly.

Ben Johnson's list was waiting on the fax machine when she returned to her office. It had eleven names on it; two of them were parolees who he'd been asked to find work for through a contact in the Justice Department. She ran them all through NCIC—the National Crime Information Center—and called Tim while she was waiting for a response, leaving the message that she would be sure to get the girls to his mother's so he could make his *commitment*. Then she called Clarke and told him she would love to take a drive up the coast.

Nothing looked interesting about the names at first. There was a man named Earl Oberlein Sykes who had done time in the Midwest for murder. NCIC had coded his homicide conviction with a vehicle reference, which meant he'd been charged with vehicular homicide; that was commonly a reference for reckless driving resulting in death. He got a lot of time, but there may have been a juvenile history of drunken driving. Sykes had no other history of violent crime, so she set it aside.

Some of the other sanitation drivers had traffic citations—one had received a DUI and one had left the scene of an accident. Then she ran Sandy Lyons, and the computer didn't stop spitting paper for a full three minutes.

Lyons had been paroled for rape and assault with intent to kill. He lived in Rio, not a dozen miles from the coast. White male, thirty-seven years, born in Elizabeth, New Jersey; four years in Lorton, Virginia, for rape, released August 1999. Two years in Alderson for rape in 1991, two years in Alderson for sodomy in 1986 when he was seventeen but charged as an adult. O'Shaughnessy had no doubt as to what his juvenile record was going to show.

There was a knock on the door. It was McGuire.

She looked up with a question on her face.

"Guess who called for you?"

She took a deep breath. "Ed McMahon?"

He laughed. "Newsy."

She folded her hands.

"He said to tell you there's a rumor Billy Weeks was with the Yoland girl the night she disappeared."

"No way."

"Way," he said.

She put a foot on her desk and looked up at the crime scene photos. "No shit," she whispered. Everyone on the force knew that Billy Weeks sold cocaine on the boardwalk. Could all this have been about cocaine? She thought about that for a long minute. "He's not the type, Mac. He doesn't have what it would take."

"Exactly what I was thinking."

"You going to bring him in?"

"Tomorrow at noon. I want to take him off the street when he's dealing. Might give us some more leverage if he's got a pocket full of dope."

"Good idea." She swiveled the computer screen toward him. "Look at this, Mac."

He read it and whistled. "Where'd you find him?"

"Drives a truck for Public Works. An orange truck."

"Jesus."

She nodded. "Keep it under your hat. I'm going to get a paint sample from his truck and we'll see what comes up."

"God, that looks good," he said, shaking his head.

"Go on," she told him. "Get out of here for tonight."

She popped a Nicorette as he was clearing the

door, and picked up the phone, dialing a number at the Public Works office. A woman answered.

"Is Ben Johnson still there?" she asked.

"Hang on."

Five minutes later a voice came on the line. "Johnson," he said, slightly out of breath.

"Sorry to bother you, Ben. It's Kelly again."

"Caught me in the parking lot. What can I do for you?"

"How can I get a look at the truck assigned to Sandy Lyons?"

"Hang on, Lieutenant," he said. "I need to get out of everyone's way here."

He came back on the line a moment later. "Sorry about that. Too many ears around. Lyons drives the meat wagon on the midnight-to-eight shift."

"Meat wagon?"

"The dead animal truck."

"Oh, yeah," she said. She'd called for it dozens of times when she was in uniform.

"Fleet number is thirty-three, but you can't miss it. It's a light dump truck with a hydraulic tail lift. Parks in the wash bay all the way at the end of the garage."

"Doors locked at night?"

"They're supposed to be," he said, "but never are. We keep everything that's valuable in the admin offices anyhow. Use the door on the west side of the building. The one closest to the parking lot."

"What does he do with the animals he picks up?"

"Takes them to the incinerator at the county landfill and burns them; last thing they do before they bring the truck in for cleaning."

"Cleaning?"

"Scrub down the bed with disinfectant. I think we use bleach."

"What happens on his night off? Does somebody else take the truck?"

"Not after the budget they gave me in September. Three men, three shifts. When one of them has a day off, the truck sits."

"Who are the other drivers?"

"Danny Ellerbee and Earl Sykes, but Ellerbee's been out for a hernia operation."

"When's Lyons's first day off this week?"

"Thursday," he said, "day after tomorrow. You'll have to wait for the evening shift to get in and out, though. They start coming in around ten, clean the place down, and everyone's gone by eleven-thirty."

"Thanks." She hung up the phone. "Yes!" She thumped the desk with her fist. The incinerator was the perfect place to dispose of a body.

Clarke looked quite handsome when he picked up O'Shaughnessy at her house. He was wearing olive dress slacks and a blue oxford shirt, loafers, no socks.

Normally she would have been nervous about a man picking her up, just as she'd been nervous about meeting a man in a public bar, but for some reason tonight she just didn't care.

She could tell that Clarke liked her outfit, too. The skirt was the shortest in her closet, but the mood struck her and it was over her hips before she could change her mind.

It was such a nice night, too. The stars were brilliant, the air was warm, the drive down to Cape May was invigorating. He had the top down and the wind made too much noise to be able to carry on a normal conversation, but they both seemed content to take it all in.

They crossed the bridge and wound along a string of lighted condominiums. Twenty minutes later they were parked near the soft-colored Victorians in Cape May—a gas-lamp community of fine dining and boutique bed-and-breakfasts.

She took his arm as he led her to a restaurant and a table reserved by a window. She was pleased when he ordered the wine and two-pound lobsters without asking.

The meal was fabulous and fun and there was nothing stuffy about Clarke. Here again he had put her at ease, just a regular guy with a mountain of money.

The drive home was heady, or maybe it was the bottle of Chardonnay and the moon, but she was definitely thinking thoughts she didn't normally think.

"Need to get right home?" he asked.

"Show me yours?" She almost giggled. "Your home," she repeated. Her hair was flying all around her face and she thought about Tim's commitment, wondering what he was doing at that moment.

Clarke's house was big—no, Clarke's house was enormous. It sat on a knoll overlooking the sea. They entered into a great room with massive marble columns and pale Oriental rugs on a red mahogany floor that reflected its shine like still, dark water.

Wooden spiral stairs ascended to a living room with a black baby grand and a staggering view of the sea. The dining room table was set for twenty, and a library overlooking the bay was stuffed with old books and heavy leather chairs.

She admired the art on the walls—rich, vibrant oils and wonderfully framed photographs and prints. An island the size of her entire kitchen sat in the middle of the kitchen and a stainless-steel refrigerator that could hold a cow took up a good amount of space along the wall.

"Come see the upstairs," he said excitedly, grabbing her hand and pulling her up the steps. The room was an octagon turret, forty feet in diameter, all of it carpeted in white and cooled by air-conditioning ducts all around the baseboard. There was a circular fireplace in its center, open on all sides and vented overhead. The walls of the octagon were glass.

The furniture was composed of two C-shaped sofas on either side of the circle and two overstuffed chairs, all of beige leather. There were four brown and tangerine pillows the size of bobsleds tossed around on the carpet. A brass telescope on a tripod was directed out to sea.

Clarke picked up a remote and clicked a button; then a fire appeared magically in the circle of stone, music started from the ceiling, and the air-conditioning hissed on, compensating for the heat.

She focused the telescopic lenses on a light off-shore, watched it for a moment, bobbing up and down on its crawl up the coast. Then she let go of the instrument and turned, taking it all in.

"Chardonnay?" he asked.

"Perfect." She dropped to the rug and curled her legs beside a pillow.

He opened a door in the wall and removed a bottle, poured, and brought the glasses to where she sat. They touched crystal and he kicked off his shoes and sat with her. "Let's rough it," he said.

"Yeah," she said softly, looking around the room. "Let's rough it."

They ended up on their stomachs facing the ocean, talking, laughing, watching ships' lights bobbing at sea. She was conscious of his arm against hers, but there was never a hint of urgency with Clarke. When their hands met, they encircled and then squeezed, and he rolled on his back, pulling her on top of him.

And this time when they kissed, she opened her mouth.

19

WEDNESDAY, JUNE 1
WILDWOOD, NEW JERSEY

The phone buzzed. "It's a detective from Philadelphia."

O'Shaughnessy nodded and picked it up. "O'Shaughnessy."

"Hey, Lieu, John Payne, Philadelphia."

"Detective Payne." She smiled. "Been a while. How's your case going?"

"Nowhere until this morning. I used the Scaglia underboss angle on the FBI and got my ballistics report back in record time. Guess what they found? My murder weapon was used in Cape May County in 1974. Open-case shooting at Atlantic and Cresse."

"Get out."

"Case name is Lisa Penn, Caucasian female, eighteen years, born in Indiana, Pennsylvania. Bullet was recovered from a 1969 Volkswagen Beetle registered to her, but that's all it says. Hoping you could tell me more."

"Man, this case is growing tentacles."

"Yeah, and they're all reaching toward you."

"Give me a couple hours."

It was in the basement in an olive-drab file cabinet, scratched and dented and covered with peace signs and "Go Navy" bumper stickers.

Lisa Penn was supposed to have been attending classes at the University of Pittsburgh in the fall of 1974. Her roommate called campus security after the girl hadn't come back to the dorm for several days and it was learned she'd been missing classes. Her parents were notified and Pittsburgh police were called to take a missing persons report. Fourteen days later a Wildwood, New Jersey, policeman running tag checks on overdue vehicles in public parking lots discovered her 1969 blue VW Beetle. The car was parked near Cresse and Boardwalk with a half-dozen traffic tickets stacked under the wipers, the first of them written well over a month before.

The police couldn't locate her. The girl's parents came to Wildwood, taking a hotel room and walking the streets day and night with her photograph. They talked with foot patrolmen, business owners, and hippies for weeks following their daughter's disappearance. When they finally gave up and left, they refused to take possession of their daughter's car and asked the city to donate any profits from its sale to a runaway shelter. They wanted no more memories of what had happened to her.

Wildwood kept the car another two months and slated it for auction. A mechanic getting it ready for inspection found an expended bullet on the driver's-side floorboard that the seizing officers had missed. A state police mobile crime unit determined that a bullet had been fired into the driver's seat. Presumptive swabs found human blood in the torn fibers on the seat cover and in the matting underneath.

O'Shaughnessy flipped the page.

Fingerprints on the driver's-side door and palm smudges on the steering wheel are not usable exhibits: items collected in the immediate vicinity of vehicle are as follows: nonfiltered cigarette, WTA stub (Wildwood Transit Authority), disposable cigarette lighter, partial plastic tail lens from American-made vehicle.

O'Shaughnessy knew that the seventies were a chaotic period for police officers everywhere. Though a child herself at the time, she had hazy recollections of the tent towns outside the city, could only imagine the minor disruptions popping up everywhere—common accidents, injuries, and illnesses, plenty of overdoses. Half of the hippies had used false or partial names, and if someone went missing it was assumed they'd only moved on to different digs.

An abandoned car and a missing girl wouldn't have remained a priority in any town in the United States for long.

O'Shaughnessy's fingers stroked the frayed red bindings of the file. She shifted a stale piece of Nicorette from one side of her mouth to the other and scanned the water-stained pages.

Then she found the list.

It was handwritten in blue ink on lined tablet paper. She read:

Venable, Marissa, *W/F/dob: 6/6/58—Beckley, West Virginia, missing 7/7/74.*
Ashley, Bianca, *W/F/dob: 3/6/54—Wildwood, missing 9/27/74.*
Melissa Last Name Unk, *W/F/dob: unk/20's, missing 2/18/76 along with a young child, all statistics unk.*

Below them at the bottom of the page and circled in red was an entry *Penn, Lisa, W/F/dob: 4/13/56, missing 9/21/74* and a line drawn up the side of the page with an arrow placing it between the names Venable and Ashley.

She flipped to Venable, who had been living in a community house on Versailles Street with eleven other people. Venable was reported missing by a man with whom she shared a bed. The man claimed he last saw her at a beach party where they had been smoking marijuana. When he woke up the next morning, she still hadn't returned. A few days later, when she hadn't come by to pick up her belongings, he walked to the police station and made a report.

Venable's parents stated that they hadn't seen or heard from their daughter in the four months prior to her disappearance. There were two photographs stapled to the inside of the jacket, one taken with her mother several years before and one with a cousin in Arizona in 1971. Standing in front of a cactus, both girls wore granny glasses and long beaded vests.

Bianca Ashley-Wells, the second missing woman, was born and raised in the North Beach section of Wildwood and was married to the owner of a local real estate company at the time of her disappearance. Case notes described the evening of the disappearance as the couple's sixth wedding anniversary. The family's Volvo station wagon was found with the hood up along the Garden State Parkway near the golf and country club. Detectives later determined that a radiator hose had come loose, draining the car's coolant and causing it to overheat. She was only two miles from the club, where she was to meet her husband for dinner, when it happened.

Ashley, along with her purse and a gift-wrapped Rolex for her husband, was never found. The jeweler who sold her the watch said that she had stopped by the store just before closing and seemed to be in high spirits. A dozen other pages concerned her husband,

who detectives ultimately determined was not involved.

Two years later in February, a woman living in Cottage Town disappeared with her daughter. She was a
dark-haired beauty shown in a photo kneeling behind
a sand sculpture of the Last Supper. "Melissa" was the
only word written on the back of the photo. She had a
child, according to housemates, a happy little girl
nearing preschool age. They said Melissa was secre-
tive about her past and never used a last name or
talked about the child's father. Her friends had the
impression she was from the northeast, but they
couldn't agree on why they thought that.

O'Shaughnessy picked up the phone and dialed the
department's laboratory. "Gus, it's Kelly. Can you
come up for a minute? I need to show you something."

"You ever heard of a cop named Andrew Markey?"

Gus looked at her oddly and nodded. "Uh-huh. He
was a captain around the time I came on. Got caught
up in the rackets in Atlantic City in the seventies; the
FBI locked him up and he did some time in upstate
New York."

"He had a daughter?"

The lab chief nodded. "I remember one."

"He's dead. Fell down a set of steps in Elmwood
first of May. His daughter was gunned down
execution-style a couple days later in Philadelphia.
Someone came into the store where she worked and
put three bullets in her. The police said no sex, no
robbery. One of the men her father testified against

has climbed the ranks to underboss of the Gambino family."

He frowned. "Hell of a long time to wait for revenge."

O'Shaughnessy shrugged. "On that everyone agrees. So here's the kicker: Philadelphia homicide got a match on their murder weapon to one of our cases."

Gus leaned forward; forensics was his specialty.

He watched her eyes for a moment, then looked at the thick red file on her desk. "Which one?" he asked hesitantly, thinking there had been no mob shootings in Wildwood in his memory.

"Lisa Penn," she said.

He shook his head. "I don't recall it."

"Nineteen seventy-four." She smiled. "I was three years old."

"Good God," he whispered. "Is that the jacket?"

"Uh-huh. It's not very helpful, though. They never found the victim."

He looked confused. "Go back to this Philly shooting."

"Andrew Markey's daughter moved to Philadelphia twenty-five years ago. The detective says she's clean, heavy into the church, good family, solid friends, no flaws that he can find. He said she never came back to Wildwood and didn't stay in touch with anyone here. Not even her father, who was in Elmwood for a decade."

Gus whistled. "What about the husband?"

She shook her head. "Born and raised in Philadelphia, good family, good education, clean as the victim. Philadelphia is hoping we can tell them something about Markey that they haven't already heard."

"May I look at it?"

She lifted the jacket and handed it to him with a smile. "I was hoping you would ask."

He put it in his lap and traced the binding with his fingers.

"What about the mother?" O'Shaughnessy asked. "Philadelphia never mentioned one."

He nodded. "Pretty woman, took a long walk off a short pier the week after the indictments were handed down. Never seen again. The daughter turned into a regular wild child after that. I remember hearing the guys talking about her around the station; they called her Crazy Sue or something like that. She got busted for drugs at least once I knew of, and she was running with some real lowlifes. Then she just vanished, or at least I never heard of her again."

O'Shaughnessy thought that Detective Payne would find that last bit of information interesting; still, like Susan's father's connection with the mob, it was a long, long time ago. "Give me a call when you're finished reading it."

"It'll be tomorrow. I've got to work up Clarke's savings and loan checks or he'll have a cow. The FBI is already driving him crazy."

THURSDAY, JUNE 2
O'Shaughnessy spent the morning developing infor-

mation on Sandy Lyons. His house was located in Rio off Route 9. It was a two-bedroom modular with one visible neighbor. A motorcycle and a ten-year-old Subaru filled the driveway; a hard-barking Doberman paced the gated backyard. According to the regular mailman, Lyons lived alone.

She'd ordered Lyons's old case summaries, which would provide details of his sex crimes; she was particularly curious about whether he had used duct tape on any of his victims and if he had transported them to any other location than the crime scene.

Just after lunch a bouquet of white roses arrived at her door, which prompted some hooting from the detectives. O'Shaughnessy took that to mean the men were starting to accept her, but it might also have meant they liked the delivery girl.

The card was from Clarke. Not Tim.

She called the DA to thank him, forgetting that he was arguing motions on the savings and loan case, and left a message. Afterward she called the girls, who were getting to her mother-in-law's from day care. Oddly, it was Tim who answered the phone.

"How are you, Kel?"

"I'm fine, Tim. You?"

She wondered why he was not at work and was curious about his damned *commitment*, but she held her tongue. They were both adults. She had been the one to suggest a separation in the first place, and after all, what was separation anyhow if not a chance to reevaluate? Besides, she had gone out with Clarke.

They talked about Reagan's birthday party for a few minutes and then he put the kids on.

"I got to bring a ferret home," Marcy said, excited.

"A ferret," O'Shaughnessy said.

"His name is Alf and we all get to take him home for a week if it's okay with our parents. Daddy said it's okay. Daddy said you wouldn't mind. Is it okay with you, Mommy?"

"Of course it's okay," she said. "How is your sister?"

"She's fine, but Alf doesn't like her as much as he likes me."

"Put your sister on."

"Reagan won a ticket to a matinee for a spelling bee."

"Put your sister on," she repeated. "I'm sure Reagan wants to tell me about it, too."

O'Shaughnessy missed hearing about their school adventures over the dinner table. She missed being a part of a family again. Had Tim really had a date?

McGuire took two of his detectives and picked up Billy Weeks in front of Lecky's Pawnshop and brought him into the office.

Weeks made a show of being put out by the experience, shirt askew, hair ruffled, scowl on his face. It wasn't the first time he'd been run in by the cops, but it *was* the first time he had a pocket full of money and three bags of dope. Not to mention an additional ten bags they'd found in an empty coffee cup sitting on top of the trash can next to him. He wasn't worried, though. He knew the search wouldn't hold up without probable cause. If there was no legal reason to pick him up, there was no legal reason to go through his pockets. The cocaine would be inadmissible. Maybe his attorney could even sue them for false arrest.

The interview room—no larger than Billy's walk-in closet—had a narrow table with two chairs on either side. The walls were covered with cork tiles to suppress sound. He waited for the interview to begin. He knew the drill. Butter him up good, then turn on the heat. He watched *NYPD Blue*. He'd wait long enough to find out what they knew and then he'd ask to see a lawyer. That would be his final word on anything.

But Sergeant McGuire wasn't ten words into the conversation when Billy started to talk, forgetting all about lawsuits and lawyers. Somehow they'd learned that he was the last person to have seen Tracy Yoland alive before she disappeared.

He told them everything he knew. If they ever found the girl's body, his hair and semen would be on her anyhow. They could haul him in front of some Baptist jury and convict his ass of murder with nothing more than DNA. And Billy Weeks didn't want to be a murder suspect, not even for five more minutes. Billy wanted to be charged with cocaine possession, not murder. Billy wanted to help!

"Didn't you see the flyers we handed out on the boardwalk, Billy?"

"Yes, yes," he told them. He'd seen the flyers. He knew it was the same girl who was missing, but it wasn't a crime just to know her, was it? He hadn't heard that her purse was found. He thought she had just changed her mind about going home and ended up with someone else that night. It wasn't like that hadn't happened before.

*　*　*

Gus was stooping over a plate-size magnifying glass when O'Shaughnessy entered the laboratory.

"S&L?" she asked.

He nodded, looking through the glass and switching documents. "Lady had some pretty big cojones if you ask me."

"Quarter of a million, I heard."

"And growing. She had more checking accounts than she had shoes."

"How's it going with you?" she asked.

"Good." He pushed the lens away. "And you?"

"I mean, how are you really doing, Gus?" She put a hand on his shoulder. It was a rare moment when no one else was around.

"I'm so-so," he answered.

"Haven't had a chance to say it, but I'm so sorry, Gus."

"We had lots of good years, Kelly. You have to look at it like that."

She thought of Tim and the girls at that moment. Nothing was certain. Not ever. "Are you sure you want to be here?"

"I could sit in that pastel hell over there waiting for her to die, but I'd rather be working. Working keeps my mind off her. Besides, she sleeps most of the day."

O'Shaughnessy squeezed his shoulder. "McGuire said you called."

Gus walked to his desk and picked up the red file.

"I remember these women," he said. "We didn't have a lot of specialists back then. In fact there was only one detective assigned to the entire department, and his job was to monitor the pawnshops' and liquor stores' licenses. Beat cops handled their own investigations and the state police assisted with murders. I know there was talk about white slavery rings out of Philly and Washington, D.C.; pimps used to roll through town in their Lincolns and Cadillacs on the way to AC. We were asked to record out-of-state tags and any activity that looked suspicious. We had some big-city detectives come over from D.C. and nose around for a while, but nothing ever came of it."

She shook her head. "And everyone just moved on?"

"That was the times, Kelly. There wasn't a clearinghouse for missing persons in the seventies. Every department took their own reports, sent descriptions across the country by Teletype, and looked for their own victims. Picture a whole country full of roaming teenagers. No one knew where their kids were. Serial rapists, killers, and pornographers were in their heyday. Victims were sticking out their thumbs and climbing into the backseat of anything that came along."

"What stopped this one, Gus? Things like this don't just stop on their own."

He shook his head. "Maybe he moved on to another part of the country or maybe he got himself arrested. Maybe he died. Or maybe there really was some organized white slavery ring and someone put the squeeze on them. Could have been a million different reasons."

She considered that for a moment. "Okay, how about the Penn girl? Why shoot someone if you're going to kidnap her anyhow? He already had a gun on her, so she was most likely going to cooperate."

"The only thing I can come up with is that she wasn't taking him seriously and he wanted to get her attention fast."

"Then it stopped?"

He nodded. "Last one in '76." He tapped the front of the file. "I checked with Youth Division this morning. There hasn't been a special-circumstances case since 1991 and that was when a maid abducted a child from the Pan Am Hotel and took him to South Carolina." He handed her the jacket. "Not until Anne Carlino last May."

"What do you think of this case up in Philadelphia? This ballistics match?"

"I'd say it's the strangest thing I've heard in thirty-five years."

O'Shaughnessy waited for the detective to pick up the phone, popped a Nicorette in her mouth, and settled back in her chair.

"Payne here."

"It's O'Shaughnessy, Detective Payne. We lost the juvenile records to our fire, but I can tell you your saint wasn't exactly a saint when she lived in Wildwood. Crazy Sue was the term I heard used. Our lab chief remembers her, said she kept some real bad company."

"You don't say." Payne cradled the phone against

his ear, pulled a pad toward him. "What about your shooting in 1974? The Penn girl."

"'Missing from college in Indiana, Pennsylvania,'" O'Shaughnessy read from her notes, "'car was found by the boardwalk. A bullet was fired through the seat. There was blood in the seat fibers, same type as the missing girl.' End of story. Girl was never seen or heard from again."

"That's it?"

"I'm afraid so." She took the gum from her mouth, made a sour face, flicked it in the trash. "There were other missing women around that time. Four in all over a two-year span. All open cases."

"Jesus."

"I'll fax you the summaries if you want." As her eyes traveled to the crime scene photo of the drain-pipe, a thought struck her like a lightbulb flash and that thought led her to a very strange place.

"Detective," she said softly.

"Yes, Lieutenant?"

"Lisa Penn's car, the one with your bullet match from 1974, it was found in public parking by the boardwalk."

"Go ahead."

"I had an abduction May first, same way. Victim's car was found in the same parking lot, bloody scene, victim never turned up."

Neither of them spoke for a moment.

"Any suspects, Lieu?"

"Two."

"Could either have come here and killed Susan

Paxton?"

"I don't know. One of them can't drive; the other doesn't know he's a suspect yet."

For a moment they were both silent.

"Lieu," the detective said hesitantly, "do you still have Andrew Markey on ice?"

"Uh-huh. I called over there after our conversation yesterday."

"Look, Lieutenant, I know this is going to sound a little off, but I was wondering, have you ever heard of a woman named Sherry Moore?"

O'Shaughnessy repeated the name. "Sherry Moore? I don't think so."

"She's been written up a lot for helping the police solve cases. She reads memories. Memories of—"

"Dead people. Yes, yes, I remember," O'Shaughnessy interrupted. She'd read about the woman while on a ferry to Martha's Vineyard last fall. The bittersweet memory of Tim's surprise anniversary vacation startled her as much as the question.

"Lieutenant, Sherry Moore is a personal friend. I asked her to assist me on the Paxton case."

O'Shaughnessy was quiet a moment. "To read your victim's thoughts?"

"Kind of," he said.

"Well, I must say you surprise me every time you call, Detective Payne. So what is it she saw?"

"A man. I have a sketch, Lieu. Sherry described him to our police artist. Young man, long hair, beard; he doesn't show up in any of our books. Neither the husband or friends or coworkers have ever seen him before."

"And you want to find out if Andrew Markey saw the same man before he died?"

"Uh-huh."

O'Shaughnessy looked out over the outer office at the men working behind their desks; Sergeant McGuire was speaking into the phone.

"My department would never allow it."

"You don't need to ask them, Lieu. Just get her into the morgue for a few minutes. That and tell me where I can show my sketch around the boardwalk. Maybe there's a connection here. Maybe my shooter is your abductor?"

"I know I raised the issue, but really, Detective, isn't that stretching it?"

"You tell me. It won't cost a dime. We're in, we're out, we either find out Andrew Markey was pushed down the steps or he wasn't. It's that simple. No one would have to know Sherry was involved."

O'Shaughnessy opened her desk drawer and shook out a cigarette. Then she took a match and lit it, blowing smoke at the ceiling.

"You're reading my mind," she said dryly.

"I know how people react to this stuff, Lieu. I'm a cop, too. I just want to find Susan Paxton's killer."

She stared at the wall. "When do you want to come—unofficially?"

"Would Friday night be inconvenient? We could go to the morgue on Saturday, and Sunday I could show the sketch around town."

"Can you share a one-bedroom? There's a sleeper sofa in the living room."

"You don't have to trouble—"

"My contribution," she interrupted. "Besides, you'll never find a summer weekend vacancy on such late notice."

"We can share an apartment just fine."

"Good," she said, looking up at the ceiling and thinking she was straying far from the beaten path. "Miss Moore stays away from everyone. I don't want anyone talking to her but me, and that's inflexible. In fact it'll be like you said. No one is to know she's in town."

"Deal," he said.

"One more thing."

"Go ahead."

"We're liable to get some weather this weekend. The Carolinas are taking a beating, and if this storm holds the coast it's not going to be pretty."

"We're not coming to vacation, Lieu."

"All right, then, Friday night. I'll give you my address and cell phone number."

O'Shaughnessy could manage the morgue easily enough; Gus had his own set of keys to the place. She would ask him for them. The condo had been sitting empty since her mother's death the previous year; it was going to be musty and need an airing out, but the linens were clean.

Sykes drove west toward the sound and then left on Desmond Drive. The call had been for a dog down in the cul-de-sac. The homes were expensive here, a couple hundred thousand to a million each; he liked to sit outside on sunny afternoons and watch the wives and daughters carry packages in from their Mercedeses in their little tennis skirts.

All those years in prison he had sat in a cage while these people went about their lives: barbecuing in their backyards, drinking wine and fucking their neighbors, cheating on their taxes and gouging the poor. How many times had he thought of them, smelling the good leather of their Mercedes-Benzes, sunbathing by their pools with *The Wall Street Journal*, while he was surrounded by steel?

They could never repay him for that. Not in a year, not in a million years.

A dog was lying in the cul-de-sac, motionless. The parkway was just on the other side of the trees. Most likely it had gotten hit and was crawling toward its home when it collapsed.

No one else was around when he made a U-turn and pulled in front of it, blocking it from view of the houses.

It was a Rottweiler and a large one; its face was black and caramel, its muzzle was covered with blood. One of its ears was split and both of its back legs appeared to be broken.

He got out, pulled on leather gloves, scratched his neck with one, and lowered the tailgate to pull the tarp back. Then he crouched and grabbed one of the animal's back legs. When he did, it lunged and clamped its jaws on the heel of his boot. Sykes kicked at its mouth with his other leg, but the dog bore down even harder, teeth buried in the leather. Sykes fell to the ground and rolled until he managed to get a hand around to his stun gun, firing it into the dog's shoulder. The animal's jaws went slack and Sykes dragged himself away from it. After a minute he got to his feet and walked shakily to the truck, reaching into the bed for a tire iron. When he returned, he beat the dog's head until he heard the skull crack. After a minute of hard breathing he threw the bloody iron in the back of the truck and kicked the dog in the belly for good measure. Then he grabbed its legs and dragged it onto the lift, pulling the lever that hoisted it onto the bed.

He wasn't injured; the dog's teeth never got through the boot. It had current rabies tags that he threw into the incinerator with the dog when he burned it.

That night he bought a six-pack and found a turn-around on the Garden State Parkway where no one would bother him.

It had hit him a little harder than he would have thought to discover that his old nemesis, Chief Lynch, had died of a heart attack while he was in prison. All those years hating a man who wasn't even alive anymore. He'd felt cheated, as if the bastard had come out of the grave and taken something else away from him.

But then he'd learned that Lynch's daughter was the city's new chief of detectives, Lieutenant Kelly O'Shaughnessy. O'Shaughnessy, the same name that was on the condominium mailbox listed to Lois Lynch. It had been her parents'. She owned it now and she also had an address on Third Avenue, just a city block away. Sykes knew how he was going to get his revenge.

20

THURSDAY NIGHT, JUNE 2
GLASSBORO, NEW JERSEY

Nicky was as drunk as Marcia had ever seen him, staggering wildly from his car and screaming obscenities at his bag of beers, which had ripped open, cans tumbling over the lawn.

"Come here, bitch!" he yelled. "Come here and bring me some lovin'!"

Not tonight, she prayed. No bruises tonight, Nicky.

She gathered his beers in the folds of her skirt and talked him into the living room, where she helped him out of his clothes, which were rank from sweat. Whatever he had been doing with his brothers tonight, it wasn't all drinking.

She kept thinking about the news broadcast she'd seen on television while she was doing her ironing. The police were looking for a gang stealing farm equipment in the area. It would be just like him, she thought. Beat her up all these years, then get himself locked up so she could get evicted and starve.

It wasn't long before he fell asleep on the couch. Marcia tiptoed into the kitchen and took a long last look at the two twenties on the counter. It seemed wrong to leave him anything. He never thought twice about drinking up his overtime and holiday pay. He never gave her anything extra that came in. Never let her buy anything for herself.

She picked up one of the twenties and walked out the door.

Something emboldened her as she crossed the yard. Maybe it was just the knowledge of the new lock and the front-end loader in the barn. Maybe he wouldn't be such a smart-ass if she mentioned that news bulletin to him.

She reached the road and her shoes scuffed across the gravel berm. There was a moon, a beautiful heavy moon, and the air was sweet. Ding, their old dog, jumped at the kitchen door and started barking. She turned back with a look of horror, knowing the dog was making twice as much racket inside.

Whatever her initial instincts, and one of them was definitely to run, she stood there, feet frozen in place and waiting to see if Nicky would come to the door.

He did.

The door swung open and Ding dashed across the lawn, squirming happily at her feet, looking up at her with his big head against her thigh.

"Where you going?" Nicky growled. He was stark naked and standing just outside the door.

"You know where I'm going," she said softly, soothingly. "Tonight's the night I go to meet Connie. Remember?"

"You're sneaking off, you little bitch?"

"I'm not sneaking anywhere, Nicky. You know we talked about this. We talked about it a long time ago. I left your money right there on the counter."

"This," he yelled, making a face and shaking the twenty-dollar bill. "Is this why you didn't say good-bye?"

"I did say good-bye, honey," she said. "You were just sleeping so soundly I didn't want to wake you. I said good-bye. I kissed you on the cheek."

He stared at her, weaving back and forth and clutching the crumpled twenty in his hand. "You said you was going to leave me fifty, bitch." He slurred his words badly. "You ain't leaving me this." He crumpled the bill in his fist.

"I never said fifty dollars, Nicky. I said I'd give you whatever I got. But you know I had to use some of the money on your groceries and beer. I thought you'd know that. I made you a meat loaf and bought you your favorite beer, Nicky. It's in the refrigerator."

He took a step forward, then stopped. "Come here," he said, pointing at the ground in front of him. A chill went down Marcia's spine.

"I'm going to be late, Nicky," she said. "Don't you want to go to bed now?"

"Come here," he said. The tone was dangerously familiar.

She started toward him slowly, wondering if he was going to strike her now or when he found the new bikini and nail polish in her bag. He would beat her until he couldn't beat her anymore and then he would destroy them.

"Come on, Nicky," she said. "You have the beer and food and some money to go out with."

She was close to him now, walking nearer all the time, and when she was within reach, he tore the denim purse from her shoulder and dumped its contents out on the ground. She watched as twenty-eight dollars floated to the grass and he stooped to pick them up. Then he looked at the overnight bag. A cruel grin came over his face.

"I'll do without it, Nicky," she said. "You need it more than me." She half laughed, half cried. "What do I need money for?"

She wiped the tears away quickly. Nicky didn't like tears.

Drunk, distracted, or feeling sick, he turned and staggered with his forty-eight dollars to the door.

She knelt and raked up the things on the lawn with her fingers, shoving them in her purse with the grass and dirt, and then she ran and didn't stop running until she was at Connie's house, where she found the keys under the floor mat of her car.

She was still trembling twenty miles later when she reached the intersection of Route 55, but every new mile brought composure, and by the time she reached Dennisville, she was actually starting to feel good. She had freedom, even if it was only for a few days. She had time to think.

She lowered the driver's-side window and felt the cool air lifting her hair like someone's caressing fingers. She was here and he was there and that was what really mattered. "Woo hoo!" she yelled into the rearview mirror, seeing the first evidence of sand along the edges of the road.

The thought of lying on a beach tomorrow was almost more than she could bear. She hadn't been away from Nicky for more than a few hours since their wedding night and then it was only to go to work so there would be more money for him to buy beer with.

She hoped that Connie was wide awake and ready

to go, but even if she wasn't, Marcia intended to go to the boardwalk. She might not have money to spend, but she wasn't going to waste a moment sleeping. She would be there in just under an hour. One hour!

When she was near Goshen she saw a police car blocking the road and beyond it a spiral of smoke rising from a dark heap of metal. She couldn't tell which way the cars had been heading, but it was apparent that no one got out alive.

The policeman's flare indicated that she should turn her car around and go back the way she came. She had concerns about getting lost, but the look on the man's face didn't invite conversation. She could guess what it must have looked like inside that wreck and thought it prudent not to ask him for directions.

She looped the small car, then pulled over and looked at the map Connie had left her. The last turnoff she saw to the east was south of Dennisville on a dirt road. It wasn't on the map, but it would take her nearer the coast; she guessed it connected with some other road that would get her to the Garden State Parkway, which would take her directly into Wildwood.

She checked her gas gauge and found the needle touching the shaded area above empty. She'd passed plenty of stations after she left her house, but Nicky had taken all of her money. Still, she was relatively certain she had enough in the tank to make it seventy more miles.

Bugs slapped her windshield and possums darted in front of the car. She came to the farm road and turned east, her headlights illuminating miles of slouching telephone lines. Fields and farms eventually gave way to forest.

The treetops soon swallowed the moon and the temperature dropped several degrees. She felt goose bumps rising on her arms as she entered the Pine Barrens. She held the speedometer at forty, always alert for deer or a car coming toward her, but there were no deer and no cars and no signs of a town or telephone if she needed it.

Connie wouldn't start to worry about her until after midnight and even then she wouldn't actually be alarmed; both of them knew there was the possibility that Nicky wouldn't let her out of the house. Marcia wished that she'd made firmer arrangements with Connie, that she could have at least let her know she was on her way, just to be safe. But Connie's mother hadn't bothered to turn on the phone in the beach house this year.

The stars continued to shine and every now and then the moon made an appearance between the trees. Thirty minutes later, when the needle was solidly in the red, she drove under a four-lane overpass and knew it had to be the Garden State Parkway. She found a parallel road, and another ten miles of mistakes brought her to an on-ramp taking her south.

Everything was going to be fine.

The needle on the gas gauge was as low as it could go. Five more miles, she kept thinking. Just five more miles, please. There was a city's pink glow on the horizon, probably Wildwood's.

But the gas finally gave out and the engine cut to

silence; she let the car drift into a wide spot off the berm.

Marcia killed her headlights and smacked the wheel with her hand, putting her head against the headrest. "Shit."

The parkway was dark, and there was little traffic this time of night. There had been no exits for several miles, so the only way to go was forward.

She considered her options. She could either get out and start walking or stay with the car until someone came along to help her. The latter made more sense, especially these days. People didn't like picking up other people at night, not the way they used to. She checked her watch and waited. It was almost ten.

Five long minutes passed and headlights appeared. She put her flashers on and got out waving her arms.

The vehicle's headlights were in her eyes, but she could see that it was a pickup truck with an emergency beacon on top. Oh, thank God!

Probably the highway department, she thought. Surely they would have a can of gasoline with them.

"Oh, thank you," she yelled as she ran up to the driver's door. "I must be close to Wildwood," she said excitedly.

"Three miles." The man nodded.

Her eyes were still trying to adjust to the darkness; she could tell he was an older man, sixty or more. She could also smell that he'd been drinking. "Do you have any gas with you?" she asked.

"Uh-huh," he said. "Right there in the back." He jerked his thumb over his shoulder. Then he opened his door and got out. The truck didn't smell very good. Like he was hauling something dead. She watched him go around the back to the passenger side, where he started fooling with the tarp that was covering the bed. He looked a little unsteady on his feet and it reminded her of Nicky. God, she thought. Is that all they do at work? Drink beer?

"Help me with this a minute, lady," he said. "I can't hold the tarp up and shine the light at the same time."

Sykes knew he didn't have much time. Another car would be coming along at any minute.

She came around back and leaned over the rail where he was pretending to look under the tarp. The smell was so bad under it, she nearly gagged.

"In the cab under the seat is my flashlight. Grab it for me, will you?"

Marcia opened the passenger door and leaned in to look under the seat. Something touched her back and a surge of electricity shot through her body like a million hot needles, shutting down her muscles and blinding her eyes as if they had been seared by the sun. She thought she could feel her body twitching, but in fact she was immobilized and the surge continued as hands went around her waist and lifted her into the cab. He slammed the door behind her and ran to get behind the wheel. Then he jammed the truck into gear and popped the clutch, lurching onto the highway. The whole thing had taken under two minutes.

He took the next exit off the parkway. The jolt tossed her head forward into the dash, where the radio microphone was cradled, and split her forehead open above one eyebrow.

He pulled her back against the seat as blood trickled down her nose, and cursed.

Marcia felt the burning behind her eyes and the torturous prickling throughout her body. Then she remembered she was in the truck and the truck was leaving the road, turning onto dirt where it entered the swamps.

The truck stopped in thick trees covered with vines. They were next to a fence; Marcia could make out a yellow diamond biohazard sign just before he shut off the lights.

Sykes got out and came around to her side, opened the door, and put her over his shoulder. He carried her through a cutout in the wire. She could see by the moon that they were in a junkyard. He stopped twice and laid her on the ground to catch his breath, but eventually they came to a section of old buses and he propped her on the steps of one, climbed in behind her, and dragged her to the rear with hands hooked under her arms.

It was black inside the bus; he dropped her on a mattress and left her lying there while he lit a match to a lantern. There was a noisy flicker, then light; she could smell kerosene and chemicals in the air.

She looked around and grew wide-eyed when she saw the metal rings welded to a rod at the edge of the mattress.

He was going to tie her down. Going to rape her.

Sykes shook a cigarette from a pack and tapped it down on the face of his watch.

The bus windows had been spray-painted black;

she could see scratches in the paint in the reflection of the lantern. Oh, God, she thought. Not this!

When he got his breath once more, he crouched by the lantern and opened a pack of plastic Flexi-Cuffs, knelt and pulled her arms and legs apart, and bound them to the steel rings. Then he produced a roll of duct tape, ripped off a piece with his teeth, and put it across her mouth.

"Daddy's got to go to work for a while, but we'll play later. I promise. Okay?"

He laughed and blew out the lantern.

John Payne sat in the living room of his apartment, feet planted squarely on the floor, rocking back and forth in faultless rhythm. His eyes were fixed on a spot on the television, but Angie knew he wasn't really watching.

They had never bothered to buy a house, though they once had talked about a small farm outside the city in Lancaster. Never went on exotic vacations, though they'd planned to visit Hawaii and Australia. For whatever reason, the desires had all gone away.

The apartment had become a place for them to meet, to pretend to believe in the marriage that had been over for years.

"She cares for you," she said.

Payne's eyes turned to meet hers.

"Oh, come on, John. You're always giving her credit for how brilliant she is. Don't you even know that much? You talk about her incredible intuition and yet you lie here night after night, wondering if she cares about you?"

Payne's mouth opened and Angie leaned forward. "I suppose you're afraid of what will happen to me. This isn't what I wanted either, John. It's not there anymore. Move on. Let me move on. Go to her. I'll find someone, don't you worry."

He'd never wanted to hurt her. The fact was, he did love her, just not in the way she wanted him to. He didn't have the kind of feelings for her that he did for Sherry.

"I know you've never cheated on me, John, not in the physical sense. You're not a bad man for wanting someone else. You're just not doing either of us any good. We can work out the details when you get back, but when you're with her in Wildwood, you tell her."

She stood and walked over to him, put a hand on his shoulder, and kissed him on the top of his head, leaving his hair wet with her tears as she walked out of the room.

21

THURSDAY NIGHT, JUNE 2
WILDWOOD, NEW JERSEY

O'Shaughnessy slapped a mosquito on her neck and turned the police radio down. The three-to-eleven shift was coming out of the Public Works garages for the night; men walked past her to get to their cars in the employee lot. Some looked in at her, others paid her little mind.

She had a picture of Sandy Lyons in her folder, but he wouldn't be among them. Sandy was on his day off. The meat wagon would be parked for the rest of the night.

She put her head against the headrest and watched the last of them walk by. Reagan had asked about her birthday party today. It was only two weeks away and she needed to arrange something with the other mothers. She'd pretty much settled on McDonald's, Reagan's favorite. She knew Tim would want to be there and it would be easier for him to slip in and out if they weren't at the house.

She wondered if Tim had heard rumors about her and Clarke Hamilton. Could that have prompted his *commitment*? If he had, he'd keep it to himself, because that was how Tim was. She honestly didn't want to hurt him, but the possibility was real once they started seeing other people. How far could it go before it became irreversible?

The separation, she'd thought, had been necessary to give her time to grieve or whatever in the hell she was doing. Maybe more accurately, to exact some form of revenge. She could see now how easily a separation could get out of hand. It might only be isolation and anger in the beginning, but then other people started working themselves into the equation, and things began to snowball until there was nothing left to salvage.

She spoke with Tim's mother almost every other day and found it peculiar that the woman never asked her about the separation. Mostly, she was thankful that her mother-in-law respected their privacy and tried not to meddle like so many other mothers-in-law might do. O'Shaughnessy knew that the woman had hope it would blow over quickly, just like her own daughters did, that they all wished she would take him back so they could get on with their lives.

Her window was down; she popped a Nicorette and was leaning over to reach in the glove box for a penlight when suddenly she sensed someone behind her. She sat up quickly and there was a man looking in her window. Not from several feet away, but right there with his head in her window! He was an older man with droopy eyelids and a frightful-looking scar across his neck. The radio crackled; he smiled and stood upright and walked away without saying a word.

She could hear her heart beating in her chest. His boots ground on the gravel until he reached a dark-colored Jeep, got in, started the ignition, and sped away.

She sat there, hands shaking. She felt her service weapon pressing against her back, but she hadn't thought of it in that moment. It had all happened too suddenly. Why would someone do that? What in the hell was he thinking?

June bugs whacked noisily against the dome-shaped street lamps as O'Shaughnessy made her way toward the garage. A veil of low clouds raced across the moon. It was light enough to see without a flashlight.

The lot was empty now and quiet but for the insects. The garage doors were closed, the evening crew gone home. She found the side entrance unlocked, as Ben had promised.

The steel building echoed her every sound—the door latch, the light switch, her shoes scuffing along the concrete. The room smelled of sour garbage and greasy machinery. She was careful not to brush up against anything, cognizant that the scratching sounds were rats climbing the steel beams. She walked in front of the trucks to the opposite end of the building and at last to a small dump truck numbered 33 sitting on a drain grate. There was a high-pressure hose suspended from a mount overhead, a do-it-yourself carwash. She removed a small plastic jar and a penknife from her pocket, and took a scratch of paint from under the headlight, then another from a rear quarter panel. She sealed the container and walked around the vehicle, playing the light over it until she reached the doors, where she stood on the running board and looked inside.

There were rags on the floor and a pair of wire snips on the seat. There was a radio under the dash, microphone off the hook, lying on the floor mat. There was a tear in the fabric of the ceiling, and the upholstery was stained black in places. She noticed the side-view mirror was cracked and the passenger-side door latch was missing. She continued around the back of it. The bed was still dripping puddles of soapy water onto the ground; she could smell bleach, and there was a bucket and a wet push broom in the corner behind it. The three-to-eleven driver would have just brushed it clean. Ben had said that was the protocol.

She used the light to look under the tarp and check the bed for anything out of the ordinary: a hair clip, a piece of jewelry, a broken fingernail. She got on her knees and looked under the chassis. Then she heard a noise outside the shed and froze in place.

Footsteps were crossing the gravel in front of the closed bay doors.

She got to her feet and reached for her weapon, quietly pulling it from her holster. Whoever was out there was just on the other side of the door. She could see the shadow moving along the crack of light along the bottom. She waited a full minute, then began creeping down the length of the garage toward the side entrance, staying behind the big compactor trucks. Rats watched her from their perches on the backs of the big trucks; she stumbled over a hose, striking her knee against a workbench. The door was thirty or forty feet from her now. There was more noise outside, more steps. Running steps. She stopped and waited. Then she ran as fast as she could to the end of the building and threw open the door.

Nothing.

She stepped outside into the lot, gun out in front of her, looking in all directions.

Insects chattered and bugs continued to batter the halogen lights. Her car was alone in the lot. No one else was in sight.

She walked toward the administration building and checked the doors. There was a swamp behind the buildings that she had no intention of entering. She waited another minute, then turned to go back inside, and when she did a car door slammed and an engine turned over on the highway behind the trees.

Sandy Lyons?

She opened the door, this time throwing on the overhead lights, and ran back to the pickup truck. The doors were locked. Maybe that was normal. She made a mental note to check with Ben. The missing door latch inside the cab bothered her, too. She'd formed a picture of Anne Carlino trapped inside the cab and unable to get out. Or maybe Lyons threw his victims in the bed and covered them with the tarp. That would make more sense if they were unconscious or already dead. The bed was disinfected and hosed down at least fifteen times a week. She looked at the drain grate and wondered if anything was trapped beneath it. Wondered if the women were already dead when he put them in the truck.

Jeremy Smyles hadn't killed that girl, O'Shaughnessy had always been sure of that, and Billy Weeks had two female witnesses who swore he was back on the boardwalk at eleven the night of the kidnapping. They knew the exact time and date, they'd said, because it was Billy's "birthday" and they had dreamed up the gift of sleeping with him together.

Weeks had also given detectives access to his car and apartment and there wasn't a drop of blood anywhere. Most convincing were the results of the polygraph he'd insisted on taking.

She played her light over the ceiling, across the back window, and up and down the seats. Then she circled to the passenger side and did it again. No, a new scenario was beginning to take form in her mind. The orange city truck parked by the boardwalk, just a regular part of the landscape, unnoticed by anyone who might have seen.

She was going around the windows for the last time when something reflected in her light and she stopped and took a breath.

"Oh, my God," she whispered.

She played the light carefully around the door. A single strand of hair was caught in the window molding. Her heart began to race. She pinched it between her fingers and pulled it gently; it came away without breaking, nearly two feet long and light brown. Just like Tracy Yoland's.

Lyons's hair was short and black and not an animal in the world could have accounted for what she had in her hand.

She patted her sports coat pockets with her free hand and found a plastic envelope. She delicately placed the hair into it. Then she sealed it and started to check the rest of the truck.

It didn't come easy; indeed, it wouldn't have come at all, if it hadn't been for the radio going off in the cab. She looked inside, shining the light down at different angles to see where the crackling noise was coming from. She had seen the two-way radio bolted under the dash, but it was unlit and obviously turned off. So what was she hearing?

The scanner wasn't visible from the driver's-side window, but leaning over the hood and shining her light down into the windshield on the passenger side, she saw a bead of green light from a handheld radio tucked under the seat. It wasn't the scanner, though, or its existence that made the effort worthwhile. It was the dark reddish spot on the dash only visible when looking down from the hood. It looked like a bloodstain.

You stupid shit, she thought. You put her inside the truck and now I've got you.

Her heart was pumping. She needed to get help right away. She needed to impound the truck and get it to the crime lab. She knew she could break in and search it without a warrant. The truck was city property. But the blood was too important to lose and a warrant was too easy to get. She was going to do this by the book. No loose ends. No problematic searches. No appeals. She had him and she wasn't letting go!

O'Shaughnessy called the dispatcher and told her to take two marked units out of service and send them to her location. She also wanted her midnight detective on the scene. Then she called Clarke at home and asked him to meet her early to approve an affidavit for Judge Vickroy before he went to court. Next she woke Ben Johnson and told him that she was going to be seizing the meat wagon and that she needed him to shut down the city incinerator immediately. Ben made it sound like she'd asked him to cap Vesuvius. "Do you know how long it takes that unit to go down, Lieutenant?"

She hated to call Gus at home, knowing he'd probably spent the night at the hospital, so she decided to wait until morning. She'd have the truck towed to headquarters, where they could process it in the police garage. She would also let Gus come up with a plan for siphoning the drain in the truck bay and sifting the ashes of the county's incinerator. There had to be bones or teeth. It only made sense that Lyons would have used the incinerator to dispose of them.

A small army grew around the Public Works garage that morning. A bleary-eyed Ben Johnson was running between the arriving day shift and the cops and trying to find a quiet place to go through his call-up list to close the incinerator. Incinerators weren't like kitchen stoves, he kept trying to tell her. It took days to cool the chamber sufficiently before anyone could handle the residue. When pushed, he reduced it to forty-eight hours but still called it a minimum.

But it wasn't only that. The community and several surrounding counties relied on the incinerator, which meant he would have to stockpile dead animals and disposable wastes without somehow violating the health codes. During some summer months they burned fifty thousand tons of waste, and income derived from other communities would be lost for any period it was down. In other words, it was going to cost the city money.

Fingerprint technicians dusted the exterior of the truck, lifting several promising prints from the passenger-side door. A police contract crane took the truck to the impound lot, where Gus's people would work on the inside. Ben Johnson had to reassign the meat wagon crew and find another truck in his fleet to handle the dead-animal pickups. The only thing that did seem to go right that night was that the new guy, Earl Sykes, called in sick. At least he wouldn't have to worry about reassigning him while his truck was out of commission.

*   *   *

O'Shaughnessy agonized all night long about whether to interrogate Sandy Lyons. If it had been a matter of paint samples, she would not have. The results could have waited. But with blood and hair she needed to seize the truck, and it was going to be plain for anyone to see that she was interested in him. If she waited, she would lose the element of surprise. If Lyons had time to think it over, he was going to have his alibi and an attorney ready.

In the end, she decided to bring him in. At 6:30 A.M. detectives were knocking at his door.

FRIDAY, JUNE 3

She watched him through the blinds of her office. He was sitting in one of the chairs next to a detective's desk, legs crossed, thumbing through a magazine. McGuire was sitting next to her.

"Looks like he's waiting to get his teeth cleaned."

"He's certainly no virgin," Mac said. "How long do you think the interview will take?"

"About as long as it takes him to say the word 'attorney.'" She shrugged. "Of course, he might start sobbing and confess. That's why we do this, isn't it?"

McGuire laughed. "I'll bring the tissues."

She stood and grabbed her jacket. "Let's get him in there before he falls asleep."

The interview with Sandy Lyons went as predicted. No tissues were needed. The moment they brought up the abductions, he clammed up and demanded an attorney. Lyons had been around the block.

O'Shaughnessy hadn't slept since Wednesday night and was heading for the door when Randall called her name.

"Lieu." The detective's voice was hesitant. "It's Celia Davis, Youth Division. She says it's important."

She picked up a phone. "O'Shaughnessy."

"Lieu, you may want to meet me in the unit block of Forty-fifth. I have another missing female."

O'Shaughnessy's heart stopped. She took a breath and replaced the phone, looked around the room for her sergeant. "Mac, stick around just a couple minutes more. I'll call you from my car."

Detectives weren't assigned to investigate missing persons as a rule; Youth Division investigators were, because 95 percent of all missing persons are juveniles. O'Shaughnessy had made it known that she wanted all missing females called in to her office first so that the detectives could get a head start if the case turned into a crime. At least until summer was over or the abductions were solved.

She drove north on Atlantic to Forty-fifth and found a parking space behind Davis's marked unit. The officer was talking to a woman by a summer cottage; two wiggling spaniels had their forepaws on the chain-link fence.

She opened the gate and the spaniels covered her thighs with dirty paw prints. "Lieu, this is Connie Riker. Connie was expecting a friend to arrive in town last night, a woman by the name of Marcia Schmidt."

Riker had the dogs by their collars and was dragging them back toward the house. She managed to get them behind a screen door that they battered with their paws trying to get back out.

"Her friend still hasn't shown, and Connie is worried something happened to her along the way."

Connie brushed her hands clean. "I wasn't sure who to call," she apologized. "I did talk to the state police early this morning around one A.M., and gave them a description of my car. They said there hadn't been any accidents in the southern part of the state involving a female last night and nothing at all on my tags. I half believed that her husband wouldn't let her come, but when I called her house a few minutes ago, I got no answer, and I'm not sure anymore. I know I'm probably wasting your time."

"There's a problem with her husband?" O'Shaughnessy asked.

"He beats her," Officer Davis said.

"I know she's probably still there and he won't let her go to the phone." Riker sniffed and wiped her eyes dry with the heels of her hands. "She gets embarrassed sometimes, too. Maybe she just didn't want to answer the phone."

"You said your car, your tags?"

Connie nodded. "We're neighbors. I left the keys under the mat for her."

"Is there any way you can check to see if your car is still at your house?"

She looked thoughtful, then shook her head. "We're out in the boonies. Our nearest neighbors, except for Marcia and Nicky, are two miles away and I don't think I've ever spoken to them in my life. My mom knows them. I told her about Marcia not showing up and she's coming back down from Atlantic City tonight. We'll head home in the morning to make sure she's okay. I just thought maybe she'd broken down or something and you guys would have known about it."

O'Shaughnessy looked at Davis, thinking about hospitals, but Davis shook her head. "I did the drill, Lieu."

"Do you think her husband could have hurt her, Connie? Bad enough so she couldn't come to the phone?"

She shrugged. "He usually knows just when to stop."

"Mrs. Riker, we can have police from the jurisdiction where you live look in on her."

Riker shook her head violently. "No, please don't do that. Nicky would kill her if the police came by. I probably overreacted. Probably she's okay and he just won't let her answer the phone. He's done that plenty of times."

"Don't you think your friend would have tried to call you if she couldn't make it? He can't be with her every moment."

"I know, I know." She shook her head in exasperation. "Maybe she has. We didn't turn on the phone this summer. Every time I call her I have to run up to the pay phone on Atlantic."

"It's your choice, Connie, but my advice is to get someone involved before your friend gets hurt too badly. Get her out of the house and into a shelter. There are plenty of those around, and they won't tell her husband anything about either one of you. I promise."

Connie nodded. "Yeah," she said halfheartedly. "I'm sorry I bothered you all with this."

"You didn't bother anyone," O'Shaughnessy said. "You do as I said."

She followed Officer Davis back to her car. "You run the tag with the state?"

Davis nodded. "Absolutely nothing."

"Get her a number for Human Services and try to stress that she call it. I'll see you later, huh."

Davis nodded.

O'Shaughnessy dialed her cell phone. "Mac. Never mind. Go on home. False alarm."

22

FRIDAY, JUNE 3
TEXHOMA PANHANDLE, OKLAHOMA

Dr. Chance Haverly sat in her office in the corner chair she usually reserved for her patients. The file in her hands was heavy and old—the psychiatric chronicles of Earl Oberlein Sykes.

Earl was the son of a career criminal. His juvenile record began at twelve and grew in proportion to his age until he turned seventeen, which was when he had begun to trifle with felonies such as auto theft and burglary. But all of them, to that point, were property crimes; Sykes appeared to enjoy destroying things to get attention.

Surprisingly, he was arrested only three times as an adult. All of the arrests were minor and none required more than a weekend's stint in jail. Sykes had either learned how to stay out of trouble or had teamed up with some brains. Haverly believed it was the latter.

Then came the accident. Sykes was tried and convicted of two murders for vehicular homicide. He had been using drugs and was running from the police when he ran a school bus full of teenagers off the road.

Had he been in Rikers or Joliet, his life would have been quite different. Private, progressive prisons like Jenson Reed were contracted by the government on the premise that they brought rehabilitation to incarceration. Modern behavioral therapy included expensive drugs and psychoanalysis not normally available to prisoners. Only lifers with nonviolent histories were eligible for the chance to rehabilitate themselves in prisons like Jenson Reed.

Time passed in Jenson Reed. One day Sykes was mentioned as a potential parole candidate, a suggestion that triggered a venomous response from the community in New Jersey where he had been arrested. Sykes was not about to have an easy time with a parole board. Not as long as the victims' parents and siblings were alive to testify against his release.

Fifteen years later, the community resistance died off and relatives moved away; doctors at Jenson Reed, examining the strange cauliflowerlike growths on

Sykes's body, discovered a whole new rationale for releasing him. Sykes was beginning to die.

Prison administrators were always under pressure to show rehabilitation results in the form of paroled prisoners, which was foremost in the administrator's mind when he prevented a board from viewing the psychiatric files of Dr. Haverly concerning Earl Oberlein Sykes. The man had only two or three years to live anyhow and most of that was going to be in a hospital bed. Sykes was the perfect candidate to put back in the community.

She flipped through the pages.

10/12/87 ES is withdrawn, highly suspicious of authority. Has the capacity to develop complex skills. Recommend grade-seven entry into GED and skill levels evaluation preceding vocational placement.
4/17/89 ES appears disinterested in bus accident that led to incarceration. ES considers the accident and the ensuing trial inconsequential circumstances of his life (he states he can't recall the accident, therefore he can't have emotion for the victims). ES similarly not interested in surviving family members. Therapy objective is to elicit remorse for the resulting deaths.

In the beginning she wanted to open the book on Sykes. To make him rediscover every negative moment in his life so that he would be better equipped to handle similar experiences in his future.

Sykes was suspicious of her motives from the start.

Session after session, Dr. Haverly explained her role in the rehabilitative process, the meaning and the purpose of psychotherapy, the laws governing privacy. It took months for him to accept that no one would use what he said against him, but once he did, once he started talking, his conversations weren't about the bus accident that sent him to prison. They were about killing a teacher's cat and raping his neighbor's daughters.

She thought at first that he was just showing off. Sykes said he was only thirteen when the first of his alleged sexual assaults took place. But then he began to talk about others and still others, and the doctor began to understand that Sykes was no candidate for rehabilitation. Sykes's was not a story about a boy on drugs and a tragic traffic accident. Sykes was a sociopath, a sexual predator; his psychopathic life had simply been interrupted by an unrelated event. That was why Sykes had no interest in the bus accident. He truly didn't care about or connect with the teenagers he'd killed.

Confidential Memorandum
To: File
From: Dr. Chance Haverly,
            Director of Client Services
Subject: 86–591
Date: 6/13/91
ES began a physical exercise routine last week. This is a new development in his lengthy incarceration, most likely a response to the notification of eligibility for his first parole hearing in

sixteen years.

ES relates the details of an adult rape in which he restrains the victim in a junkyard. He states he keeps her there for several days and threatens to dispose of her in a bottomless pit. He likes the reaction he gets from her. He likes to see her diminished.

This is the second time he has mentioned a bus and the third time he has mentioned the pit.

All those years ago she had been fooled. Her first thoughts were that the bus was a symbolic representation of the accident and that the women he claimed to abuse represented the teenagers he hurt. She thumbed back to her notes on the conversation.

While there is no indication that Sykes has a religious aspect to his life, the woman begging for her life represents his own need for forgiveness. The pit under the bus is unquestionably his hell.

She snorted.

She had thought he was going through a "loosening up" phase at the time. To her it was a sign of progress that he was talking, even if he was making up stories to veil the turmoil that was going on inside his mind.

Here was the key to his success, she'd told him. You are about to unearth the hidden obstacles that prevent you from being productive in society.

Reading her own words made her sick.

Confidential Memorandum
To: File
From: Dr. Chance Haverly,
          Director of Client Services
Subject: 86–591
Date: 12/20/96

Graphic rapes are meant to shock me. His accounts grow more fantastic all the time. Is it just me, or does he try to impress others as well? A side note to speak with Captain Ridenour on A block.

It is difficult to accept that ES raped and tortured several women as he claims. The number of missing bodies would have prompted intercession by the law. Neither is there a foundation for sexual history in his juvenile records. Is he only having fun with me, or is this for real?

With time she saw the folly of her efforts.

Week after week, month after month, she began to see the extent of his depravity. *He* had been leading the sessions all along. *She* was his plaything. For eighteen years he was symbolically masturbating and making her watch.

Then he was diagnosed with skin cancer and cancer of the pancreas. The surgeons removed part of the organ, but only to relieve the symptoms. Cancerous cells had already spread into the stomach and small intestine. In time they would spread to his kidneys and spleen and finally his upper organs, his heart, and his lungs, which would signal the beginning of the end.

So they intended to release him, never mind what a sociopath with a year left to live was likely to do. Never mind what his psychiatrist said.

A phone rang in the corridor and she jumped. She reached to switch on a reading lamp, turned the ringer off, and flipped through the contents of his file, thinking the thing had become as vile and corrupt as he was.

She remembered the last time he spoke to her. His eyes traveled slowly down her body, stopping at the hemline of her skirt. "I'm getting out, Doc," he'd said, head bent low toward the ground. He smiled and the ugly scar slid to one side of his neck. "Will you miss me?"

23

FRIDAY, JUNE 3
WILDWOOD, NEW JERSEY

Sykes stuck a cigarette in his mouth and pulled back the curtains of his kitchen window. The news said there would be a few more hours of sunshine before the storm rolled in.

He'd panicked in the early-morning hours when he called to report in sick. Ben Johnson was already there, which meant that something was up. Fortunately Ben knew about his chemo treatments; calling in sick wouldn't seem so odd, unless the cops were looking for him and then it was already too late.

Still, here he was, and no one had come to get him.

How in the fuck had she caught on to the sanitation truck anyhow?

He could hear the groans of old springs as his neighbor settled into a chaise longue. She was tanning, which was all she ever did besides sleep; she said she lived off her old man's Social Security benefits so she didn't have to work unless she needed something extra. Sykes had seen her pole-dancing at the Lucky Seven.

She was lying belly down now on a towel, beer resting on the bumper of a long deceased pickup. Her bra was on the ground next to her and an orange cat was draped over the truck's headlamp licking its paws.

Her name was Denise and she'd once invited him to see the Harley-Davidson Sportster dripping oil on a beach towel in the living room. Her husband, who was in heaven now, would have wanted her to keep it, she'd told him.

Sykes took a book of matches from his shirt pocket and lit a cigarette, blowing smoke up into the air and rolling the sweat out of his scanty whiskers with the side of a filthy thumbnail. He scratched his bleeding neck and tossed the match into a pink flamingo ashtray. He was unshaven and hadn't bothered to shower. The backs of his hands and wrists were flecked with the short hairs of the Rottweiler from the night before.

He'd taken a chance, sticking his head into O'Shaughnessy's car window like that. He knew he'd startled her, but he just had to look into those eyes. He'd also taken a chance sneaking back to the garage. It had been so tempting to take her out right then and there, but then she'd heard his footsteps and he lost the element of surprise.

It was hazy, hot, and humid. The wind would pick up dramatically, according to the weather report. Coastal flooding was a possibility.

The orange cat dropped to the ground and went slinking under his neighbor's trailer. It was a cat much like his English teacher's cat. Same color. Same startled eyes.

He'd hung Miss Carney's cat from the hook of her porch swing—Miss Carney, who said he couldn't go on to the fifth grade with the rest of his class. When he tossed the cat's collar on her desk the next day and told her he'd found it in the hall, she grabbed him by the arm and manhandled him into the principal's office, demanding in a tearful rage that he be expelled.

But as it turned out, she was wrong. And people came to visit his trailer after that. Smiling perfumed people with nice clothes and leather satchels. The social workers looked around in disgust and, feeling sorry for him, told him they would deal with the principal and they did.

So Sykes went on to fifth grade with his friends, and Miss Carney—much to the administration's surprise—packed her things and moved to New Hampshire.

Carney wasn't a fool. She had been stalked before and a straight-shooting but cynical detective had finally told her to either kill him in the act or move as far away from him as she could possibly get.

Sykes walked to the back of the trailer to use the toilet again; Xena Warrior Princess was fighting a skeleton on the big-screen TV as he walked by.

He hadn't forgotten about Bianca Ashley, either. Bianca, in the black Mustang convertible who had wanted to hear him beg for a ride in front of the high school. It took only a moment to wiggle the clamp loose on her radiator hose and then follow her Volvo station wagon until her antifreeze was gone. Bianca had wanted to please him, oh, had she begged to please him in the end.

He pulled up his pants and zipped himself. The window was open; he could smell the creek stinking up to high heaven. He opened the medicine cabinet, found a bottle of aspirin, and emptied it into his hand. Then he tossed five of the pills and Marcia Schmidt's gold wedding ring in his shirt pocket.

He returned to the kitchen, took a bag of candy bars from the counter and a bottle of water, grabbed his keys, and started down the rusty steps, looking at his neighbor, who had flipped onto her back. Her legs were getting heavy, but her tits still looked great. She opened one of her eyes and looked at him, then closed it again, stretching her arms to yawn.

Maybe his luck was holding, but it wouldn't hold forever. It was time to take the offensive.

A marked police car pulled into the parking lot next

to Lecky's Pawnshop. A young officer waved and Sykes raised a hand. He had noticed an increase in patrols this summer, cops getting out of their cars, shining their Kel lights into the shadows, checking parked vehicles. They were not at all the happy-go-lucky cops of the seventies, twirling their batons and having their pictures taken with tourists. These guys were intense, always in a hurry, always looking for someone.

He took Marcia Schmidt's wedding ring inside and got forty dollars for it, then spent the afternoon drinking beer in the Anchorage across the street. He took Marcia her chocolates and some aspirin to keep her from getting a fever in the bus. Just another day, he thought. Just hang on another day. Then it will all be over.

It was dark by the time he reached the boardwalk. Young couples strolled by arm in arm. The sea mist rolled heavily across the street. The town was busy in spite of it.

As he climbed the ramp to the boardwalk, he watched the demon's eyes roll back in its head, its huge black talons clutching the gates of Strayer's Pier. Rap music blared as a great gyrating disk appeared then vanished behind the rooftops. A moment later he could hear the rise and fall of the passengers' screams.

Bodies passed by in waves, old and young, rich and poor. They were from all walks of life, mingling together as one, the patient and the surgeon, the teacher and the dropout.

No one paid much attention to Sykes as he stood

in the shadows. The demon's hooded eyes opened and its head turned menacingly, tongue lolling to one side. A young girl stood beneath it, hands connected to her father, her pink hair bands dividing long blond hair into pigtails. A pink shirt ended inches above her belly button. She was teasing him, making him want her. Was she fifteen or only thirteen?

A crowd of leathered bikers passed, obscuring the twosome from his view; behind them a crowd of Midwestern salesmen and their pudgy wives bellowed their way up the boardwalk. He stood and joined them, riding the sea of bodies, then stepped out quickly into the shadows by the restrooms. Two leathered lovers groped in the darkness behind him. He spat at a pigeon, then tapped the end of a cigarette on the glass of his watch, admiring the curves of the naked woman on his bicep.

Couples were walking with their hands on each other's asses. Tour groups stampeded along four abreast, feeling safety in numbers.

A young couple stopped to buy snow cones, and Sykes felt an ache in his groin when the man slipped his hand up under the back of the girl's T-shirt. He scratched hard at the base of his skull, finding blood on his fingernails when he brought the cigarette to his lips again.

The girl was braless and wearing low-rider jeans. He could see the band of a black thong above her belt. She must be sixteen, he thought. Just like the girl who had choked on her own puke that night under the boardwalk. What a piece of ass she would have been.

The sea of bodies flowed in and out of shops,

swarming around the food vendors with their sausages and french fries and pizzas. The smell of it all lay heavy on the dense air.

Two uniformed cops cut through the crowd, eyeing a gang of teenagers huddled around a park bench. The slick kid who had been with the girl that night was among them, the one who'd left her under the boardwalk before Sykes shot her with the stun gun.

As the girl in pink with pigtails stepped away from her father, a line of large-bellied men in Mellon Bank T-shirts came by; the policemen continued up the boardwalk, casually gesturing as they carried on a conversation.

Sykes took the Rio Grande exit ramp down to his Jeep and drove the half mile to Third Street, where he made a right turn and parked. He took a section of newspaper from his jacket pocket and unfolded a photograph of O'Shaughnessy, ran his fingers over it. His collar was damp, the open sore on his neck oozing blood. Her car was in the driveway and there were lights on in the house.

24

FRIDAY, JUNE 3
PHILADELPHIA, PENNSYLVANIA

Sherry had mixed feelings about Payne's invitation. For one thing, they'd never done anything like it before, never gone away together. She knew that John was circumspect about their friendship at work, but he would have been totally open with Angie about the trip. He told Angie everything.

What John didn't realize was that innocent or not, women applied different rules to friendships than men. Angie might not say anything, but she certainly wouldn't have approved.

Then there was the fact that she felt guilty about her feelings—guilty and perhaps vulnerable. Reining in her emotions was one thing when you were obliged to say good-bye each evening. Could she do it if he was staying in the same room?

Not that there was ever a doubt of Sherry accepting. The decision had been made the moment she took Susan Paxton's hand in the funeral home. From that moment on, she had become utterly and irrevocably involved. She was concerned about what she might learn, but she needed to know the ending. At any cost.

She was waiting for him when he got off work. She was wearing black slacks and a sleeveless black top, black bracelet and black earrings. She smiled as he came into the room.

"You look like June Carter Cash," he told her.

"June Carter Cash?"

"Never mind." He reached for her bag. He thought she still looked a little off color, but didn't say anything.

He took her arm and led her to the circular drive, where he put her small bag in the car.

"It's not going to be nice, I hear," Payne said.

"The worse the better," she said. "I love a good storm."

Philadelphia rush hour was in true tangles with weekend revelers out in force. It was well after eight before they broke free of the suburbs. Payne was torn between telling Sherry now about the conversation he'd had with Angie or waiting until they returned. The last thing he wanted to do was make her feel that he had an ulterior motive for asking her to go. But there was another reason. If anything ever did come of their relationship, if Sherry really felt the same way that Payne did, he wanted them to have a fresh beginning. He wanted the experience to be unique, free of anything they had ever experienced before. Free of cops and corpses.

Difficult though it would be, he would wait until they got home.

Traffic was sparser near the coast, and what little there was of it was heading toward them, away from the beach. They didn't reach the city limits of Wildwood until almost eleven. Payne called O'Shaughnessy from his cell phone.

The white stucco building was nestled between two towering hotels. It was a three-story building with blue spotlights in an oyster shell drive, illuminating a wooden sign that read DRIFTWOOD. Parking was directly under the condos at street level; a stairwell and elevator led to the eighteen units above.

O'Shaughnessy was sitting on the steps when they arrived. She wasn't exactly sure who she had been expecting, but it wasn't the woman in the passenger seat.

She got up and walked toward the car with Pennsylvania plates, went to the driver's window where Payne stuck out his hand. "Good to meet you, Lieu. This is my friend Sherry Moore. Sherry, meet Lieutenant O'Shaughnessy."

"Call me Kelly." She crouched. The woman's head turned, but the eye contact wasn't right. O'Shaughnessy knew something was amiss even before her eyes dropped to the walking stick.

Oh, my God, she thought, running around the car and opening the woman's door. "Here, let me help." She grabbed the woman's arm and guided her out.

"I'll just follow." Payne smiled, knowing Sherry hated to be coddled. He pulled two small bags from the trunk. "Is that an elevator?"

"Yes, and we're lucky," O'Shaughnessy said. "It's actually working."

The ocean smell was strong off the front of the storm. The elevator doors opened and closed again, the platform raised and jolted hard to a stop. O'Shaughnessy led them down the concrete hall and unlocked the door. "Come right in," she said, dashing ahead. "The bathroom is back here." She was grabbing anything that Sherry could trip over. "There's no tub, I'm afraid, just a shower."

She picked up things as fast as she could, nudged furniture against the walls: an ottoman, a magazine rack, a small iron stand with plants on it. What an idiot I am, she thought. She hadn't even researched her guest, which would have been all too easy. Of course, the detective could have said something, too.

Or maybe she was just overreacting. Maybe they didn't behave as if she was blind. Maybe she should ease up.

"There's a can of coffee above the sink and a coffeemaker on the counter. Regular old thing, filters are next to it. Linens and extra blankets, soap, toilet paper are all in the hall closet. I made up the bed with clean linens this afternoon."

"It's really nice," Payne said. "I had no idea we would be on the ocean. I hope you didn't go to too much trouble getting it."

"Actually, it's mine; it was my mother's before she passed away. I still can't bring myself to rent it, so it's just sitting here, going to waste."

"Oh, I hope we're not imposing," Sherry said. "I don't want—"

"Hush," O'Shaughnessy said. "I'm thrilled to have you. You'll breathe some life back into the place. Sorry it's for a storm instead of sunshine, but storms can be pleasant if the worst of them stay out to sea. I read about you in *The Boston Globe* once. Your life must be very interesting."

The Boston Globe meant she'd read about Norwich.

"Sometimes," was all Sherry could manage to say.

O'Shaughnessy looked around. "Yes, well, the couch is right here; it's a pullout." She glanced at Payne; his wedding ring was visible on his left hand. "Over there is the kitchenette; dishwasher's under the counter. Dining room table here and just to the side are sliding glass doors to the balcony. It's not enormous, but there's room for two to sit comfortably." She made a face and shrugged. "Don't know how long the rain will hold off, though. Do you want me to move the coffee table out of the room?"

"We want to pay you," Sherry said.

"I won't hear of it," O'Shaughnessy replied. "And I mean that."

"No, no, this is far too much."

"We'll talk about it later, then. As for tomorrow," she said, turning to Payne, "I suggest we kill two birds with one stone. I have a one o'clock appointment in Vineland, about an hour north, and won't return until after three. If you have no objections, I'll have my sergeant take you around to show your suspect's sketch. When I get back I'll take Sherry to dinner and then later, when no one is around, to the morgue."

"Sounds fine," Payne said.

"Good. You must be tired." O'Shaughnessy headed for the door. She couldn't tell if there was something more between the detective and Sherry Moore or if she was just being overly suspicious. Ever since Tim's tryst in Saint Paul, it seemed she had been dissecting every couple she met.

"There's a phone on the dresser next to the bed and another on a stand by the chair. Number for me is easy, 228-2800. If you forget it, I'm in the book."

"Thanks," Payne said.

Sherry stepped back into the room from the open balcony. "Yes, thanks." She waved.

The whole thing had taken only forty minutes, but O'Shaughnessy was utterly exhausted. She crossed Atlantic and started up the block toward her house, turned, and looked back at the condo. Blind! What a shocker. There was something between those two, she thought once more.

She looked north toward the pink and yellow lights on Strayer's Pier to the revolving Ferris wheel; it was where she and Tim had first met.

She was wearing shorts and a sleeveless T-shirt; the air was sticky with salt, just cool enough to raise goose bumps. You could see the sea mist hanging under the glare of the street lamps.

She hadn't thought she could forgive Tim for what he did. Two months ago, she was only sure that she wanted him out of the house. Now she wasn't so certain she'd done the right thing.

The woman he'd slept with owned one of his company's affiliates in Saint Paul. The trip was to celebrate their first-year financials and the board wanted photos of the two management teams for propagation to new acquisitions. The Saint Paul woman had planned the dinner and drinks for the out-of-town visitors. She was divorced, and Tim said there were just too many bars and too many cocktails and he didn't remember all of how it ended except that he woke up in her bed and not in his hotel room, where O'Shaughnessy had been leaving messages throughout the night.

He should have spared her his need to confess. She would have forgiven him the damned night, if only he had waited to tell her. A month, maybe two, and the pain would have been bearable. Right now it hurt, and when people hurt they make bad decisions. Oh, God, she thought. Was that all she was doing? Were

Jeremy Smyles and Sandy Lyons and Clarke Hamilton all just bad decisions?

The street was quiet. Most of the tourists were already in their rooms for the night. She could see lightning bugs blinking in the community playground across the street. Her daughters were at their father's again.

She walked into her driveway and tapped the contentious coach lantern until it stopped flickering. Then she opened the unlocked door and closed it behind her. She heard a thump in the kitchen, the cat leaping off the counter and slinking through the dining room, seemingly uninterested in her return.

She put a pot of water on the burner and took a celery stalk from a cup in the refrigerator.

She thought about Sherry Moore; the woman was nothing like she'd expected. No wonder, she thought, that the press liked her so much. She was simply beautiful.

She ran the dishwasher. Then she put laundry in the machine and pushed the vacuum around. The girls' things were strewn all over the house, but that was because they didn't have a house anymore. They had stopovers where they sometimes ate and slept.

She called Tim's; no one answered. Then she called her mother-in-law's and found that Tim had dropped the girls and gone out for the night. *Bastard!*

She poured tea and turned on the eleven o'clock news. Clarke had left a message on her answering machine, but it was Tim she wanted to hear from. The television was on mute and she could see a weatherman pointing at the hurricane stuck over the

Carolinas.

Tim, the girls, the Yolands—everyone exasperated her. She thought about making herself a drink but decided against it. Not with the way she'd been handling nicotine lately.

She picked up the phone and dialed. Headlights approached from a side street; a bar of light drifted across the dining room ceiling before it vanished. She punched in the last number and Clarke answered after a couple of rings.

"Too late for dinner?" she asked.

"I've retired my apron." He laughed. "But I do have numbers for all the best carryouts."

"Actually it wasn't the entrée I was interested in. How are your desserts?"

"I have a wide variety of excellent desserts. Hang on a moment, please." She heard footsteps on tile, a freezer door open and close. "How do Popsicles sound?"

"Sexy."

It was almost 2:00 A.M. before she left Clarke's and started for home. What had compelled her to call Clarke like that, right out of the blue, she didn't know. Anger? Frustration? The fact that she couldn't reach her husband whenever she pleased?

Oh, yeah, that's right, she told herself. Project the blame on Tim. Make him responsible for her throwing herself into Clarke's arms. How long could she keep telling herself that one?

She turned the corner onto her block and saw that she'd left an upstairs light burning.

What she really wanted Tim to know was that she hadn't been able to go through with it in the end. That she'd taken off her clothes only to lie in Clarke's arms and bawl about how much she missed her husband.

Why did she want to confess to Tim so badly? Was that what happened when you loved someone so much? Was that the reason Tim had hurried to confess to her when he returned from Saint Paul? Was his need to reconnect with her stronger than the risk of estrangement? Were his feelings so strong that the knowledge of what he had done wrong hurt him more than the consequence of telling his wife?

Oh, God, she thought. If only she had continued to communicate with him. It wasn't like she had to come right out and forgive him, but she could have kept them talking. If only they had been talking, things might not have gotten to where they were.

She closed the door and a breeze met her from the kitchen; she walked toward it, stuck her head inside, and saw the back door standing open.

She backed up, looking up the stairwell to the second floor, cautiously passing through the dining room and into the foyer, where she reached to open the front door and ran to retrieve her Glock from her car's locked glove box. Then she dialed 911 from her car phone.

Two marked units sat in O'Shaughnessy's driveway while a third made circles around the neighborhood, sweeping its spotlight through neighbors' lawns and into the dark park across the street.

Dillon happened to be the midnight sergeant who

greeted her at the door.

She reached the top of the landing with two uniformed officers behind her, guns drawn. One of the officers turned the corridor in the direction of the girls' bedrooms. The other followed her.

The windows were all raised; distant breakers pounded the shore.

She checked the closet, an empty bathroom, another closet, the master bath and master bedroom—and she gasped.

An American flag had been draped over the down comforter on her bed. She approached it cautiously, grabbed a corner, and slowly pulled it away.

"Oh, my God!" she whispered.

One of her dress blue uniforms had been laid out under it. Navy slacks, white shirt under navy jacket with the buttons done up, tie knotted at the neck, lieutenant bars on shoulders, sleeves folded one over the other—just like a corpse. She lifted the waist of the trousers to reveal a white silk thong from her dresser drawer and panty hose that stretched to the hems of her trousers.

She dropped the flag, shocked and embarrassed.

"Looks like someone was imagining you lying there dead in your thong, probably one of them desperados you been scaring the hell out of. Of course maybe it wasn't work-related. You'd be surprised how many domestic situations get out of hand. Woman starts dividing her attention between two men and, bang, someone wants to see someone else dead. That's always a possibility, if you know what I mean."

Dillon was leaning against the door frame behind

her, toothpick in his mouth, hand in pocket.

"Sergeant, would you mind waiting outside?"

"Why, no, ma'am, I wouldn't mind that at all. Frankly I've seen all I need to see. You have a good night now. You have yourself a very good night."

Dillon whistled loudly and the other officers came to the landing. "Come on, Mike, Vinnie, let's get the hell out of here."

25

SATURDAY MORNING, JUNE 4
WILDWOOD, NEW JERSEY

Dillon was just checking off the night shift when O'Shaughnessy arrived for work the next morning. He watched her enter her office, avoiding his stare, and heard the door close behind her. "Big shit lieutenant," he told a rookie. "Women cops are all the same, son, seen it a hundred times. Give them a job to do and all you get is lots of drama. If you want results, ask a man. That's the way it's always been in police work. We should never have hired the first of them and we sure as shit shouldn't promote them 'cause their daddy happened to be a fucking chief."

He finished checking off the last of the officers and closed the section log. "Hey, what say we get a couple of beers? I'll tell you about the time we found them crispy critters in the Video Hut fire." He looked up with a smile. "Tell you what Lieutenant O'Shaughnessy wears under them britches, too."

"Sure," the kid said enthusiastically.

Dillon and the rookie took off their uniform shirts and drove to the harbor in T-shirts with their guns on their hips. Jeremy Smyles was just stepping out of the door of the Crow's Nest with his Styrofoam cup in one hand when they arrived.

"Find any more rings under the boardwalk, asshole?" Dillon poked a finger into the man's chest as he was reaching for his paper spear.

"You know what I think? I think you're not as stupid as you let on. I think they're going to electrocute your ass when Jason Carlino gets a real investigator on you. You may be able to fool a bunch of stupid detectives, but you ain't fooled me, boy. I saw them earrings and panties in your room. You're a fucking pervert, and you're lucky I don't take you out in the Pine Barrens and shoot you right now. You hear me, you crazy sack of shit?"

Jeremy wobbled, looking distraught, not knowing if he was supposed to leave or listen to the rest.

Fortunately he was spared the decision when Janet threw open the door. "Thought I heard someone," she said.

Dillon smirked and pushed his way past her. "Come on, kid. Let's get upwind from this asshole."

O'Shaughnessy left the office before ten and went home to sit alone in the dark living room. The house felt different now. It was no longer the safe little place it had been. Not Tim's, not hers, not the girls'—it was just a cold little box filled with rooms. And memories.

She hadn't slept and shook with a coldness that penetrated her very bones.

She'd been grilled by the chief and hounded by reporters who had overheard the radio call for a break-in at her house. And then came the bad news. First, from the forensics lab and then from the city manager's office. That and the persistent memory of taking off her clothes for Clarke and crawling into bed with him were enough to make her morning utter hell.

She looked at the picture of herself in the newspaper. A regular old celebrity, she thought miserably. Most of the article had been about the incinerator fiasco. Gus's people had sifted it for hours and found no bones, no teeth, no guns, no knives—nothing but cold white ashes and lumps that had once been dog tags. The shutdown had cost the taxpayers eleven thousand dollars and a selectwoman friendly with Jason Carlino complained that the department should pick up the tab, if not O'Shaughnessy personally.

The blood on the windshield was type A-negative; both Carlino and Yoland were positives, one A and one O. The hair caught in the window glass was not similar to samples they had collected from the Carlino residence, nor to hairs collected from the scene where Tracy Yoland had been kidnapped.

FBI reports on the paint sample hadn't come back yet, but with the way things were going, O'Shaughnessy didn't hold out high hopes for a match on the truck, either. Not anymore.

Her mind kept going over it. Lyons had been perfect. Everything about him had been perfect. He had opportunity—he was the night-shift driver. He had means—he drove a city disposal truck. He had motive—he was a convicted sex offender. There was evidence—the female hair and bloodstain found in *his* vehicle. And his truck was orange, just like the vehicle Anne Carlino came into contact with the night she disappeared off the face of the earth. What more could you ask for? she wondered. This was Probable Cause with a capital P.

But the town's leaders didn't think so, nor were they convinced of the wisdom in closing down the county's incinerator. Not on the thread of a single human hair, which, as Jason Carlino pointed out to the *Patriot*, was far short of finding a victim's ring in the apartment of a known sex offender.

In the city manager's reasoning, it would have been harmless to charge Jeremy Smyles and keep him in jail. For one thing, it would have appeased Jason Carlino and the Yolands. For another, it would have made the public feel better. If evidence developed to the contrary, or if another suspect turned up later, she could always release him. Smyles not only had the evidence, he admitted to having it. He was a known sex offender—albeit for peeping in someone's window— and he couldn't explain his whereabouts on the night of either crime. He belonged in jail! *And for God's sake, Kelly, he's a retard. He's not going to complain to anyone. You'd be off the hook if it turned out he was innocent.*

O'Shaughnessy couldn't even formulate a proper response for that one.

Tears brimmed in her eyes. Even a paint match for Lyons's truck wouldn't mean much right now. Paint pointed to a particular group of vehicles, not a particular vehicle. To get Lyons, she needed a direct link to his victims. She needed physical evidence. She needed to match the hair and the bloodstain she'd found in that truck to another human being. But to whom?

She set her coffee cup next to the recliner. And now someone was stalking her. Or trying to make her look like a fool. She wondered if Dillon would have that kind of nerve, that much hate. And decided he would.

There was mail in the mailbox—she hadn't opened it in two days—and the message light was flashing on the answering machine: undoubtedly Clarke.

She looked around the house and thought of all the tears her family had shed in those rooms. Good tears and bad tears, the life and laughter of a family. She missed being a family. Nothing seemed to be working without them. And now she didn't know if she should let the girls come back home or stay with their father. How safe was it to be with her now?

Suddenly the tears spilled over and she began to bawl. Deep throaty sobs erupted as she wondered how life could change so suddenly. She wanted Tim back. She wanted Tim to hold her. She knew that Clarke would come to her in a minute, but Clarke didn't know her like Tim did. Clarke hadn't shared the ups and downs that made her who she was. Clarke wasn't part of her family and that's what she wanted back. Her family.

She closed her eyes, squeezing back the tears. Gulls screamed outside. She could hear the thrum of traffic inching its way down her street. Rio must be backed up to the bridge, everyone trying to get out of town before the storm hit. *Everyone going on with their lives while hers had stopped dead.*

She set the cup on the stand and stood, grabbing tissues for her face and depositing them in the kitchen garbage. She took her sneakers from beside the back door. Then she pushed herself out the front door and sat on the steps to lace them up. The humidity was oppressive.

She ran to the sidewalk and east toward Atlantic Avenue, where fifty cars waited for their turn at the light.

She looked at the people in them, the children, the toys, the dogs, the luggage, everything mashed up against the windows. Families . . .

She crossed Atlantic under the shadows of the towering Dunes, jogged an alley next to the Driftwood, where Sherry Moore would be getting up and making coffee. O'Shaughnessy's mother had lived in that condo until her fatal heart attack last fall. Now it was just a reminder of someone else lost.

Vendors rolled carts of soda and cigarettes into the hotel's side doors; she could smell the remains of breakfast bacon, which for some reason reminded her of Tim.

She was jogging down the beach, fighting heavy sand until she reached the shoreline, and then she turned north and picked up her stride toward Strayer's Pier.

The waves were large and explosive and the tide washed well up on the beach.

She'd fucked up. It was that simple. She'd wanted something positive to happen in her life, and when Lyons was the only thing in her sights, she came out shooting. Probably she'd jumped too fast with Clarke, too.

There was a line of reeking seaweed to follow; a tenacious family determined to get in the last hours of their vacation played among it. She zigzagged her way past them and startled a threesome of shorebirds pecking in the receding tide. O'Shaughnessy's tears started to well again and sweat began to pour from her brow. After another mile she started looping for home.

God, she wished she could call Tim. Just to talk to him. Just to have him hold her. She turned up her street and into the driveway and up the steps to the house. Maybe it was too late for that now. Maybe she'd screwed that up as well.

She showered and drove to the men's shelter on the harbor where the city had temporarily placed Jeremy Smyles. From there she drove him to the psychiatric clinic in Vineland, where he underwent his voluntary evaluation. She was sitting in a waiting room, ruminating over whether or not to call Tim on her cell phone, when McGuire called.

"I dropped Payne at your condo for lunch. No luck with his sketch yet. I talked with that cab fleet in Ocean City. They don't have an orange car that's older than three years. He says they sell them off at ninety thousand miles, about every twenty months. All the big fleets do the same, he said. The vehicle we're looking for could have been sold to a private citizen by now. Just one more thing we need to take into consideration."

There was a noise outside his office door just then. "Hang on a minute, Lieu." McGuire cupped his hand over the receiver and yelled, "Yeah?" but no one responded. A moment later he was back on the line. "Sorry, Lieu, I thought someone came in. So what do you make of all this psychic stuff anyhow? I mean, what's Sherry Moore like? Can she really talk to the dead?"

"She's blind," O'Shaughnessy said, "and she doesn't talk to the dead, she sees memories." Suddenly she wondered if it had been prudent to involve McGuire. For his own sake.

"You're kidding."

"Uh-huh. And she's beautiful, not at all what you'd expect for a psychic. By the way, I'm taking her to Kissock's tonight if you need to reach me. I'm leaving my phone in the car."

"Well, have fun, Lieu. My Philly friend and I should be heading toward the boardwalk about then."

"Take him out to dinner if you want. I'll voucher it."

"You sure?" He was thinking about the incinerator debacle.

"I'm sure," she said.

"You know this guy in the sketch is pretty twisted-looking. Anyone who had seen a face like that wouldn't forget it."

"That's about what I thought."

"Maybe it's not even a real person?"

"You're not telling me anything I haven't already thought of." She sighed. "Thanks for working with him, by the way. I'll make it up to you."

"No problem, Lieu. He's a good guy. We're heading over to Jennie Woo's next, then Carlino's boyfriend. Tonight we'll look for the gang around Strayer's."

"Don't forget Newsy."

"I'll try him on the way to Jennie's."

McGuire heard a noise in the outer office again. "Sorry, Lieu. Got to go, someone's in the outer office."

McGuire picked up a stack of mail and opened the door into the outer office, almost running into Dillon's boots around the corner. The fat man was draped over one of the detective's chairs with his feet propped up on a desk. There was mustard on his T-shirt and he reeked of booze.

"You need something?" McGuire asked.

"Yeah, I need a blow job," Dillon slurred, grabbing his crotch. "But I see the lieutenant ain't here right now." He looked up at the ceiling. "Maybe that was her on the phone just now? Calling in from the nail salon?"

Dillon pushed himself back from the desk and stumbled to his feet, knocking over a ceramic coffee mug that read "Best Dad"; it shattered on the floor. "You know why you suits make me so sick?" He staggered in place. "Because you all think you're smarter than the rest of us, giggling on the phone like a bunch of little girls; none of you have the nuts to know what real cop work is all about. Sorry-ass detectives," he mumbled, weaving toward the door.

McGuire closed his eyes and said a silent prayer. A prayer that Dillon hadn't heard him talking about Sherry Moore.

Sherry was wrapped in a towel and sitting on the balcony when O'Shaughnessy arrived. "Enjoying the storm?" she asked.

Sherry nodded. "I can't remember the last time I slept so well. We left the sliders open all night."

And indeed it had been her longest night of sleep since the incident at the funeral home.

"It's getting dark out there. The brunt of it won't hit until midnight, but the tides are up and the beaches are covered with seaweed."

"I can smell it," Sherry said. "Would you like coffee, Kelly?"

"Yes, I'd love coffee, but I'll pour. What do you take?"

"Black," the blind woman said.

O'Shaughnessy grabbed the woman's mug and found herself one in the cabinet.

"This was your mother's place, you said?"

"Yes," she answered. She carried the cups to the balcony and took a seat next to Sherry. "She had a thing for white. Everything here is white. White rug, white furniture, white walls, white, white, white."

"I'm sure it's beautiful."

"Actually, it's not so bad. I used to buy her art every Christmas, just to get a little color in here." O'Shaughnessy sipped her coffee. "My sergeant said no luck with the sketch."

Sherry shook her head. "John came back at lunch and told me the same. I'm not always comfortable that I interpret what I've seen correctly, Kelly. I've had some bad experiences in the past."

"You can hardly be expected to be perfect at such a thing, I would imagine."

Sherry hugged herself. "Sometimes you can hardly afford not to be."

"You're nervous about tonight. The morgue?"

Sherry nodded.

"And that's not like you."

She shook her head.

O'Shaughnessy sensed there was far more to visiting Andrew Markey than the woman could share.

"I'm hoping you'll want to join me for dinner tonight before we visit the body. I told my sergeant to take Detective Payne out as well. I think they'll be at it late anyhow."

Sherry waved her hand. "Please don't rearrange your life for me. I'm quite content to do nothing, and John brought a bag of sandwiches in case I get hungry."

"Well, my children are at their father's, and quite frankly I'd rather not spend the evening alone. All right?"

"Only if I get to pay," Sherry said.

"Payne didn't tell me you were so stubborn."

26

Marcia was able to free one of her wrists by dislocating her thumb and tucking it under her fingers, a stunt that Nicky made possible the night he threw her out of a second-floor window.

The bus was overrun with rats—not your typical farm rats, but pale, sluggish creatures with yellow eyes. They looked for all their worth like small opossums. She could only tell when it was night or day by the color of the scratches on the painted black windows and when sunlight illuminated the front steps of the bus. Sykes had already given her the tour; she'd seen the pit, which was all you really needed to see to understand what went on in here.

There were no highway sounds, no horns or sirens, but airplanes crossed frequently and she could hear the whopping blades of a helicopter throughout the day. At first she thought they were looking for her, but later she began to recognize a pattern. It was a tourist's ride, going out over the coast and back.

He'd taken her clothes and dropped them into the pit in front of her. He poured water into her mouth from a plastic Coke bottle and fed her candy bars that he cut in small bites with a dirty paring knife left by the side of the lantern. He told her that if she got too weak to keep him happy he'd throw her into the pit. After that he left her naked but covered with the tarp.

Once she managed to slip off the handcuff, she could roll to the side and tear the tape from her lips and scream if she chose to. She could also reach the lantern on the floor next to her and the little paring knife that was next to it.

The first time she'd done it she could see the lipstick stains on the mattress under her head and the scratches along the rod where someone had fought the cuffs. She was not the first woman to lie here waiting to die.

He'd raped her that first night, but yesterday he had looked sick, flushed like he had the flu, and paid minimal attention to her. Nicky's sister looked that way when she didn't get her fix. She thought he might be on medication.

But medication or not, he was planning something. He brought back a policeman's hat and a pair of glimmering black shoes he kept against one wall of the bus. They were small shoes, lady's uniform shoes. He told her he was bringing some entertainment for her soon. He told her she would be part of the show.

When he let her use a bucket, he emptied it into the pit; the smell of that hole when he removed the cover was as if he'd opened the throat of hell, a gaseous cavity into the detritus of mankind. The mere thought of being pushed into it alive was more than her mind could bear. How many others had suffered that fate? How many others had he pulled kicking and screaming across the floor?

She grinned as if demented herself, rolling, reaching, and touching the small knife by the lantern. Slip, roll, reach, grab. She could do it every time. It was strange, she thought, but she had spent a lot of her time alone thinking of Nicky. Nicky who had dominated her life, Nicky who had raped and beaten her, and humiliated her in front of his family and friends. It was amazing how clear it all seemed now, like she'd had an out-of-body experience where one part of her was looking down upon the other and there was finally no more uncertainty about what was right and what was wrong. What she was going to accept and what she wasn't.

She had learned something else in the last two days as well. She wouldn't lie here and scream like a Schmidt wife would do. She wouldn't risk the only chance she had. She was ready for him. She could take anything he threw at her; Nicky had prepared her for that.

They would have found Connie's car by now and Connie would be all over the authorities. She'd have the whole damned state looking for her and she wouldn't back off until it was done.

Marcia knew she wasn't all that far from the parkway. She knew she'd been carried into a junkyard. Someone would be along soon, some kind of official person or the owner or an employee, maybe just kids fooling around. And when she saw who it was and she knew it was safe, she'd slip off the handcuff and call out for help. If no help came, she would wait and practice her roll and jab, waiting until the next time he crawled on top of her. If he ever did it again, she was going to give him the screwing of his life.

27

"I love all the smells," Sherry said, taking in the aroma of Kissock's kitchen.

They were seated in the dining room, halfway between the back wall and the bar, where, O'Shaughnessy recalled, not too long before she had met Clarke for drinks. She'd been so nervous that night about bumping into someone she knew. Now she was worried she might bump into Tim and another woman.

She'd tried to pump the girls for information about their dad's comings and goings, but neither seemed to know anything. Or maybe they were oblivious to the possibility that he could be out with someone else besides their mother.

She knew he kept her picture on his nightstand; the girls made it a point to tell her so. She knew he still wore his wedding ring, or at least he was wearing it every time she had seen him since the separation.

"What's good?"

"Everything's good, but the lobster is outstanding."

"Say no more." Sherry put her hands together. "I haven't had lobster in months. Are we having cocktails or are you on duty?"

"Cocktails," O'Shaughnessy said. "Lots of them." She was in a slightly better mood this evening. The doctors at the psychiatric clinic agreed that Smyles was both physically and emotionally incapable of the crimes. "He couldn't deceive you if he tried," the doctor said. "He couldn't contain a secret."

Sherry sat quietly, calmly, as the candlelight flickered over her glasses. O'Shaughnessy saw how people were drawn to Sherry—first her looks, then the fact that she was blind, then the fact that she didn't look like she was blind. Her expressions were free and animated, her hands and head followed conversation easily. She was in great shape; you could see it in her muscle tone, in the way she carried herself. Sherry had told her about the various things she did to keep herself busy: workouts in her home gym, martial arts with a sensei twice weekly, sunning herself in her winter solarium and during summers on the lawn behind her house. O'Shaughnessy thought it sounded like a lonely life.

The waiter took their drink orders and left them alone to decide. They both ordered Cobb salads, boiled lobster for Sherry and crab-stuffed flounder for O'Shaughnessy.

"You two seem to have a close relationship. You and John, I mean."

"He's the nicest guy you'd ever meet," Sherry said. "He cares, Kelly. He really does care. It's not just a job to him."

"You've known each other a long time?"

Sherry nodded. "Almost fifteen years now. We met on my very first police case, although I didn't know what was happening to me at the time. I guess it was the way he treated me. He was sensitive when anyone else might have laughed at me."

O'Shaughnessy heard it in her voice, a weak moment perhaps, but she seemed to have let her guard down. Sherry's tone suggested that there was definitely more between them than a friendship. She wanted to ask but didn't want to hear there was a wife waiting at home for him somewhere.

"He's serious about this victim of his, Susan Paxton," she said instead.

"He feels responsible to the victims," Sherry answered. "He's always talking about the ones he didn't close, like he'd never done enough for them. I know it drives him crazy. He keeps telling me that I am God's gift to victims." She laughed. "So you're married?"

O'Shaughnessy nodded. "Uh-huh."

"Long time?"

"Seven years."

"Children?"

O'Shaughnessy swallowed; she was going to have to take the question. "Two, both girls."

Sherry's head was down, facing the corner of the table; her expression was wistful. "You're lucky, you know," she said. "Really lucky."

"I know." O'Shaughnessy put her fork down. Sherry looked so alone, so vulnerable for just that moment; then it seemed to pass.

"John said there were women missing. Here, this summer, from the boardwalk."

The waiter arrived with their drinks: O'Shaughnessy had a margarita and Sherry had an India Pale Ale.

"These are on Chief Loudon." The waiter pointed to the bar. "He said to tell you both to enjoy. He didn't wish to intrude, but if you have a moment, Lieutenant, he'd like a word with you at the bar."

O'Shaughnessy craned her head toward the bar, raised her glass, and smiled as the chief waved back. "My boss," she said. "I should dash over there before our food arrives. Do you need to go to the ladies' room? I can take you with me."

"I'm good, Kelly, but thanks."

"I tried to reach you on the radio," Loudon growled. "McGuire told me you were here." His expression was dark. "I thought today might be a good day after you gave me the news on Smyles's psychiatric tests, but instead I get a call from Jason Carlino."

O'Shaughnessy groaned.

"Who told me he got a call from a highly intoxicated Sergeant Dillon who told him you were meeting with fortune-tellers about his daughter's case. Of course Carlino wanted me to know what idiots he thought we all were."

She groaned louder, but the chief wasn't done.

"I got Dillon out of bed and asked him where he got the harebrained idea he could call private citizens to talk about cases. He told me that he and Carlino are friends and that he overheard Mac talking to you about a suspect in the Carlino abduction, thought maybe Carlino would be interested to know we had a break. Dillon told him there's a Philadelphia homicide detective in town showing a suspect's sketch and a psychic named Sherry Moore you're consulting." His eyes flickered to the table and back. "Dillon may not be the smartest guy on the planet, but he knows how to use the Internet, Kelly, and guess what he found?"

O'Shaughnessy slumped against the bar. "I'm so sorry, Chief. I should have told you before I did it."

"Is there anything else I need to know, Lieutenant?" Loudon looked at the blind woman at O'Shaughnessy's table and this time he stared.

"You know the Lisa Penn case we talked about, the one from 1974 with the ballistics matchup to Philadelphia? The detective who has the case is a friend of hers." She nodded toward Sherry. "His victim was born here. That's it. I swear it. We help out other departments all the time."

"It doesn't explain Sherry Moore." He scowled.

O'Shaughnessy put her hand on the bar and looked at the floor, thinking she wouldn't dare mention Andrew Markey in the morgue. "All right. It's her sketch. His suspect. She inspired it."

"Ah, well." The chief smiled, sitting back and taking a deep breath. "That makes it all so much easier. It's a sketch from the dead that you're showing everyone. I can explain that easily enough when the city manager calls back. He'll understand." Loudon thumped the bar with his fist and leaned into her face. "Didn't you think it would come out, Kelly? Didn't you know they would use it against you? Jason Carlino's been burning up the phone all afternoon. I know you think what you're doing is right, and I know you must see all this as being very innocent, but this is just the kind of ammunition Carlino's been looking for. This is what will hang you when it hits the streets."

"Streets?"

"Oh. Didn't I mention that I was only Carlino's second call of the day? The first was to the *Patriot*."

"Oh, shit." She groaned. "Jack, I'll fix things with Carlino. I'll go over there and see him myself tonight. He should be glad someone is trying to do something about his daughter."

"He thinks you already did, Kelly, and that you blew it when you let Smyles out of jail. That's what he's been howling about ever since you started this investigation. That's why he wants you removed. Stay away from him, Kelly, and if you're real smart, you'll put some distance between yourself and your Philadelphia friends, too. Now that may sound a little draconian to you, but this is getting to be about your job. Do you understand what I'm telling you?"

O'Shaughnessy nodded.

Loudon put a five-dollar bill by his half-empty beer and stood. "City manager wanted me to suspend you. Dillon filed a formal allegation with the police union that you staged the burglary scene at your house. He says you wanted to divert attention from your failed search and seizures over at the sanitation yard. He's asking them to support Carlino's petition for an attorney general's audit because in his words, the district attorney in Wildwood is unlikely to put the evidence from the Jeremy Smyles house fire before a grand jury."

O'Shaughnessy shook her head. "I'm not following."

Loudon coughed. "He said, Kelly, that you're having an affair with Clarke Hamilton."

"Oh, my God." She moaned. She could no longer spare Tim and the girls. Now they'd drag her relationship with Clarke into the papers. Dillon would know it was a no-win situation for her. How could she actually prove that an intruder had put her uniform on the bed? How could she defend against the fact that she'd been seeing Clarke Hamilton? People in town had already seen them together. She'd received flowers from him in front of an office full of detectives.

And it wasn't about whether what she did was right or wrong. It was the suggestion that she was incompetent. The attorney general could not ignore Carlino's demands for an audit much longer.

She knew that if it was ever discovered that she'd kept Andrew Markey on ice for Sherry Moore's sake, she would be back in sergeant's stripes, riding the streets with Dillon on midnight shifts before the end of the summer.

"What do you think?" she asked. "About me."

"Well, I've got a uniformed officer in the park across the street from your house twenty-four hours a day. What do you think I think?" He shook a finger at her. "What should concern you, Kelly, is not what I think. I won't be able to say no to him if there's a next time. I won't be able to save you."

Loudon took the finger out of her face. "I don't know what you're planning to do with Miss Moore, Kelly, and quite frankly, I don't want to. I just want you to know that everyone in town is waiting to see what you're going to do next. Have a good dinner."

O'Shaughnessy returned to her table as the entrees arrived. She picked up her fork and made noises on the plate, drank her drink a little fast, and failed to answer something Sherry had asked.

"Something wrong?"

O'Shaughnessy looked up at the blind woman. "I'm okay."

"The hell you are."

O'Shaughnessy sighed, looked around at the other tables, and smiled weakly. "You don't miss much."

"Am I a problem? That happens more than you know."

"It's part of it," O'Shaughnessy admitted. "But it's really only an excuse, too. The problem was here long before you arrived."

"Can I do anything?" Sherry asked.

She shook her head. "One of my victims' fathers learned that you and Detective Payne are in town. He's been riding my ass since the day his daughter disappeared. Now the newspapers are going to pick on you and he'll play it to his advantage."

"John and I should leave."

"Absolutely not. You only came to help, Sherry. If my daughter was missing, I would want people to explore every possible means of finding her. This man's problem is with me. He's a powermonger. He wants the state to take over the case and he'll use the fact that I invited you here to do it." She put her fork down. "I had an incident at my house last night. A break-in."

O'Shaughnessy told her the story about finding her uniform on the bed, leaving out that she had been in the district attorney's home at the time it happened.

"They're trying to say it was staged. That I staged it to divert attention away from the abductions."

"Kelly, that's a very serious allegation. If they're not looking for whoever did it, you could be in danger."

"No," she said thoughtfully. "The chief put an officer outside my door, but I'm sure it's someone I know, a cop who thinks he can score political points before this is all over." She raised a finger to signal for the check and settled back in her chair. After a few seconds she leaned forward again. "Before we go to the morgue, would you like to go under the boardwalk with me, to feel what it's like, to see where my victims were abducted?"

"Of course I would," Sherry said. "Of course. I just want you to be sure."

"It's . . . dark," O'Shaughnessy started to warn, then put a hand over her mouth and giggled. "Oh, fuck."

"Yeah, it is, isn't it." Sherry giggled back.

O'Shaughnessy stood and looked to the bar where Chief Loudon had been sitting. "And as long as we're at it," she said, "we'll stop by the condo and get a bottle of wine on the way. Okay?"

"Good deal.

9:15 P.M.

The rain had stopped; the sea was eerily calm. O'Shaughnessy parked in the lot where they'd found Carlino's Explorer. She opened the glove box and removed a flashlight. "I'm leaving my shoes in the car," she said.

Sherry nodded and kicked off her own.

"You'll want to watch your head. It gets low in places."

"Got it."

There were only a handful of cars in the lot; most of the tourists had left in advance of the storm. O'Shaughnessy guided Sherry to the drainpipe where it disappeared under the walk.

"Okay, grab my belt and remember your head."

Sherry took a loop of O'Shaughnessy's belt and reached out to find the edge of the walk.

Sherry could smell urine as they stepped under the timber, then a whiff of something decomposing, a sea-gull or a rat. The sand was cold, mushy under their bare feet. They stepped into a puddle, then heavy sand that was dry and caked around their ankles.

O'Shaughnessy took Sherry's hand and laid it on the side of the drainpipe. "We'll follow the pipe about twenty feet."

"Got it."

Footsteps clomped overhead. A dull, hollow quality about the enclosure seemed to intensify the farther under they went from the parking lot. The smells changed to those of the barnacles, seaweed, century-old pilings.

O'Shaughnessy raised the light to the boards over-head. "The kids spray graffiti here. There are lots of cigarette butts and beer cans lying around. We found a blood trail the whole way down the pipe, handprints and hair that matched the victim's. Right up here, just another few steps." She rapped on the side of the pipe with her knuckles. "Her wristwatch was on the other side, buried in the sand. Her ring was wedged in the boards above where her head would have been. The blood marks on top of the pipe tell us that he grabbed her from this side and pulled her back over."

"What did she look like?"

"This one was seventeen, long hair, very pretty; her friends called her the conservative one, simple jewelry, no tattoos, no body piercings. From what we could tell, she was attacked in the parking lot where we came in. That's where her car was found. Tire punched. The blood trail ended here, just on the other side of the pipe."

O'Shaughnessy turned the flashlight's beam upward, bathing them both in a halo of light that circled the dark sand around them.

"You said there was graffiti."

"Uh-huh." O'Shaughnessy took Sherry's arm and tugged her back in the direction they had come. "We can sit here, the sand's dry."

Sherry let herself down cross-legged and O'Shaughnessy sat opposite her, their knees touching. They had already pulled the cork on the wine bottle in the car, so it came off easily. O'Shaughnessy raised the light and Sherry raised the wine, taking a drink from the bottle and handing it back.

"'Beatles, Kurt Cocaine, EP loves FS, Green Day Dookie, Bay Side Blows, Allison loves Christy, Stop the War, Wishbone, Beejun's suck, SSM 96, Syko Sue, Peace.'" She shifted, took another drink and continued reading. "'LCMR High—'94 Champs, Surfers

DRule, Fuck Gerald, Pat loves Rocky, BH is a cunt, Curly and Moe,' and on and on. I never imagined that people hung out under here." O'Shaughnessy lowered the light and turned toward her companion. "I lived here all my life and— Sherry, Sherry, are you all right?"

Even in the poor light she could see a troubled look on the blind woman's face. "Sherry?"

"I've seen it before," Sherry whispered. "Psycho Sue, only the word *psycho* was spelled wrong. I saw it through Susan Paxton's eyes in Philadelphia."

O'Shaughnessy turned the light on Sherry's face, recalling a conversation with Gus Meyers. *They called her crazy Sue . . .*

"Spell it out like you saw it."

"S-Y-K-O," Sherry whispered.

O'Shaughnessy looked at her, wiped her forehead with a gritty hand. "You mean she was here? Sitting right here where we are?"

"It's the same spelling, isn't it?"

"It's the same," she whispered. "It's exactly the same."

10:00 P.M.

O'Shaughnessy was grateful to find the morgue dark and the parking lot empty. She parked her unmarked car in a space reserved for the medical examiner behind an ivy-covered brick wall. She led Sherry to a basement entrance, where she took out a set of keys and tried several before the door opened. A half-dozen steps ascended to a spotless linoleum floor;

their shoes tapped loudly down the corridor until they reached a set of cool double doors. She took a breath and tried more keys, and the doors swung open.

Anyone who had ever seen Sherry at work would hardly forget the moment. Andrew Markey's head was draped with a sheet; O'Shaughnessy had seen the autopsy reports and knew his face had all but been cleaved in half when it struck the edge of the bottom step. There was no reason to see it now and so it remained draped as Sherry took his hand and tilted her head to one side.

. . . an old woman was sitting on a rocker, she was holding out her arms for a hug . . . a pig hung butchered from scaffolding behind a barn, there was blood dripping from its ears . . . a young woman, a beautiful woman riding a bicycle, same woman on the beach, same woman naked in a bed . . . a stage with small children dressed for a Christmas play . . . man mopping a floor, she could see his face, turning up to her, grinning . . . a name on the back of a boat, something luck . . . a young woman, it was Susan! A prison . . . the man with the mop again, crooking a finger at him, beckoning him down the hall.

Oh, my God! It was the older man in Susan Paxton's memory, the man with the floppy hat and raincoat who had been picking up sweaters.

"Sherry?"

"I've seen him before," Sherry whispered huskily. "He was in the store where Susan Paxton was killed. It was the second time she'd seen him that day."

"The same man in the sketch you gave to Payne?"

Sherry shook her head. "No, this was an older man; he was picking up a stack of sweaters and handing them to Susan. I thought he was a customer. I picked the younger one because I saw a gun in his hand. I saw him last."

O'Shaughnessy closed her eyes for a moment and then opened them again. "Describe this man."

"Fifty, sixty, short gray hair, long white scar on his neck—you wouldn't miss the scar."

"I know who it is," O'Shaughnessy said quietly. She took Sherry's arm. "We've got to get back."

O'Shaughnessy's mind was racing. It was the man who'd stuck his head in her car in the sanitation yard parking lot the night she searched the meat wagon. She had been right about the truck all along, but wrong about Lyons. It hadn't been Sandy Lyons driving the truck. It had been the man with the scar, one of the other drivers. And she'd missed it!

28

SATURDAY, JUNE 4, 10:45 P.M.
WILDWOOD, NEW JERSEY

"Randall, this is Lieutenant O'Shaughnessy. Anyone talked to McGuire? I can't get him on the phone," she said into her cell.

She had to reach McGuire and let him know he was showing the sketch of the wrong man.

Streets had begun to flood; fallen tree limbs and branches appeared and disappeared in her headlights.

"Haven't heard from him, Lieu, but a Trooper Mc-Callis keeps calling for you from Cape May barracks. Something about a missing person." Randall rummaged around his desktop for a sticky note. "Marcia Schmidt ring a bell?"

O'Shaughnessy sighed. She didn't have time for this now. "Yeah, she was a friend of the lady who was trying to make a report yesterday to Celia Davis. This friend was supposed to visit from the other side of the state and never showed. We checked the tags and got nothing. She thought the friend might have been delayed by an abusive husband."

"Well, the trooper's got her car impounded, and he spoke with the owner in Glassboro, New Jersey. The driver's a critical missing person as of two hours ago."

Her heart stopped. "They have her car?"

"They found it on the parkway yesterday. He acted like you might know what he was talking about."

"Randall, find McGuire. I'll call you right back." She hung up the phone and called Youth Division.

"Is Davis there?"

She was told the officer was on leave and got her home number. A minute later she had the officer on the phone. "Celia, sorry to wake you. Do you remember the woman who reported her friend missing yesterday? Connie something?"

"Connie Riker. Yeah, sure, Lieu. What's up?" She yawned.

"What happened when you ran her car through

NCIC?"

"Nothing. It came back clean. I gave her the social service numbers like you asked and went on leave. What's up?"

O'Shaughnessy sighed. "I'll call you later." She hung up the phone.

Was everything she touched going to turn to shit? She dialed the operator. "Give me the Cape May State Police Barracks." When she got through, after identifying herself she said, "Trooper McCallis, please."

"Just a minute," the clerk told her.

He was on the phone a minute later.

"Trooper, this is Lieutenant O'Shaughnessy, Wildwood. Detective Randall said you called about Marcia Schmidt."

It turned out that Riker's Ford Escort had first been seen on the Garden State Parkway early Friday morning by a New Jersey state trooper. When it was still not moved by noon, they towed it off to their impound lot. That's when it was first entered into their records, which was why NCIC wouldn't have had the tags when Connie Riker called to check on it the night before, the night that Marcia Schmidt was supposed to have arrived in Wildwood. Celia Davis couldn't have found anything on it the following morning, either. It simply hadn't gone in the system until noon.

McCallis said he had asked a trooper to go by the Rikers' home in Glassboro—on the other end of the state— yesterday to leave a message for the owner that her car had been impounded at the Cape May State Police Barracks, the closest barracks to the city of Wildwood.

When Connie and her mother returned that afternoon from Wildwood, they found the message to call Trooper McCallis's number, but no car. Marcia Schmidt wasn't at her home, either.

"She said she talked to you."

There really was a missing woman.

O'Shaughnessy felt a chill come over her. Thursday night she had searched the truck in the highway shed. It had to be Marcia Schmidt's hair and blood she'd found in the meat wagon!

She turned the wheel sharply and took an eastbound street toward Atlantic. "Trooper McCallis, can you get the barracks in Glassboro to send someone out to the Schmidt residence right away? I need hair exemplars and fast."

O'Shaughnessy wheeled into the Driftwood garage off Atlantic.

"Sherry," she said as she jumped out and came around to the passenger door, "I've got to get you back in the condo and find Mac."

Within the hour, two state police officers were sent to collect combs and hairbrushes from the Schmidt house in Glassboro. When they arrived, Nicky and his older brother were driving a John Deere front-end loader onto the back of a spotlit flatbed with Delaware tags. The tractor looked like one on a flyer the troopers had on their clipboards; its serial numbers matched those of a machine stolen from a dairy farm in nearby Tylertown. The troopers placed the Schmidt brothers and the driver of the flatbed under arrest and got into the house long enough to remove hairbrushes from both bathrooms.

29

SATURDAY, JUNE 4, 10:00 P.M.
WILDWOOD, NEW JERSEY

Sykes recalled an FBI agent commenting during the sniper shootings in D.C. that law enforcement solved only 47 percent of all murders in the United States each year. That meant one had a better than even chance to kill someone, even a cop, and get away with it.

Sykes knew, too, that if one could permanently dispose of the bodies, he could split the odds even further. No bodies, no evidence. And that was a hard case to prosecute. They'd be tripping over themselves for months trying to figure out what happened. And even if they suspected him, those months meant all the time in the world. At least all the time in his world. He was going to make the lieutenant go away—permanently.

The storm had unexpectedly turned inland. Garbage flew through the streets; winds turned unfettered furniture into dangerous missiles. City workers and emergency personnel had been held over into the midnight shift; Sykes, who'd reported back to work, was supposed to use the meat wagon to collect debris from the flooding roads along Cottage Town. He piled the back of the truck high with picket fencing, bicycles, and Big Wheels, but not nearly enough to fill it. Only enough sticking out of the back to appear as if he had.

* * *

Thank God O'Shaughnessy knew the man Sherry had seen in the vision in the morgue; she even knew where he worked.

Sherry took a drink from the bottle of wine she'd opened when she returned to the condo, set the bottle on the vanity top, and hung her wet clothes on the bathroom door. She was already tipsy from the night's drinking, but the boardwalk and the morgue had unnerved her. She'd been wrong about the man in Philadelphia. She'd given Payne the wrong suspect to go after.

By tomorrow, though, O'Shaughnessy would have the man arrested and Payne would have his suspect in the Susan Paxton murder. So, yes, she had made a mistake, but it had turned out all right in the end. She wasn't infallible. She was human just like everyone else and would make more mistakes before it was all over.

She raised the bottle and drank some more. Somehow, the feeling was liberating. She had always taken life so seriously, always lived in fear she might do or say something wrong. Now, tonight, she thought, putting the bottle down unsteadily, she would do something selfish for once in her life.

She would be honest with John.

She stepped into the hot shower, thinking of what she might say when he came through the door.

She lifted her hair, thinking of young lives cut short, dreams unfulfilled. She felt changed by it.

She shut off the water and wrapped herself in a towel, brushed her teeth, and combed her hair, which she let hang damp on her shoulders.

Maybe it was his touch last evening, the way he took her arm and put a hand on the small of her back; John had never touched her like that before.

She let the towel drop to the floor and put on one of John's dress shirts appropriated from his luggage; she fastened two buttons midway to her navel.

He'd talked differently, too, as if there was something on his mind and he couldn't yet bring himself to say it. Let it hang there like a question mark between them.

The energy in the little apartment was palpable. She could feel it even after they said their good nights. Lying under the covers, hearing him toss and turn in the living room, her own guilty desire that every noise was him coming through her open door. But he hadn't, and by morning her fear was that the spell had been broken. That both would be returned to the reality that he was married, even if, as Sherry suspected, the marriage was not a happy one.

But it hadn't been broken. Morning found them in the tiny kitchen together, brushing against each other unnecessarily, tangling fingers when she handed him a coffee cup. They were like strangers caught together, the tension unbearable, then McGuire phoned to say he was downstairs. And suddenly John was gone.

She stepped into lace panties and a pair of shorts, put gloss on her lips.

There was a knock at the door. She took a deep breath.

She must not waste any more time. Come what may, she wanted him to know just how she had felt all these years.

"I'm coming," she called.

"God, don't let me be wrong," she whispered, walking to the living room, stopping to take a breath, undoing one of the two buttons that held her shirt together.

And opened the door.

Sykes kicked Sherry in the chest, knocking her over the packed suitcase sitting by the coffee table; she heard the telephone stand splinter and the telephone receiver fly off the hook as her head struck the floor. Then he stepped inside, dropped a tarp, and closed the door. She heard him throw the dead bolt. He flicked on lights and ran to the bedroom to make sure they were alone. Another suitcase was packed and waiting in the hallway.

Sherry had already pushed herself off the floor and was dragging the phone by the cord toward her when he kicked her in the side and leaned across to tear the phone from the wall. Then he knelt and put a hand over her mouth. Her eyes were open; they looked normal, but they didn't move. They never moved. "My, my," he said, glancing around the room again. "You're not Lieutenant O'Shaughnessy." He looked down at her open shirt and bare legs. "Pretty little thing and blind as a bat, too."

Her forearm shot forward with a barely perceptible flick of the wrist, driving three fingers underhanded into the soft part of his neck. The Japanese called it *nukite*, the spear hand, and it sent him sprawling backward into the kitchenette, where he struck his head on the cabinet doors. He grabbed his throat trying to get a breath of air. She cocked one leg for a side thrust and used her fist to pound the floor. "Help!" she screamed. "Help me!"

He had his stun gun on his hip but was afraid to get close enough to use it. Whatever she'd done to his neck was some serious shit, some kind of judo or something. He couldn't let her daze him long enough to call for help or gain an advantage over him.

Wind and rain battered the sliding glass doors, drowning her screams. He searched for a broom or a pan or anything he could use to defend himself. Then he noticed the open cabinet under the sink; the door had popped after his head struck against it. He grabbed a can of ant and roach spray from in front of the cleaning supplies and started spraying a stream in her face. She put her arms down and he moved closer and closer until the poison was foaming over her nose and mouth, and when she started to gag, he slammed his fist into her face.

Sherry snap-kicked, but this time he was ready, catching the leg and rolling on top of her. She lunged for his eyes, raking skin from his cheeks and slamming her knees into his sides simultaneously. The move used so little motion that the power behind it shocked him.

He knew he didn't have a chance in a prolonged struggle with this woman; he stretched to reach the leg of the broken telephone stand and brought it down across the bridge of her nose hard enough to crack bone. He managed to reach the stun gun in his belt before she recovered and jabbed it into her side. She went limp.

He took a roll of duct tape from his jacket and tore off a strip, which he put across her foaming mouth. If she died of the insecticide poisoning, it was what she deserved. Fuck her after all that shit.

"Think you're so tough," he heaved; his heart was racing and sweat doused his shirt. He wrapped tape around her ankles, then laid her wrists together over her pelvis and bound them tight.

He got to his knees and dragged her toward the door, pushed the coffee table on its side, and opened the tarp next to her, then rolled her body in it. He didn't know who she was, but he knew by the suitcases that she was only visiting. And he knew now how he was going to get the lieutenant here.

He unlocked the door and looked down the hall before he dragged her body along the rough concrete hall. The sky was dark, and many of the windows had been taped or boarded with plywood before the tenants fled the coast.

The elevator was waiting. A moment later he was dragging her across the parking lot and onto the hydraulic lift behind his truck. Once she was in the bed, he shoved her behind fencing he'd stacked against the tailgate. Then he got behind the wheel and activated the yellow roof beacon, pulled out of the lot, and turned the corner onto a side street.

All city employees had been authorized overtime tonight. He wouldn't have to return the truck as long as he was involved in the storm cleanup; they would simply reassign Sandy Lyons until he got back.

When he'd first parked the meat wagon in the condominium garage, he'd believed that O'Shaughnessy was inside. Her Third Avenue address was dark and the driveway was empty. A police car assigned to watch her house was still stationed in the park across the street, had been ever since the night he'd put her uniform on the bed.

Then he'd seen lights on at the Atlantic Avenue condo and decided she had moved in there, thinking it safe.

He checked the back of the truck; the body wasn't visible and neither could the truck be seen from Atlantic Avenue, which was the way O'Shaughnessy would come in. He returned to the garage, unscrewed the four bare lightbulbs on the ceiling, and dragged his tarp back to the elevator.

Payne's and McGuire's luck never improved. The wind was gusting to forty knots, the boardwalk and most of the beachfront hotels and condos were virtually empty. By 10:30 they had called it a night, McGuire heading to the office, Payne to the condo to collect Sherry, thinking there was little else to be done in Wildwood.

Maybe Sherry had gotten the face wrong, or maybe Susan Paxton never knew who her shooter was. Maybe she really had been killed by a stranger who had come in to rob the store and panicked before he got the money.

Maybe, he thought, Payne would tell Sherry how he felt about her tonight.

10:35 P.M.

Sykes stuffed a paper towel in his mouth and lifted the receiver.

"Police Department," a woman answered.

"Detectives." He snapped the latex gloves over his hands.

A few clicks later he was transferred.

"Detectives," Randall answered.

"Lieutenant O'Shaughnessy, please."

"Just a minute."

Randall watched her come dripping through the door, raised three fingers, and mouthed "Phone."

O'Shaughnessy nodded and picked up the nearest receiver. "Hello," she answered, staring down at the puddle at her feet.

"Yeah." The voice sounded froggy. "This is maintenance down at the Driftwood. I got a soaking wet blind woman, says she locked herself out of her apartment. I'm just here to unblock the drains; they don't give me no keys, lady."

O'Shaughnessy stifled a groan. "Tell her I'll be right there. And stay with her if you can." She hung up and looked for McGuire. "Anything at all from Mac?"

He shook his head. "I left a message on his voice mail."

She turned for the door. Damn, she thought. "Tell him to wait for me if he beats me back."

30

Seagulls beat their wings, buffeting in the night winds, relentless in their pursuit of food. Street signs wobbled on their stanchions; rain pounded the sides of windows and cars, sheets of it white as ice.

O'Shaughnessy was just pulling into the Driftwood lot when a vertical streak of lightning sizzled over the ocean. The street lamps flickered off and back on; a thunderous boom shook the ground.

She turned on the defroster and bent forward, trying to look out the windshield; she shut off the wipers and searched the garage. Everything was dark. All of the lights had gone out; the power must have failed.

Maintenance kept a small office in the garage, but their lights were off as well.

The police radio had earlier announced a power line down on Thirteenth Avenue, just half a mile away. Another flash of lightning preceded a thunderclap; she could feel its vibration traveling through her knees to the floorboard beneath the steering column.

She left the car by the elevator and ran up the stairs to the second floor, turning down the hall toward number four.

No one was waiting outside for her. The hallway was unlit like the basement. She came to the door and tried the knob. It turned.

"Sherry," she called, her voice lost in another report of thunder. She pushed the door open and saw a blur; a hail of needles took her legs out from under her.

Strong hands gripped her arms and pulled her inside. The door closed behind her. Fire pulsed through every pore of her skin, burning her like a billion pinched nerves. She could not move or breathe. She could not see what was going on behind her. Had she been struck by lightning?

Raw heat began to build under her skin; white-hot pain filled the void behind her eyes. She began to lose consciousness.

Suddenly she was flung on her back and someone was standing over her, something dark in his hand, his face going in and out of her badly impaired vision.

A figure of a man began to form, a leering man with an ugly scar that divided his chin and ran across his Adam's apple into his collar. Something dark was sticking out behind his right ear. He was the man from the Public Works' parking lot—the one who looked in her car window! The man in Sherry's vision. The last person Susan and Andrew Markey ever saw alive.

Another burst of light illuminated the deck outside the window, followed by a boom that rattled the dishes in the cabinets. She caught an eerie negative of the man in the light, then nausea struck her stomach and she tasted bile.

His face descended like an apparition. His hands touched her body, taking her gun, putting it into his waistband. She felt nothing. He left her there, moving around the room, returning, straddling her, something gray in his hands, a roll of duct tape. Yoland had been duct taped to the piling! Why couldn't she move? Why couldn't she speak? What was making her burn so badly?

The face dropped to within inches of hers. "Well, Lieutenant," he said. "We meet at last." The scar on his neck slid to one side of his throat.

"Just a little jab, Lieutenant. Won't keep you down for long." He was kneeling now, fooling around with something on the carpet. She heard tape ripping. "I've got your little blind friend, too," he said, cutting the tape off with his teeth. "You'll get to see her real soon." He put the tape over her mouth.

"You know, I've been thinking about you, Lieutenant." He laid the roll of tape down beside her and undid the top two buttons of her blouse, slipping his hand beneath her bra. "You know why?"

She just looked at him, every inch of her paralyzed.

"Of course you don't, so let's just say you can thank your daddy for that. Your daddy and me went back a long way."

He squeezed her breast hard, then removed his hand and got to his feet, spreading a tarp on the floor next to her. He picked up the tape and bound her ankles and wrists in front of her.

"I was disappointed about your daddy's heart attack. I was hoping to see him again. But things seem to have a way of working out, don't they?"

O'Shaughnessy's mind raced to Tim, then to the girls. She wanted them to know how much she loved them. She wanted Tim to know she had never stopped loving him.

"I had to park on a side street so you wouldn't see the truck; you were the only one who would have understood its significance. So you wait right here like a good little girl and I'll be back in a minute."

The door closed; O'Shaughnessy tried to move, but nothing happened.

Oh, my God! She fought to gain a breath of air, the first conscious breath she'd taken since she'd come through the door. She tried her right hand and then her feet. Nothing. Her entire central nervous system was scrambled, the muscles silenced. He had shot her with a stun gun.

She lay there for what seemed an hour but was only a few minutes. The door opened. She tried her left finger again and then her arm and this time it moved. The effects of the stun gun were wearing off, but much too slowly to help her. Now he was back. She exercised the fingers back and forth, took a slow deep breath, finding that the burning was receding behind her eyes as well.

She felt something against her side—a knee? A man was bending over her. Detective Payne!

31

McGuire walked into the detectives' office, shaking his umbrella as Randall was hanging up the phone. Another line lit up and he punched the button.

"Sarge," he yelled a minute later. "Lieu said to tell you she'll be back in ten, and someone on the phone wants to talk to whoever is in charge."

McGuire turned and started walking. "I'll take it in my office."

Chance Haverly put her head against the back of her chair. There was a cardboard box on the floor stacked with pictures and plaques. She would be forty-eight next month—forty-eight and childless. Her husband made more money than either of them could spend in a lifetime and she hadn't done so badly herself.

She swiveled in the chair and stared at the file in front of her. Then she looked at the wall clock. It was almost eleven on the East Coast.

A voice came across the speakerphone. "Sergeant McGuire speaking, how can I help you?"

"Sergeant, I've been reading your crime reports in Cape May County. You have two young women missing in Wildwood."

"May I ask who is calling?"

"My name is not important, Sergeant. Only what I have to tell you."

McGuire sat rigid at his desk, still trying to assemble what he'd heard on the phone. The name Earl Sykes had come up on the list of drivers from the Public Works department, but where in the hell was Blackswamp?

He punched the intercom for Randall's desk. "Randall, I need to know where every junkyard is or ever was within twenty miles of Wildwood, and I want to know where anything that has ever been called Blackswamp is supposed to be. Within the hour!"

McGuire was just beginning to enter Sykes's name into the computer when the door to his office flew open.

"You know where she is?"

McGuire looked up at Chief Loudon, who was shaking a sheet of paper in his face.

He shrugged. "Randall said she'll be back in ten."

"Is this supposed to be some kind of joke?" The chief tossed the paper on his desk. It was a copy of the sketch that he and Detective Payne had been showing around town.

"I beg your pardon?"

"Do you know who this is?"

McGuire looked down at the wild-looking youth, then back up at the chief, his eyes widening in astonishment.

"You mean you do?"

11:00 P.M.

O'Shaughnessy's eyes were screaming up at Detective Payne, but she still couldn't speak. He was working on the tape around her wrists. "Are you alone?" he whispered. He had come around and was kneeling, facing the door in order to study her face.

Her eyes moved up and down. "Sherry, where is she? Sherry—where is she, Lieu?" Her eyes remained still.

The door flew open and shots rang out. Payne leaped to cover O'Shaughnessy as tufts of material blew out the back of his jacket. His chin hit the floor next to O'Shaughnessy's chest; she felt his arms slide down next to her sides to prop himself up. His elbow bucked against her right side when he fired his gun, and Sykes's pistol crashed to the floor as a 40-caliber bullet struck the base of its grip, propelling lead splinters into the palm of his hand.

Payne's whole body slumped to the floor. Sykes stared at the mess that was his hand, kicked the door closed with his foot, and staggered toward them. Pink foam frothed on Payne's white shirt. Payne was looking up at Sykes, but his gun lay motionless in his hand. Sykes got to his knees and pulled a pillow off the couch, put it over the detective's head, and with his left hand picked up the gun and pulled the trigger. O'Shaughnessy closed her eyes in horror.

You son of a bitch! You goddamned son of a bitch!

Sykes knelt there a moment, squeezing his hand against his chest. Then he managed to get himself to his feet and to the kitchen, where he bound the bloody hand in a towel. He could no longer close his fist the whole way; fragments of the bullet had severed the nerves along the thumb.

But that had to wait. Sykes tucked O'Shaughnessy's Glock back in his belt and rolled her onto the tarp. He needed to move now and fast. He couldn't know if someone had heard the gunshots and didn't want anyone to see the sanitation truck near the scene. But first he had to clean up his own blood.

32

SATURDAY, JUNE 4, 11:00 P.M.
WILDWOOD, NEW JERSEY

Janet had complimented Jeremy's hair again this morning; he was glad she couldn't see him now, though. He'd lost his hat in the winds and his wet hair was plastered around his face. He'd spent the morning chasing papers and cans, but it had only been raining then, no lightning. When Jeremy saw the first sizzling bolts strike the ocean, he crawled as far under the boardwalk as he could get.

The winds kept changing and sand pelted his face. Paper and cans and cartons rose and spiraled in the air. He saw one of the orange Public Works trucks with its flashing lights pull into a nearby garage. He ran out into the street and toward the structure before it went away, but by the time he reached it, the cab was empty. It was a dump truck with a tarp over the back, just like Mr. Johnson's truck, only bigger.

Jeremy took his spear and his sack and pulled himself up into the back, then crawled under the tarp past the heap of children's toys and picket fencing, just like he did when Mr. Johnson picked him up after work. He heard the elevator doors open just about the same time he realized he was not lying alone. Something was in the bed next to him and it had moved!

Jeremy started to crawl back out, but then he heard more noises: something was being dragged across the floor. Maybe he shouldn't have gotten into the back of the truck after all. Maybe whoever was driving it would be mad at him and tell Mr. Johnson what he did. He drew his knees into his chest and hugged himself in a fetal position. Maybe if he just hid there long enough, no one would see him. He could wait until the truck got to wherever it was going and sneak back out. Then after the rain stopped he could go back and clean the rest of the beach like he was supposed to.

The hydraulic tailgate began to whine as it was being lowered. Something was rolled under the tarp, striking the bottom of his boot. The hydraulics groaned again as the tailgate ascended and an ear-shattering *clank* indicated the gate was closing. The truck bounced as someone entered the cab. The engine turned over, and the vehicle lurched forward.

33

Sykes put a match to the lantern and looked at Marcia Schmidt on the mattress; she was still covered with the tarp, one hand and one elbow exposed, just the way he had left her. He dropped Sherry Moore's body on the floor of the bus next to her, ankles taped and bent awkwardly beneath her, wrists bound in front. Then he went out in the storm to get O'Shaughnessy, hauling her in last.

The bus was illuminated by the tiny flame in a kerosene lantern. O'Shaughnessy could make out Sherry sitting by a dark flat form in the back on the floor. Sykes dragged her roughly with his left hand to mid-bus and dropped her next to a sheet of plywood. The fumes around it seared her throat and burned her eyes.

The skies opened up, rain hammering the roof like millions of falling beads. Sykes looked down at the policewoman and swallowed. A wave of pain passed through him, creasing his brow as he knelt in front of her. He pinched her cheeks with one hand and forced her to look up at him. "You were just a little cunt back then, all proud of your daddy in his uniform."

He picked up the plywood and leaned it against the wall; then he grabbed her by the hair and pulled her to the edge of the hole. Rancid odors rising from the pit nearly caused her to puke.

"This is your fate, down there in the shit and bones. Down there with all my other cunts." He grabbed the back of her head and pushed her face into it. "This is where you'll spend eternity, you and your little blind friend. This is how it ends."

He looked past her, into the blackness, mindful that the hole was responsible for his own end as well, that death had risen out of it and invaded his very being. In a sudden burst of despair he backhanded O'Shaughnessy with his good hand, slamming her head against the wall of the bus.

Things would get hot for a while. The police would go over the truck again and one day they would bring him in for questioning. He'd need a lawyer when they linked the truck to the girl on the parkway, but without a witness and a body their case would be circumstantial. No one had seen his truck on the road. No one could say that he had been driving it when that woman's hair had gotten caught in the window. And anyone with access to the keys could have taken the truck out after he went off duty. Who could say any different? Not the night supervisor, who stayed in his office staring at his computer screen.

As for tonight, he'd only been out doing his job. He'd been seen picking up trash and he'd been heard on the Public Works radio. He'd need to deal with his injured hand. But that could wait. He wore gloves every day. All the workers did. No one would ever have to know.

No, he would have his year of life and he would

have his revenge. And tomorrow morning, when the cops were combing the state for the man who had shot a cop and kidnapped a police lieutenant, he would be sitting right here, drinking a beer and watching O'Shaughnessy dance, three short miles from Wildwood, three short feet from eternity.

He thought about the police hat and shoes he'd taken from her house. She'd resist at first, but then he'd throw the bitch on the mattress into the hole and the other two would do anything he asked to save their own asses. They always did.

Sykes stood and walked to the front of the bus, took one last look, and stepped outside. Now he had to make sure he was seen at the sanitation yard, dumping his storm debris, disinfecting the bed. He'd be back in Blackswamp in less than an hour.

He found a pair of gloves beneath the seat, put the truck into gear and looped back onto the path, missing sight of the shaking man in a filthy raincoat cowering at the foot of a tree.

O'Shaughnessy managed to kneel in front of Sherry and pull the tape from one side of her mouth. The blind woman's face was covered with crusty blood, distorted by her broken nose. She gagged and spat.

"You okay?"

Sherry nodded, taking big gulps of air. "What do we do?"

"Can you move?"

"Yes." She opened and closed her hands into fists.

O'Shaughnessy thought she looked awful. She'd really bungled it. She'd put all of her chips on Sandy

Lyons and was wrong. She should have paid more attention to the other drivers. She should have known something was wrong when that man looked in her car in the sanitation lot.

"I'll cut you loose," a voice hissed from the mattress in the corner.

Both women turned toward the lump in the back of the bus. "Bring me your hands," Marcia whispered. "I have a knife."

O'Shaughnessy watched as a small hand pulled aside a tarp and a young woman's face appeared. She could see now that one of the woman's wrists and both ankles were bound to the frame of a mattress. The other hand did indeed hold a knife.

"Hurry," the woman coaxed. "Give me your hands."

Sherry started sliding herself across the floor in the direction of the woman.

"No. Wait," O'Shaughnessy commanded. She was familiar with the heavy-gauge Flexi-Cuffs used to shackle the woman to the bed. Without wire cutters they would not be able to set her free. If they cut their own bindings, they would still have to stay and protect her, and O'Shaughnessy wasn't sure they were in any condition to do that. Not as long as Sykes was armed.

"What's your name?"

"Marcia."

"Listen to me, Marcia. The first thing he'll do when he gets back is check our wrists. How strong are your legs, Sherry? Can you move your legs?"

"Yes," Sherry answered tentatively.

"Okay. I've got an idea." O'Shaughnessy took a breath, a long one. "But you've got to be ready, Sherry. If anything happens to me, you've got to get back to Marcia and the knife. You got it?"

Sherry nodded tentatively.

"Marcia?"

"Yes," she answered. "Got it."

"Okay, let me tell you about his hand."

34

SUNDAY, JUNE 5
WILDWOOD, NEW JERSEY

Chief Loudon was notified that a "shots fired" call had come in to 911 at 11:10 P.M. Officers responding to the area of Atlantic and Third located Lieutenant O'Shaughnessy's empty car in the basement lot of the Driftwood condominiums. Everyone was aware that she kept a unit there, but there was no answer at her door and the patrol officer guarding her house on Third Avenue confirmed she had not returned to that address, either. They decided to break down the door.

An ambulance and several other cars were already in the garage by the time Chief Loudon and McGuire arrived; all was dark but for their blue strobes and the flashlights of police officers and medics on foot.

Puddles rippled in the wind, reflecting lights continued to amass as cars arrived on the scene. Radios crackled everywhere; first units on the scene found a body in O'Shaughnessy's condo. It had a Philadelphia PD detective's shield on it.

"Sarge," said a uniformed officer, holding up his radio. "It's Randall. He says he's got something for you."

McGuire took the radio and turned his back to the crowd. A moment later he put it away and started jogging toward his car.

"They found Blackswamp, Chief."

O'Shaughnessy used her shoulder to guide Sherry closer to the center of the bus, placed her back against a wall, feet facing the hole. She positioned herself between Sherry and the pit and told her to pay attention to two things: the location of Sykes's voice and her signal. Marcia Schmidt replaced the knife, dislocated her thumb, and slipped her hand back in the Flexi-Cuff.

Thirty minutes later they heard someone approaching, boots grinding on the front steps of the bus. Sykes appeared in the murky light, head dripping wet, hand scratching furiously at the back of his neck.

He started for the lantern next to the mattress, staggered some, and then knelt. A look of concern crossed his face. Where was the paring knife? He looked at Marcia Schmidt on the mattress, still handcuffed to the rod above her head; no way could she have reached the knife. He looked back over his shoulder at the policewoman; it had to be her. The other one was blind.

He drew his pistol from his belt, walked back to the policewoman, and shoved the gun under her chin, grabbing her arm with his free hand, jerking it high in the light where he could see the tape. The wrists were still bound.

He pushed her aside and grabbed Sherry by the wrists, checked the tape, and pulled her away from the wall to look behind her.

Nothing.

He shoved her back.

Cautiously he returned to the lantern, keeping the gun pointed at O'Shaughnessy, patting the floor behind him and around the lantern; he smiled as his hand came to the knife at last.

Fucking nerves were getting to him. It had been there all along.

"Kneel in front of her." He came back to O'Shaughnessy and kicked her in the side. "Do it now, bitch."

She pivoted so her back was to him.

"Undress her. Use your fingers and be quick about it." He coughed a deep, racking cough that pulled something up from his lungs.

She hesitated.

"Five more minutes and this cunt on the mattress goes into the hole." He pointed the gun toward Marcia.

O'Shaughnessy leaned toward Sherry, undoing the last button on her shirt, pulling it off her shoulders until it fell and draped around her waist. "Now her shorts; open her shorts." He came closer, leaned over O'Shaughnessy's shoulder, and put his lips against her ear. "You like that, don't you? You want some of that yourself, don't you, Lieutenant?"

His laugh reverberated around the metal walls of the bus. O'Shaughnessy's knees scraped the bare metal floor as his thighs pushed against her back, his fetid breath on her neck. "You'll get your chance. You'll both get your chance, and soon."

O'Shaughnessy waited, taking her time with Sherry's shorts. Sykes squeezed the tops of her shoulders, leaned down, and licked her neck; she could smell sickness on his breath. He laughed quietly. "You know, you were even easier than I thought."

"Now!"

O'Shaughnessy ducked as Sherry snap-kicked, tape flapping from her unfettered ankle as the heel of her foot shattered his nose. O'Shaughnessy spun, ramming him with her elbow, knowing that if he didn't go down, she would need to plant her heels into the floor and push him into the hole with her back. Most likely falling in with him. But he toppled and Sherry leaped forward and gave him a two-fisted shove that pushed him over the edge.

Sykes's own weight worked against him; he tried but failed to keep from rocking backward on his heels. His feet went out from under him as he went over the edge. Clawing for anything to grab hold of in that last possible second, he snagged the tape around Sherry's wrists. And took her down with him.

O'Shaughnessy leaped to grab Sherry's legs, catching them at the ankles just before she disappeared.

They all froze as the human chain snapped to a stop. Everyone holding a breath to see if the chain would hold.

Then Sykes started to swing his legs, trying to catch a toehold on the side of the pit.

"I die, you die," he panted up at Sherry.

Thunder cracked and the bus shook. It was a deafening explosion with a blaze of white light. Shadows seemed to move around them; silhouettes came and went like ghostly apparitions.

O'Shaughnessy looked down and could see the top of Sykes's head, illuminated by the ceiling's reflection of the lantern.

Jeremy wasn't actually aware that his legs were transferring weight or that his disjointed footfalls had started to reconcile. He didn't know that he was running as he passed between the seats or that his hand was gauging weight or that his elbow was setting or that his torso was twisting for power as he lunged over the hole and thrust the paper spear at the man who was hurting the women.

Sykes heard the footfalls only a second before Jeremy appeared, reached up to block the attack, and swiped to grab the pole with his right hand. But without the use of his thumb, the spear slid easily through his glove and buried its steel tip in the scar that creased his throat.

Sykes looked up at the disheveled man in astonishment. Then blood began to pump from the hole around the spear. He hung there a minute longer, dark stains spreading across the shoulders of his T-shirt, and then his body began to convulse.

Sherry could feel his grip on her wrists weakening as his head tilted forward. And in the final seconds between the time Sykes's hand went limp and his body plunged into darkness, a collage of screaming faces exploded in front of her.

She was seeing his victims fall.

35

SUNDAY, JUNE 5, 1:00 A.M.
BLACKSWAMP

Blackswamp had become a city of strobes; every available emergency vehicle in the county was called to the scene. Gus Meyers and his crime-scene technicians set up a command post near the bus. Police alerted the FBI, the state police, and the Centers for Disease Control in Atlanta. Men and women were donning protective suits and bringing cameras on cables and crates of detection equipment to the bus.

O'Shaughnessy's lips were dark in the bright glare of the emergency room lights. She was missing one of her shoes. There was a heavy bloodstain on her blouse and dried blood in her hair. The backs of her arms were black and bleeding; her lip had been cut, and there was a mass of green and black swelling on the side of her face. "Tim," O'Shaughnessy whispered.

"It's me, Lieu. It's Mac."

"Call him, Mac. Call him for me." Her words were so faint he had to put his ear to her lips.

"I'll call him right now, Lieu. You're going to be just fine."

McGuire took the radio and stepped away from the gurney, placed a call to the office, and directed one of the detectives to find O'Shaughnessy's husband and bring him to the hospital.

Marcia Schmidt was badly dehydrated and suffering internal injuries; she had been wrapped in blankets and flown to the university hospital in Vineland.

Sherry Moore was in the cubicle next to O'Shaughnessy, both eyes black and nose bound in tape.

Jeremy Smyles sat in the back of a police car staring at the puddles forming in the swamp. His face looked oddly serene, his arms unusually still.

Chief Loudon stood at the gates of Blackswamp. The air was fetid with the smell of decay. He took the sketch out of his pocket and unfolded it. Sherry Moore had described him perfectly. Earl Oberlein Sykes. Just as he had looked thirty years before.

Loudon balled up the paper and threw it away.

Life went on that year. Sykes managed to get his picture in the papers one more time, a headliner for several weeks until the public tired of reading about him.

The pit regurgitated its own tragedies, reminding the world of a time when men knew as little about the things they were putting in the earth as they knew about men themselves. A time of innocence when words like *carcinogen* and *serial killer* were yet unknown.

From a morass as black as its name, they sifted its bones and belt buckles and keys and teeth, one by one transforming them into names: Venable, Ashley, Sharp, Able, Sanderson, Rutledge . . .

O'Shaughnessy returned to her position as commander of the city's detective unit. She was studying nights for the captain's exam, and Tim surprised her with a return trip to Martha's Vineyard to celebrate a new beginning.

Dillon didn't lose his job, but he did lose his sergeant's stripes. It was Corporal Dillon now, and he preferred the night shift where there were fewer officials to order him around.

Nicky Schmidt was convicted of interstate theft and sentenced to seven years in Lewisburg Penitentiary, where Sykes had started out thirty years before.

Marcia Lamb, who dropped the name Schmidt,

filed for divorce and moved to Wildwood, where she manages a small hotel.

John Payne was commended posthumously. The shot that disabled Sykes's hand in the second before Payne died helped to save the lives of three women.

And Jeremy Smyles has a medal from the city hanging over his new dresser. It's the first thing he sees each morning when he rises to go to work.

Dear, dear John. What would you have thought if I told you that night in the funeral home I saw Susan Paxton as a young woman putting a big, red fisherman's sweater on a little girl like me? Or that she watched the little girl climb an icy set of stairs toward an angel; I never knew that a statue of an angel looked down on the landing where I was found.

Susan was with me that day, the one in my nightmares when I saw my mother's face on the windshield. Susan was supposed to guard me until Sykes returned.

They identified her, you know, my mother—her name was Melissa Rutledge. I still dream of her, but it's a different dream these days. I see more of her than I used to. I see her face more clearly than before. Not the terrorized woman on the windshield; she is standing on the side of the road, one arm hooked around a bag of groceries, the other around my shoulders. She looks down at me, smiling and beautiful, and when a van appears on the horizon she raises her eyebrows and makes a silly face, and then puts her thumb out toward the road.

Sherry sighed and reached for an object on the

sofa next to her, picking it up.

And what would you have thought if I'd told you that I loved you, John? That I always loved you.

A chunk of ice fell from a gutter and landed dully outside her window. Sherry pressed the gold badge between the palms of her hands, just as Angie Payne had pressed it into her hand at the cemetery after the funeral; Angie had told her everything that day.

The hardest part of my life was keeping my feelings from you, even when I suspected what you were thinking.

She sniffled, reached for a tissue, and covered her mouth with it.

I blame myself, John. If I hadn't been wrong about Sykes, you would still be here. We would be together right now.

Tears spilled down her cheeks.

It's especially hard without you this time of year. You know how I hate winters. How can I do this without you, John? How can I let go of the guilt?

Sherry kneaded the badge between her forefinger and thumb. She lay down on the sofa and put her head on a pillow; she hadn't left this spot in her living room for weeks.

Brigham says I can't go on like this. That you wouldn't have approved. He said that if I give up, I give up all that you worked for. I turn my back on all the lives that Sykes took; even on Susan Paxton, whose own life changed the day that she first met me; even on my own mother.

He said, dear John, that I have an obligation to those who can no longer speak for themselves.

"He said"—she sobbed loudly, face contorted, lips trembling and barely able to utter the words out loud—"that you liked that part of me."

She wiped her eyes with the backs of her wrists and put the badge to her lips.

I was so afraid of what I'd see when I took your hand at your funeral. Afraid of how I might react in front of the others. Afraid that perhaps I had been wrong about us.

She laughed and wiped her eyes and put the badge on the table.

Did you know that it would be your last gift to me? Did you know it would be the first time I ever saw my adult face?

Garland Brigham looked at Sherry in the dim light of the fire, set his glass of port on the stand, and began to slit another envelope open.

This one was about a rapist who suffocated his elderly victims in their beds with electrical cords. It was the third such case in a small Arkansas community in as many months. The police wanted to know if Sherry could help identify the killer.

The occasion was momentous; Sherry hadn't allowed him to read the mail since last fall, had avoided his calls throughout the winter, wondering no doubt if the sunshine would ever return to the Delaware River.

"We should answer it, shouldn't we, Garland? Maybe I could help."

ACKNOWLEDGMENTS

A number of people endured my years of literary trials and tribulations. You know who you are, and I will never forget your patience and contributions. I am especially grateful to my agent, Paul Fedorko of Trident Media Corp., for making dreams come true; it is an honor not only to work with you, but simply to know you.

To Shannon Firth, for your first little nudge.

To Rob Weisbach, who reached out and finally pulled me in. I won't disappoint you.

To Simon & Schuster's own Terra Chalberg and her tireless efforts to bring the best out of this work and me. You rock, Terra!

To all the wonderful and talented people at Simon & Schuster who so graciously and enthusiastically embraced me and my work.

To the citizens and police officers of Wildwood and Cape May, New Jersey, I apologize for my extremely liberal interpretations of your communities and professions, both of which I hold dear to my heart.

Last Breath

GEORGE D. SHUMAN

For a preview of George D. Shuman's
second thriller featuring psychic
Sherry Moore, turn the page. . .

Chapter 1

She didn't feel quite right about the red dress; it wasn't a red dress kind of a day. The blue one was nice. She'd tried on the blue one twice already, but the more she thought about it, the more she knew it had to be green. Yes, green would be best for today.

"Green," she said satisfied, laying it out neatly on the bed. She put nylons, panties, and jewelry next to it and went downstairs in her slip to vacuum the living room for the third time this morning.

By nine she was at the kitchen table, stirring a cup of tea that she had no intention of drinking. She got up twice—once to search for cigarettes, forgot what she was looking for and came back empty handed; once to answer the doorbell, but as usual there was no one there.

She chewed the skin on her knuckles, studying the refrigerator, conscious of the passing time. The rubber seal down the side of the doors was dappled with mold, a job for Mr. Clean or Clorox or Natural Citrus, she could never remember which.

Her nerves were shot, she thought, laughing out loud, "silly, silly me." She pinched her wrist until it hurt, glanced up at the second hand sweeping the yellow sunburst wall clock. "One," she said out loud, waited for it to touch the "two," but by "eight," she couldn't get the words out anymore, and the first tear of the day plunked into her tea.

She stared at the muddy ripples in the cup, looking for a sign. Why couldn't she feel anything? Why couldn't she remember anything? What was she missing that the rest of the world seemed to have?

She breathed in the warmth rising from the cup, the sweet cinnamon and sassafras collecting around her nostrils and formed a crooked smile. She would liked to have had people think of her as eccentric, eccentric was fashionable these days, but in truth she had a screw loose. That was the problem and everyone knew it.

The ripples in the tea went still, she watched her reflection transforming into a gingerbread girl, silver candied beads thumb-pressed into a tiara. She smiled at the memory of rolling dough with her grandmother, but only for a second. There was a shadow behind the woman and it portended bad things to come.

The gingerbread girl began to sponge up the tea and an arm broke away, then a leg, and at last the head sunk into the muddy liquid and the girl with the tiara was no more.

The noon bell tolled from Our Lady of Joy on Madison Street. Her eyes snapped up to the clock, then to the telephone on the wall, then to the grocery list on the refrigerator. She had been thinking about the refrigerator off and on all morning but she didn't know why.

She took a deep breath. Where had the morning gone, she wondered? It seemed like there was never enough time to get anything done.

"Groceries and green," she said evenly, "groceries and green." That's why she'd picked the green dress for today. It was to remind her of something, but what?

Maybe John knew? John knew everything. She wanted to call John, but they would only tell her he was at work. That's what they always told her. Work, work, work, couldn't they see when she needed to talk to him?

She shivered. The house suddenly felt cold.

She looked at the telephone again, then the door to the living room. Maybe she should turn on the television and check the weather. Maybe she would need a raincoat when she went out. "No, no, silly girl. It's not supposed to rain all week. You're just trying to think up excuses not to go upstairs."

She put a hand on her chest, took a deep breath and slid her fingers beneath the silk slip. She closed her eyes and massaged her breast, thumb exciting the nipple until it was hard, tears running down both cheeks now and slowly she stood. With her hand still on her breast, she started for the stairs.

The mask was in a bottom drawer under a yellow sweat suit she had bought in Neiman Marcus. What she planned to do with a sweat suit, she had no idea.

She'd never worn anything but knee-length dresses all her life. That was about the only thing she was allowed to wear as a child. That was all she cared to wear as an adult.

Besides, she was the same weight now that she had been in high school. Sweatpants were for women who were either trying to loose weight or who had accepted the fact that they weren't going to. That's what her neighbor Celia was always saying.

Celia? Why did she just think of Celia? Why did Celia make her think about the grocery list?

It was Friday. They needed everything, even though she had just been to the store on Tuesday. What in God's name had she'd been thinking about on Tuesday, she didn't know? It must have been one of those senior moments, like Celia was always joking about.

She closed her eyes and pursed her lips. "Concentrate, concentrate," she told herself. John says you never concentrate enough. That's why you never get anything done.

A moment later she sighed, pushed Celia from her thoughts and looked down at the mask, not unlike a junkie looks at a tourniquet, wanting it, repulsed by it, repulsed by herself. She lifted her hair and pinned it behind her ears. Then she picked up the mask and held it in both hands, thumbs kneading the rubber collar, tracing the cast of the rubber face piece.

It was Soviet-made and as obsolete as its designers, but everything John handled was obsolete, from dated medical supplies to archaic military gear, things that could only be qualified for sale as novelties. In fact the only thing he handled that was new was ice cream in a truck he drove on weekends and which their son forbade him to bring into their neighborhood lest one of his friends might see him.

The mask had a frightening quality, she thought. She remembered the first time she had seen the boxes in the basement. The cartons were labeled "Red Army-SchM-1 M38–1941." Someone had written HELMET across the box in magic marker. It wasn't a helmet of course, but more of a hood and the face was made to look like that of a giant insect or one of the aliens you see in vintage comic books. It was black and smooth, broad forehead and triangular chin. Its eyes were round glass panes and over its mouth there was a respirator hose attached, which was supposed to match up to a filter canister, but canisters would be in other boxes that weren't in the house and you didn't need one anyhow unless you were trying to breath pure air.

She couldn't explain why she had to put it on, but she knew the moment she saw it that she had to. That was almost a year ago. By now she had gotten very good at it.

She tilted her chin and slipped the hood over her head, pressed the face piece against her cheeks and sucked the air out of the mask until it was snug.

She grasped the foot-long hose that protruded from the mouthpiece, took a deep breath and heard the rushing of air through the intake hose. Then she cupped off the open end of the hose with her hand and felt the stifling discomfort of a vacuum. This was a world where you couldn't bring your little problems, your little idiosyncrasies. This was a place of the present, of focus, where you thought about yourself and nothing else. This was the amateur walking the high wire.

Things looked different when the senses were ratcheted up to the nth, the world looking alien through the lens of the round glass eye portals. She was on the other side of the continuum, anonymous and looking back in. She was no longer Mary Dentin. She was no longer bad.

She put her hand on her face, caressing the slick black rubber. Her husband handled the masks all the time, but John would never have appreciated the beauty, would never have considered putting one on. Poor dismal John in his world of gray. He saw no good, no bad; no happy, no sad. She knew she was to blame. She knew that she weighed heavily on his mind. John who worked three menial jobs to support her and all the while she was forgetting or burning his dinner, spending like she was out of control, having no interest in his hands, his lips, unable to respond to his slightest attempts at affection. She knew all that.

She knew too that he loved her, even though he had long ago discovered there was no love inside of her to give back. It wasn't that she didn't love him in particular. She had no love for anyone. She was emotionally devoid of the feeling and there was nothing he could do, no matter how hard he tried, to make her happy. They had come to terms with that long ago.

He would be horrified to look at her now. He knew that she had secrets. He knew there were nights she walked the streets alone, was not at the movies with friends.

He knew she drank and she did, but only to anesthetize her racing mind. She used the mask when she was home alone, because when she put it on, she wasn't responsible anymore. She wasn't the disgraceful wife and mother. She wasn't a bad girl anymore.

She pushed the straps off her slip and let it fall to the floor. She took an old terrycloth belt from one of John's bathrobes and walked mechanically to the bathroom where she closed the door and pulled the old wicker clothes hamper to the middle of the floor and stepped up on it.

One end of the belt had been fashioned into a noose and this she slipped over her head, pulling it snug around the collar of the gas mask. The other end was knotted around a large S-hook she'd bought at a Home Depot. She slipped the S-hook through the antique iron ring that held the fixture and let her knees bend until the fixture took the weight of her body.

Slowly she picked up her feet and put her hands down, closing her eyes to a faint field of stars, nerve endings prickling. She put her hands on her breasts, then on her stomach and goosebumps began to rise on her arms and thighs. She felt her head begin to clear, the clutter of her craziness dissipating into the vacuum of space.

She groaned at the pleasures, put a foot on the

hamper and pushed to take the weight off the noose. She found the slightest bit of oxygen in the air she sucked through the plugged hose, prolonging the experience, then she dropped again, and again until she was nearing climax. One more minute, one more breath, she arched her foot, toes on the hamper, pushing off one last time when she heard a loud snap and a leg of the hamper skidded across the bathroom floor and under the space beneath the closed door.

She fell five inches fast and jerked to a stop, arms shooting upward to grab the light fixture, legs kicking frantically to find the hamper again. She couldn't die like this, she couldn't be here; she couldn't let them see how pathetic she was. She swiped up at the hook above her head, breaking light bulbs. Glass rained down over her head.

She began to get dizzy, the glass eye windows fogged, she thrashed about some more, then her arms fell to her sides, muscles contracting, spasms contorting her back. Her fingers were clenched into fists, legs swinging over the broken hamper, feet trying to catch the edge and then suddenly she managed to touch a corner of the hamper with a big toe.

The doorbell rang.

She hung there still as possible, arms at her side, one leg out in space, the other supported by her big toe on the hamper now leaning precariously to one side.

The doorbell rang again.

Celia?

She put pressure on the toe, gently managing to

rise a quarter of an inch. The old wicker groaned under her weight. It was enough to relieve the pressure at her neck, but she was panicking and there was little oxygen to be had through the plugged tube. She tried to calm herself, to hold off as long as she dared without breathing, then put pressure on the toe again to rise and catch another breath, letting herself down again.

Someone was knocking now, knocking persistently on the door and no one ever came to her door but Celia anymore. What had she forgotten this time? Was she supposed to do something for Celia?

Suddenly she thought of the grocery list on the refrigerator. Was she supposed to go to the store with Celia to buy something?

The doorbell quieted. The knocking stopped. Whoever it was had given up.

She raised herself an inch on her toe and took a careful breath.

How many more could she get before the basket broke?

It was Friday and the end of a week of school. The first hint of orange tinged the leaves around the old brick schoolhouse. The sun was low on the horizon, casting long shadows of the maple trees into the city streets. He ran his hand along the iron picket fence that went around the playground, kicked a tennis ball lost by a dog and jumped over a fire hydrant. Horns persisted on distant Freemont where people rushed home from work to the suburbs.

His father would be at work until midnight, at

his second job stocking nursing homes with medical supplies. On weekends his father drove an ice-cream truck. He was never at home to take him anywhere. They had never played ball together or gone to a game. The family had never taken a vacation together. It seemed there were always bills to be paid, groceries to buy. He couldn't understand why the other boy's fathers were able to do things they couldn't.

He stopped in his tracks.

The newspaper was still rolled and stuck in the door. The old blue Nova was still parked at the curb.

His mother must not have gone shopping. His heart sank in a long moment of wretched disappointment. Then he realized she must have taken everything around back. She would have used the back door. That would make sense. She wouldn't want him to see if she was carrying anything to Greg's house. It would just have been easier, so much easier to use the back door.

He started for the house again, crossed the street and tried not to doubt her. The windows looked dark at Greg's. Greg's mom, Celia's little white Toyota was not in front of her house either.

Stop it, he told himself. She won't forget. She wouldn't forget this time.

He took the steps two at a time. "Home," he yelled, letting the screen door bang.

He opened the fridge and grabbed a Pepsi, snapped the can, and climbed on the counter, looking in the space above the kitchen cabinets for something to eat.

His mother often bought junk food and hid it from herself. She was forever buying things and forgetting about them. He knew most of her hiding places—candy in the well on top of the kitchen cabinets, new clothes under the basement stairs, shoes under the twin beds in the extra bedroom. She had a way of acting like there were different people inside of her, all fighting for her attention at the same time, all disagreeing. She'd buy a television for the kitchen and put it in the attic. She'd light cigarettes only to stamp them out. She'd fix a drink and pour it down the sink, open a savings account and close it in the same day. She never wore the same clothes all day long, never returned clothes that didn't fit, never read the books she purchased or watched the movies she rented. It was as if she were guided by opposing voices.

"Mom?" he yelled, grabbing a handful of Oreos from an open pack, guzzling the soda. "I'm going next door to Greg's."

He was only kidding of course. He couldn't go next door until everything was ready. Until his friends got home from school and changed and picked up their presents and got rides back to Greg's.

He knew about the surprise birthday party two weeks ago. Greg had heard his mother suggest it to Greg's mom, who offered to have it at her house so it would be a surprise.

She would make him clean his room or do homework or something to take up the time.

"Mom?"

No answer.

Maybe she was still over at Celia's? Maybe she was putting candles on the cake or tying a ribbon on a new bicycle? Maybe she was hiding in the dining room with the blue eighteen-speed waiting to yell surprise? She had a hard time keeping things to herself. Sometimes would give Christmas presents to people at Thanksgiving.

He peeked around the corner and saw a library book on the dining room table, a dollar bill taped to the cover.

It wasn't really his birthday, not until tomorrow, but Greg was going to Six Flags with his parents in the morning so it was the only time he could be there and Greg was his very best friend.

He knew he'd be getting the blue bike he saw in the window of City Cycles, because his mother felt so bad about last year. She promised she would never forget one of his birthdays again. She'd go overboard on Game Boy cartridges and other things too, as she was prone to do. Never able to make up her mind, she ended up buying everything she looked at rather than select one thing.

He looked in the laundry room, walked into the living room, then back through the dining room into the kitchen.

"Mom?" he looked up the stairs.

He grabbed the handrail. "Mom?" he said a little less loudly, a little less enthusiastically.

He took the steps two at a time, walked the hall toward the bedrooms. Her door was open and a green dress was laid out on the bed. He saw nylons and jewelry lying next to it. Her purse was hanging on the doorknob, an envelope with one of his father's paychecks sticking out of it. She should have gone to the bank to deposit the checks before she went shopping.

He checked the other bedrooms, all empty, looked down the hall and saw the bathroom door was closed. He walked toward it, frowned as he bent over to pick up a piece of broken white cane protruding from under it.

"Mom?" he opened the door slowly.

He screamed.

She was hanging from the old light fixture naked, her face, her hair covered with a black rubber mask with glass eyes and a respirator hose for a mouth. There was something stuck in the end of the hose, a rag perhaps or a kerchief.

The clothes hamper was on its side beneath her feet, spilling yesterday's underwear and towels on the floor.

She had a toe on it; he could see her foot arched like a ballerina's, muscles quivering to hold her weight up long enough to catch a breath.

He stepped into the room, could see her eyes now through the round glass windows. She was looking down at him, eyes wide, wild, intense.

The phone rang.

He heard the wicker groaning beneath her trembling foot as she tried to raise herself up again.

He looked at her eyes for the longest time, then he backed up and sat on the toilet seat and stared at her.

The telephone rang again. It would be Greg, calling to tell him the bad news. That his mother hadn't come through, once again.

And for what?

He knew very well what this was. He'd seen it in the movies. The boys had laughed about it around school. This was what his mother had found more important than his birthday. This was what she woke up and decided to do rather than call Celia and go to the bank and the stores.

The telephone continued, the doorbell rang, someone knocked, and he ignored it all.

He could still see her eyes from where he was sitting. She was watching him, eyes never blinking, toe trembling on the corner of that hamper. Finally he got up, walked over to the hamper and kicked it out from under her.

She dropped fast, their eyes locked together as she bounced. He stood there a few feet away until he was sure she was dead, until there was no more soul inside looking out.

He heard a knock at the door, persistent now. He walked to the window and looked out to see Greg's mother, Celia. She would have known all along it wouldn't happen. Just like all the other mothers would have known. There never was going to be a birthday party. There never was going to be an eighteen-speed bicycle. She'd forgotten about him again. Just like the times she forgot to pick him up at school, or when she was supposed to take him to a movie or come to parents' day, or the soccer game or the school play. He had all but stopped saying it.

That his mother was going to be somewhere or she was doing to do this or do that. He couldn't stand that look on the other kids' faces.

"You didn't forget to do this, did you?" he said to his dead mother, his chin trembling. "How in the fuck did you remember to do this?" he wiped angry tears from his eyes with the heels of his hands. "Was this more important than me?"

He went to his room, got his pocket knife and came back and cut her down. She collapsed in a heap at his feet. He grabbed her under the armpits and dragged her down the hall where he put her on her bed.

It took thirty minutes to get her into the clothes she had laid out, brushed her hair and cleaned the mucus and smeared lipstick from her face.

He put the noose back around her neck then took the mask to his room where he hid it between his mattresses.

Back in the bedroom he sat in a corner chair and looked at her until his father got home.

It was nearly midnight.

The newspapers called it suicide and no one seriously questioned the fact. Mary Dentin had a screw loose, the neighbors told the police. Mary was just like her own crazy mother who stepped in front of a metro bus on Christmas morning.

Mary's grandfather was the only next-of-kin she had, save husband and son, and he looked less than happy to be drawn into a funeral. That didn't really surprise the boy, his mother was always uncomfortable around the old man and it seemed there was no love lost between them. When he left after the service that day, the boy never saw him again.

His own father was an outsider, even to his mother. He lived with her and he loved her, but he knew less about her than anyone in the world.

Life changed after that. His father quit all three of his jobs. He would sit in his threadbare recliner all day with a newspaper in his lap and a pen in his hand. He had taken up his mother's erratic habits of smoking Pall Malls and drinking Maker's Mark whiskey. He filled the borders around the printed articles with random words like ROOM ROAD AUTOMOBILE BREACH GERMANY KOREA COLD. He would write the words in bold print, turning the paper sideways and upside down, until there was no more room in which to write. Then he would fall asleep in his chair. He would still be there in the morning, staring vacantly at the paper as he bade him goodbye for school.

For weeks it went on. The house remained silent, the lamps sparely lit. The phone never rang, friends never came to visit. It was as if they had all had died together.

One day his father showed up at school, the station wagon packed tight with boxes, and they drove west.